R

Rogue

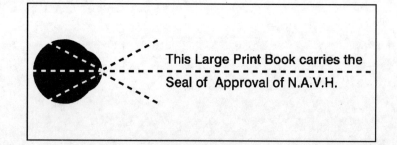

This Large Print Book carries the
Seal of Approval of N.A.V.H.

ROGUE

MARK SULLIVAN

THORNDIKE PRESS
A part of Gale, Cengage Learning

Detroit • New York • San Francisco • New Haven, Conn • Waterville, Maine • London

GALE
CENGAGE Learning

LIBRARY OF CONGRESS CATALOGING-IN-PUBLICATION DATA

Sullivan, Mark T.
  Rogue / by Mark Sullivan.
    pages ; cm. — (Thorndike Press large print thriller)
  ISBN-13: 978-1-4104-5625-0 (hardcover)
  ISBN-10: 1-4104-5625-0 (hardcover)
  1. Thieves—Fiction. 2. Undercover operations—Fiction. 3. Large type books. I. Title.
PS3569.U3482R64 2013
813'.54—dc23   2012046947

Published in 2013 by arrangement with St. Martin's Press, LLC

Printed in the United States of America
1 2 3 4 5 6 7 17 16 15 14 13

For Victor Daloia, whose street smarts
taught me to recognize thieves

ACKNOWLEDGMENTS

This book was born from a letter my then sixteen-year-old son, Connor, sent home after he'd traveled through the slums of Buenos Aires. His description of the mountains of garbage and the children living on them haunted me and fired my imagination.

I am likewise indebted to my wife, Betsy, who shared with me her impressions of Cyprus.

I also need to thank my friends Jim Sullivan, who advised me on all things international; National Public Radio's Pentagon Correspondent Tom Bowman, who answered many question on special forces teams; Richard Vietze, who was once again a great help with money matters; and Jim Erickson, who helped me grasp a basic understanding of particle physics.

David Robarge, the chief historian of the Central Intelligence Agency, was of great aid, as were CIA officer George Little and several other former intelligence and special forces operators who quietly helped me devise the character of Robin Monarch.

Any mistakes in description or technique are my own.

Fellow writers Joseph Finder and Gregg Hurwitz kept my spirits up during the second and third drafts. Gentlemen, I'm honored by your friendship.

My thanks go out as well to Meg Ruley, my agent, and to Danny and Heather Baror, who fought so hard to see *Rogue* published overseas.

My overwhelming gratitude, however, goes to all the great people at St. Martin's Press, especially Keith Kahla, my brilliant editor and champion, who cajoled and prodded *Rogue* into existence.

Crazy as it sounds, I can't wait to do it again.

The thief is no danger to the beggars.
— Old Irish Proverb

PART I

1

TWO *A.M.*

ISTANBUL

Robin Monarch leaned over the balcony railing, peering out into the darkness toward the Bosporus Straits that separate the Black Sea from the Sea of Marmara. The smell of the straits came to him on the east wind, saline and brackish in the heat that gripped the city.

Monarch wiped a sleeve against his brow, closed his eyes, and breathed deep and slow, trying to clear his thoughts. He took another deep breath and fell into a clean place. Stubble bearded, with short dark hair and a dusky tone to his skin, Monarch was smoothly handsome. He was six-foot-two, muscled, and a bit more than two hundred pounds. Hunched over the railing, eyes closed, breathing slow in deep meditation, Monarch gave off the impression of a panther dozing.

Gloria Barnett walked through the French doors behind him. "Robin," Barnett said softly. "Slattery says it's time."

Monarch roused and turned to look at Barnett, a ginger-haired crane of a woman in her thirties. She wore a white shirt and jeans and was barefoot. A pair of reading glasses hung on a chain around her neck.

"Why's he here, Gloria?" Monarch asked. "Why the secrecy?"

She shrugged. "Slattery's a big enough dog — it's gotta be a big enough hydrant that he wants to pee good and hard on it."

"Anyone tell you you're the best?"

Barnett smiled. "Only you, Robin."

He bent over and kissed her on the forehead. "Watch our backs," he said.

"Always," Barnett said.

Monarch went by her through the bedroom, out into the living area of the luxury suite. He took in the suite and its inhabitants in a sweeping glance. The coffee table was strewn with the remnants of room service. John Tatupu, a Samoan-American, was working his massive arms into the sleeves of a dark blue work coverall. A former linebacker at Ohio State, Tatupu sported wavy mahogany hair gathered in a ponytail, virtually no neck, and a tightly cropped King Tut beard.

14

Chanel Chávez sat on the sofa opposite the Samoan, dressed in a dark skirt and blouse with a black scarf over her short dark hair. She was dismantling a rifle and putting the pieces in foam compartments inside a suitcase.

Abbott Fowler was eating the last of a sandwich at the room's only table while studying an aerial photograph. Like Tatupu, Fowler wore a dark blue coverall. He was in his early thirties, shorter than the Samoan, and more slope shouldered, with a meld of features that, similar to Monarch's own, made him look like he could be from any number of racial backgrounds.

"You sure this is the latest we got, Yin?" Fowler asked.

"It's the latest," insisted Ellen Yin, a petite Asian-American woman with a perpetually intense air about her. "Just before sundown."

"Put it on the wall."

The voice came from the hallway on the other side of the suite. Jack Slattery rounded the corner, his eyes darting around the room before fixing on Monarch, who watched him, calm but alert. Monarch did not like Slattery much. The man was a manipulator and opportunist, traits that had helped him in his climb to his current posi-

15

tion of power. According to agency scuttle-butt, Slattery had also been helped by connections. He was a college classmate of Congressman Frank Baron, a senior member of the House Intelligence Committee. Still, according to the rules that Monarch lived by, working with a man did not have to involve liking him or envying him, especially if that man was your boss and your boss was the CIA's chief of covert operations.

A projector attached to one of Yin's computers threw the satellite photograph of three large buildings on the wall. Monarch glanced at it and said, "You going to give us what's inside, Jack? Or are you going to send us in blind?"

Slattery was a lean white man in his early forties, with salt-and-pepper hair; dull, pewter eyes; and an acne-scarred face that revealed nothing. At last he said, "You're after the secret archives of Al-Qaeda. Copies of every document that organization has generated since its inception, accounting records, personnel files, histories, plans, safe houses. Everything."

Chávez whistled in appreciation.

A gold mine, Monarch thought. He was beginning to understand why Slattery was here to personally oversee the mission. He asked, "Where's the intel coming from?"

"Highly reliable Turkish police sources," Slattery replied curtly, walking to the suite wall and tapping on the middle of the three buildings. "They say the archive is listed as *Green Fields* in the computers in the office of an engineering firm owned by a Turkish national named Abdullah Nassara."

Slattery explained that Abdullah Nassara was the president of Nassara Engineering Ltd., and an inventor with several patents. Nassara held doctorates in both electrical engineering and astrophysics from MIT. Before founding his company, he had worked for CERN, the nuclear science research center in Geneva. He posed as a moderate Muslim and a firm supporter of secular rule in the Turkish state. But Slattery's sources believed Nassara had a secret and deep hatred of the West nurtured during his years in the United States and Switzerland. His company had become a front for an information repository crucial to Al-Qaeda's international operations.

"Why not just have the Turks arrest Nassara and seize the files?" Monarch asked.

"Because we don't want Al-Qaeda to know what we know," Slattery said with more than a hint of condescension. "And in any case, you're not here to make strategic decisions, Monarch. You're here to see them carried out."

"True enough," Monarch said.

"Then get to it," Slattery said, tapping his watch.

An hour later, in the dry hills above the east shore of the Bosporus, Monarch slipped from a Renault sedan driven by Abbott Fowler. John Tatupu followed Monarch, carrying a mason's bag. Monarch wore a black baggy shirt over his shoulder holster and pistol, and carried a black fanny pack around his waist. As Fowler drove away, Monarch and Tatupu scanned the empty street, and then vaulted a brick retaining wall that held back a steep bank tangled in vine and brush.

Monarch had excellent night vision and led the way uphill through the thicket into a stand of aromatic cedar that choked a ravine he followed in a low athletic crouch, his felt-soled shoes as quiet and as carefully placed as the pads of a hunting cat.

Rule Number Four, Monarch thought. *No sudden moves. They attract attention. Sudden moves say you are afraid and unaware, listening to that voice in your head instead of paying attention to what's around you, which can get you killed, man. No sudden moves.*

Monarch came to the edge of the canyon and peered through a high chain-link fence across a short lawn to an empty parking lot behind three factory buildings. Tatupu eased up beside him. Monarch slid on a black face mask, instantly overheating. He felt on edge, which was not normal. But he'd had no hand in the plan. His team was brought in to execute a mission Slattery had scouted and designed.

"Looks straight forward, soft target," Tatupu murmured to Monarch. "Cameras, a single guard on duty at a front desk. No problem."

"On paper," Monarch whispered. "But if this is a terrorist archive, where are the armed guards? The dogs? No razor wire on top of the fence?"

The Samoan shrugged his great shoulders. "Sometimes the best security is just lying low. It looks like what it's supposed to be: an engineering firm."

Before he could reply, Chanel Chávez's voice came over the Bluetooth communication bud in Monarch's ear. "Settled in. Wide-angle view. Ready to rock."

Monarch had a microphone taped to his neck. He turned it on and said softly, "Roger that. We are ready, Base."

■ ■ ■ ■

If Jack Slattery had been a professional poker player, he would have been a card counter, a statistics and odds man. The CIA covert ops chief was forever gaming in his head, playing out scenarios and ranking them in terms of their likelihood. Gaming was Slattery's gift and his task as he paced behind Gloria Barnett and Ellen Yin, listening in on the headset he wore.

Barnett and Yin were working side by side in the hotel suite, watching the computer screens showing various video feeds from the tiny fiber-optic cameras worn by operatives in the field. Monarch's and Tatupu's cameras showed different angles on the west side of the Nassara Engineering Building. Chávez's camera faced the building from the northeast, and from the vantage of a cedar tree that abutted the industrial park. The barrel of her rifle was visible in the bottom of the feed. Fowler's camera showed the view through the windshield of a sedan as he slowed it to a stop outside the gated entry to the complex. In the corner of the screens, there was a small diagram of the Nassara Building with a moving red dot that showed Monarch's position.

Nothing on these screens moved Slattery to shift his thinking. The scenarios he was gaming emanated from two thrilling and fearful thoughts that kept repeating in the covert ops chief's mind: *I'm taking the biggest risk of my life, here. What happens here seals my fate.*

Slattery summoned cold reserve, flashed on the odds one more time, and then said, "Send him."

Barnett nodded and said into her microphone, "Monarch, you are go."

On a screen in front of Barnett, Slattery followed Monarch as the agency's top field operator bumped knuckles with Tatupu and then started loping toward the fence.

Monarch leaped up onto the fence and snagged his gloved hands in the mesh. Tatupu had followed him and gone to his knees carrying a portable high-intensity laser light that he aimed through the fence at the lens of the camera above the loading dock doors. Monarch got over the top of the fence in seconds, dropped, and landed softly in a crouch.

His heart began to race. He reminded himself: *Rule Number Three: Pay attention. There's nothing else at these moments. You have no past. No future. Just attention. It's the only thing that will keep you alive.*

Time seemed to slow for Monarch. He crossed the parking lot, hugging the shadows, aware of everything around him: the sound of his feet, the humid spice in the air, the rustle of birds in the trees he passed, and the blinding beam of light Tatupu kept trained on the security camera's lens. Monarch got up on the loading dock and moved past the locked roll-up doors to a stainless steel door in the corner. There was no knob, just an electronic key slot. He pulled a flat plastic card attached by a cable to his iPhone.

He stuck the card in the slot and murmured, "Can opener, Yin?"

"We got an app for that," Yin purred in Monarch's earpiece.

Monarch heard a soft whine in the door and then a sagging of mechanisms. He pushed the door open, slipped inside, and shut it behind him. He paused, still, letting his eyes adjust to the glowing red auxiliary bulb that softly lit the interior of the loading dock, seeing a forklift and tanks of welding fuel — acetylene and saturated oxygen.

Monarch had a photographic memory. He could see the blueprint of the building clearly in his mind. He eased through a second door into a hallway also lit in red light. He smelled oil and brazed metal in the air, and moved toward the odors to a set of locked metal double doors. Monarch fished out a small kit that held thin picks, worked two into the lock, played with them, sensing the teeth and teasing them open. He was inside in less than fifteen seconds.

Shutting the door behind him, Monarch looked over a laboratory and machine shop a football field long, replete with industrial lathes, grinders, shapers, benders, welders, acetylene tanks, and what appeared to be a small unlit blast furnace at this end and a simple glass cubicle office at the far other. Monarch moved by the mouth of the blast furnace, noting the bags of various ores, and smelting tools on the benches nearby that told him that Nassara Engineering, among other things, dabbled in experimental alloys.

He checked his watch — 3:15 A.M. According to Slattery's intelligence, the security guard would not make rounds until at least four thirty.

"Perimeter?" Slattery said in his earbud.

As Monarch wove through the machines, he heard Tatupu, Fowler, and Chávez calling out, "Clear and quiet."

Monarch came upon something strange near the center of the lab: a heavy metal tube about eight inches in diameter and ten feet long, which had been bent, shaped, and welded into a shape like a Q with the tail coming directly off the center. The tube was bolted into the cement floor. Beyond it was a second Q, only smaller, about six inches in diameter and half the length of the other. A third, smaller still, was bolted to the floor beyond the second one, close to the office door.

Monarch found the door locked, and picked it open. He slid an LED headlamp on, and hit the switch. There were two desks inside the office, one where Abdullah Nassara seemed to handle the affairs of his business, and another — more a table, really — that was covered with four large computer screens all tied to a server beside a stand-up safe. After digging in the fanny pack for a small broadcast modem, Monarch connected it to one of the server's USB ports. He flicked on the device's power and saw a green light.

"Yin, run the Chomper," Monarch murmured.

"Give me a second," Yin said.

The Chomper, as Ellen Yin liked to call it, was a mainframe computer network at the National Security Agency that employed the most sophisticated algorithmic cryptography software in the world. Once the device was attached to a computer, it could probe its hard drive and pick up digital ghosts that would lead to a password.

While the Chomper gnawed at Nassara Engineering's security system, Monarch looked at a framed picture of a man he assumed was Abdullah Nassara, kind of a geeky-looking guy, dressed in a business suit, his arms around wife and children on what looked like a graduation day. It was hard for Monarch to imagine Nassara as a terrorist sympathizer. Then again, what did they look like these days? He'd seen the —

The largest of the computer screens blinked and jumped to a desktop.

"We're in," Monarch said. "What was the password?"

2

Back in the hotel suite, Slattery was interested as well.

"Al-Kindi," Yin said. "Ancient Islamic mathematician and one of the first cryptographers."

"Clever," Monarch said. "She's all yours."

"On it," Yin said, typing on her keyboard. She hit ENTER. When nothing happened, she tried again with no better luck. "It's balking. A security wall I'm not breaching."

Slattery felt acid in the back of his throat, but then Barnett said into her microphone, "We're a no go from here, Robin. Try flash."

"Roger that," Monarch said.

On the screen, Slattery watched Monarch replace the wireless transmitter with a flash drive, then return to the keyboard and type instructions that would begin copying the files to the drive. He could not see what was on the computer screen in Nassara's office because of glare.

"No luck," Monarch said. "You want me to take the server?"

"No," Slattery said emphatically. "We want them to continue business as usual while we get the files analyzed."

"Don't know what to tell you, then, Jack."

There was a pause before Slattery said, "Do a search for *Green Fields.*"

"Arabic or English?"

"Both."

On-screen, Monarch typed on the keyboard.

Then John Tatupu's voice came over the headsets: "We got company."

Slattery's attention shot to Tatupu's video feed, seeing a late-model Mercedes station wagon roll to the front gate. A man leaned out the window to stick a card in a security reader.

"Shit," Slattery said, feeling as if things were slipping away from him. "That's Nassara two fucking hours early. Move, Monarch."

On Monarch's video feed, Slattery saw Monarch tap one of the screens in Nassara's office and heard him say, "Green Fields. There's a shitload of files here."

"Front gate's opening," Gloria Barnett warned.

Slattery said, "Copy what you can in five

27

minutes and get out, Monarch."

"I've got subject coming toward the parking lot," Chávez said.

Monarch said, "The files won't export. I'm going to open one and try 'Save As.'"

Slattery yelled, "Don't open them! Get out! We'll try again later."

"Lost visual on subject," Chávez said. "He entered the underground garage."

Monarch knew that the parking garage was quite a ways from the machine shop. He wanted to take home something from the foray, a taste of the Al-Qaeda archive at least. So rather than follow Slattery's command to flee, he clicked the first file on the list: GREEN FIELDS -1.

A CAD-CAM file launched and filled the screen. Monarch was looking at a three-dimensional design that looked like the Q-shaped devices bolted to the floor. He clicked a hyperlink on the design. It broke open to reveal an intricate piece of technology. Notes in Arabic appeared on the side of the design page, and Monarch started to read them.

"Monarch," came Slattery's insistent voice in his ear. "I'm ordering you out."

Monarch shut off his camera and microphone, effectively blinding and deafening

Slattery, and then opened two more files on the list. They were documents that described the purpose of the device and its design; and Monarch grasped enough to understand what Nassara Engineering really did, and what Green Fields really was.

"Monarch," Slattery said in his earpiece. "We've lost your visual. Talk to us."

Monarch flashed back to the terrible things he'd had to do recently, especially in Africa. His brain flooded with disillusion and disgust. He shut off his earbud and thumbed off his iPhone and beacon. Monarch had once seen his job as a noble calling, one done for national security and the greater good of the American people. Now, however, he saw it for what it was — or at least what it had apparently become. And right there, right then, Monarch decided his job no longer fit within the rules by which he lived.

Light burst on all around the machine shop.

Monarch turned off his headlamp and spun out of the chair and into a crouch. He spotted two men entering the machine shop through the same doors he'd used. Monarch recognized Abdullah Nassara in a white tunic shirt and black slacks. The engineer was carrying a metal briefcase that he cradled in his arms like a child. The man next to him was considerably younger, dressed in a khaki outfit that suggested a uniform and carrying a carbine rifle.

Monarch pulled down the face mask and drew his gun from the holster under his shirt. His weapon of choice was a Heckler & Koch USP .45-caliber pistol, which felt strangely obsolete at the moment.

When the two men passed behind one of the huge tool lathes, Monarch scuttled low out of the office, hoping to take cover behind one of the bigger grinders and then escape unnoticed. Monarch made it to cover just as they appeared about forty yards away.

He could hear them speaking in Arabic, which he understood. The younger man seemed interested in what ever Nassara had in the metal case, and was wondering if the safe in the office was the very best place to keep it.

Their footsteps came closer. Monarch glanced over his shoulder and started to ease backwards softly, his pistol up, braced with both hands. His toes led every step, feeling for the floor, rolling to the heel. He'd taken six slow movements back when the loose fabric of his pants caught on the jagged end of a metal tube jutting out from a stack of them. The jostle was enough. The tubes all came down in a clang and clatter.

Even as he heard the younger man shouting for him to stop, Monarch spun and took off. He charged across an opening between two of the larger machines, catching sight of the younger man aiming the carbine at him from a position at ten o'clock to his own. Just before the first muzzle blast, Monarch dodged behind a shaping machine. The round smacked metal behind him.

"Kill him!" he heard Nassara yell.

Monarch scrambled toward the exit on the other side of the three Q-shaped devices, gun up, intentionally aiming at a high angle, shooting one of the shop lights. The bulbs exploded and rained glass. Monarch veered away from the blast furnace, shooting twice more at the ceiling before heaving himself, shoulder first, through the double doors even as the second muzzle blast ripped from the carbine. The round shattered the glass in the porthole window next to Monarch's head before he fell to the floor in the outer hallway and the doors swung shut.

Back in the hotel suite, Slattery was outraged. Monarch had shut off communications and his beacon. Now they did not know his location.

"Shots fired inside," Tatupu said over the headset. "Three of them."

"Make that five," Chanel Chávez said.

"You want us in, Jack?" the Samoan demanded.

Inside the factory building, on the hallway floor outside the machine shop, Monarch heard Nassara shouting something, and then an alarm went off. Monarch sprinted not back toward the loading dock, but down the long hallway toward the staircase that led to the garage. As he ran, he felt as if he might be shot at any moment. When the third shot came, Monarch flinched mightily, but then realized it was muffled, as if the blast had come from back inside the machine shop.

Monarch knew he could think of nothing but escape now. An alarm had been triggered, and police would be coming. Years of training impelled him to get away. He blew through the door at the top of the staircase and jumped down four risers at a time, hitting the landing, spinning, and leaping again.

Midjump, Monarch heard a fourth shot followed by a tremendous explosion that shook the building all around him.

Slattery saw the flash of the explosion on Tatupu's video feed, a searing white clap that blew out windows followed by rolling balls of flame. The covert ops chief felt a raw, flaring pit open in his stomach.

"For Christ's sake, Jack!" Barnett yelled. "Send Tats and Abbott!"

The covert ops chief glared at her. "We have no idea where Monarch is now. I have no idea where to send —"

Another explosion erupted deep inside the factory, sounding to Slattery like a giant gate slamming shut on a once bright future.

After the first detonation, Monarch landed by the door to the garage, shaken and off balance. He stood there, hunched over, trying to regain equilibrium when the second explosion went off, much bigger than the first, and then a third, as if the floor above him were being bombed in segments.

Monarch's instincts took over and drove him through the door and out into the garage. Chunks of wood and plaster had fallen from the ceiling. Other sections were crumbling, and filled the place with billowing dust. Monarch went to his knees, fixed his face mask, and then scrambled forward on his belly. He could not risk exiting by the garage gate for fear of getting caught by the firemen and police who had to be coming.

So he groped toward the only other viable escape route.

A fourth explosion rocked the building. More cement fell and crumbled away. He had to keep his eyes closed to the dust as he crawled on. At last, Monarch's gloved fingers found the holes of a metal grate. He stuffed his gun back in its holster and then, eyes still closed, got to his feet. He laced his fingers in the grating and pulled upward with every last ounce of strength.

The grate budged and then lifted. Monarch heaved it away, then groped around the lip of a drain well. He jumped in and fell six feet. As soon as he landed, he could feel the wind blowing at his thighs. It took several attempts at contorting his position until Monarch could get his head and shoulders into the horizontal drainpipe, and then he began to squirm and squiggle forward.

Rule Number One, he thought. *You have the right to survive.*

On the screens in the hotel suite, flames

were leaping from the roof and licking out the shattered window casings of the Nassara Engineering Building. Slattery felt handcuffed by events completely beyond his control.

"Sirens coming," Chávez said.

"I'm going in," Tatupu grunted

"The hell you are, John!" Slattery shouted into his microphone. "That place is full of chemicals that aren't going to stop blowing anytime —"

Slattery caught a flash of movement on Tatupu's video feed. One of the loading dock's overhead doors splintered outward. A forklift shot off the dock and landed in the loading zone. Seconds later, a figure staggered out from the hole the forklift had made. He was coated in grime and dust and hunched over, one hand holding his stomach, the other a carbine rifle.

"Is that him?" Yin cried into her microphone. "Robin, do you read me?"

But then the figure stood up and started to hobble away. He was much younger and had darker features than Monarch. His clothes were tattered. He was bleeding from the forehead and from cuts about both shoulders. When he was seventy-five yards away from the loading dock, there was a tremendous flash and Tatupu's feed died.

The acetylene and pressurized oxygen tanks in the loading dock exploded, sending a fluorescent orange fireball high into the sky. Monarch crouched and threw up his hands to shield his eyes from the light. He had just climbed out the other end of the pipe, and was down the bank in the brush about 150 yards west of Tatupu.

Monarch stood and stared at the flames as police cars raced by on the road below him, horns blaring and lights flashing. He was dazed and mystified by all that had happened in the last ten minutes, but dead sure of what he now had to do.

Monarch picked the bud out of his ear and threw it away into the brush. He tossed the iPhone after it. He walked away from the burning factory, feeling cored through and orphaned for the third time in his life.

3

SIX DAYS LATER . . .
THE WILLARD HOTEL
WASHINGTON, D.C.
Jack Slattery lay under rumpled sheets, watching a statuesque redheaded woman get back into her lavender lace bra. Ordinarily, Slattery would have let his mind game on that gesture for as long as it lasted. But his brain whirled with various blends of anger oozing from one question: *How did it all go so fucking wrong?*

"Jack?" the woman said, shaking Slattery from his thoughts. She was looking over her shoulder at him, holding the waistband of a tight black skirt at the midline of her near perfect bum, her expression demure.

"No round two tonight, Audrey," Slattery replied.

Audrey pouted, then shrugged and pulled her skirt to her waist and buttoned it, saying, "Should I not dress this way in the future?"

"No, it's great," Slattery said. "I've just got a lot on my mind."

The redhead slid a black sleeveless sweater over her head, picked up the envelope on the dresser, and tucked it in her purse. She came to Slattery's bedside, leaned over, and kissed him on the lips. "You'll call me?" Audrey asked.

"How could I not?" Slattery replied.

When Slattery heard the hotel door shut behind her, he told himself once again that Audrey and the others were good for him, fantasy games he could control and then leave behind so he could focus when it came to his real work.

But as the CIA's cover tops chief got into the shower, the release and clarity he normally felt after Audrey simply was not there. He was tenser than ever, and finding it almost impossible to consider what had been lost when Nassara Engineering exploded and burned. The prize had been within his grasp, and then — *poof* — it was gone. He wondered if he would ever have a chance like that again, and felt saddened and anxious because he was exactly who he had been before the explosions: a powerful invisible man with a purposeful life. And yet, he was still no closer to fulfilling dreams he'd had as a boy, dreams he'd fondled like a security blanket for most of his life.

Slattery was dressing and trying not to turn bitter about his turn in fortune when his work cell phone rang. He picked it up, listened, stiffened, and then reddened.

"Are you sure?" he asked.

He listened again, before barking, "I'll be there in twenty minutes. Have everything on my desk."

4

DAWN, THE NEXT DAY . . .
GRAVELLY POINT PARK
ALEXANDRIA, VIRGINIA

Sitting in his Chevy Tahoe, dressed in the same clothes from the day before, Slattery saw a familiar figure jogging in the predawn light along a paved path just west of Reagan National Airport. He climbed out of his vehicle and trotted across the grass to intercept the runner, who wore shorts and a sweatshirt, hood up.

"Frank?" Slattery called.

The runner startled and tugged back his hood. Congressman Frank Baron of Georgia, a ranking member of the House Intelligence Committee, was a photogenic white man with an extremely large head and normally affable face. But today he seemed displeased to see his old college chum.

"This is my time, Jack," Baron said, going past him. "Only time I get to think."

Slattery ran after him. "I've got news, Frank."

The congressman did not slow. "It was all just a bad dream?"

"No," Slattery said.

"Then we've got nothing to talk about," Baron said. "Now, do we?"

"Frank —"

Baron cut him off. "Do you know what you've done with this fuckup, Jack? You set us back twenty years at least. C.Y. can't even talk about it. A complete fuckup."

Slattery said, "Monarch's not dead, Frank."

That stopped Baron in his tracks, hands on his hips, chest heaving as he regarded Slattery with deep skepticism. "You said that place was blown to smithereens."

"It was," Slattery said. "But he apparently escaped."

"Apparently, or he's been seen?"

"Not seen," Slattery admitted. "At least not yet."

"What's your evidence?"

Slattery told Baron how the Turkish press had revealed that the man who staggered out of the burning building was Ali Nassara, eldest son of the youngest brother of the late Abdullah Nassara. Istanbul police discovered the engineer's nephew wandering the grounds shortly after the fire trucks arrived. He was bleeding and concussed.

Ali Nassara, twenty-seven and recently discharged from the Turkish Army, was working part-time as his uncle's bodyguard because there had been a rash of kidnappings of wealthy Turks lately. And his uncle had taken to coming into work hours before anyone else to tinker with a secret project with which he'd become obsessed, but about which the nephew seemed to know little.

Ali Nassara said he and his uncle entered the building through the parking garage and took a shortcut to the machine shop. They turned on the lights, heard a clatter of noise, and then spotted a masked man carrying a pistol running through the shop. The nephew said the man shot at them, and he returned fire. The intruder shot again and mortally wounded Abdullah Nassara. His nephew fired a third time, missed, and then watched in horror as the intruder shot at two acetylene tanks as he went out the door.

The explosion hurled the nephew off his feet and set off a raging fire in the shop. He tried to get his uncle's corpse out, but could not. He escaped the machine shop before the second and third eruptions. He made it to the loading dock, but the alarm system had locked down all doors. In desperation, he fired up the forklift and sent it crashing through one of the doors to make his escape before the entire place exploded into fire.

"What about Monarch?" Baron asked when Slattery finished.

Slattery replied, "Forensics teams combed the wreckage and found the charred remains of Abdullah Nassara and the security guard at the front desk. No other bodies."

"How'd Monarch get out?"

"We think he used a storm drain out of the parking garage," Slattery said. "But to my mind, *how* is not as important as *why*."

Baron thought about that. "Any theories?"

"Three so far," Slattery said, and then explained his thinking.

Upon hearing the third scenario, the congressman lost color. He swallowed hard, looked away, and said, "That won't do. Even the remote possibility of that won't do."

"It's why I came to you first, Frank," Slattery said.

Baron gazed at Slattery. "Shut this thing down, Jack. For all our good."

It took twenty-six hours before Slattery was able to get an audience with Willis Hopkins, a former professor of mathematics at Stanford and the current Director of the Central

Intelligence Agency.

Hopkins, a rail thin black man, had a superprocessor for a mind. He remembered everything, and he saw things differently, analyzed them differently from any other man Slattery had ever known. So Slattery made sure he was razor sharp in his version of events in Istanbul, placing emphasis on Ali Nassara's contention that Monarch shot his uncle and then the gas tanks to cover his escape. He concluded with raising the possibility that Monarch had sympathy for the terrorists.

Hopkins listened without comment during Slattery's presentation. When he quieted, the director pushed his glasses back up onto the bridge of his nose and said, "If he does have sympathies, why kill Nassara, a supposed terrorist? No, I've seen the raw mission feed, Jack. And it occurred to me that Monarch might have seen something in those files he did not like."

Slattery's head retreated slightly, surprised that the director had gone to the effort of watching the raw feeds of the mission. "Well, sir, I should think so," he replied. "I'd imagine there were many things in them most people would not like to see, beginning with me."

Hopkins leaned back, flipping a pencil

between his fingers, considering Slattery. He asked, "Monarch ever show signs of instability before this fiasco?"

"No, sir. He was our finest asset. It's why I chose him to be point on this mission."

"What about his team? Did they see anything to indicate he was a sympathizer?"

"They claim to be as bewildered as I am. But as a precaution, I've put them all on administrative leave or reduced duty pending investigation. Just as a precaution."

"Seems prudent," Hopkins said.

"Yes, sir," Slattery said. "The question is what to do about Monarch."

The director thought a moment. "I'd like to see him brought in for questioning."

Slattery nodded. "I've put out a watch for him under his name and all his known aliases, but I'm also advising that he is to be considered armed, dangerous, and not to be approached by local police."

"Smart," Hopkins said, and then he paused before refocusing his penetrating gaze on Slattery. "Jack, how good was the intelligence regarding the archives?"

The covert ops chief bobbed his head sharply. "Excellent, sir. The source has been impeccable in the past. Turkish National Police."

Hopkins watched him, blinking slowly,

before saying, "Keep me posted."

Slattery left the director's office feeling like he'd just sprinted a mile. The fact that Hopkins had watched the feeds made him feel like people higher up the food chain were second-guessing his decisions. But now, after talking to Hopkins, he felt like he was back in control. With a little luck, he could make things almost right.

Slattery went downstairs and through the CIA's main cafeteria, which he had always considered a bizarre place. There were hundreds of people, analysts, assets, and support staff, all eating side by side. Many knew each other by sight. Some were friends. Yet hardly any of them knew what the other did for a living, and never would. And that was how Slattery liked it. At some level, it made him invisible, mostly free to do as he wished, and that suited him more than anything in life.

Entering the long hallway that led to the agency's operations command center, Slattery heard the slap of shoes against the marble floor. A deeply tanned woman in her forties, with an attractive face, but the unfortunate build of a bulldog, was running at him. Her name was Agatha Hayes. She'd recently joined Slattery's team as an analyst and mission runner.

"Don't you wear your beeper?" she demanded in a low breathless voice.

"Not when I'm briefing the director, Agatha," Slattery replied.

"We got him," Hayes said. "Monarch. He's in Algiers."

Slattery began to run toward the operations center. "You're sure?"

"Came in on a cargo boat from Istanbul under one of his known aliases."

5

FORTY HOURS LATER . . .
ALGIERS

French and Arabic rap and reggae thudded from windows high over Monarch's head as he entered the warren of alleys that climbed into the Casbah, the oldest part of the city, a maze on the steep hillside above the Great Mosque and the Place of Martyrs. The air drifting in the Casbah smelled of simmering garlic and lamb and tobacco and the sea. Fruit vendors called to him. So did fishmongers, and rug and curio dealers, and restaurant owners, who stood outside their empty establishments, spitting, and praying for relief from the merciless sun.

It was Monarch's fourth day in Algiers, and the fifth day of the holy month of Ramadan, the fifth day of fasting from dawn until dusk. The hardship of the fast already showed in the faces and postures of the people he saw. He matched himself to their manner. He did not swallow his spit; and he acted on edge as he climbed deeper into the Casbah, heading toward a familiar address. It was also Friday, the day of giving, and Monarch went out of his way to put coins in the jars of the beggars who sat in the doorways, crippled or blind or half-crazed by the life Allah had given them.

In the fourteen days since leaving Istanbul, Monarch had let his beard grow. His skin was darker from long hours in the sun on the voyage he'd taken across the Mediterranean. And he'd made sure he wore clothes that let him fit in: gray slacks, black lace-up shoes, and a white cotton dress shirt he'd bought on the docks in Tripoli. To the casual observer, he could have been anybody from a merchant on break to a government *fonctionnaire* out for a midafternoon stroll.

Monarch thought most clearly when he was moving, especially when he walked long distances. During the six-day voyage from Istanbul to Benghazi and on through Tripoli and Tunis, he'd walked the decks of the ship from dawn until dusk. And he'd walked all over Algiers since his arrival, six to eight miles each day, considering his life, and feeling like it was out of balance, that he'd done too many things society would consider negative. And yet all that walking, all that thinking, and Monarch had moved no closer to understanding what he wished for his future other than this issue of balance.

He had the freedom to do whatever he wanted. He'd stashed enough money away over the years to live comfortably for the foreseeable future. While some people might have found those prospects inviting, Monarch felt as if he'd had too much freedom already. Twice before, extreme liberty had come to him like an earthquake cracking open the earth, leaving a fissure, sudden, fathomless, and dark. Each time he'd been cut off from his prior life, leaving him to figure out a way forward.

That's how Monarch felt at some level as he climbed through the old city, cut off from his friends and support, alien and adrift and, he assumed, pursued. The boys at Langley must have figured out he was not dead by now. Someone would come searching, wanting to talk. Monarch decided that when it happened, he'd be honest; and he'd tell them he had no intention of going back inside the fold. As far as he was concerned, when the earth cracked open like this, it left you on one side or another.

Monarch's thoughts broke when he noticed a group of seven teenage males coming down the narrow street at him. He caught the hunger in one of their eyes and recognized its flavor. They were a pack. They were hunting.

The urchins swarmed in around him, bumping him, and turning him as they passed. Monarch spun with them, keeping his pockets just ahead of their fingers, his own hands plucking a wallet from one and a wad of cash from another.

He held both up and glared at the boys. "Rule Number Six: Know your target," he said to them in Arabic, and then tossed the wallet and the cash back at the stunned pickpockets.

Several of them began to laugh and clap. One of the older ones, a boy with a gold tooth, asked, "Where you from? Where'd you learn to do that?"

"Rule Number Thirteen: Keep your secrets secret," Monarch replied, and then turned and strolled away from them, happy that his skills had not dulled.

In his office in Langley, Virginia, Slattery felt a cheap prepaid cell phone ringing in his pocket. He got out the phone and answered. "Yes?"

"We've located the cat you lost," a woman's voice said in a mild French accent. "As you suspected, looks like he's heading to

Rafiq's."

Slattery nodded, pleased. "It's where he would go in Algiers."

"And so he has," the woman said. And the line went dead.

Slattery left his office and climbed down a metal staircase into the agency's operational command center, which featured three tiers of desks and a wall of video monitors. Agatha Hayes was sitting on the top tier, headset on.

"Agatha," he said. "Give me Lynch's feed, split upper left."

Hayes typed on her keyboard, and the upper left quadrant of the screen jumped to show the view out the window of a car traveling past the Great Mosque of Algiers.

Slattery spoke into his headset: "Lynch."

"Right here," a hoarse male voice came back. "We've checked the manifests on the docks, but —"

Slattery cut him off. "I think I know where he might go. A fabric shop west of Boulevard de la Victoire, due south of you, up the hill, no more than four kilometers."

He gave them an address, then said, "Get there and sit on it."

"On our way, boss," Lynch said.

"No fireworks," Slattery said.

"We're just there to assist him home."

Slattery took off his headset, feeling pleased with himself. The choreography he'd just set in motion felt pitch-perfect, all of it logical, acceptable, and defensible.

Agatha Hayes was watching Slattery. She asked, "What makes you think Monarch will be going to this fabric store?"

Slattery replied, "He entered Algiers under one of his known aliases, which means eventually he'd have to seek a new identity. That fabric store belongs to Sami Rafiq, of the Beirut Rafiqs. The family has fabric shops all over Africa and the Middle East. The Rafiqs are also the finest document forgers in the world, and Sami is one of their best. We've used him quite often in a pinch, as a matter of fact."

"The agency?" Hayes asked, surprised.

"There's a push to outsource everything these days," Slattery said. "Keeps the overhead low."

Rafiq's Magazin de Tissu Extraordinaire bustled with clerks and customers, women mostly, some modernly dressed, others in traditional robes and veils, examining bolts of expensive cloth stacked on long, short-legged tables and in bays attached to the walls. Monarch paid it all little mind as he headed to the rear of the store to a staircase that led up to an office that overlooked the sales floor.

He climbed the staircase, hearing a man barking at someone in French, "You call Sami thief? I gave you a fair price. I always give a fair price. Sami Rafiq is no thief! I am an honorable businessman!"

Monarch rounded a corner to look into the office, where a short, portly Lebanese man with glasses, a shirt opened too far down his hairy chest, and a rash of gold chains around his neck was listening to his cell phone. The man shouted, "You slander me!" He thumbed off his cell phone and slammed his fist on his desk.

"That temper of yours will get you, Sami," Monarch said in English.

The fabric merchant's head rose, and his face broke into a grin. He lurched to his feet, his arms open. "Robin Monarch!" he cried. "My dear, dear friend! How are you?"

Sami came around his desk, shaking Monarch's hand warmly before appraising him. "Who lets you wear these clothes? Come, we go to the floor and pick out a fine light linen and —"

"— I'm kind of in a hurry, my old friend," Monarch said.

"Of course!" Sami cried, before bustling around his desk. He retrieved a padded envelope and handed it to Monarch. "Six, just as you ask in your e-mail."

Monarch opened the pouch and fingered through passports from Chile, Brazil, Canada, Morocco, India, and Australia, seeing his face over names he would soon learn to respond to flawlessly. He studied several of the other documents in the pouch, and then nodded, satisfied. "Beautiful work, Sami, as always."

The fabric merchant beamed a moment, then remembered to lean over to another drawer. He pulled out a bundle of blue cloth that smelled of oil. He tossed it to Monarch, saying, "Wasn't easy to find this particular make and model on such short notice."

Monarch caught the bundle and felt a familiar weight and shape. "H and K .45 USP," Monarch said, putting a hand to his heart. "I'm touched that you remembered, Sami."

The Lebanese merchant smiled. "The Rafiqs take care of old and dear customers."

"Ammunition?" Monarch asked.

Sami slid two boxes of bullets and two clips across his desk.

Before picking them up, Monarch tugged out a cashier's check drawn on the Bank of Algeria. "Your fee, as agreed."

Sami took the check with a bow and quickly slipped it into his pants pocket. "Always a pleasure doing business, Robin," he said. "Can I interest you in some coffee?"

"It's Ramadan," Monarch said.

"I'm Christian," Sami said. "You?"

"A lost soul," Monarch said, who was loading the clips with the bullets.

"A lost soul who drinks coffee?"

Monarch shook his head. "As much as I'd like to, Sami, I'm pressed for time."

"Where are you going so fast?" Sami asked.

"Trying to figure that out."

"You still with the agency?"

"Nope."

"Working freelance?"

"That's a possibility," Monarch allowed, taking a shopping bag advertising Sami's store off the windowsill and dropping the passports and the extra bullets inside. The gun he stuck beneath his shirt in his waistband at the small of his back.

"I hear of any jobs, I'll let you know," Sami said.

"Appreciate that."

Sami bowed again. "Let me at least walk you to the door, my old friend."

■ ■ ■ ■

Back at Langley, Slattery paced inside the CIA's operations center. Agatha Hayes typed on her keyboard, and a satellite image of Algiers popped up on the central screen. She zoomed in on the Casbah, and now Slattery could see a red dot flashing on the Boulevard de la Victoire. Lynch's position.

"Can you give me a visual on the shop?" Slattery said into his microphone.

"Coming at you," Lynch said.

A moment later, the screen to the right of the satellite image filled with the street scene outside Rafiq's Magazin de Tissu Extraordinaire, looking at the business from a block away at a steep diagonal angle. Pedestrians crowded the sidewalks on the store's side of the street. On the near side, two women in dark robes and veils were moving slowly toward Lynch's position. A boy on a bike pedaled down the middle of the narrow street, with a taxi coming up behind him.

Through the front windows of Rafiq's fabric shop, Monarch saw the boy on the bike pass at the same time he heard the muezzin's cry begin to echo out over the city, calling the faithful to pray and an end to fasting. He stopped beneath the transom. He turned, meaning to shake Sami's hand and bid him farewell. But as he did so, ingrained habits forced him to scan the shop around him, looking at the customers and clerks.

All seemed well until he caught a woman in dark veil and robes standing up against the plate glass windows at the far end of the store next to the other exit. She was trying not to show it, but she was watching him.

Monarch stuck his hand out to Sami. The forger took it and pumped it, saying, "You sure you would not like to buy some fabric? I have a tailor who could be finished with some fine clothes for you by noon tomorrow."

"Not this trip, Sami," Monarch said, releasing his grip and turning once more, letting his attention drift past the veiled woman. She was no longer watching him. She was looking out the window and nodding.

Monarch's attention slipped to the crowded sidewalk just outside the store, to the taxi honking its horn and to the other side of the street where two other women in dark robes and veils were talking. One of them faced roughly toward the storefront. Something about the situation felt wrong, but he said, "Until next time, my old friend."

Monarch decided that the sidewalk was crowded enough to let him slip in, move with the flow toward the nearest mosque, and catch anyone trying to follow him. But he'd no sooner stepped out onto the sidewalk than he realized he'd emerged into a gap in pedestrian traffic. The taxi had turned onto the Boulevard de la Victoire, and the veiled women on the other side of the narrow street were reaching inside their robes and crouching to face him.

Their silhouettes dropping into athletic postures was enough to throw Monarch into action. He ducked, spun, and dived back toward the entrance to the fabric shop and a startled and puzzled Sami Rafiq. Monarch tackled the forger and drove him to the wooden floor of his shop just as automatic gunfire broke out, shattering the plate glass all around the entrance.

6

Slattery watched the surreal scene unfolding on the big screen inside the CIA's operations center. Monarch had clearly stepped out onto the sidewalk from the store. And then he had twisted and dived back inside as the two robed and veiled women drew machine pistols and opened fire, blowing out the shop's windows. The feed went shaky.

Lynch shouted into the covert ops chief's ear, "Who the hell are they?"

"No goddamned idea," Slattery shot back, transfixed by the veiled women moving in combat crouches toward the store, letting go with controlled bursts of fire.

"What do you want us to do?" Lynch demanded.

Slattery said, "Nothing you can do. Hold your ground."

"But they're trying to kill Monarch!" Agatha Hayes protested.

"Or Rafiq," Slattery snapped. "In any case, I'm not putting my men in harm's way. We'll let it play out."

Monarch scrambled forward off Sami Rafiq and threw himself behind one of the tables laden with fabric. He retrieved the pistol and clips while customers and clerks screamed and ran for cover. Another burst sounded from the street, splintering the wooden doorframe.

Monarch got to his knees, threw the .45 up and over the bolts of fabric, firing three quick shots at the door and another two out the front window. Out of the corner of his left eye, he spotted Sami dragging himself under another table.

A burst of gunfire came from Monarch's far right. He heard it thudding into the rolls of cloth over his head. He sprawled on his belly, peering beneath the low fabric tables and seeing a pair of dark sneakers beneath the hem of a dark robe. Monarch aimed at the sneakers and fired.

He heard her scream, and jumped up, seeing her let go her gun, twisting, trying to get to the ground. Monarch shot her in the chest, then swung the pistol hard and fired twice in the direction of the street. He kept swinging, using the momentum to hurl himself away from the front entrance. He landed, slid, and then pushed himself up, running crouched toward the rear of the store and the door at the bottom of the staircase, the pistol aimed behind him, shooting the last two rounds in his first clip.

He'd almost made it to the door when the two veiled women attacking from the street opened fire again. Their rounds pinged off the metal staircase and blew holes in the drywall, but none hit Monarch, who barreled through the rear door to the fabric shop and out into a whitewashed alley. He cut hard to his right. More shots ricocheted behind him.

He ran, dropping the first clip and shoving it in his pocket, coming up with the second clip, and slamming it into the magazine. He reached another alley. This one was more like a tunnel, with a roof overhead, and ancient stone stairs that dropped downhill. He ducked around the corner into the alley and waited, panting and refusing to let his mind seize on the obvious questions: *Who are they? Why are they trying to kill me?*

Monarch heard people shouting, and then police sirens wailing in the distance. He thought about fleeing, but felt compelled to take a look around the corner, back toward the rear exit from Sami's store. Before he could, a chicken came squabbling up the alley behind him. He grabbed the chicken, which scolded and clawed at him. He underhand tossed it about head high out into the air in the main alley.

The bullets came immediately, spraying the alley side to side. Monarch shifted the pistol to his left hand, aimed it blind around the corner, and fired. On the second shot, he heard the unmistakable punch of a bullet striking flesh and a soft cry, before the corner he hid behind exploded under fire. Shattered plaster and brick stung his face and hands.

He ran down stone stairs past a line of brightly painted Moorish doors. He reached a T where the covered alley ended, glanced back up the long stone staircase, and saw the veiled woman appear, her weapon held hip high as she readied to fire. Monarch jumped out of her line of sight, but his shoe caught on cobblestones. He stumbled and fell, the gun clattering from his hand.

He struggled forward on all fours, hearing the police cars wailing closer now, and knowing that the veiled woman was coming. He reached for the pistol, but a sandaled foot stepped on it.

Monarch looked up and saw one of the pickpockets, the one with the gold tooth.

"Follow me," the boy said in Arabic, and kicked the pistol at Monarch.

Monarch snagged the gun and jumped up, sprinting after the pickpocket, who dodged hard left into another descending alley, with three- and four-story buildings pressing in from both sides. The boy skidded to a stop in front of a low, green Moorish door, twisted the knob, and pushed.

He went in and Monarch followed hard at his heels, ducking so as not to hit his head on the low arch. The boy let him pass, then eased the door shut and slid the bolt. Monarch looked around himself. He was in the courtyard of an old villa badly in need of repair. The boy silently signaled to a staircase that climbed the interior of the wall to a small landing before shifting directions and rising to a second-floor colonnade.

The pickpocket stopped on the landing in front of a small piece of wood carved in the same shape as the door and set into the plastered wall. He hooked his finger in the iron ring attached to the piece of wood and gently tugged. It pulled out, revealing two iron bars that crossed the opening horizontally. Through them, and from above, Monarch could see people coming out onto the alleyway. He could hear their frantic voices wondering about the gunfire. Then he spotted the last veiled woman descending into the alley, her shooting hand tucked beneath her robes alongside her hip.

The pickpocket touched Monarch's shoulder. He twisted his head to see the kid with the gold tooth smiling at him and holding his fingers to suggest a gun.

Monarch moved closer to the hole, watching his assailant move beneath and past him, hurrying by the other people in the alley and then out of his sight. It was many moments until he was convinced that she'd gone. He slid the cover back into the hole.

Monarch turned and looked at the pickpocket, who was watching him the way some might a master magician. "What's your name?" Monarch asked in Arabic.

"Bassam," he replied.

"Why'd you help me, Bassam?"

The boy shrugged. "Why do they want to kill you?"

Monarch hesitated, and then said, "I don't know."

"Why didn't you kill her?"

"Because then you'd have a dead body outside your door and questions to answer. And I don't think you or your neighbors would like that."

Bassam seemed to respect that. "Who are they?"

"I don't know."

"Who are you?"

"Just a guy."

"Where you from?"

"All over."

"You got supersecret enemies, then," Bassam said.

Monarch thought about that, came up with a short list of possibilities, and then decided he had flush out whoever was behind the attack.

"You want to make some money?" he asked.

The pickpocket looked interested. "What do I got to do?"

"I need clothes, scissors, a razor, and a cell phone off a tourist."

Slattery said, "Lynch, go have a look before the police cordon off the place."

"Roger that," Lynch said.

On the big screen at the front of the operations center, Slattery watched Lynch's point of view as the operator left the car and crossed the street toward the six or seven people brave enough to look into the shop so soon after the shooting stopped. He could hear the police sirens coming.

"Hurry up," Slattery said.

Lynch's camera went to the front door and scanned inside. Glass lay all over the floor. Several people were wounded and moaning. A veiled woman in black sprawled dead on her back, half on, half off one of the fabric tables, blood pooling beneath her.

Sami Rafiq climbed out from under another of the tables, brushing glass off himself and trying not to break down in tears. He turned and looked right at Lynch. "Who are you?" Sami demanded.

Lynch pivoted without answer and left the shop, moving through and away from the crowd building outside.

"Did you see Monarch?" Slattery demanded.

Lynch crossed the street to the car, saying, "That's a negative."

Slattery snapped, "Circle the Casbah. There are only so many roads where you can drive. He'll head for one eventually."

With that, the covert ops chief threw down his headset. He looked over at Agatha Hayes. "I want everything our other people in Algiers can find out about what happened inside that store. ASAP."

Hayes was new to Slattery's team and shocked by the violence she'd seen explode on the streets of Algiers. She nodded dumbly, but then said, "Shouldn't we alert the Algerians to the threat?"

"What threat?"

"Monarch?"

Before Slattery could answer, the cheap prepaid cell phone buzzed in his pocket. Without speaking, he turned away from Hayes and stalked out of the room. He climbed the staircase to his office, digging for the phone. He flipped it open, entered his office, closed the door, and growled, "What happened?"

"He killed two of my best operators and escaped," said the woman with the French accent, sounding tense, exhausted, and angry.

Slattery felt like kicking something. Instead, he squeezed his free hand into a slow, deliberate fist. "I warned you he was good before you took the job."

"Not that good," the woman said coldly. "It will take me at least six months to replace them. So I'm out. And I damn well expect final payment."

Slattery said, "For a botched job? Not fucking likely."

He clicked off the phone, sat down hard on his leather couch, and stared at the ceiling. The game had changed. Monarch knew he was being hunted now.

68

Slattery closed his eyes, considering Monarch, trying to imagine and predict what his possible moves might be. As the special ops chief always did, he started with the history of anyone he was trying to game. He filtered through everything he knew about Monarch from his files, and then let his imagination carry forward to the man as he was today, as he might be at that very moment, trying to anticipate his attitude, his thoughts, and therefore his direction. After several games smoked out, a new one ignited, burned through his mind, and made Slattery bolt upright.

Monarch would go on offense.

Slattery jumped to his feet. The director had to hear his version of events first.

7

"Australian," the pickpocket said. He tossed the cell phone to Monarch and then handed him an old gray suit on a hanger. "Razor and scissors in the pocket."

"That was fast," Monarch said.

Bassam shrugged. "I clipped the phone the other day. The suit used to belong to my grandfather, Allah bless his soul. Only thing I had to do was get the razor."

"Any sign of the one who followed me out on the street?" Monarch asked.

Bassam shook his head. "Police are all over Rafiq's, though. Everyone's talking about it. People think it was a drug deal or terrorists or something."

They heard a low rumble of thunder. Lightning flashed. A peculiar electric smell, one of ozone and rain, came to Monarch on the quickening wind, pushing his thoughts hard to his early adolescence, to a night spent huddled under a cardboard box to stay out of a rainstorm that smelled just like this one.

Monarch looked at the pickpocket in a new light. "How old are you?"

"Sixteen," Bassam said.

"Who lives here with you?" he asked.

"Depends on the night. But mostly my grandmother."

"No one else?"

"Like I said, depends on the night."

Drizzle started. Monarch said, "Where can I shave and make a call in private?"

Bassam pointed to the second floor, where louvered metal doors were flung open to the colonnade. "Use that room, and the toilet there," he said. "I'm going to check on my grandmother."

Monarch climbed the stairs to the second-floor colonnade and walked its length, seeing how at one time the villa must have been a grand place, with mosaic tile floors and copper fittings on the banister. Now, many of the tiles were missing and the rest were coated in filth. Plaster sagged from the walls. The rooms he passed were musty. Spiders had spun large webs in the rafters. He reached the room with the open shuttered doors and looked in. There was little inside save a sleeping pallet and blankets, a stool with a radio on it, and a pile of books.

The drizzle turned to a steady rain. Monarch paced the colonnade back and forth, thinking through the course of actions he needed to take in order to survive. When he got it straight in his head, he punched in a number with a 703 area code just as a loud knock came on the door down in the courtyard. Monarch drew his pistol from his belt, listening to clicking on the cell phone, watching Bassam go to the door and open it. One of the other pickpockets Monarch had seen earlier in the day darted through, carrying a bag of groceries. Bassam patted him on the back, and the boy moved across the courtyard.

"Welcome," a computer voice said on the cell phone. "Enter code."

Monarch typed in a code. A moment later, a human came on the line. "Central Intelligence Agency. How may I direct your call?"

"Director's office," Monarch said.

There was a moment's hesitation before he heard the line reconnect and ring. Down in the courtyard, Bassam was answering another knock and letting in another of the boys who'd tried to steal from Monarch.

"Dr. Hopkins's office," came a woman's voice in his ear.

"Hi, Kris," Monarch said. "It's Robin Monarch."

"Monarch?" she replied in surprise. "He's in a meeting — about you, actually."

"Break in for me."

The phone went silent. Monarch watched as Bassam let in a third and fourth boy, each carrying a bag of one sort or another.

"That you, Robin?" The director of the CIA's hoarse voice was unmistakable.

Inside his office at CIA headquarters, Dr. Willis Hopkins leaned toward his speakerphone, listening.

"I understand you were having a meeting about me," Monarch said.

"Something about a gunfight in Algiers," Hopkins said, looking across his desk at Slattery, who sat with an impassive expression on his face, and the tips of his fingers pressed together in a thoughtful prayer pose.

"Who's there with you?" Monarch asked.

Hopkins raised an eyebrow. Slattery said, "I'm here, Robin. It's Jack."

"You guys trying to have me killed?"

Hopkins lifted a hand to stop Slattery from responding. "Not us, Monarch. We were attempting to find you, but the attack was not us."

"You've got some third party after you," Slattery said.

"And you know that how?"

"I had men watching Rafiq's, looking to bring you in to answer questions about what the hell happened in Istanbul. They saw the attack. We saw the attack. Muslim women in veils."

"Where are you, Monarch?" Hopkins cut in. "We would like you to come in. Slattery has a team in your area. They can meet you, get you out of there."

"I don't think that's a good idea," Monarch said.

"Why not?" the CIA director asked.

"Because before it all went to hell inside Nassara's lab, I opened a few files on his computer. I saw what Green Fields really was."

"What it really was?" Slattery sputtered. "What the fuck does that mean? It was an archive."

"What's your source? Who gave you that information?"

Slattery looked at Hopkins, who nodded. Slattery replied, "Someone very high up the food chain in Turkish Intelligence."

"And his source?" the CIA director asked.

"Someone inside Nassara Engineering," Slattery said, his eyes never leaving Dr. Hopkins. "An engineer who has known my source his entire life. The engineer said one day last month, Abdullah Nassara forgot to sign off from his computer in his personal laboratory. The engineer noticed it, and because he'd been curious about the strange hours Nassara seemed to be keeping, he started going through recently opened files, all of them named or referring to Green Fields. He opened twenty, and realized he was looking at detailed files from Al-Qaeda. That's why you were sent in there, Monarch. How many files on Nassara's computer did *you* open?"

In the Casbah, Monarch watched Bassam let in more boys, feeling suddenly unsure of the decisions he'd made in Istanbul. "Three," he said. "But three was enough."

"Three?" Slattery shot back. He was almost shouting. "How many files came up on that screen when you searched Green Fields?"

Monarch thought back and admitted, "A lot."

"You said a shitload," Slattery replied. "Isn't that the term you used?"

Monarch winced before saying, "Sounds right."

"So you actually have no idea what the other files in that *shitload* of files may have contained, isn't that correct?"

Doubt surged through Monarch. "That is

correct," he said.

Slattery showed Dr. Hopkins his palms. The CIA director nodded.

"What is it that you saw in those three files, Monarch?" Hopkins asked.

"Did the computers in Nassara's office survive?"

"Nothing survived," Slattery said. "Everything burned or melted."

"Were there backups of the files outside the building?"

"Not that we know of," Slattery said.

"What did you see, Monarch?" Dr. Hopkins pressed.

Inside Bassam's villa in Algiers, Monarch squinted, thinking one last time before answering, "I'm going to hold that card close to my chest for now. The way I figure it, Nassara's plant burning down was a blessing, a place that needed to be erased, and we should all just move on from here."

"Why?" Dr. Hopkins demanded. "Stop being so obtuse, Monarch."

"Sometimes it pays to be vague," Monarch replied. "Let's just say that I saw enough to know I didn't want to go on with my job, sir. And I knew it before Nassara and his nephew ever came into his laboratory."

Slattery elected to say nothing.

Hopkins said, "Did you kill Nassara and blow the place because of what you saw in the files?"

"Absolutely not," Monarch said. "On both those counts it was the nephew. I heard him shoot well after I'd escaped the lab. He blew the place to cover his tracks."

Slattery demanded, "Why the hell would he do that?"

"Don't know," Monarch said. "But he seemed real interested in what ever was in the steel attaché case his uncle was carrying."

Dr. Hopkins looked at Slattery. "Any information about a metal case?"

"No," Slattery said. "And the nephew certainly wasn't carrying one when he exited the factory. Tatupu would have mentioned it."

The CIA director said, "What do you think was in this case, Monarch?"

After letting in one last boy, Bassam turned from the gate to follow him through the puddles across the courtyard. The pickpocket paused in the pouring rain to look up at Monarch before nodding and disappearing from sight.

"No idea," Monarch said.

Dr. Hopkins said, "Why did you run?"

"I didn't want my teammates involved with my decision to leave. How are they?"

"Feeling betrayed," Slattery said.

"It's a moot point now, anyway. The files are gone," the CIA director said. "Monarch? What do you want to do now?"

Monarch replied, "Leave the agency, Dr. Hopkins. Start a new life."

"Why?"

"The job simply doesn't feel right anymore, and it hasn't for a while. There are other things for me to do. A better use of my time and talents."

"Such as?" Slattery asked.

"I honestly don't know, Jack. That's what I hope to find out."

"And the people who tried to kill you?" Dr. Hopkins asked.

"I'm hoping they really weren't after me," he said. "I'm hoping Sami Rafiq was the target and I just happened to get in the way. If not, I'll deal with them as they come."

Slattery said, "With no help from us."

"I understand what walking away is. But let me be clear about something: As long as there are no more attacks on me, I'll keep what I saw in those files to myself. Someone else tries to kill me, I'll change the policy."

"We had nothing to do with that attack," Slattery insisted.

"Just the same," Monarch said. "I have nothing more to give the CIA, and the CIA has nothing more to give me. Mutually agreed separation."

There was a pause on the line before Dr. Hopkins said, "You'll need to send us a letter of resignation to make this official, Monarch."

"I'll take care of it in the next day or so, sir," he said.

"Know also that if we find even a shred of evidence that you were responsible for Nassara's death, we will come after you," the CIA director added.

"Understood," Monarch said. He ended the call, dropped the phone on the bathroom floor, and crushed it with the heel of his shoe.

8

The CIA director rose from his chair in his office back at Langley, saying, "And that is that. We're down one of our best assets."

"Monarch can be replaced," Slattery said, rising as well. "If his mind was no longer in the game, we did not want him anyway."

Dr. Hopkins said, "I agree. But is Monarch telling the truth?"

"About his motives?" Slattery asked.

"I believe his motives," Hopkins replied, coming around his desk. "I've been through these kind of sea changes in my own life. I heard it in his voice. No, I'm wondering about the rest of it."

"The rest of it, sir?" Slattery asked.

The CIA director looked sharply at his covert operations chief. "What is the name of your Turkish source, Jack?"

Slattery had been expecting the question. He replied, "Muktar Otto, director of criminal intelligence for the Turkish National Police. I've known him for twenty years. I can send you his file if you'd like, as well as the report he slipped to me regarding Nassara Engineering and Al-Qaeda."

Dr. Hopkins nodded. "Just to close up loose ends."

"And Monarch?" Slattery asked.

"Leave him go."

"There are loose ends about his story, too."

The CIA director thought about that, then said, "There are, but I don't see how any of them threatens our national security anymore. We lost the archives and what ever Monarch saw in those files, but so did Al-Qaeda, and that has to have thrown them in some disarray. Unless we learn of evidence linking Monarch to Abdullah Nassara's death, let's set this one down, Jack, move on."

"Is that an order, sir?" Slattery asked.

"Yes, Jack, for the time being, it is."

In the Casbah, Monarch shaved off his beard and changed into the gray suit. When he was finished, he returned to the breezeway and stood there in the gloom, listening to the rain splattering in the courtyard, understanding that he had no idea what he was going to do other than get out of Algiers. The CIA had been all consuming for eight years, and U.S. Special Forces for nine years before that. Seventeen years of taking orders. Seventeen years of someone else giving him direction.

Monarch felt rudderless, and that sensation triggered once more the memory of huddling under a cardboard box in a rainstorm. A moment later, over the drum of the dwindling rain, he heard boys laughing. The sound, so unexpectedly familiar and yet so different, came to him like a horn blowing in a fog.

He saw himself the month before, standing in shallow water in a rainstorm, looking down at the bodies of three boy soldiers he'd been forced to kill in the Congo in order to escape with a valuable diamond the government wanted for scientific purposes. He felt sick again and then shook it off.

Monarch hurried down the stairs and crossed the courtyard. He slipped into a cluttered hallway lit at its far end by a soft glow.

The light flickered from kerosene lanterns in a room that was a kitchen at one end, where the boys were crowded, working or watching, and joking. Bassam was at the center of the activity, shouting orders, tearing a lit cigarette from the mouth of one of his friends, taking a drag, and then picking up a tray with a bowl of soup. He headed toward couches and chairs and a coffee table nearer to Monarch, who stood in the shadows watching, the scene triggering a dozen wretched and tender memories.

Bassam set the tray on the coffee table in front of one of the couches turned lengthwise. Monarch shifted his position and saw for the first time that someone was lying on the couch, someone small and frail, an old woman in a threadbare white robe and a matching veil and shawl. A clean, ironed sheet lay across her waist and legs. She was watching Bassam and making soft moans.

Monarch took a step into the room. The old woman caught the movement. Her eyes shifted and refocused on him. Then they widened, and she began to whimper. Bassam glanced over at Monarch and then at the other pickpockets who had stopped their banter and joking to watch the intruder in their midst.

"It's all right, Nana," Bassam told his grandmother. "He's just here to pay me money he owes me."

She whimpered at him insistently. Bassam shook his head, saying, "Of course that's not grandfather's old suit. Let me see him to the door. And when I come back, your broth will be cooled enough."

Bassam patted the old woman's shoulder as her complaint died back to soft moans. The pickpocket came to Monarch and walked by him into the hallway. Monarch nodded to the old woman and to Bassam's friends, who watched him in some awe.

The rain had stopped. Bassam slowed near the fountain. "She is dying," he said.

"I'm sorry," Monarch said. "Your parents?"

"My father left for France when I was two," Bassam said. "My mother died when I was nine. I have lived with my grandmother since."

"The other boys?" Monarch asked.

"I give them a place to sleep. They give me a cut of what they earn."

Monarch felt moved. "All of this will make you stronger than you think," he said, fishing for his wallet and drawing out five one-hundred-dollar bills. "For the phone, the razor, and your help, Bassam."

The boy snatched the bills. "Five hundred!" he cried. Then he calmed and looked closely at Monarch. "I don't even know your name."

"Call me a friend," Monarch said. "That's all you need to know." He gestured back at the house. "Those other boys?"

Bassam put the money in his pocket, nodding.

Monarch said, "Rule Number Two: Trust your brothers unless they prove otherwise. They are your family. They'll save your life."

"What's with the rules?" Bassam said, going to the door.

"It's complicated," Monarch replied. "A story for another time."

Bassam unlocked the door. "Good luck, thief."

"You, too," Monarch said. He slipped out the door.

By then, the entire Casbah had awoken and come out into the streets after the rain had passed and night had fallen. The alleys were crowded with people. So were the restaurants and coffee shops and the markets, which bustled against a blare of music that seemed to come at Monarch from all angles. His attention was everywhere, making sure no one was following him as he dropped downhill through the alleys, deciding he could not return to the hotel where he'd spent the last few nights. He'd get a bus if he could, heading toward Morocco, and sleep once he was across the border.

These thoughts were becoming plans, a direction in which to move, anyway — when he heard a jingle of coins.

"*Cadeau?*"

Monarch glanced down and saw a girl in ragged, filthy clothes sitting on the ground, shaking a begging can at him. She was no more than ten, a Bedouin of some impoverished lineage, with pale gray eyes that seemed to look right through him.

"*Cadeau?*" she cried in a pleading tone. "*A manger?*" (A gift? To eat?)

Monarch dug in his pockets and came up with several dinar bills and some coins that he dropped in her can. For some reason, he wanted to know more about her, where she came from, why she was begging alone in the streets. But he knew he had no business talking to her for long. It would only attract attention.

He reluctantly walked on, feeling upset. He stopped, looked back, and saw the silhouette of the girl shaking her can, calling for alms. He felt her despair and her plight as if it were his own. And then he felt anger that bore up out of memories of his adolescence. He flashed on the image of the dead African boys and felt deep shame. Those three emotions — despair, anger, and shame — fused in him. They became a conviction.

And in that moment, Robin Monarch envisioned the course of his future.

■ ■ ■ ■

PART II

■ ■ ■ ■

9

ST. MORTIZ, SWITZERLAND

It was the last day of racing on the frozen lake for the winter. The peaks around the Engadin Valley glistened like jewels set in platinum. So did the chiseled stone façade of the fortresslike tower of Badrutt's Palace Hotel, the standard of luxury in St. Moritz for more than one hundred years.

Wealthy spectators jammed the stands erected out on the ice in front of the hotel. The air smelled of grilled bratwurst, hot chocolate, and spiced wine. Oompah-pah beer hall music brayed. Fashionably dressed in ski gear and dark sunglasses, Robin Monarch had taken a seat in the third-to-highest row of the grandstand.

"They're vulgar, Robin," sniffed the petite and handsome woman in the ermine ensemble to his right. "I saw one vodka-addled Natasha lighting her Boris's Cuban cigar with a five-hundred-euro note last night outside King's Club."

Lady Patricia Wentworth sported a Kensington accent and vernacular, refined and precise enough to be as cutting as a scalpel. She was somewhere around fifty, give or take five years, artificially blond, but very put together and attractive. Her late husband, Sir Harold Wentworth, left Lady Pat 150 million pounds sterling upon his death. She was also half sister to the Earl of Gloucester and possessed an encyclopedic knowledge of the moneyed families that formed the nucleus of old St. Moritz. She'd been coming to the winter playground of British nobility since she was a child, and her gossip had been of great help to Monarch already. But after they found their seats that day, Monarch had stopped getting anything useful out of her. Lady Wentworth just kept going on and on about the bloody Russians and how they were ruining the resort.

She finished her tirade and then asked, "Is it too late to pad my wager?"

"I imagine someone would still take your money," Monarch replied, his attention cast out into the sea of fur below him in the stands. It had been nearly a year and a half since Algiers, and there had been no further attacks. But old habits were hard to break, and Monarch actively scanned the crowd around him.

He looked down near the rail and spotted a lovely fair-skinned woman in her late twenties, with shoulder-length hair the color of freshly shredded ginger. She wore a red down vest, a white cable-knit sweater, and coal-colored wool slacks and boots.

She held her hand to her brow, looked up, and spotted Monarch. She waved and came up the stairs. She gave Lady Wentworth a peck on either cheek. "Auntie, you look ravishing in dead animal skins."

Lady Wentworth smiled. "Wonderful to see you up finally, Lacey."

Lacey Wentworth slid around her aunt and into the seat to Monarch's left. She snuggled against him and said, "God, it's cold."

Lady Wentworth glanced at her niece. "You could have worn your mother's mink coat and hat as I offered."

"I don't do fur, Aunt Pat, even if it was mummy's," Lacey replied.

"Then don't bitch about the cold, dear," Lady Wentworth said, stroking the arm of her ermine coat. "I'm nice and toasty."

"Robin," Lacey said. "What's your take on women in fur coats?"

Monarch really didn't want to get between

an aunt and her niece, especially when he was a house guest of the former and a new lover of the latter.

"Depends on what they're wearing beneath," Monarch replied.

"Sensible man," Lady Wentworth said. "Fur, silk, and lace. Tactile aphrodisiacs."

Lacey's face screwed up. "Is everything about sex, Aunt Pat?"

Lady Wentworth shot her niece a condescending look. "Well, of course, dear. What ever did you think?"

An amplifier blared to life. A man speaking German welcomed them to the races on the White Turf, a tradition started by the British aristocracy who flocked to St. Moritz in the late 1800s. A trumpeter blew a fanfare. Horses and riders skipped out onto the ice, trotting across the packed snow surface, cautiously parading past the stands.

"Number three, the blue colors there, Argent," Lady Wentworth said, gesturing with her white mitten and program at a big roan. "I have fifty francs on him to place."

"Not to win?" Monarch asked.

"She bets to win only on sure things," Lacey informed him.

"I'm good at understanding the odds," Lady Wentworth agreed.

Monarch looked over the horses. A bay in

yellow colors with a female jockey caught his eye, and he suddenly felt something good ripple through him. "The yellow horse will take it," Monarch said. "Number eight."

Lady Wentworth made a puffing noise. "That old nag?"

A few minutes later and several furlongs away, the horses were lining up. Lacey, Monarch, and Lady Wentworth stood on their seats.

The flag dropped. The horses lunged forward, kicking up snow, slipping, and trying to find sure footing. But three, including Lady Wentworth's roan in blue and Monarch's bay in yellow, sped sturdily off the line, hooves throwing up snow clods as they accelerated.

"Go, you son of a bitch!" Lady Wentworth cried.

The crowd shouted along with her in ten languages. A forest of fur-clad arms, gold bracelets, and kid leather fists made whipping motions as the horses came on, the blue stallion running right off the shoulder of the yellow. As the horses pounded toward the crowd, dull, deep, unnerving thuds sounded from beneath them. The stands shook.

"One of these days, we're all going in the water," Lacey moaned.

"Nonsense," Lady Wentworth snapped. "It's just the ice settling."

The lead horses thundered abreast of the stands, throwing contrails of snow that lingered in the air behind them, a sparkling cloud that shrouded the rail and the first three rows of race goers. It was so unusual that Monarch's attention slipped from the horses.

A woman stepped from the haze at the rail and climbed several stairs.

She stopped, tugged off her spattered sunglasses, and brushed snowflakes from long ebony hair that cascaded and blended seamlessly into the jet tone of her ankle-length mink coat, which was open, revealing a blue denim shirt, jeans, and cowboy boots. Her build was tall and athletic, her posture a dancer's. Her deep mahogany eyes were large, almond shaped, and Asiatic. Her lips were naturally pouty, her cheekbones high, gracefully set, and blessed with flawless skin the color of clover honey. She climbed the stairs in the proud knowledge of her extraordinary beauty.

"Yes!" Lady Wentworth cried in Monarch's ear. "He showed! He showed!"

Monarch felt an arm loop his. "Aren't you happy?" Lacey asked.

Monarch startled and looked to Lacey.

"What?"

The cheering had died to post race hub-bub, chuckles, and groans.

"Your horse won," Lacey said, studying him. Then she glanced to the stairs and spotted the woman. "Oh, well, she is stunning."

"The horse?" Monarch said.

Lacey was watching Monarch more closely now. "Ms. Exotic Hot to Trot."

"Where?" Monarch said, making a show of looking around before settling on the woman, who had turned again and was now facing slightly toward the rail, looking into the crowd of people stretching between races. "Oh, her?" Monarch said. "If you like that sort of woman."

"Who, dear?" Lady Wentworth asked. "Of whom are we talking?"

"The bombshell in the mink coat and the Western wear, Aunt Pat," Lacey said.

Lady Wentworth scanned the crowd, picked up on her immediately, and snorted, "She dresses for Santa Fe, but by her features, I'd say she's Russian tainted with Mongol blood. Some new money's trollop, I'll wager."

"Trollop?" Monarch said incredulously. "I know what a trollop's supposed to look like, Lady W. That woman does not look like a trollop."

Monarch immediately knew that those were the wrong things to say with such emphasis, and he glanced at Lacey to find her getting stonier by the moment.

"And here's the trollop's benefactor," Lady Wentworth said. "Just as I suspected. I'll bet he can't get a rise for her without a little blue pill."

"Aunt Pat!" Lacey cried.

"What?" Lady Wentworth said.

The man in the sheepskin coat was taller, heavier, and at least fifteen years older than Monarch. He was deeply tanned, blockish, and sported close-cropped iron-and-salt hair and a stubble beard. He had his hand on the woman's back. He was whispering something in her ear. She was laughing.

"They are interesting specimens, aren't they?" Monarch said.

"Certainly different from the old crowd," Lacey said.

"Russians," Lady Wentworth said, almost spitting. "They're flooding in here, ruining St. Moritz. They all stay at that garish Kempinski's, but they're spending their money everywhere. Jewels, fashion, houses. It's obscene."

"Is it?" Monarch asked, growing irritated. "Their economy was in shambles twenty years ago. The Russians here now are the ones who risked everything. If they got rich, they deserve to be rich. How they spend their money is their business."

Lady Wentworth pursed her lips, as if deciding how best to tongue-lash Monarch for his impudence. But as usual, she surprised him: "I suppose you're implying that those born rich are not as worthy as someone who has made it himself," she said.

"Depends," Monarch said.

"On what?" asked Lacey, who had an ample trust fund.

"On whom we're talking about," Monarch replied. "I do admire someone who starts from scratch and makes millions far more than someone who is born rich or married rich but does nothing constructive with his or her life. I also admire someone with privilege who actually tries to make a difference." Monarch paused. "Like you, Lacey, and you, Lady Wentworth."

Lady Wentworth raised her eyebrow and nodded. "Smooth recovery, Robin, and point taken. I suppose St. Moritz will change no matter what I do."

"Life is change," Monarch said. "Every moment's new."

Lady Wentworth studied him. "Lacey says you won't be joining us this evening."

"A client is in town for the weekend. We're meeting for dinner."

Lady Wentworth hesitated, and then smiled coolly as she got up. "Well, then, I'm going to cash in my winnings and head for home, Lacey. Dinner is at eight. Maggie Cosgrove and her latest consort are coming. Don't be late."

"You're not staying for the rest of the races?" Lacey asked, frowning.

"I always believe in quitting when I'm ahead, dear," Lady Wentworth replied curtly. "Perhaps you should think about doing the same."

Robin Monarch and Lacey Wentworth left the white turf an hour later, walking up the hill under the shadow of the tower of Badrutt's Palace looming above the Tyrolean maze of old St. Moritz.

Lady Wentworth had told Monarch about the luxurious suites in the tower. One of her closest friends, Dame Maggie Cosgrove — her dinner guest for that evening, as a matter of fact — was staying there. But Monarch never gave it a second glance.

They got around the hotel and into the narrow village streets. They passed a pub bustling with the après-ski crowd. Monarch asked, "What did your aunt mean about you quitting while you were ahead?"

Lacey did not answer.

"Sore subject?"

"She was talking about you, Robin."

He laughed. "I thought she liked me."

"She does," Lacey replied. "She just can't see us ever working out."

"What do you think?"

Lacey stopped near a bakery. The aroma of fresh bread and pastries whirled around them. "Undecided. You?"

"We've known each other only a few months, but I'm having fun."

"Exactly," Lacey said, looking relieved. "Fancy a nap?"

He kissed her. "I'm in the mood for a walk. Why don't you take my car? I'll walk back and wake you when I come in."

"Clothed?"

He smiled and handed her the keys. "Your wish is my command."

"Starkers," she said, kissed him, and took a left at the next intersection, heading toward his car.

Monarch watched her walk away a few strides, then sobered with purpose. He maneuvered his way northeast through the crowded streets to Via Serlas, the high-end shopping district in St. Moritz. He got to Cartier, doubled back, and found a narrow, winding lane called La Suretta. From there, he had an unobstructed view of the tower of Badrutt's Palace to his southwest. He had to work quickly. Daylight was fading and dark clouds were gathering. He studied the gray stonework on the first six floors of the towers, then the rust red balconies on the next six floors, and finally the top, with its swooping green roof rising to a snowy peak.

Monarch then moved several hundred yards west to Via da Scuola. He turned left, glancing across a ravine and over a rock wall to the tower rising above the west wing of the hotel. Finally he walked to the Via Gerlas, the lakefront road, and repeated his inspection a third time.

Several minutes later, it started to snow. Monarch headed northwest through the streets toward Lady Wentworth's chalet, the entire hotel tower etched precisely in his brain.

Rule Number Six: Know your target.

10

Lady Patricia Wentworth's Chalet was a formidable stone-and-beam structure set amid the exclusive estates on the heights above the Survetta House, as elegant a private address as there is in St. Moritz. Monarch and Lacey's suite upstairs was alpine rustic and cozy, with whitewashed walls, a red duvet on the sleigh bed, dark exposed beams, and a gas fireplace that bathed the bedroom in a soft warm glow. It was dark outside the leaded glass windows. Oregano and thyme scented the air, rising from the kitchen. The only sounds were Lacey and Monarch trying to catch their breath after making love. They lay spooned under the duvet, Lacey in front of him.

"You're a mystery sometimes, Robin," Lacey said, stroking his forearm, fingertips near a tattoo that featured a hand extended as if to pluck something on top of the letters FDL.

"I'm an open book," Monarch said.

"What's *FDL*?" she asked.

Monarch's arm tightened, but he said, "A fraternity I was part of growing up. The stupid stuff that boys full of testosterone do."

Lacey looked at the tattoo, kept stroking her finger across it. "What were you working on for Stanley?" she asked.

"Sorry, client privilege," said Monarch.

"Is Stanley in any danger?"

"No more than you, I should imagine," Monarch said. "There were some things he wanted checked out in Australia. I checked and made my report."

Stanley was Lacey's boss, the head of one of the largest publishing houses in En gland. Lacey was an editor at the house. Monarch met her in an elevator one day after a meeting with Stanley. There'd been an immediate attraction, dinner, and well . . .

"Do you like flitting about all over the world?" Lacey asked.

"I enjoy the people I meet," Monarch replied.

"Like me?" she asked, reaching for him.

"Exactly like you," Monarch said, and rolled her on her back.

While Lacey finished showering, Monarch

checked himself in the mirror. Black slacks, black turtleneck, and black dinner jacket. He'd fit in wherever he went this evening. He entered the bathroom. Lacey was toweling dry.

"I'm off," he said.

"You'll meet me at Dracula's at midnight?"

"That's the plan."

Lacey wrapped a towel around her body and another around her wet hair. She gave him a quick kiss. "Good luck."

"Right. You're fine with me using the car?"

"I'll use Aunt Pat's. Where are you eating?"

Monarch hesitated. "He's made the arrangements."

"We're having Tuscan duck."

"I can smell it," he said. "Say hello to Dame Maggie for me."

"You don't even know her," Lacey said, plugging in her hair dryer.

"I feel like I do. Lady W. told me so much about her yesterday."

It was past seven when Monarch headed for the front door. The lower house was quiet and saturated with the smell of the Tuscan duck simmering. Lady Wentworth was still getting ready for dinner. Not even the maid saw him leave.

Monarch paused to survey the driveway that led down to the gate. No one. It was cold, and snowing steadily. He retrieved a black knapsack from the unlocked trunk of his rented BMW, got in the driver's seat, and drove off. He did not glance back.

Monarch took a left at the Survetta House, drove several hundred yards up a forested road, parked, and set about changing. He opened the knapsack and removed a pair of black gummy-soled shoes that fit him as tight as a glove. He strapped black neoprene gaiters over the shoes and his ankles.

Monarch tugged out a small black fanny pack. He clipped it on. The weight of the tools of his trade settled on his hips and disappeared beneath his turtleneck sweater. He stuffed a white ski mask in his coat pocket and put on tight, thin, neoprene gloves. He put loose wool gloves over them. He tugged out a Hermès plastic shopping bag and checked the white workman's coverall inside.

The drive to the Kulm Hotel in St. Moritz took less than five minutes. He valet-parked. Holding his shopping bag, he passed doormen in livery, admired the lobby, wandered through the hotel, and ducked out a side entrance. There was more foot traffic than

106

he anticipated on the Via Veglia, so he decided to take a left.

Rounding the corner, Monarch bumped hard into the side of a big man in a long dark wool overcoat. Monarch picked his head up in surprise. The man had a flattened nose, as if it had been broken many times. A fighter. But that was not what surprised Monarch; he'd felt something metallic under the man's coat.

"Bitte," Monarch said in German. (Sorry.)

The man looked offended at first, but then nodded.

There were two other men with the one he'd bumped. They all looked Slavic at first glance, blond, intense, all of them wearing similar long coats. Monarch bowed his head and moved down the lane, heading south as if nothing had happened, but knowing what was beneath the biggest man's coat, some kind of weapon. He'd felt the barrel and receiver of it clearly. He wondered if they were undercover agents of the Swiss Police, who were among the few allowed to carry guns in Switzerland.

Despite all the years of training, despite all his experience, Monarch's pulse quickened, and he was aware that his pace had increased. He forced himself to slow down, and he refused to look back until the lane bent to the right. The sidewalk ahead was clear and he glanced back up the street. All three men were gone.

Monarch forced himself to focus. He had only one goal to night. So he strolled on. Passing the formal entrance to Badrutt's Palace Hotel on the opposite side of Via Serlas, he slipped in behind a group of younger Swiss who took a left onto Via da Scuola, heading down toward the frozen lake.

Monarch let them get ahead of him, aware of the tower rising above the west wing of the hotel and the ravine. He glanced over his shoulder, saw the route behind him was deserted, and leaped off the bank of the ravine. He dropped and slid fifteen feet and landed in snow up to his knees. He leaped again, this time plunging into darkness. When he reached the bottom of the drainage, he dug out the coverall, put it on, and then tugged on the white wool head mask.

Finished, he clambered up the opposite bank to a stone-and-mortar wall perhaps seven feet high. Monarch stayed tight to the wall and walked the exterior of it to a snowed-over path near the southwest corner of the hotel.

Monarch squeezed into the bushes against the stone face. The rock was rough and scored enough that his practiced hands and feet found steady purchase as he climbed. Two minutes later, he reached the top. He pulled himself up on the lip slowly, breathing hard and steady, and looking at a terrace covered in snow.

The tower rose at the east end of the terrace. The tower's west wall featured a bowed extension of woodwork and windows below a covered balcony on the tower's fourth floor. There was another balcony on the fifth floor below the overhang of the upper roof. No lights shone on the first or second floor. The third floor showed a weak glow. The upper two floors were dark.

Monarch peered through the falling snow and made out security cameras mounted above the north and south corners of the terrace. From this distance — about 150 feet — Monarch could not tell if they were on. He crawled forward along the ledge through the snow toward the tower, praying that the coverall and white hat in the snow would be enough to let him pass beneath the cameras unseen.

When he got close to the cameras, he slowed to a creep, shifting, pausing several moments, then shifting his way forward again. At twenty past eight, Monarch reached the deep shadows where the ledge met the tower's south wall. He rolled on his back. He blinked at snowflakes, watching the cameras. They hadn't moved.

When he was sure of it, he rolled to his feet and took several steps to where the tower's stone façade met wood. He turned his back and braced his left gloved hand against the rough rock, feeling it grab. Monarch wedged his right forearm against the wood extension, then raised his legs and jammed the gummy soles of his climbing shoes against nubs in the opposite rock wall.

He shifted his weight and slid his forearm up three inches; and then his left hand, and then his feet, over and over again as if he were climbing the inside of a chimney. A difficult minute later, Monarch felt the top of his head against the bottom lip of the fourth-floor balcony. He grabbed hold of the floor of the balcony. Monarch pulled his head and then chest up enough that he could snag the balcony's railing. He was wriggling up onto the balcony when the exterior light flipped on.

Monarch froze, unsure what to do. His upper body was so fatigued, he didn't think he could hang off the side of the balcony again, and a jump to the terrace would definitely break his legs. So he stayed where he was when the balcony door opened, head bowed, pressed against the stone face, holding on to the railing, feet dangling below him.

Out of his peripheral vision, he watched a young boy in pajamas and boots step out in the snow, throw his hands toward the snow sky, and squeal with delight, *"Il neige encore! Vingt centimeters, au moins, Mama!"*

Monarch spoke eight languages and understood what the boy was saying to his mother. (It was snowing again, at least twenty centimeters.)

The boy turned and took a step toward Monarch.

But then the boy's mother appeared in the door, dressed in eveningwear, a rope of pearls at her neck. *"Claude,"* she scolded. *"Vien dedan maintenant. Tu etais malade, hier!"*

After hearing his mother tell him to come back inside, a pout grew on the boy's face. He seemed to look right through Monarch before reluctantly moving toward his mother.

"Je suis en plein form, ce soir," the boy complained.

"Dedan," she said, pointing a finger inward. The boy trudged inside.

Monarch heard the lock snap in place and breathed easier. He waited several moments.

It was snowing hard now. He could barely see down through the storm to the streets north of the palace, where pedestrians hurried past, heads bent over. Any other night, Monarch might have been spotted as he continued his climb. But in the squall, wearing white, he might as well have been a ghost.

He reached the uppermost balcony at a quarter of nine. Monarch crossed to a casement window and dug in his fanny pack for a large suction cup, a disposable cigarette lighter, and a small canister. Affixed to the canister was a horse-necked copper torch fitted at the base with a black twist control. Monarch opened the gas valve and thumbed the lighter; and with a soft pop, a flame shot out the torch, short, thin, and intense as a laser.

Monarch pulled on the suction cup. Then he stroked the flame to the glass in a precise arc. It was like a razor passing through skin, turning the triple-pane glass molten as it passed. He made a quick cut beneath the suction cup and lifted out an oval-shaped piece. The edges glowed orange. He set it and the suction cup in the snow.

Monarch stuck his hand through the hole and found the window crank. Moments

112

later, he slid over the sill and parted the drapes.

It was the living room of one of the palace's finest suites, scented with an older woman's perfume and a younger man's cologne. The passage to the suite's elevator lay to the right of a media center and was softly lit. The French doors to the bedroom were open, revealing a four-poster bed. A soft light shone in there as well.

He cranked shut the window. He got a throw pillow from the couch and stuffed it against the hole in the glass. He didn't want to change the air temperature significantly. If he did this right, he'd be able to weld the glass back in place. If he was lucky, it would be morning at least before they discovered his intrusion.

Monarch got out a small LED headlamp and clicked the red bulb on. He padded toward the bedroom. He knew he was leaving melting snow as he crossed the wood floor and the oriental rugs, but he didn't care. It was barely 9 P.M. He'd have plenty of time to clean up before he left.

Monarch's instincts took him to the cantilevered doors that filled the walls on both sides of the bathroom. He tugged the one closest open. A man's wardrobe. Ski gear. Several suits. A blue blazer. A tuxedo.

Several pairs of fine British-crafted shoes. Shelves of sweaters and socks. Dame Maggie's latest consort.

Monarch closed the doors, passed the bathroom, and opened the next closet. A dozen couture dresses. Twenty pairs of shoes, from ballroom slippers to rubber-bottomed boots and a ski suit with fur trim. The shelves held negligees, lingerie, and the object of Monarch's desire: a safe, a Herald, one of the toughest in the world.

The locking mechanism was digital, and featured a keypad that allowed each patron to set a special entry code. Monarch snatched a ziplock pouch from the fanny pack. He opened it and removed a vial of talc blended with fluorescent dust. He shook the vial, then unscrewed the top and drew out the brush. He dabbed each number on the keypad with the fluorescent powder. Then he screwed the brush back into the container. He flicked his headlamp switch. A blue halogen glow spilled on the safe. Monarch used a lens puff to blow at the talc. He smiled. The legendary service at Badrutt's Palace was as good as its reputation.

The maids had polished the face of the safe's keypad when they'd cleaned the room in the morning. Sometime since then, Dame

Maggie had punched in the code that opened and locked the safe. The fluorescent talc had clung to the oil her finger had left above the numerals *1-5-8-9.*

Unless the safe operated on a five-digit sequence, there were a considerable but limited number of configurations to try. But Monarch knew the right combination immediately. With his gloved finger, Monarch tapped out *1-9-5-8,* Dame Maggie's birth year. He heard the mechanism unlock and saw the steel door sag ajar. After the effort it had taken to get to that point, it seemed almost too easy.

He opened the safe and found a stack of black velvet boxes. He grabbed the first, a ring box, and found a multicarat, brilliant-cut diamond set in platinum. He snapped shut the case and set it on the shelf above the safe. Monarch didn't trust diamonds. If they'd been micro-etched, they were traceable. He was looking for something much more anonymous and therefore more negotiable.

The next box held a diamond choker, and he left that as well. The third box was square, Cartier, and empty, though the padding indicated it held a string of pearls and matching earrings.

The fourth box held a pair of large emerald earrings and matching ring. Seeing them, Monarch felt like everything was suddenly right in the world. Softer stones than diamonds, emeralds were rarely laser-etched and largely untraceable. These emeralds were of such size and quality that they had to be worth at least twenty thousand euros. He dropped the earrings and the ring in his fanny pack and set the box beside the others.

He took up the bottom box, about ten inches long, eight inches wide, and heavy. He snapped open the case.

The necklace was spectacular: forty-eight multicarat emeralds set in filigreed white gold and arranged in a wing pattern around a ten-carat emerald-cut emerald, a piece far too ornate for a simple get-together with Lady Wentworth. Monarch plucked the necklace from its silk bed and dropped it into his fanny pack.

Ding!

The elevator car that served the suite was arriving.

11

Monarch clicked off his headlamp, shut the safe door, and pushed into the back of the closet, hearing a woman's voice with a German accent call out in English, "Halloo? Housekeeping!"

He shut the closet door. A light came on. Monarch peered through the slats.

The maid wore a blue and white uniform. She had sallow skin, thin dark hair, and tired eyes. She drew down the duvet and folded it with Swiss precision. A moment later, she laid chocolates on the pillows, turned, and seemed ready to leave.

But then she halted not a foot from where Monarch watched her. Her attention drifted downward. Monarch's gaze went with hers to the carpet. A small puddle of water sat up on the carpet nap, and tablespoon-sized droplets led toward the living room. The maid tensed. Her head came around. She looked at the closet door.

Monarch pushed hard on the joints of the cantilevered door, causing them to buckle outward. The maid stepped back to scream. Monarch was on her before she could utter a sound. His hand clamped across her mouth as he drove her back onto the bed, pinning her with his body. She was terrified and tried to squeal and twist from him.

He held her tight and spoke to her first in Chinese, growling. "I don't want to hurt you. Do you understand?"

She looked at him in complete incomprehension. *Perfect.* "English?" he asked with a Chinese accent. "Speak English?"

She nodded, tears dribbling down her cheeks.

Monarch said, "You stay quiet or you die. Yes?"

The young woman's brows knitted in deeper fear, but she nodded.

Monarch relaxed and moved back off her. He kept one hand on her upper arm and the other over her mouth. He lifted her to her feet and led her into the bathroom. He shoved her inside the shower stall and turned on the water.

"You stay here," he said. "No talk. Quiet. If no, I kill you."

"Bitte," the maid said in a half sob, shrinking to the back wall, already soaking wet. "I

say nothing."

"Give me cell phone," he said.

She trembled as she handed it to him. Monarch took her phone and shut the shower door. He crossed to wall phone by the bath and unclipped the receiver. He twisted on the bathtub faucets and dropped the receiver and the cell phone in the water.

He turned on the sink faucets and the exhaust fan before glancing back at the shower. Through the steamy glass, he could see the maid had sunk to the floor and drawn up her knees, fetal in her surrender. She would be unable to hear anything and would not move until someone came for her. Monarch grabbed a towel. He shut the door.

The encounter had taken less than two minutes. He took a long, shuddering breath before realizing that he had no idea how long it would be until a supervisor came looking for her, which meant he could not afford to go out the laborious way he'd come in.

Rule Number Fourteen: All plans have weaknesses. Improvise.

An alternative came to him in an instant. He tore off the coverall and face mask, went to the other closet, and grabbed a hooded red ski jacket and a wool ski cap.

Monarch spotted a pair of men's reading glasses by the bed. He crammed them in his coat. He grabbed the coverall, mask, and the towel. He went to the edge of the bedroom carpet, stepping onto the towel with both shoes, and began wiping up the water and smearing whatever tracks he might have lain coming in.

Monarch circled back to the window he'd torched. He cranked the window wide open. Snow blew in on him. He leaned his body through and out until he could snag the suction cup and the disk of glass he'd cut. He tugged the suction cup loose, grabbed the glass like a Frisbee, and snapped his wrist. The disk sailed off over the balcony and disappeared into the storm.

He shut the window and remained on the towel, shuffling to the entry hall where the maid's cart rested by the closed elevator door. Monarch spotted a canvas bag, snatched it up, and stuffed the clothes inside. He buried the towel in the maid's hamper. He got out the reading glasses, put them on the bridge of his nose, and then drew the jacket's hood over his head before pressing the elevator button. He knew he'd probably be on camera, so he hunched over, with the canvas bag hanging from his right arm.

The elevator door opened. Monarch stepped into a wood-paneled carriage with brass railing and turned to the control panel. Every floor except the first floor required a key. He punched *1,* and waited, head down as the door closed and he dropped.

There was a guard-cum-concierge likely to be sitting to his right when he exited. The guards changed shift at eight, and Monarch prayed that Dame Maggie had left the hotel before then.

Deception is a delicate, suggestive art. As the elevator drifted by the second floor and slowed, Monarch rolled his shoulders forward and gathered all the saliva in his mouth to the center of his tongue. The second the elevator slowed, he inhaled hard.

He choked and started coughing. The door opened. He hurried forward, hacking hard, bent over. He aimed straight ahead, not stopping, not even when he heard a woman's voice call, "Herr Reynolds? Are you all right?"

"Something caught in my bloody throat," Monarch managed in a gurgled British accent. He never missed stride and never looked back to see the guard's reaction. He just kept coughing and moving toward the hotel entrance. He shivered like he had a chill as he entered the reception lobby. He coughed again as he approached the front door.

A doorman in livery bowed and opened the door. *"Danke,"* Monarch said.

A second doorman stood at a valet station. *"Ein taxi, Herren?"* he asked.

"Nein, bitte," Monarch said, and walked away, head down into the storm.

12

Monarch ditched the white coverall and face mask in a Dumpster behind a restaurant as he walked back toward the Kulm Hotel and the car. He tossed the canvas bag in a trash can outside a bar. He went inside the bar and had two shots of agave tequila neat. He purposefully engaged the bartender in small talk, told him that his client had stood him up, and left a large tip.

He retrieved his car then, drove north toward the ski slopes at Diavolezza, parked at the deserted tram station, and worked quickly. He turned the defroster on high. He put his gloves, spats, and tools in the fanny pack; and then he slipped them into a large mailing pouch with the correct postage for the weight, and a Swiss customs declaration taped to the front, identifying the contents as dental tools. Address: a post office box in London.

Next, Monarch removed the emerald

necklace from the velvet pouch and laid it in his lap. He rummaged in his pack and found a rectangular cardboard box about three inches deep, ten inches long, and eight inches wide. The lid advertised a chocolate shop in St. Moritz and featured a pretty red bow and a birthday card addressed to MARTA taped to the top. He lifted off the lid.

A sheet of confectioners' paper covered what appeared at first glance to be a slab of Swiss chocolate cradled in petals of gold foil, nearly two pounds' worth. Monarch took hold of the edges of the chocolate slab and lifted off what proved to be the top of a chocolate box with a hollow core.

Monarch set aside the top, carefully picked up the necklace, and spread it out inside the core. He put the earrings and the ring in as well. Then he opened a ziplock bag containing three quarters of a pound of chocolate slivers and spread them over the necklace until the core was filled. The chocolate cover fit snugly into place. The gold foil wrapped it tight.

Monarch went to his fanny pack again and found a thin electric cord that he plugged into the lighter. The cord's prongs slid into a tiny socket in the inside corner of the box. Monarch set the chocolate shop's box top in place, and then placed the box on his dashboard. The foil was expensive stuff, NASA stuff. It made his little contraption into the heated chocolate mold that it was.

He exited the tramway parking lot, driving back toward St. Moritz, one hand holding the box on the dashboard as the temperature inside the car became stiflingly hot.

It took him roughly six minutes to reach the train station directly west of Badrutt's Palace. He parked across the street. A train had just arrived from Geneva, and the entry bustled with taxis waiting for wealthy tourists on holiday. He paid them little mind as he rested the box in his lap, removed the cover, disconnected the plug, and pushed the tiny socket down between the cardboard box and the warm foil. The chocolate and the necklace had become one. Now all it needed was to cool.

Monarch taped the cardboard cover solidly in place before sliding the entire box into a larger padded mailer. It was addressed to SEÑORITA MARTA MÉNDEZ and carried enough postage stamps to get the package to a post office box in Buenos Aires, Argentina. The customs papers taped beside the address declared that the package held a kilo of Swiss dark chocolate worth fifty euros. At the bottom, it read in

Spanish and German, *Birthday Present for My Granddaughter.* Like the Swiss, the Argentines have a love affair with chocolate. Swiss chocolate meant for a little girl's birthday present would not be tampered with. At least he hoped not.

Monarch opened the door, slid the mailer beneath his car, and shut the door. In the bitter cold, the chocolate would solidify quickly. Fifteen minutes later, when the debarking passengers had cleared the area, he put on the wool cap, got out, retrieved his packages, and crossed the street.

He walked straight to a postal box with his head down to thwart the security cameras. He pulled open the hatch and dropped the pouch that contained his tools into the postal box first. The mailer containing the chocolate and the necklace he treated more delicately, however, reaching his arm in as far as he could, almost to his elbow, and holding the package like a plate before letting go.

Monarch trotted away, drawing his jacket collar up around his ears like a man desperate to get in out of the cold. Several minutes later, he entered a pub on a side street. He spent an hour there, eating a roast beef sandwich and drinking a beer. He told the bartender the same story about having his client stand him up, tipped him well and left.

At two minutes to midnight, a techno-beat dance song echoed as Monarch strode down a long snow tunnel lit by candles toward the entrance to the Dracula Club, the private nightspot in St. Moritz for has-been royalty in search of money and the newly super-rich in search of old-world credibility.

The front doors to the nightclub opened. The music blared at Monarch and put him on edge. Since escaping from Badrutt's Palace nearly three hours before, he had been hyperaware of everyone and everything around him, inspecting them, gauging their level of threat. The maid had changed everything. There would be an investigation. Someone would come looking. Someone official. There could be police already on the scene.

Monarch went inside. It was only midnight, a young hour by Dracula Club standards, but the place was already packed with revelers drinking heavily from bottles of Absolut Cristal. The dance floor was filled with writhing wealthy bodies.

Monarch scanned the crowd and then frowned. Lacey was usually very punctual. He heard cheers and spotted people moving through open doors at the back of the room. He followed them outside onto a raised deck.

People hung over a railing, roaring in six languages, "Go! Go!"

Below the deck some ten feet, lit by torchlight, a rough-skinned man in a blue parka and a ski helmet plopped down on a rectangular stainless steel restaurant tray. Five feet in front of the man loomed the entrance to the St. Moritz Olympic bobsled run, built in 1903 and still one of the most challenging in the world.

The man snagged a bottle of Cristal and swigged from it.

"Go! Go!" the crowd chanted.

Monarch smiled. There was an engaging insanity about watching a man prepare to propel himself down a high-banked ice course on a steel tray. The man pushed off and leaned back as his sled gained speed. His eyes were wide and utterly awake. The cheers of the spectators swelled. And then he was gone.

The crowd fell quiet, listening. Above the last few murmurs, Monarch caught the rattling of the tray over ice and the man howling like a wolf. Monarch broke into laughter, and the tension that had so tightly gripped him these last few hours fell away.

"Go! Go!" the crowd began again. A new victim was preparing himself.

Monarch felt a tap on his shoulder. He startled, pivoted cautiously, and found Lacey standing before him in a purple ski jacket, jeans, and spike-heel boots. She was listening to her cell phone. She held her finger up in the air toward him.

"Of course, Aunt Pat," she said. "You'll ring when you know more?"

Lacey snapped shut the phone in disbelief. "A cat burglar climbed the tower at Bad-rutt's Palace, broke into Dame Maggie's room, cracked the safe, and stole her necklace. It's worth about six hundred thousand euros."

Monarch feigned astonishment. "That's over a million bucks!"

"Emeralds," she said. "Beautiful ones. Lots of them. It was one of a kind."

"When did it happen?" Monarch asked.

"While she was eating with us," she said, all the more astonished. "William Reynolds, Dame Maggie's gentleman friend, found the maid in the shower when they got back. She'd surprised the thief. Said he was masked. Wearing all white. Some kind of Asian. He put her in the shower, told her he'd kill her if she moved."

"That's wild," Monarch said.

"Aunt Pat's going to Badrutt's to fetch Dame Maggie and William back to the house. Can you believe it? He climbed the tower in the middle of a snowstorm and then cracked the safe like it was a toy?"

Monarch put his arm around her. "Do you want to go there, too?"

Lacey's face pinched. "That would be a good idea, wouldn't it? If only to help haul the luggage home."

"Agreed," Monarch said, and he felt a mild thrill go through him at the idea that he might actually get to see the crime scene postmortem.

They exited the nightclub. There was a long line of people now waiting to get inside. It stretched almost to the other end of the snow tunnel. As they made their way toward the valet station, Lacey said, "I'll bet Dame Maggie's petrified."

"Why?" Monarch said. "She wasn't there."

"She could have been," Lacey said.

"I would imagine he'd have waited until she was gone," Monarch said. "I'll bet he wasn't happy when the maid came in."

"My point exactly. That could have been Dame Maggie that surprised him."

Monarch thought it best not to argue. "Point taken."

"Aunt Pat said she's heartbroken," Lacey

said. "Her late husband, Harold, gave her the necklace shortly before he died. Did I tell you?"

Rule Number Eight: It's never personal. Still, Monarch felt a brief pang of remorse. He thought he had taught himself to ignore the sentimental value people placed on the things he stole, but there was no avoiding it now, and it made him feel off-kilter.

He felt even odder when he and Lacey stepped from the tunnel to the valet station. A black Porsche Cayenne was pulling up. Through the windshield, Monarch saw to his surprise that the driver was the Russian in the sheepskin coat from the horse races earlier in the day. Beside him was his woman in the mink coat.

The valet cut in front of Monarch and Lacey to open the car's passenger door. It distracted Monarch enough that he looked over the roof of the Porsche to the Russian climbing out the other side. Monarch happened to glance beyond him and spotted three men hurrying out of the shadows on the opposite side of the circular driveway.

The one leading was the same man he'd bumped into earlier, the one who'd been carrying a weapon beneath his long dark overcoat. The sleeve of his right arm flapped in the wind, empty.

Monarch's internal alarms went off. He barely registered that the Russian's woman was standing right in front of him. The men were running at them now, their left hands no longer holding their coats shut, their right hands bringing up guns.

13

"Down!" Monarch bellowed, grabbing Lacey and the Russian's woman by the shoulders and hauling them to ground behind the Porsche.

The machine guns opened up, shattering the car's windows, blowing holes through the doors, exploding ice off the snow tunnel. The valet fell dead next to Monarch. The Russian dived on top of the valet. His woman was screaming and holding on to Lacey. Other people were screaming, too.

"Inside!" Monarch shouted. "Get in the tunnel!"

But Lacey couldn't move. The Russian's woman was holding her too tight. Monarch could hear the guns laying down short bursts, coming closer. If he lay here, he was a dead man. He did the only thing he could think of: He played shot and rolled out from behind the Porsche's front bumper and into the gutter.

One of the gunmen was right there, not five feet away and coming hard around the car, weapon up. Monarch waited until he was in range, and then lashed out with his foot, kicking the gunman in the kneecap. The man buckled.

Monarch grabbed the assassin by the hair and hammered him with the butt of his palm right at the base of his neck. He felt bone crunch and the man slumped. Monarch grabbed his gun and came up on his knees.

The second gunman rounded the back of the Porsche, gun up, his focus on the Russian. Monarch fired. The assassin danced and jerked before falling.

The third man, the one he'd bumped into, was starting to retreat. Their eyes locked and Monarch saw that he'd recognized him from earlier in the evening. He let loose a burst of fire at Monarch, who ducked and then jumped up, ready to shoot.

But the third assassin had dragged a woman from the car behind the Russian's. She was screaming and he was using her as a shield held tight to his chest, dragging her down the entry road and then into the snow toward the corner of the building.

"He's going to kill her, Robin!" Lacey cried.

They disappeared around the corner. In an instant, Monarch's intentions were split by two opposing instincts. The thief in him told him to stop and let things play out. But the soldier in him drove him to pursue.

Monarch sprinted down the entry road and jumped into the snow, following the tracks they'd left. He darted his head around the corner and spotted the third assassin dragging the woman around the rear of the building. Sirens sounded, far off, followed by screaming and widespread panic closer by.

Monarch ran to the rear of the nightclub, ducked his head around, and saw the gunman on the platform above the start of the bobsled run, watching his back trail, gun under the woman's arm while other people scattered. Monarch didn't dare take a shot. He took another quick look, seeing the gunman throw his hostage down and jump onto one of those restaurant trays that slid into the track.

It was another of those split instant decisions, to stop or go on? Monarch ran forward, snatched up another tray, threw it onto the bobsled ice, and hurled himself onto it, belly, head, and gun leading.

There was no steering the tray. It wobbled, shook, made a racket, and threatened to spin sideways. Halogen floodlights lit the track every twenty meters. The course was steep and icy, and Monarch was soon traveling twenty, thirty, and then forty miles an hour. He held tight to the front of the tray with his left hand, kicking out his feet, trying to use them like rudders. He dug the tips of his shoes into the ice as the track banked left.

He banged off the wall. The action threw him sideways. As he fought for control, he spotted the gunman flash beneath a light ahead about forty yards, and then disappear into a tunnel. Monarch got the tray going straight again. He rattled down the ice chute, moving the machine pistol to a ready position.

He flew toward the tunnel, seeing that the roof was tent canvas stretched over a wooden frame to keep snow out. He sailed into it blind, feeling the track veer hard left again. The ice inside was free of snow, and he accelerated wildly up the curved wall. For a heartbeat, he thought for sure he'd flip.

Monarch shot from the tunnel pushing fifty miles an hour. He hurtled through a pine forest. The course fell away right, and then into a straightaway.

A bridge spanned the track. The gunman,

sitting upright, skimmed beneath it. Monarch could see people up on the bridge. They shouted and hooted encouragement. The gunman looked over his shoulder and spotted Monarch behind him. He reached back with his gun and fired.

Ice exploded right beside Monarch before he sailed up the side of a tight bank curve, feeling the centrifugal force pry at him, almost spilled, but then felt launched out of the turn. He went airborne and ricocheted off the opposite ice wall. Flames erupted in the track ahead. Bullets whizzed over his head.

Monarch was already shooting when he came out of the next turn. But there was barely a straight there and the gunman was already through it and his bullets rattled off the ice where the course angled hard right and hard right again.

The assassin disappeared into another of those canvas-covered tunnels. Monarch sailed in blind again, accelerated, and blew out the other side, instantly aware of the openness around him. They'd left the forest. He could make out the lake far ahead.

Based on his speed, Monarch figured he had to be catching sight of the killer again. But then he skidded into another of those steeply curved and tented parts of the course. The threat of repetition registered, and he reacted in a microinstant.

Monarch arched himself up on his left side and aimed the gun overhead. The tent disappeared. The gunman was right there balancing on the wall of the track, raising his gun. Monarch fired first. The gunman jerked. His gun went off.

Monarch felt clubbed to the head and fell into darkness.

14

EIGHT P.M.

THE NATIONAL PORTRAIT GALLERY
WASHINGTON, D.C.

Slattery hurried up the stairs to the museum's main entrance with Audrey, who was looking stunning in a black evening dress and a gold choker. But Slattery was paying her little attention. His mind was gaming positive scenario after positive scenario, all of which left him breathless with renewed opportunity.

Slattery flashed his CIA identification to the police officer outside the entrance. The cop nodded them through, and they were soon enveloped in the happy din of a joint affair for the benefit of the National Endowment for the Arts and the Smithsonian Institute. A string quartet played in the corner. Several hundred men in tuxedos and women in their finest gowns mingled, ate gourmet appetizers, and drank cocktails.

Slattery adjusted the bow tie of his tuxedo and, with Audrey, circled the perimeter of the party. He felt slightly resentful of the patrons — rich, powerful, and able to boast of their deeds in public. *If they only knew what I've done, what I'm capable of,* Slattery thought, and smiled at that idea. He felt it ground him with confidence before he spotted a tall, gaunt, bald, and pasty-skinned man in his sixties exiting the hallway from the National Portrait Gallery. Congressman Frank Baron walked at his side. Both men carried tumblers of scotch. Baron was listening intently to his companion.

Slattery told Audrey to go have a drink, and then walked to them. "Congressman Baron," he said. "And C. Y. Tilden, I presume?"

Tilden was a Georgia billionaire industrialist. He was also Frank Baron's biggest political benefactor. Slattery stuck out his hand to Tilden, whose facial skin stretched thin over his cheekbones, revealing pitted silver eyes that showed irritation at the unwanted interruption.

"And you are?" Tilden said in a soft Southern accent.

"My friend at Langley, C.Y." Representative Baron said stonily.

"Oh," Tilden said, as if he'd tasted something old and gamey. "Yes. Too bad. A disappointment. What a coup that would have been." He was already looking beyond Slattery, scanning the crowd.

Baron clapped Slattery on the shoulder and said, "Well, good to see you, Jack, but we have several important people we need to speak with."

"Not tonight, Frank," said Slattery. "Tonight, I am the most important person in this room, maybe the most important man inside the Beltway."

Tilden shifted his gaze to Slattery in laconic amusement while Baron's expression twisted toward hostility.

Slattery ignored Baron, leaned closer to them, and said, "Green Fields is not dead. I suggest we find a place we can talk."

Fifteen minutes later, Slattery sat in a plush seat in the back of C. Y. Tilden's limousine as it pulled away from the museum. Tilden pressed a button that raised a soundproof barrier, and then he said, "I thought that all information pertaining to Green Fields technology was destroyed in that fire."

"I thought so, too," Slattery said. "But no longer."

"Prove it," Congressman Baron said.

Slattery poured himself a scotch from one

of the crystal decanters in the back of the limo before explaining that for the past eighteen months he had kept tabs on Ali Nassara, the nephew that Monarch claimed killed the physicist and blew up his private laboratory. Ali Nassara acted the grieving relative during this time, continued his work as a bodyguard for various private clients, and never once left Turkey.

Slattery set down his drink, reached into his breast pocket, and brought out a Black-Berry, saying, "But then, about a week ago, my contact in Istanbul told me that Nassara had purchased an airline ticket to Odessa."

On the screen of his BlackBerry, Slattery called up a grainy, long-lens photograph of a man pushing a luggage cart into Istanbul's Atatürk International Airport. He handed the BlackBerry to Tilden, saying, "That's Ali Nassara on his way to check in. Notice what is second to the top on his luggage cart."

Tilden held the screen so both he and Baron could see it. The congressman squinted. "A metal case?"

Slattery nodded.

Baron said, "But I thought you told me that the only thing this guy had was a rifle when he escaped that burning factory."

"My men said he was hunched over, *hold-*

ing his stomach, and carrying a rifle."

Tilden shook his head. "That case is too large to hide under any shirt."

"Agreed," Slattery said. "But I don't think that's the same case that Abdullah Nassara was carrying the night he was killed. I think that case was left somewhere inside the factory before the explosions began and melted."

Now Baron nodded, handing Slattery back his BlackBerry. "You think he got something out? Something to do with Green Fields?"

"Consider this, and draw your own conclusions," Slattery replied. He called up another photograph on his phone. "This is a crime scene photo of the hotel room where Ali Nassara was murdered in Odessa three days ago. Drugged and strangled. No sign of forced entry, no sign of struggle. Notice what is lying open and empty on the bed."

"The case," Baron said.

"Zoom in on it," Slattery said. "See the foam interior? The cutouts?"

Tilden said, "I see them, but so what?"

"I think Monarch was right. Ali Nassara killed his uncle for what was in that case," Slattery said. "Then he waited more than a year and a half to try to sell it."

"Sell what?" Baron demanded. "A copy of the files?"

"Better. A prototype."

Tilden understood immediately. "And whoever's got that prototype can reverse-engineer it."

"That's right."

"Any idea who has it?" Tilden asked.

"Not yet, no," Slattery admitted. "But something like this will not stay long in one person's hands. It will be sold and bought, and soon."

Tilden looked out the window. They were moving through Foggy Bottom, heading in the direction of Georgetown when he looked back at Slattery. "Then we find it before that happens," he said. "Find it, buy it, and my offer to you still stands."

Slattery cocked his head to one side, considering that approach; then he shook his head and said, "If whoever has this thing understands its value, he'll have a discreet auction. It will go to the highest bidder. The payment could be enormous."

"Then find the prototype and steal it before the auction," the industrialist said.

Slattery smiled. "Exactly my thought, C.Y. You should have been a spy."

Tilden seemed to find that amusing, but the congressman crossed his arms and said,

"You can't put anyone into the field officially on this. You said Monarch told Hopkins that Green Fields was not Al-Qaeda's archives."

Slattery nodded. "Which is why I did not come to see you when I first got word of Ali Nassara's murder. I could not figure out how to go after the prototype, or rather *whom* I could get to go after it without alerting Hopkins."

"And now you have?" Tilden said.

"Ask and ye shall receive," Slattery replied. "About two hours ago, I was served with an information request from Swiss National Police via our consulate in Geneva. There was an attempted assassination outside a St. Moritz nightspot last night. An American security consultant foiled the attempt. Robin Monarch."

"Monarch?" Baron sputtered. "You want to get *him* to track down the prototype? No. He'll never do it."

"If the situation were handled delicately, he might, Frank," Slattery insisted.

The congressman shook his head. "Monarch is not a stupid man. Once he figures out what you're up to, he'll bail, or try to ruin us."

"Which is why it has to appear as if none of us are involved, especially me, until it's too late," Slattery said.

Tilden scratched his thin lip before saying, "How you going to do that?"

"The way you corner any predator, C.Y. With bait and dogs."

15

NOON
HOSPITAL CLINIC
ST. MORITZ

Hans Robillard was in his early sixties and afflicted with a general sagginess that made him look worn out and disinterested. But the man's intelligence was evident in hazel eyes that flickered constantly, as if they were lightbulbs linked to synapses in his brain.

"Do you often engage in firefights with automatic weapons?" Robillard asked in slow clipped English. He stood next to Monarch's hospital bed.

Monarch was sitting up in the bed, left hand handcuffed to the rail. He had white gauze wrapped around his head, which was pounding. He wanted nothing more than to sleep, but he forced himself to focus all his wavering attention on Robillard, who Monarch understood was not someone to be trifled with. Robillard was an inspector with

Swiss Police, a national force like the FBI.

"I do when I'm shot at by automatic weapons, Herr Inspector," Monarch replied.

Inspector Robillard blinked. "Why did they want to kill you?"

"They didn't. They were after the Russian."

"And you knew this how?"

"By the angle of their attack and their eyes. Their attention was on him. I don't even think they knew I was there."

The inspector put his chin in his hands. "Lucky for Herr Belos that you were."

"Belos? Is that his name?"

"You do not know him?"

"I saw him earlier in the day," Monarch admitted. "At the horse races. But, no, I've never met him. Or his girlfriend."

"Iryna Svetlana," Robillard said. "You do not know her either?"

"No."

"And yet you risk your own life to save them," the inspector said, more a question than a statement. "You kill two men and then you chase a third man onto a bobsled track, where you have another gunfight."

"I killed them in self-defense. I went after the third man because he'd taken a hostage, and because I don't like getting shot at. I figured to try to apprehend him, but then

148

he started shooting at me on the bobsled track. So I returned fire. And then I got hit. I think I hit him, too. End of story."

Robillard thought about that before saying, "Lacey Wentworth says you were on your way to Badrutt's Palace at the time of the attack."

"That's right. We'd heard one of her aunt's friends had been robbed."

"A million-dollar burglary," Robillard said. "An emerald necklace."

"Heard that, too," Monarch replied, meeting the inspector's gaze.

Robillard asked, "Don't you find it odd that there is a theft of such magnitude and a dramatic shootout on the same night in little St. Moritz?"

Monarch felt throbbing pressure building in his skull, but kept his eyes relaxed and on Robillard. He shrugged with just enough nonchalance. "You'd be the expert on the crime rate here, Inspector. I'm just a visitor."

"You are a security consultant?"

"That's right," Monarch said.

"For?"

Monarch shrugged. "Corporations. Wealthy individuals."

"Governments?"

"Not anymore," Monarch said.

"You served in the U.S. Army?" Robillard asked.

"That's right," Monarch said. "Military police."

"So you are a mercenary now?"

"Security consultant," Monarch said.

Robillard laughed and patted the railing of the hospital bed. "Please, Herr Monarch, spare me the cover story. I know who you are, or were."

Monarch showed confusion. "Who am I?"

"Oh, Robin Monarch is your name," Robillard said. "But you were never a military police officer. You were U.S. Special Forces and then CIA. You left the agency a year and a half ago, and from what I can gather, under difficult circumstances."

"A difference of philosophy," Monarch said.

"What sort of difference?"

"A touchy subject. And certainly not germane to the matter at hand."

Robillard sat back, looking at him in admiration. "I think you are a genuinely dangerous man, Mr. Monarch. Capable of anything."

Monarch laughed. "I'm a teddy bear, Inspector. Really."

"You could be charged, you know."

"With what? Defending myself? Saving lives?"

"There are three people dead," the inspector insisted.

"I saved at least five people, counting myself," Monarch said. "The valet was theirs. If you're looking for a fall guy, I'm not it. You should be trying to find that third guy. The one who shot me."

"We did try to find him," Robillard said. "But he escaped in the snowstorm."

Monarch thought about that. Then he said, "Identify the two dead shooters and figure out how they link to the Russian, this Belos character."

"We already have identified the shooters," Robillard replied. "Members of a powerful drug-smuggling syndicate based in Chechnya."

"And Mr. Belos?"

"He poses as a legitimate businessman from St. Petersburg."

"I hear a *but* coming."

"The Russians say he is the leader of the Vory v Zakone in St. Petersburg."

"Vory v Zakone, 'Thieves in Law,'" Monarch said, suddenly very curious. He'd known about the Russian Mafia since adolescence, been fascinated by them for years, but had never actually met a member in person.

"Correct, Herr Monarch," the inspector said. "You've just saved the life of someone I suspect just might be more dangerous than you are."

Before Monarch could reply to that, there was a sharp knock at the door to his hospital room. It opened, and a young officer poked his head in. "Herr Inspector?"

Robillard closed the file, rose reluctantly, and left the room.

Monarch's thoughts swam as he tried to figure out how much Robillard might know about him. Probably not a whole lot more than what the inspector had said — that he'd been Special Forces and CIA.

The door opened. Inspector Robillard scowled as he entered. "You have powerful friends, Herr Monarch. You are free to go when the doctor will allow it." The inspector unlocked the handcuffs.

Monarch rubbed his wrists. "Not even going to tell me not to leave the country?"

"Are you planning on it?" Robillard said, stiffening.

"Day after tomorrow, from Zurich," Monarch said, standing. "I have a meeting scheduled in Buenos Aires."

The inspector studied him the way some

men might a shadow. "We are in touch with your government. I can find you if need be."

An hour later, Monarch had changed back into his street clothes and been taken by wheelchair to the clinic's ambulance entrance where Lacey and Lady Wentworth were waiting for him.

Lacey ran to him and kissed him. "I can't believe they were holding you."

"Nothing that could not be worked out," Lady Wentworth said curtly. "We'll have to exit this way. The press is waiting out front."

"Press?" Monarch said, not liking that. His head ached fiercely.

Lady Wentworth glanced at him like he was an imbecile. "You engage in open warfare on a bobsled run and you didn't think the press would come?"

Lacey offered her arm to Monarch for support. He took it. Lacey said, "Aunt Pat used to be a trial barrister, you know. She got you out."

"I thought she didn't like me," Monarch said as the overhead door opened, revealing a snow-covered parking lot.

Lady Wentworth turned. "I heard that," she said. "And perhaps yesterday, I did not like you, Robin. But when you risk your own life to save my only niece's life, I believe I have to give you the benefit of the doubt."

"Why, Lady Wentworth, that's the nicest thing you've ever said to me."

Lady Wentworth almost smiled as they crossed the lot toward Lacey's car.

"Are you Monarch?" a male voice with a thick accent demanded.

"No press," Lady Wentworth snapped.

Monarch turned to find a brutish man with a high forehead coming toward him in a black leather jacket. "My name is Artun. I work for Constantine Belos," he said in Russian-accented English. "He likes for you tomorrow night, dinner, so he gives you thanks for his life."

Monarch was aware of Lady Wentworth's expression of open distaste, but he said, "Tell Mr. Belos I'd be happy to have dinner with him."

The man nodded. "Eight o'clock. At Kempinski's." He bobbed his head at Lacey. "And bring lady friend."

16

Kempinski's Hotel des Bains was the more relaxed of the five-star luxury establishments in St. Moritz. The hotel's setting was spectacular, north of town at the base of the Engadin Range. Chords of piano jazz could be heard in the crisp cold air when Monarch helped Lacey from the car. His head felt much better. The pain had dulled to a throbbing, and he'd shed most of the big bandage in favor of two Band-Aids. Stars glimmered overhead. Floodlights lit the hotel's creamy exterior.

Lacey kissed him and smiled. "Ready?"

"Always," Monarch said, taking her arm. "Do you know what would have made this better?"

"What's that?" Lacey asked.

"Having your aunt along, bringing her into the dreaded Russian lair."

"Stop," Lacey said, laughing. "I think she was more upset with his criminal ties."

"All we're doing is breaking bread with the man."

"Right," Lacey said, but with some uncertainty.

Monarch put his hand on Lacey's back and followed her through the doors into a dramatic lobby. The ceilings were vaulted and richly lit. The colors were subdued themes, all earth tones. A loose crowd filled the place, drinking, laughing, many of them speaking in Russian. In a sweeping glance, Monarch took in the people, spotting gold everywhere, and diamonds and every other sort of precious stone.

"Mr. Monarch?" The man from the hospital parking lot came across the lobby. "Artun. Is good to see you. Constantine waits you in bar."

Monarch thought of speaking to the man in Russian, but then decided it might be an advantage to be able to listen incognito. "We looked forward to it."

Artun nodded, then leaned in closer to Monarch. "You have gun?"

"No permit to carry one in Switzerland," Monarch said.

"Does not answer question," the Russian said.

"No," Monarch said. "No gun."

"Good."

Artun led them into a bar with dimmer lights, plush velvet sitting areas, and wood wainscoting. It was a warm place, filled with people happy in their new money. The women were dressed in the couture of Paris, Milan, and Rome. Their jewels were breathtaking in their audacity. Monarch wanted to pluck every one.

In a deep corner of the bar, away from the piano, he spotted Constantine Belos at a setting of two sofas separated by a cocktail table. Belos wore a dark suit with a starched white shirt, and no tie. He faced Monarch and the door, a wary man, who studied him as he approached. Expressionless. Calculating. Monarch glanced to Belos's left and right, spotting pairs of men, watching him as well. Bodyguards. The night before last had spooked Belos.

Until they were close, Lacey had blocked Monarch's view of the woman Inspector Robillard had called Iryna Svetlana. But then she stood up to greet them. Her mahogany hair was drawn back in a French braid, accentuating her dramatic cheeks and almond-shaped and -colored eyes, the pupils of which matched the hue and mystery of the strand of gray pearls dangling around her neck. Her evening dress was a coal gray Givenchy with spaghetti straps. A hint of black lace showed at her bosom. Black stockings and stiletto heels completed the ensemble, along with a stunning bracelet featuring four braided rows of matching pearls. It took everything in Monarch's power to give her no more than a glance and a nod before reaching for Belos's outstretched hand.

"Mr. Monarch, it is pleasure to meet you," Belos said in English, beaming at him and taking his elbow with the opposite hand the way politicians do. "You save Constantine's life. Iryna's life. We never forget this."

Monarch was usually very much attuned to his surroundings. But now, this close to Belos, looking directly into the man's olive eyes, Monarch felt cut off from everyone else in the bar. For a moment, Monarch was thrown, but then he realized that Belos was one of those rare men with the gift of making everyone he met feel like he was the only other person on the planet.

"I just reacted, Mr. Belos," Monarch said. "I don't like getting shot at."

Belos burst into laughter. "I do no like this myself. And please, call me Constantine."

"Robin," Monarch said.

"Robin Monarch," Belos repeated, as if they were wondrous words, and then broke into a wider grin. "Yes."

He turned to Lacey, took her neatly beneath the arms, and blew kisses past her cheeks. "My friend," he said. "It is the much better to see you like this."

Lacey replied, "You mean not in the snow with dead people and bullets flying?"

Belos threw back his head and roared as if it was the greatest comeback he'd ever heard. "I think so. Very much! Yes!"

Iryna had broken into a radiating smile and cast her lovely eyes at Monarch. They watered, and she choked out, "I cannot thank you this much for saving my life, Robin. For all our lifes."

"You're welcome," Monarch said, still feeling off from the bullet grazing his head, a sensation amplified by Iryna's beauty.

"Sit, my friends," Belos said, gesturing toward the chairs. "And do not cry, Iryna. We are alive. Life is for the living, is it not, Robin Monarch?"

"I've always thought so, Constantine," Monarch said, helping Lacey to her chair.

"What will you have for the drink?"

"I would love a mojito," Lacey announced.

"I never have. Is good?" Iryna asked as she eased back into her chair.

"Wonderful," Monarch said, taking a seat opposite her.

"Four mojitos," Belos grunted to Artun.

Artun nodded and headed toward the bar. Belos pointed to a platter of crackers, cheese, spreads, and chips surrounding a silver urn of caviar. "The finest beluga," he said.

After Lacey and Irina had helped themselves, Monarch obligingly took a plate and several crackers. He scooped several dollops of the caviar onto the crackers and ate one. It was by far the best he'd ever tasted.

"God, I could eat that every day for a year," he said.

"I own part of this company," Belos said, pleased. "I send you a case."

"I'll take you up on that," Monarch said, popping another cracker in his mouth and winking at Lacey.

Artun returned with the mojitos. Monarch took his and sniffed the scent of gasified mint leaves, sugar, and rum.

"To Robin Monarch," Belos said, holding out his glass.

"To Robin Monarch," Lacey said.

"To Robin," Iryna said, and then brought the glass to her lips. Her eyes locked with Monarch's for a moment as she sipped.

He wanted to gaze openly at her, but instead shrugged as if he didn't like the attention and said, "Thank you one and all."

"Oooh," Lacey said, examining the drink. "That's a good one."

"This I like, Constantine," Iryna said to Belos, holding her glass out to him.

Belos took a drink, pursed his lips, and set his down. "Too sweet."

"It's an acquired taste," Monarch agreed.

Belos smiled and sobered. "Inspector Robillard talks to you?"

"Briefly," Monarch said.

"He looks like old dog, the inspector," Iryna said, and started laughing.

"An old tired dog," Monarch said, smiling.

"A fool," Belos grumbled.

"Who were they, Constantine?" Lacey asked. "The gunmen?"

Iryna's face tightened and she looked at her lap. But Belos just wearily laughed. "In my country, some men think killing enemies is good business. Like Wild West."

"So you think they were sent by one of your competitors?" Monarch asked.

He shrugged. "In Russia, nothing is as it seems. Like you, I think, Robin."

"What you see is what you get," Monarch said, raising his glass again.

Belos propped his elbow on the arm of his chair, and trained his telescopic focus on Monarch. "You are trained much, I think."

"Nine years in the military will do that to you," Monarch said offhandedly.

Belos did not reply for a long uncomfortable moment while he stared at Monarch with that unreadable expression. Then he glanced over Monarch's shoulder, nodded, and said, "Artun takes us now to restaurant. Is very good. The best."

The restaurant was on the outskirts of St. Moritz, a characterless structure in the middle of a parking lot. After the opulence of Kempinski's, Monarch was surprised to find La Barraca's interior unconcerned with pretense or style. But the place was packed with all sorts of interesting-looking people. Tourists. Sham nobility. The new, new rich. The chatter was friendly and relaxed, the aromas sublime and intriguing. They sat at a round table. Constantine Belos again took the seat with the best view of the exits, and again Artun and the four men took tables close by.

Belos began by ordering a three-hundred-euro bottle of Friuli, a rare Italian peasant wine, and an assortment of delicacies for appetizers. A salad bowl came to the table, followed by pastas and fine Chianti. Monarch did his best to keep the conversation turned away from him, trying instead to learn everything he could about the mobster and his girlfriend. Belos claimed he'd made his mark importing high-end consumer electronics into Russia in the aftermath of the fall of the Soviet Union. The economy was in chaos at the time, but Belos said he'd thrived, relying on his wits, embracing the freedom he'd been given after the Kremlin collapsed.

"Now Russia is best place in world to do business, even with Putin in charge," Belos boasted as the entrées were served. "Everyone work hard because everyone can work hard and make more money. Before, with the communists, who gives the shit? Work little as you want, work hard as you want — no difference, no more money. Takes a while, but now everyone in Russia understands life is there for taking, yes, Robin?"

Monarch was biting into a delicious chunk of chicken marsala at the moment the question was posed. He had been thinking that Belos had a nicely detailed cover story, complete with an appeal to hard work and fortitude. He looked up to find the crime lord studying him again.

"Life for the taking?" Monarch said. "Yes, I think if you don't take control, life ends up controlling you."

Lacey had been listening during most of

the conversation. But now she set down her fork and said, "But sometimes when you try to control life, it backfires and it ends up controlling you anyway."

Belos smiled in a way that Monarch interpreted as that of a man not used to being intellectually challenged by a woman. "Like when?" he asked.

"A death," Lacey replied. "An accident. Someone trying to kill you."

"I am Russian," Belos said. "I know this temptation to believe in fate."

"You don't believe in fate?"

"No," Belos said. "I believe fate we make. Fate we, how you say, design."

Iryna played with the pearls at her wrist and said, "The way I meet you, yes, Constantine? This is fate?"

He thought about that, and then nodded. "Now this was fate, Iryna."

Iryna hardened ever so slightly. She'd been drinking a fair amount, and her words came out laced with boozy irony: "My fate is to be mistress, not wife."

Belos acted as if this were old, bitter terrain between them. He said to her in Russian, "Have the class you always say you want to portray."

"Fuck them and you, too," she shot back in Russian with a smile. "When are you going to leave that bitch you call a wife?"

Monarch understood it all. He glanced at Lacey. If she didn't understand the words, she was catching the subtext.

Belos looked over at Monarch and Lacey. "She is lucky girl, Iryna," he said in English. "But she does not understand her luck or give thanks for it."

Iryna gripped her wineglass as if she wished to break it, but she looked at Lacey and said in English, "I need to visit the toilet."

Lacey, who'd turned uncomfortable, nodded and pushed back from the table. Monarch said nothing. And for almost a minute, neither did Belos. The Russian just stared ahead in defiance of the unpleasant events that "fate" had just served him. At last, he sighed, looked at Monarch, and shrugged. "Iryna, she makes me happy. She makes me angry. Sometimes at same time."

"The curse of womanhood," Monarch said, trying to make light.

"Yes," Belos said, regaining composure. "She is like this, too? Lacey?"

"She's complicated, like all women," he allowed.

"Iryna is complication inside complication," Belos said. "But she is most beautiful woman I have ever seen. And strong in the bed. Like young mare." Belos laughed softly, pouring another glass of wine. "It makes for distrust."

"How so?"

"Other men."

"I could see how that might be the case."

"You are security consultant, yes?"

"I am," Monarch said.

"I have estate. . . ."

Before Belos could go on, Iryna and Lacey returned to the table, acting like old friends. Monarch stood to get Lacey's chair, but Belos stayed seated while Iryna found her place. Iryna leaned forward toward Monarch, smiled, and said, "So what you talk about while we are gone? Me?"

"You think whole world around you?" Belos sniffed. "We talk of the estate."

Iryna's eyebrow shot up and she glanced at Lacey and then lingered on Monarch. "You should see it. The both of you."

"I was just about to say this," Belos said to Monarch. "Last year I buy estate on water near Paphos, in Cyprus. Tomorrow we flies there in my jet. You come as my guest. Lacey, too. See place and tell me what I must do for security. Of course, I pay very well."

Just then, beneath the restaurant table, Monarch felt toes rub up his shin. For a split second, he thought it was Lacey, but then realized from the angle that that was impossible. He shifted his leg back out of range, never looked Iryna's way, and tilted his head in deference to Constantine before saying, "I appreciate the offer, Constantine. And I'd love to see the estate and help you in any way I can. But I'm afraid I'm going to Buenos Aires tomorrow to see another client."

"Cancel meeting. Make other time," Belos said.

"That would be impossible," Monarch said. "They are my oldest clients." He saw Belos's face cloud before adding, "However, I have meetings in London later in the week that I could rearrange, and then fly to Cyprus on my own. How long will you be there?"

Belos smiled. "Don't worry, my friend, I wait for you."

"I will, too," Iryna said softly before nodding to Lacey. "For the both of you."

17

THIRTY-SIX HOURS LATER . . .

CIA HEADQUARTERS LANGLEY, VIRGINIA

Slattery crossed his arms and stared at the wall of flat screens flickering with various video images inside the special ops command center. His headset hung around his neck, and he was monitoring the chatter as three of his agents moved into position inside the Buenos Aires airport. The Director of the CIA had all but ordered him to stay away from Monarch eighteen months ago. It was true that there had been contact made by Swiss Police regarding Monarch, but Slattery had never raised the subject with Dr. Hopkins, preferring to use it as a pretense only if necessary. Keeping Hopkins ignorant was the best course of action. Slattery had a loyal group of people around him, and as long as he made no big moves in their presence, this should all sail smoothly.

"Flight's down, they've cleared immigration, heading into customs," said Thompson over the headset. Thompson was Slattery's top asset in Argentina.

Slattery turned to Agatha Hayes, who was sitting at a computer, her big shoulders hunched over her keyboard.

Slattery said, "Patch me into Argentine customs?"

"Already got a feed," Hayes said. "Screen nine."

One of the screens blinked to a grainy wide-angle shot of customs at Ministro Pistarini International Airport. The area was jammed with arriving passengers.

"Can you blow that up?" Slattery asked.

Hayes gave her keyboard instructions. The screens on the wall became one giant screen that displayed the Argentine customs area in virtual life size. Slattery spotted Monarch almost immediately. He was fourth row in, second in line, wearing a dark business suit, no tie, and wheeling a carry-on suitcase.

"You have any idea why he's here?" Hayes asked.

"He told the Swiss he had business in Buenos Aires," Slattery said. "But his mother was Argentine, and I believe he lived there when he was a teenager."

Hayes had been listening as she typed on her keyboard, and now she studied the screen. "Records show him entering Argentina the last time about ten years ago."

"On a U.S. passport, anyway," Slattery said.

On screen, the Argentine customs officer appeared to ask Monarch several questions before waving him through.

"He's coming at you, Thompson," Slattery said into his headset.

"Roger that," the agent replied.

"Give me Thompson's camera," Slattery told Hayes.

Hayes made two keystrokes. The bank of screens fragmented again. The feed on the screen front and center showed the scene in the Buenos Aires airport just outside the double doors that visitors move through after clearing customs.

Monarch pushed through the doors. He looked out of place wearing the dark business suit when people waiting were dressed in summer wear. Monarch passed Thompson's position, looking here and there for no one in particular.

The camera wobbled as Slattery's operator fell in behind and well to Monarch's left. Another of Slattery's crew appeared near the escalator, a woman who slipped directly behind Monarch for an instant, and then broke away.

"On his carry-on," Thompson said in Slattery's ear. "Solid plant."

"We reading it?" Slattery asked.

Hayes typed. A screen displayed showed a map of greater Buenos Aires. A bright orange dot blinked at the airport.

"Strong signal," Hayes said.

"Beautiful," Slattery said.

The other screen now showed Monarch on the lower floor of the terminal. He did not turn toward the baggage carousels, but crossed the room, pulling the carry-on, appearing ready to exit out onto the street. But then he slowed and rubbed his stomach. He paused and looked around before looping the baggage carousels to a men's room.

"Hang back," Slattery instructed.

Several minutes passed with Thompson's camera in a long shot of the toilet entrance from the other side of the baggage carousel. The restroom was a busy place. Eight or nine men had entered. Five others had left. Slattery watched them go by. A young boy left the restroom, tugging at his father's arm. An older, bald tourist with a goatee and sunglasses shuffled out next, hunched over, dabbing his sweating forehead with a handkerchief. Then two teenagers came out punching one another. A businessman in his fifties came next. A woman was waiting for him. They kissed and left. Slattery glanced at the clock.

"We're getting a strong signal," Hayes said. "He's in there."

Another four minutes went by. Slattery pursed his lips before saying into his head-set, "Thompson, take a stroll."

The camera closed on the entry to the men's room, then turned left and right again. It was a typical airport lavatory, with long rows of stalls on one side, urinals on the other, and sinks in a separate area. The camera revealed many of the people Slattery had seen enter the men's room, washing up now, getting ready to leave. The feed jiggled, showing the ceiling and then the walls, before leveling out at about two inches off the floor, showing under the lavatory stall doors.

"He's crawling on the floor in a public restroom?" Hayes asked, incredulous.

"The camera's embedded in the tip of his pen," Slattery said, putting his hand over the mic. "He probably stuck it through his shoelaces."

Slattery saw a pair of sneakers beneath lowered jeans and black legs in the first stall. The second stall revealed sandals and toes obscured by lowered shorts and white calves. In the third stall, he spotted the tips of loafers, beneath the rumpled cuffs and pants of a dark business suit. A strip of toilet paper dangled between the pant legs. Monarch's carry-on stood beside them.

"That's him," Slattery said, breathing a sigh of relief.

The camera circled through the lavatory and returned to the baggage area.

That image of Monarch's shoes and pants and the toilet paper and the carry-on kept Slattery confident another five minutes. And then he couldn't take it any longer. "Thompson, hit that stall," he ordered.

In a moment, Slattery was looking at the door of the third stall on his screen. He saw a hand come up and knock and then knock again. The camera shook, and then climbed and peered over into the interior of the stall.

The toilet was unoccupied. The waist and belt of Monarch's business pants were pinched between the seat and the bowl. His coat hung on the hook.

"That son of a bitch," Slattery said.

18

BUENOS AIRES

In the back of a taxi speeding along a crowded highway toward the city center, Robin Monarch spit out the wads of cotton he'd stuffed in his cheeks, dropped the tinted sunglasses in his lap, and peeled off the latex skullcap that had made him look so convincingly bald.

"Eh, *señor,* you an actor?" asked the taxi driver. He'd been watching Monarch's transformation in the rearview mirror.

"Auditioning for a commercial they're shooting at the airport," Monarch replied in a flawless Rioplatense Spanish. "I'm going to the Melia Hotel."

"The Melia! A fine establishment, *señor.*"

Monarch did not reply. It was midmorning, and the temperatures already hovered in the mid-nineties. The scents that drifted in his open window were familiar and haunting.

Monarch, however, was focused on the fact that he'd picked up a tail coming out of customs. He'd suspected a tail after leaving Switzerland. Robillard had contacted someone to get the base information on him, which meant the CIA had a fix on him again. Sure enough, when Monarch had pushed through the doors, he'd seen a man by the newsstand with an unlit cigar in his mouth and a pen behind his ear catch sight of him and drop his head.

When he felt someone bump his carry-on at the escalator, he'd rightly figured there had been a bug planted. So he went to the men's room, locked the door, and found the bug, a tiny pin stuck in the fabric of his suitcase. Monarch stripped and got out the baggy clothes, the sandals, and the skullcap and beard he'd stuffed into his carry-on as protection against just such an event.

He'd unzipped the floor of the carry-on and fished out his packet of passports. He stuffed them in his underwear, then balled up cotton wads and pushed them high in his cheeks. He grabbed a jar of makeup, smeared some on his handkerchief, and patted down the seam of the skullcap. He arranged the pants, shoes, and toilet paper to give the right effect, and then waited.

Thirty seconds later, the man in the stall

next to him left. Monarch got up on the toilet, took a quick glance around, saw no one, and climbed over the stall divider. He put the glasses on, stooped over as if in sciatica, and started the slow, crooked shuffle that had taken him out through the baggage area and onto the street where he'd hailed the cab.

In the taxi, Monarch sat sideways now, monitoring the traffic behind them. No one followed, and he relaxed and glanced out the side window. They were on 9 de Julio Avenue. The sidewalks were jammed with Argentines strolling in the sweltering heat.

Noticing the cabbie checking him out in the rearview mirror again, Monarch said, "A day for the beach."

"Or the mountains," the cabbie agreed. "Is Buenos Aires home, *señor*?"

Monarch glanced out the window. The sidewalk cafés were crowded. He saw boys chasing one another down the street. "I spent part of my youth here."

"What neighborhood?" the taxi driver asked.

Monarch hesitated, and then said, "Villa Miseria."

The cabbie's mouth opened in awe. "You grew up in the Village of Misery?"

"For a few formative years," Monarch said.

"And now you stay at the Melia? It is one of the finest hotels in the city!"

Monarch nodded appreciatively. "A lifetime can change in a moment."

"How did you survive that terrible place and get out, *señor*? Villa Miseria?"

Monarch replied, "I learned to fight, cheat, and steal."

The cabbie frowned; then he looked in the rearview mirror, saw Monarch was serious, and broke into uneasy laughter. "Yes, *señor*, I imagine you had to."

Despite Monarch's attire, the concierge at the Melia recognized him instantly as Raul Rodríguez of Santiago, Chile, an import–export agent and valued guest. They gave him his favorite room. Monarch placed an order for some clothes before going out on a balcony that looked toward the harbor and the hazy mountains that surrounded it. He got a phone and used a calling card to dial a number in area code 703. Virginia. Langley.

A computer voice asked for a password.

"Ruby Tuesday," he said.

There was a short series of clicks, followed by a woman's familiar voice saying, "Leave it after the beep."

Monarch waited for the tone, then said, "How's the fishing by the bay? I'll be there at nine fifteen." He hung up and waited, fighting not to drowse.

Two minutes went by before the phone rang. Monarch snatched it up.

"Are you insane?" Gloria Barnett said. "And using my password?"

"Go somewhere you can talk," Monarch replied, seeing cranelike Barnett in his mind and smiling. It had been a long time.

He heard the line go dead, relaxed, and closed his eyes. Fifteen minutes later, he was on the verge of sleep when the phone rang again. He could hear the sound of a bar in the background.

"Qué pasa?" Monarch asked.

"This is the way you contact me after all this time, Robin?" Barnett demanded.

"I'm sorry, Gloria," Monarch said. "But it was necessary for reasons that are best explained in person."

Her response was cold. "Then why are you calling?"

"I thought I had a truce with the agency, but I had people on me this morning."

"I wouldn't know," Barnett said. "I haven't been stateside in five months."

"Where are you?" he asked.

178

"London."

"Tough duty."

"Actually it's a demotion. I'm back working analysis."

"I'm sorry, Gloria."

"So am I, Robin."

Monarch said, "I need your help."

"You didn't need it in Istanbul."

Monarch said nothing, letting the silence fill the telephone line until she said, "What do you want?"

"Whatever you can give me on Constantine Belos. Supposedly he's a kingpin in Vory v Zakone, Russian Mafia in St. Petersburg."

"You're working for Russian Mafia now?" Barnett asked archly.

"He's asked me to review security at his estate in Cyprus."

There was another long silence before she said, "Give me some time."

The line went dead. Monarch hung the phone up, shut his eyes, and promptly fell asleep. He awoke shortly after noon, exercised in the hotel gym, refused to eat, and then slept again.

It was nearly 4 P.M. when he awoke the second time. He put on linen slacks, a white cotton shirt, and the running shoes the concierge had purchased for him. Monarch exited the Melia by a back door, hailed another cab, and asked to be taken to a cemetery in one of the more elegant neighborhoods in the city.

He got out fifteen minutes later, paid the cabdriver, and then entered through the archway of the cemetery. After buying flowers from a vendor at the entrance, he walked off through the crowded gravestones along a gravel path that took him deep inside the sprawling cemetery, making every turn by memory toward a knoll that faced south.

Leaves rustled in the hot breeze. Sprinklers chattered as he climbed the knoll to a polished black granite gravestone that read MONARCH. Two smaller stones were laid flat and flush with the grass in front of the monument he'd purchased a few years before, after moving the bodies of his parents from a paupers' cemetery to this place of tranquillity. The stone on the left read, FRANCESCA DEVILLE MONARCH. The stone on the right read WILLIAM FRANCIS MONARCH. Between the stones, a vase had been set in the ground, its lip flush with the lawn. Withered flower stalks jutted from the vase.

At the sight of the graves, Monarch's mind rippled with random images of himself with his parents: at a café in Paris when he was eight, laughing at his father who was painting his mother's lips with the froth from a cappuccino; in a train crossing Italy when he was ten, lying in his mother's lap, watching his father count money; and, not far from the cemetery at all, when he was thirteen and gangly, running out of a theater where he and his parents had gone to watch the latest *Star Wars* installment, slashing his imaginary light saber past the crowd gathered for the final show of the night, then spinning around halfway down the block, meaning to slash his way back to his parents, who were just exiting the building.

Robin's mother, Francesca, was a classic Latin beauty who wore her black hair back in a tight bun above a stylish leather jacket his father, Billy, had bought for her earlier in the day. Robin's father had his arm around his mother's shoulder and was whispering something in her ear. Monarch's mother was laughing, her hand traveling to her mouth, her mischievous and glistening eyes finding her son.

Robin locked eyes with his mother, raising his imaginary sword at the same instant two men dressed as police officers stepped out from a car idling on the curb. He saw the panic in his mother's eyes before he noticed the shotguns, before she shouted, "Run,

Rob — !"

They cut her down with buckshot, and his father, too. The boy's overwhelming urge had been to run to them, but then he saw the killers turn and spot him. The thirteen-year-old began to sprint away so hard and so fast that his lungs burned.

Monarch's parents were con artists and thieves, but he had loved them fiercely. Francesca spoke six languages and possessed remarkable acting abilities. Billy was a smooth talker from Miami with a keen knack for plotting swindles. Monarch's father had also been a cat burglar of the highest order. They, in turn, taught their son their skills and more; and by the time Robin turned thirteen, by the time he ran from his parents' murder scene, he'd been part of several of their more successful scams.

Their life had been a roller coaster, always traveling, always either broke or awash in cash. They'd been in some close calls in Europe, and decided to return to Buenos Aires to let things cool down. The summer of their death had been the closest Robin had ever been to a normal existence, and his parents seemed to have more money than ever. The afternoon and evening of their murder may have been the best moments of his life.

Then they were gunned down. And Robin's life turned to nightmare; he was unable to go to the police for fear they'd kill him, unable to do anything but run and hide.

Standing at his parents' graveside more than twenty years later, Monarch felt his eyes water at the thought of himself as a boy, sprinting through the streets as it began to rain, hysterical with loss, and petrified that the killers were still after him.

Monarch knelt and took out the old, withered flowers from the vase and put in the new ones. He lingered a few moments on his knees, and then murmured to the spirits of his dead parents, "God knows I haven't turned out to be a perfect man, but I'm trying to do what's right these days, not taking orders blindly, trying to do some good."

He paused and then got to his feet. "I thought you'd want to know that."

19

At a quarter to five, Monarch climbed from another cab and stood before the ornate façade of the Sarmiento post office, the central facility in Buenos Aires. He gazed across the street to a park. There were couples walking among the flowers and several kids throwing coins in the fountain. No one watched him.

He entered the post office, finding himself in a vaulted space with gilded cornices and marble floors. His eyes swept the area until he was satisfied he was not being watched. Then he moved into line, scanning the workers behind the long counter until he spotted a man roughly his age with glasses and a wispy mustache.

Monarch maneuvered and stalled through the waiting line so he stood up front when the light above that clerk signaled him forward.

"I believe there is a package here for

Marta Méndez," Monarch said softly.

The post office worker startled, then peered at him closer through his thick glasses before saying, "I'll go look."

Two minutes later, the clerk slid the mailer addressed to Marta Méndez across the counter. "Say hello to our sister, Robin," the postal worker said.

"I will, Javier," Monarch promised, and left.

Monarch took a series of buses from the post office to La Boca, a working class neighborhood of Buenos Aires brilliantly painted in greens, yellows, and reds. The sidewalks were choked with people going home from work and shopping. He got off near La Bombonera, the home field of the Boca Juniors soccer team.

There was no game scheduled, so the plaza in front of the stadium was less crowded than usual. Nevertheless, he sought out and bought a Boca Juniors cap from one of the vendors on the plaza. The sun was setting. La Boca after dark could be a rugged place, not as bad as Villa Miseria, he thought, but it never hurt to cheer on the home team when you're on the home team's turf. *Rule Number Five: Fit in.*

Monarch walked toward the river as night

came on. Music blared from a hundred open windows. Tango dancers performed in the streets. Hawkers called to him to inspect their wares. But Monarch had places to go, and important people to see. He reached the riverbank and rented a rowboat for fifty pesos.

Fifteen minutes later, he pulled up on the opposite shore, left the rowboat and climbed up into the city of Avellaneda, which was considerably more upscale than La Boca. Satisfied now that he wasn't being followed, Monarch wove through the streets to an address in a neighborhood high on a steep hillside.

He entered a luxury apartment building, greeted the doorman by name, and headed to the elevators. He got off at the eleventh floor and went to the second door on the right. The Gipsy Kings' "Bamboleo" blared inside, so he hit the buzzer hard.

A tall dark-skinned woman, pretty, early twenties, in the barest of bikinis, answered the door and looked at him blankly. The music was deafening.

Monarch shouted in Spanish, "Claudio's expecting me!"

She regarded Monarch with mild contempt, turned, and jiggled away. He followed her into a hallway and shut the door.

Beyond a kitchen, Monarch emerged into a glass-walled room with a panoramic view of the city. Outside, the lights of Buenos Aires were switching on in swaths.

The air in the room smelled of paint and was set up as a studio. A man in his late thirties hunched over a black canvas set on an easel before the window. He was barefoot and bare chested, clad only in a pair of paint-smeared shorts. Paint spattered his entire torso. It glistened in his hair and on his hands.

The artist worked feverishly, glancing out the window at the lights of Buenos Aires coming on, and then slashing at the canvas with the six or seven paintbrushes he held in each hand. The paint exploded against the black canvas in iridescent violets, silvers, reds, and golden swaths and points.

The effect was stunning. Monarch stood there watching, aware that the painter was moving in sync with the pulsing music, pushing himself harder and faster as the song built toward climax. When the last guitar strum faded, he threw down his paintbrushes, looked at it in disgust, and cried in Spanish, "It's shit!"

He stepped toward the canvas as if he meant to put his fist through it. But Monarch took three quick steps and caught him by the wrist and turned it slightly to reveal a tattoo of a hand outstretched above the letters FDL.

"It's brilliant, Claudio," Monarch said. "Let it dry."

Claudio Fortunato struggled a moment, glaring at Monarch wall-eyed before the tension gushed out of him.

"Is it good, Robin?" he asked, yearning in his voice.

Monarch looked at the canvas. He saw an instant of the city greeting night rendered with deep emotion. He looked around at the base of the walls, seeing thirty other canvases along the same theme. "These are your best," he said.

Tears came to Claudio's eyes and he hugged Monarch. "I missed you, my brother," he cried, and kissed him on the cheek. "I thought about you the other day, very clearly. I felt like you were in danger."

"I followed the rules," Monarch replied. "I came out fine."

"What happened?"

"I got in a thin place, that's all."

"You're sure?"

"Clean," Monarch said, handing him the chocolate box. "Lose the trollop."

"Huh?" Claudio said, and then spotted the girl in the bikini watching them from the kitchen. He dug in his pocket and came up with some money. "Esmeralda. Put some clothes on. Go out. Eat. Come back later."

The girl looked like she wanted to argue, but then sullenly came forward and snatched the money from his hand. Two minutes later, the front door slammed shut.

"Isn't she kind of young?" Monarch asked.

"She's teachable," Claudio said, heading toward the kitchen.

Claudio set a pot of water on the stove and lit the fire beneath it. Monarch got them each a beer from the refrigerator while Claudio unwrapped the chocolate. When the water boiled, he set the block of chocolate in the pot. Two minutes later, he fished Dame Maggie's emerald necklace, earrings, and ring from the runny brown water.

He ran hot water over them in the sink for several more minutes before spreading the necklace on a towel. Claudio rummaged in a drawer and came up with a jeweler's loupe. He set it on his head, lowered t he lenses over his eyes, and flicked on the light.

The emeralds glimmered and shone as Claudio cast his attention about and over the necklace, his lips forming silent words. Monarch knew better than to interrupt him. He sipped from his beer and watched.

It was a full five minutes before Claudio

sat back, snapped off the light, and flipped up the visor. "Six hundred fifty thousand dollars for the stones," he said. "Platinum throws in another ten, fifteen grand. Six hundred sixty-five."

"It was appraised at over a million," Monarch said.

"Maybe as a piece," Claudio said. "I'm just telling you the broken-up value."

"Half now?" Monarch asked.

Claudio nodded and headed toward the hallway, adding, "And half on sale."

Monarch followed him into a back room cluttered with art supplies. Claudio moved around several wooden frames and bolts of canvas leaning against the wall before kneeling and pushing on the wooden floor. An edge came up. Claudio lifted out a square piece to reveal the door to a safe.

He quickly spun the lock mechanism, saying, "Use the soccer bag."

Monarch looked around, spotting a canvas bag sporting the Adidas logo. He grabbed and unzipped it. Claudio was already stacking packets of fifty- and hundred-dollar notes. Monarch began stuffing the cash into the bag.

"Three hundred and thirty-five thousand U.S. dollars," Claudio said, setting the last bundle of bills in the bag.

"Sister will be happy," Monarch said.

"Send her my love," Claudio said.

"Where will I find her?"

Claudio's face tightened. "She's working near *el ano* tonight."

Monarch left the apartment building and hailed a cab. He gave the driver the address, and the man said, "That's fine. Long as I don't have to drive in there."

They drove through miles of the stylized neighborhoods that gave Buenos Aires its nickname: the Paris of South America.

Ten minutes into the ride, Monarch's cell phone rang.

"Your friend the Russian is a walking target," Gloria Barnett said.

"Tell me something I don't know," Monarch replied.

Barnett spelled it out for him. As a young man, Constantine Belos had been a helicopter pilot in the Red Army in Afghanistan. Like many, he was demoralized by the Soviet defeat and withdrawal, and infuriated at the way the government treated veterans as the Kremlin's hold on power began to disintegrate. In the political and economic chaos that ensued, Belos joined Vory v Zakone as a foot soldier in St. Petersburg, working the docks. Within a year, he had eliminated his rivals and controlled shipping and customs at the port on behalf of the syndicate. Belos rose swiftly up the ranks of organized crime, relying on an unflinching eye for potential criminal profit and a willingness to use whatever ruthless tactic necessary to see those profits realized.

He seized leadership of the St. Petersburg mob when he was forty-two, and had ruled it with an iron fist the past ten years, melding his criminal and legal pursuits into an empire reputed to be in the hundreds of millions of dollars. With that success had come enemies, lots of them. And at least one of them appeared deadlier than Belos.

Barnett said, "His name is Omak. He's the leader of Obshina, the Chechen Mafia. They're fighting over drug and weapons routes to the Middle East."

"It fits," Monarch said as he watched out the window of the cab leaving the elite neighborhoods of Buenos Aires. "The people who tried to kill Belos were Chechens."

"There's more about Omak and Belos in a file I can send you."

"Extensive?" he asked.

"Both of them have been on our radar for several years through shared criminal intelligence with the GRU," Barnett said.

The GRU was the Intelligence Director-ate of the Russian Armed Forces General Staff, the equivalent of the CIA, Defense Intelligence Agency, and National Security Agency all rolled into one. It made sense to Monarch that the GRU would share crimi-nal information with the United States. And then he flashed on the feeling of toes in silk stockings rubbing up his shin.

Monarch asked, "Was his mistress, Iryna Svetlana, mentioned in the files?"

"Not that I saw. Why?"

"Just trying to understand all the pieces of the puzzle."

"Swiss Police are very interested in you," Barnett said.

"Is that why I got a tail?"

"I don't have access to that kind of infor-mation anymore."

"How much are the Swiss getting?"

"Not enough to shed your skin."

"You'll tell me if that happens?"

"Maybe," Barnett said, and hung up.

20

It was nearly 10 P.M. when Monarch stepped off the bus at the outskirts of Villa Miseria carrying a gym bag with $335,000 in it. The Village of Misery looked and stank worse than ever.

Bolivian and Paraguayan music blared from the open windows of mud-block homes and shops with tin roofs. The air reeked of urine and feces and rotting garbage. Monarch's head reeled at memories the smells triggered. Babies cried. Chickens stirred in their roosts in the trees above ill-lit streets. A woman was shouting at her husband. A girl, no more than fifteen, passed with a pig on a leash.

She was scrawny and haggard with rheumy eyes. She offered to have sex with Monarch for fifty pesos. He declined. Hawkers called to him from their kiosks, pitching him on cigarettes, booze, food, anything he wanted. Somewhere a radio or a television set shouted the details of a soccer match. The smell was getting worse, but Monarch continued deeper into the slum, heading toward the source of the stench.

He rounded a corner and spotted two boys, eleven or so, dressed in ragged, filthy clothes. They were hunched up against a wall, smoking short, stubby cigarettes. Their heads lolled. One of them talked nonsense. The other threw up and laughed.

Monarch stopped in front of them and asked, "Where's your home?"

The puker thought that was funny. "You're looking at it," he snorted.

"Parents?"

The one who had been talking nonsense now said, "Ain't none."

"What have you been smoking?" Monarch demanded.

"Paco, man, what you think?"

Paco was a nasty by-product of cocaine manufacturing. A pale yellow paste that contained more kerosene than cocaine, paco was cheap and highly addictive. It didn't do much for your brain either.

"Got some money for our next hit?" the boy who'd thrown up on himself asked.

Monarch thought of the money in the bag he held and said, "Sure, follow me."

"You a pervert?" the other one said.

"Last thing on my mind," Monarch said.

He reached down to haul the boys to their feet. They stood there a moment, wobbly. "What are your names?" he asked.

"Juan."

"Antonio."

"Follow me, Juan and Antonio," Monarch said, and started down the street.

"Paco man's over there," Antonio said, gesturing in the opposite direction.

"Money's over here," Monarch said, and kept walking.

He did not look back. For several moments, he heard nothing; then he caught the sound of them falling in behind him. He smiled as he led them down streets and alleys that were achingly and depressingly familiar. He passed a certain door stoop and in his mind saw himself there several days after his parents' murder, hunched under a cardboard box, hiding from the pouring rain that had liquefied the Villa Miseria.

Monarch's stomach cinched up at the memory. The feeling intensified as they approached an open pit area. The locals called it *el ano,* "the asshole," because the pit was the garbage dump for the Village of Misery and other nearby shantytowns. There were flashlight beams and lantern lights playing in the pits. Monarch could see people picking through the garbage, many of them children, clawing for anything that might fill their starving stomachs. He stopped and watched, unable to block out the memories that tore through his head in response to this scene of utter desperation.

Out there on the garbage piles, Monarch saw himself at thirteen as Robin, several weeks after his parents' murder, ragged, filthy, starving, digging through that same garbage. The first night had been the worst. The rotting food he ate made him violently ill, and he learned to look closely at what he put in his mouth. Two days later, he got into his first fight with a boy who attacked him for getting too close to where he was digging. Robin took two punches to the face before something awoke in him, something primal and instinctual, and he'd beaten back the boy, kicking him and throwing him down the side of the hill. The next day, he fought two boys and won. And did the same three days later. But on his seventh day in the pit, Robin strayed too close to the claim of a man twice his age. The man attacked him from behind, hitting him with a pipe, once in the ribs and once upside the head.

Robin came back to consciousness on one of the trails in the garbage pit sometime later. Blood matted his hair and he could not get to his feet.

He noticed an older boy sitting on a nearby paint can. He was watching Robin with interest. "I am Claudio," the boy said. "I been living in the Villa Miseria on my own since I was six, and I have not had to dig in *el ano* for nearly nine years. And I certainly don't let old men hit me with pipes."

"What?" Robin mumbled. He looked up at Claudio. "You saw me get hit?"

"Don't you know how to fight?" Claudio said.

"I know how to fight. That was a cheap shot."

"Wouldn't have happened if you'd been following Rule Number One," Claudio said.

The pounding in Robin's head got to his stomach. He vomited. When he was finished, lying on his side, heaving and panting, Claudio came over and squatted by him.

"I'm telling you that you don't have to live like this, brother," Claudio said.

"My parents are dead," Robin said, wanting to cry but holding it back. "No one knows I'm alive. No one cares."

"No one cares unless you care," Claudio said.

Robin thought about that. "What can I

do, then? How else am I supposed to live?"

"The way I do," Claudio said, lifting him to his feet. "By the eighteen rules of *la Fraternidad de Ladrones.*"

Claudio told Robin that he had survived because of the eighteen rules of the Brotherhood of Thieves, a way of thinking that had been passed to him on a night like this, in almost this very spot six years before by a very smart guy named Julio Sánchez, who was the founder and leader of La Fraternidad.

Robin said, "You steal stuff?"

"We take what we need. You have a problem with that?"

Robin shook his head. "No, actually."

"Good," Claudio said as he led Robin from the pit. "Rule Number One: You have the right to survive."

"They're rats."

The boy's derisive voice ripped Monarch from his memories. He startled and glanced around the garbage pit in rising alert.

"They're in there with the rats," Juan was saying. "They are rats."

Monarch looked down at the paco smoker who was watching the people in the dump with contempt. Antonio, however, was staring at the ground in a way that made

Monarch think he'd been forced onto the garbage heaps at some point in his young life.

Monarch said, "It's where life has led them."

"I'll never be a rat," Juan said.

"You would do a lot of things if you were hungry enough," Monarch said, and then moved on.

Monarch led the boys up a tangle of lanes that climbed a hillside above the pit. The dwellings on the hill were built like children's tree forts, slapped together with odd pieces of plywood and plank, tin and tree limb.

About halfway up the hillside, near one of the few streetlights, four men got up off wooden boxes and stepped in the way. Monarch could see that they all had beer bottles in their hands. He heard the click of a stiletto knife. The bearded muscular man in the sleeveless T-shirt held the blade.

"What's in the bag, man?" he asked.

Monarch said nothing, his attention flaring from the leader to his men, one of them large and beefy, the others lanky and much amused by the situation.

"Money," Juan said from behind Monarch. "He told us he had money."

"That right?" the leader said, emboldened. He raised the blade toward Monarch while his men flanked.

Monarch watched them, rotating his right arm to expose his tattoo.

The lanky one to Monarch's right saw it and turned uneasy. "La Fraternidad," he said to his companions.

The bearded one spit. "Fuck the Brotherhood. They are no more. What's in the bag?" He took a step and pushed the blade toward Monarch's throat.

In a lightning move, Monarch spiraled his free hand up and grabbed the man's knife hand by the outer edge of its palm. He twisted, throwing his weight over the wrist. Bones shattered. The man fell to his knees, screaming.

The big beefy one threw a quick hook at Monarch's face. Monarch saw it coming, spun off the line of the punch, and elbowed the boxer low and hard in the ribs. He felt several crack. The man choked and fell to his knees, the wind blasted out of him so hard, he sounded like he was being strangled.

Monarch twisted again, looking for the lanky guys. But they were backing up, hands up, saying, "We're cool. We're cool."

Monarch shifted the bag of money to his other hand and looked back at the boys.

Antonio's mouth was open. Juan was backing up, bursting into tears, saying, "I'm sorry, *señor*! I'm so sorry!"

Monarch growled, "Follow me."

At the top of the slope, the wind was better and the odor of garbage was blown away. He smelled food frying.

So did Antonio, who said, "I'm hungry."

"I want to find some paco," Juan complained. "Where are we going?"

"In here," Monarch said, stopping before a mud-brick building. Beaded curtains hung in the doorway, obscuring the interior, where lights blazed. Women were talking in there. A baby was squawking. A wooden crucifix hung above the transom.

"That ain't no paco house," Juan complained. "What's in there?"

"Hope," Monarch said. "Go inside."

Antonio glanced at his paco partner, climbed the stairs, and pushed his way through the curtains. Juan hesitated, and then reluctantly climbed after him. Monarch followed, stepping into a single room about fifty feet long that smelled antiseptic. There were metal folding chairs near the entryway. Posters promoting clean water and health lined the walls. Beyond the chairs there was a counter, and beyond that a rudimentary medical clinic. White sheets hung as dividers in the clinic's long hall.

An older woman in a denim skirt and a white laboratory coat stepped from behind one of the dividers. She had a stethoscope around her neck and was looking at a medical chart. She had long gray hair that had been braided and a handsome face weary enough to be called wise. Seeing her, Monarch felt his heart thaw and warm.

As she came to the counter, she glanced up from the notes and saw him. She broke into a look of relief and then a grin. "Robin!"

"Hello, Sister," Monarch said, returning her smile.

The woman rushed out and hugged him. Monarch hugged her back.

"I hadn't heard from you in so long. I was worried," she said, beaming up at him a moment before noticing the boys. "And who are these fine young men?"

"Candidates, I think," Monarch said.

She crouched down to their level, examining the filthy boys with a smile.

"Where are you from?" she asked gently.

"Nowhere," Antonio said.

"No parents?"

Both boys shook their heads. Juan pointed angrily at Monarch. "He said he'd give us money."

"Money," she said. "Let me guess. For paco?"

"That's right," Juan said.

"Why do you like paco?" she asked.

Antonio shrugged. "I dunno."

Juan said, "Makes so you can't feel nothing."

"And you want to feel like nothing?" she asked.

"I don't want to feel like nothing. I just want to feel nothing," Juan said, scratching hard on his arm.

She looked at Monarch. "They look hungry."

He nodded. "I told them we'd get them something to eat."

"We'll have to go for a car ride first," she told the boys. "Would you like that?"

The prospect of riding in a car seemed to perk Antonio's interest. But Juan asked suspiciously, "Where are we going? Who are you?"

She smiled again. "You can call me Sister Rachel. And we'll go to where I live with boys and girls just like you and get you something good to eat and a warm bed to sleep in. Would you like that? Or do you still want to go look for paco and sleep in the streets and wake up with no food in your belly?"

Antonio appeared stunned. "A real bed?"

"A real bed," Monarch said.

21

El Hogar de Esperanza, "the Refuge of Hope," was a compound on seven acres in the foothills west of Buenos Aires. A high brick wall surrounded the place.

Driving Sister Rachel's van through the gate, Monarch glanced in the rearview mirror and saw how terrified and curious the paco smokers were.

"The main building," Sister Rachel said. "They'll have to be examined."

"I'm hungry," Antonio said.

"I have a headache," Juan said.

"There'll be food waiting," she assured them. "And the pain in your head's the paco wearing off. You'll feel better in a day or so."

Monarch parked in front of a two-story stucco-walled building with a veranda. Two women in jeans and T-shirts came out of the building. The younger one opened the back door and said, "We have meat and eggs and fresh milk."

Antonio nodded cautiously and made to get out.

"My head hurts," Juan said again.

"He's starting withdrawal, so detox protocol," Sister Rachel said, climbing from the passenger seat. "Sister Gabriella, will you give me a report when they are settled? How much they were able to eat. Get their history, too."

"It may be late, Sister," the older woman said.

"I don't sleep anyway," Sister Rachel said.

The boys disappeared inside with the two women. Monarch watched them go. Sister Rachel studied him. "You're remembering the night I brought you here."

Monarch nodded. "I was angry at you."

"You were wounded and afraid. Anger is just another form of fear."

"I have something for you."

For the first time she looked to the gym bag he carried and then up to Monarch, who watched her impassively. Finally she said, "We'll go to my office."

Sister Rachel's office was on the second floor of the main building, above the kitchen, where the scent of meat frying stirred Monarch's own growing appetite.

He set the bag on her desk, piled high with papers and books. The walls of the room were almost completely covered by framed photographs of young boys and girls in clean white clothes interspersed with pictures of Sister Rachel and various adults hugging her. She sat down in an upholstered chair behind the desk and sighed.

"You look tired, Sister," Monarch said.

"Paco is a plague upon us, Robin," she said. "Ever since the collapse of the economy, we're seeing more and more kids like Juan and Antonio — abandoned, hopeless, numbing themselves into death. They are looking for ways not to feel sadness. Not to cry anymore. You remember what that felt like, don't you, Robin?"

"I do," Monarch said.

"But there was nothing like paco back then. Worse than crack. It literally robs you of the capacity to feel anything. The paco smokers will tell you they're after the void, chasing it. What makes a child want to chase the void?"

"Hopelessness, Sister," Monarch said. "Loneliness and hopelessness."

She sighed again, taking off her glasses and rubbing her eyes. "They both spread like diseases. We just can't seem to keep up with them."

"You don't need to work so hard in the clinics, Sister," Monarch said. "Your work is here. This is where you make a difference."

"The clinic was where I found you."

Monarch thought of the first time he saw Sister Rachel. He was seventeen, and she was crouched over him while he lay on his back making choking noises because there was a knife in his chest and it had collapsed his right lung.

Monarch set the bag in front of her. "I hope this makes a difference." He unzipped the bag and shook the money out on the desk. "Three hundred and thirty-five thousand dollars," he said.

Sister Rachel was dumbstruck. Her hand went to her mouth, where it hovered for several beats before lowering slowly toward the money. "My God, Robin," she said, starting to cry. "This is so much more than ever before. Do you know what this can do?"

Monarch nodded, happy.

She wiped at her tears, smiling. "We'll be able to keep the outreach programs going. We'll be able to rescue more of them."

"That's the idea," he said.

She shook her head in wonder. "Wherever did you get so much money?"

"My business is doing well," he said. "So is Claudio's. And some of the others."

Her smile faded somewhat. She bit at her lip, looking away from Monarch.

"What's wrong?" he asked.

"Please tell me it's not from drugs."

Monarch shook his head. "No drugs. Like I said, my business is going well. This place saved my life, saved our lives. It's the least that we can do."

Sister Rachel's eyes searched his face.

"I have more money than I need and this makes me happy," Monarch said, unable to stand the silence. "Please. It will do good in your hands."

"Why do always bring me money in dollars and in cash?" she asked.

"Because it's a hard currency," he said. "If you put it in the bank, they'll exchange it for pesos, and the value of our currency disappears every day. I give you the money like this, and you keep it hidden, except when you need it, I know it will do the most good."

Sister Rachel hesitated again, but only for the briefest of moments before putting her hands on the packets of money and bursting into tears again. She came around the desk and hugged Monarch. "Thank you, Robin. Thank you from the bottom of my heart."

"There's more where that came from,

Sister," Monarch said, hugging her tightly. "I promise you."

PART III

22

TWENTY-SIX HOURS LATER
LANARCA, CYPRUS
The jet from Madrid lowered its wheels. Monarch felt the rumble of them locking into place as the aircraft made its final turn before approach. He brought his seat into an upright position, still conflicted about his decision to come to Cyprus.

On the one hand, Gloria Barnett had been right. Following the firefight in St. Moritz, he'd definitely lost the low profile he'd maintained since Algiers. Was going to the vacation house of a Russian crime lord the smartest choice at the moment? Probably not.

On the other hand, a job was a job. As long as he kept all business between him and Belos at arm's length, selling the mobster advice on his security system was a fairly benign transaction.

But then he forced himself to admit that a

part of him had been drawn by the sensation of Iryna's toes on his shin. She was easily the most beautiful woman he had ever met, but how could the mistress of a Russian mobster not be dangerous?

Still, as the plane touched down, he told himself that these things were manageable. He'd learned to rely on himself twenty years ago, received years of training to do so, and remained confident that he could handle any situation life threw at him.

Monarch left the plane, went through immigration, received little scrutiny as Samuel Carter, a Canadian tourist visiting friends, and saw no evidence of a tail when he exited into the waiting area.

Constantine Belos, however, stood off to one side, a grin smeared across his face. "So happy to see you," he growled, clapping Monarch on the back. "I think you are not coming."

"Little jet-lagged, but I'm here," Monarch said.

Belos looked around. "And Lacey?"

"She had a meeting today and could not get off work," Monarch replied. "She's coming tomorrow morning. I hope that's not a problem."

Belos gazed at him with that poker face and said, "No problem. Come, come. Helicopter is on other side of airport."

The helicopter swung away from the bluest sea, heading inland over dry plains, olive orchards, carob groves, and dusty tan villages built millennia ago. Monarch had never been to Cyprus before, had never encountered its rare beauty, a cross between France and Greece, with a southern horizon that looks out to Africa over the Mediterranean, where it is at its most impossibly blue. Belos told him about the estate and its security challenges as they flew toward the southwestern reaches of the island, where the plains gave way to whitewashed beach resorts and then to a sparsely populated coastline.

The Russian's estate took up thirty remote acres above a rocky cove ringed with a reef where waves broke offshore. The house was sprawling and *V*-shaped, three-storied, twenty or thirty rooms, and the same dun color as the soil. The hills behind and above the estate were terraced with orchards. They landed on a pad near a barn and corral.

Monarch waited until the rotors wound down, then followed Belos's lead and climbed out, smelling horses on the breeze. Artun appeared, wearing a pistol in a shoulder harness.

"Iryna has lunch for you," Artun said after shaking Monarch's hand respectfully. "I have business with Constantine. He comes to you soon."

Belos nodded and followed Artun toward a veranda grown up in flowering vines. Monarch went with the servants into the house. The interior boasted terra-cotta tile floors, simple wooden furniture, and primitive art on the walls. They passed through a large sitting area with a fireplace, bar, and television before entering a solarium, where Monarch spotted Iryna. She was sunbathing in a bikini on a chaise longue.

"You make it!" Iryna cried, snatching a robe and a pair of dark sunglasses.

She threw the robe on and went to him, barefoot, her lush hair back in a ponytail. She pressed her terry cloth–covered breasts against him as she leaned in for air kisses.

"Constantine worries you not come," Iryna said. "I worry you not come. We is . . . we are very happy when you call."

"I try not to break promises," Monarch said.

"Constantine remembers such things," Iryna said, tapping her temple. "He like — how you say? — loyals?"

"I'm just here to take a look at the security," Monarch said. "A favor."

"Lacey, she comes?"

"Tomorrow."

"Oh, good. You like mojito? I learn how to make just for you."

"I'd love one later, but how about a beer for now?"

Iryna pouted. "You promise me you try later?"

"I promise," Monarch said.

She grinned and told the servant in Russian to bring two beers with lunch.

"You bring your help with you?" Monarch asked.

Iryna clouded as she took a seat at a table in the sun. "Constantine brings them. They worked for him years. He does not trust others."

"That could make life a little claustrophobic," Monarch remarked.

She smiled, puzzled. "I do not know this word."

"Claustrophobic? Afraid of small places. Like in a cage."

Iryna's smile evaporated, but she nodded and said, "You have no idea."

"Tell me," Monarch said, taking a seat opposite her.

The lapels of her robe had loosened, revealing the swell of her tanned breasts. Iryna seemed to struggle with whether or not to speak.

"You've been shot at, probably for the first time," Monarch offered. "You're afraid. People meant to kill you. They may still mean to kill you. Is that part of it?"

Iryna's lower lip quivered before her response. "I cannot sleep. I hear noises, and I get awake. I go down to the cove at night where ocean kills all noise."

"And Constantine?" Monarch asked.

Iryna's face distorted through anger, disbelief, and envy. "He sleeps like bear in cave. But he only needs five hours. Short. Deep."

"So you'll want better security in your bedroom, bars on the windows, alarm system?" he asked as the servant returned with a platter of food: kebabs of barbecued lamb, onions, and red peppers; steamed rice; salad; and fresh fruit.

"This helps," she allowed.

But Monarch heard doubt in her voice. "What else?"

The servant left. Iryna took her beer. She took a deep draft of it, and then said, "Got some thing to stop bad dreams?"

"About the attack?" he asked.

"Mixed with other things," she said.

"Like?"

Iryna shrugged, picked up a kebab, slid

the meat and vegetables from it, and ate several pieces before drinking again from her beer. Monarch learned long ago that if you wanted people to talk, you shut up. Silence is a void, and voids like to be filled.

"When I am sixteen, my parents die in food riot in Siberia," she said. "I have no family. So I wander. I steal things to stay alive. I sleep in streets. Hungry all time. I ride trains. I sell myself. People steal my money. I get to Vladivostok with nothing. I meet girl who tells me where to go to sell sex. It is night. First car, first man is Constantine. He saves me, teaches me things, like to speak English. He gives me books. He helps me survive." A tear dribbled from beneath her sunglasses. "These are other nightmares."

Monarch heard deep pounding echoes of his own childhood in her story and felt compelled to tell her some truth about himself.

"My parents were murdered when I was thirteen," he said. "I was left orphaned in Buenos Aires. I ended up living beside a rat-infested garbage dump in the worst slum in the city, scrounging for anything I could. I believed I was going to die there."

Iryna's fingers had gone to her lips. "How do you live through this?"

Monarch thought of what he'd told the cabdriver in Buenos Aires, that he'd survived by learning to fight, cheat, and steal, but told her another facet of the truth. He said, "I followed rules, and I had help."

"From?"

"Other boys like me. We banded together. We protected each other."

"How long you live like this?"

"Almost four years."

"And then?"

"I was stabbed in a street fight," Monarch replied. "A woman who ran the clinic in the slum healed me and took me in from the streets. A friend of hers had died and left her a farm in the foothills above Buenos Aires. She took me there. She saved me."

Iryna was nodding at him in a way that made Monarch feel as if he were staring at a reflection of himself, a person who wore many layers of invisible armor. The biggest barrier of all was belief, belief in anything other than the lengths it took to exist one day to the next. Even behind the glasses, he could see that about Iryna as plainly as her beauty. She was a survivor, just as he was.

"Where is she now?" Iryna asked at last. "This woman who saves you?"

Monarch flashed on Sister Rachel and said, "She's still there helping kids."

Iryna studied him a moment, then casually reached back to peel off the band that held her hair in a ponytail. Her dark hair fell about her shoulders and framed her extraordinary face. She leaned forward, resting her chin in the palm of one hand. The other came to rest flat on the table. Her shoulders rolled forward. "Tell me about Lacey."

Monarch found himself drawn to her. He leaned slightly forward, his face belying nothing. "Lacey's a good friend. Tell me about Constantine."

He saw the pulse at her throat quicken and felt his heart gently hammer.

Iryna cocked her head, suddenly amused. A beguiling grin crossed her face, and she murmured, "You like to play dangerous games, I think, Robin."

"I don't know what you're talking about," Monarch said, but he glanced at her left hand and had an irrational desire to touch it. He looked back into her eyes and felt his hand lifting.

At the last second, Monarch spotted Belos coming through the doorway onto the terrace. His hand deftly broke course and grabbed a pepper mill. He made a show of cracking pepper over his lamb kebab, while Iryna scratched herself behind the neck.

"You don't like food?" Belos asked as he sat down and put a napkin in his lap.

Monarch glanced down at his plate, untouched, and wondered how much Belos had seen. There'd been no actual contact, no words of betrayal spoken, but Monarch guessed their body language might have been strong enough to raise suspicions.

"I thought we'd wait," Monarch said, picking up his knife and fork. "I knew you'd be along shortly. It all smells wonderful."

If Belos had noticed anything, he didn't show it, but instead dug in, eating several helpings. Monarch made sure to comment on the food, which really was quite good, and steered the conversation toward the security system and what could be done, including alarms, cameras, and a wall around the entire estate.

"Is that enough?" Iryna asked.

"She get scared at night," Belos said. "Can not sleep."

"I could design a safe room."

"How good is safe room?"

"How much steel and cement do you want to pay for?"

Belos's eyebrows rose and fell, and then he sighed, "I'll think on this." He paused and then asked, "You want look at place from water?"

224

23

The Russian had a cigarette boat docked at a marina closer to Paphos, and that afternoon the Mediterranean was calm enough to open up the engines. Monarch stood at the passenger seat when Belos threw the throttle. The entire hull of the boat vibrated, hesitated, and then exploded like a sprinter coming off the blocks, almost knocking Monarch off his feet.

Belos glanced at Monarch and laughed. Soon they were going so fast, they were skipping swell to swell, roaring up the coast. Fifteen minutes later, Belos cut the throttle and swung the bow of the boat toward land. They settled and drifted with the tide, not four hundred yards from the cliffs. Belos's cove came into view. Above it, Monarch made out the mansion. He spotted movement on the balcony on the top floor of the south wing. Iryna was waving to them.

"She sees us," Monarch said, waving back.

Belos glanced at her, then at Monarch, nodded and said, "So what do you think?"

Monarch studied the points of the cove and gestured at the walls. "You'll need sensors, six meters below the rim, lasers aimed diagonally across the back side of the reef, beyond the white water. You'd pick up most intruders."

"Most?" Artun said.

Monarch shrugged. "I don't think there's any way to block a submerged swimmer — No, I take that back. You could install a steel net across the cove."

"Under the water?" Belos asked.

"Sure," Monarch said. "Why not?"

"We snorkel to the reef."

"Put a gate in it," Monarch said.

Belos considered him a long moment, then said, "You think like thief."

"Part of the job."

By the time they returned, it was late afternoon. Belos disappeared into his office after telling Monarch that dinner would be at seven. Artun went with Belos. Monarch changed, stretched, and went for a run. He usually exercised every day, but the travel lately had cut into his routine.

He left the estate, crossed the highway, and headed up a dirt road toward the hills.

Apricot orchards flanked him on both sides of the road. After ten minutes jogging, Monarch stopped, stretched, and then sprinted two hundred yards fourteen times with two-minute intervals of jogging between each dash.

After the last sprint, he slowed to a walk. He was sopping wet, and his heart thudded in his chest. The long walk and stretch back to the estate were relief to his body, but his mind remained edgy and prone to drifting toward Iryna. Ordinarily, Monarch had the ability to keep women where he wanted them, especially in his thoughts. But Iryna was different. She was like him. She'd endured many of the same things he had as a teen. And her beauty was unlike any he'd ever experienced. She was trouble, and he knew it; and yet he found himself imagining how she might feel in his arms.

Monarch went back to his room, finished stretching, showered, and changed. He headed downstairs shortly after sundown and found Iryna behind the bar, wearing a flowing green blouse, bronze pantaloons, and gold sandals. Her hair was braided and pulled up in a bun. She was breathtaking.

"You try my mojito now?" she asked.

"It's all I've thought about," Monarch said.

"I learn from Internet," she said proudly, reaching for fresh mint leaves.

He sat at the bar, watching her add the mint and powdered sugar into a mortar and then pestle the mixture. The scent of mint flared in the air. She spooned out the mixture into two glasses, added ice and rum before pouring chilled club soda into the concoctions.

She set the drink before Monarch, who watched her as he raised the glass and poured. The carbonated flavor shot through his mouth, and he moaned as he set it down.

"Is no good?" she asked, worried.

"That may be the best mojito I've ever had."

Iryna grinned in triumph. "I find recipe from bar in Havana."

"You mastered it," he said.

Iryna made a flirtatious bow before raising her own mojito to her lips. Her eyes never left his when she lowered the glass after drinking. "I am happy you like this."

"What is this?" Constantine rumbled.

"Mojito," Monarch said. "She's incredibly good at it."

The Russian looked at his mistress and said, "We all must be good at something, and now you have found it, Iryna."

Iryna's face turned bitter, and ready to

spit something back at Belos. But instead she said, "And you, Constantine, are still looking for something you are good at."

Belos laughed, but it was not genuine, and then he invited them to dinner, where they dined on roasted guinea fowl in front of a roaring fire. The Russian was in rare form, drinking multiple vodkas and then glass upon glass of red wine while telling Monarch raucous stories of his life on the docks.

Dessert plates were being pushed aside in favor of snifters of brandy, when Monarch felt Iryna's toes on his shin under the table. He glanced at her. She had both elbows on the table and held her snifter in both hands. She was drinking from it and looking at him, slightly smashed.

Monarch returned his attention to Belos, who was laughing and slapping the table. Monarch started laughing, too, though he had no idea at what. "Very good story," he said.

Belos wiped tears from his eyes. "Yes. Yes. I take a piss." He got up from the table and wandered away.

"He only drinks when he knows he will win at something," Iryna said.

"When do you drink?" Monarch asked.

She looked away and said softly, "When I need courage."

"Feeling courageous?"

Her lips parted, her nostrils flared slightly, and she glanced at him. "A little."

Monarch poured them each another glass of cognac. He drank from the snifter, feeling the liquor bite and warm his tongue, watching her watching him.

"When do you drink, Robin?" she asked.

"When I'm in the presence of impossibly beautiful women," Monarch said.

She drew her head back and smiled. "You are feeling courageous, I think."

Belos returned unsteadily, mumbling in Russian, "I am tired, Robin, and I must sleep if I am to fly to get Lacey in the morning."

He came around the back of Iryna's chair and put his hand on her shoulder. Iryna's gaze passed by Monarch and then tilted so she could see Belos. She put her hand on his and said, "I'm coming, too, then."

Monarch nodded. "I should hit the sack. Long flight."

Iryna said, "Do you ride horses, Robin?"

"I do."

"Would you like to ride in the morning while Constantine goes to get Lacey? I ride almost every day alone." She looked at Belos and said, "It makes me feel better."

"Yes, yes," Constantine said with a wave

of his hand. "This you must do, Robin. There is fantastic view of coast up the mountain from the orchards."

Monarch smiled. "Then I'd love to go. What time?"

"Whenever you get up," she said.

Shortly after midnight, Monarch lay in his bed, watching out the window across the lawn toward the third floor on the opposite wing. The lights behind the curtains had died almost an hour ago. He thought of Iryna and felt a thrill go through him at the idea of riding off somewhere alone with her. He thought of Lacey and was conflicted. He liked Lacey. She was fun to be with, smart, beautiful, and great in bed. But even her aunt understood their relationship would be fleeting, as all his relationships with women had been over the years.

With Iryna, however, it felt like it could be more. But then Monarch's cold rational side took hold, reminding him that Constantine Belos was not a man to cross. Thinking about a Russian mobster's mistress was one thing. Pursuing her was another.

The breeze had picked up and with it the surf pounding out on the reef. The moon was near full and cast shimmers on the night sea. Monarch looked into the empty shadows. Iryna was a survivor. He was a survivor. But surviving often left you alone, edgy, and unwilling to believe in nearly anything except constant change. He wondered if this was the sum of his lot: to be skeptical and suspicious of every moment, of every now.

Monarch shook his head, trying to break that train of thought. Ordinarily it led to a period of moroseness where the subjects firing through his brain turned circular in their pattern, devolving into questions he was incapable of answering. Why had he been cast adrift in the streets? Why had he become what he had become?

The sound of running feet jarred him alert. He got out of bed and went to the window, looked out and caught movement near the pool diving board. Iryna had wrapped herself in blankets and was hurrying toward the staircase to the cove.

24

The sound of the surf all but swallowed the creak of the wooden stairs at the top of the cliff. Monarch peered down at the white sand beach, trying to spot her. But all he could see were shadows. He climbed down soft and easy, but not trying to hide at all. At the bottom of the staircase, beneath the shelter of the cove's cliff-work, the wind died. He stepped out onto the sand. He peered at the footprints she'd left.

Monarch had taken no more than two steps after them when Iryna emerged into the moonlight. She held her blankets around her. Silently she watched him approach, as if she had expected him to be there.

Monarch stopped several feet from her. "I remembered you said that when you couldn't sleep, you came to the cove — where the sound of the ocean kills all noise. I wanted to hear that for myself."

Iryna hesitated, but then opened the

blankets to reveal herself in her nightgown. She extended her arms. He walked into them.

Later, Monarch collapsed beside her. "My god," he managed.

Iryna turned her head to him in the moonlight. "Better than mojito?"

"A mojito does not rank in the same universe as you."

She thought that was funny and laughed. Then she pushed him away, saying, "I must go. I am away too long."

She urged him to his feet, picking up the blanket, shaking it, and wrapping it around her shoulders again while he put back on his jeans. "You wait here until I have been gone some time," she said.

Monarch nodded. "Are we still going riding?"

"Of course," she said, then kissed him and was gone up the stairs.

Monarch watched her go, feeling like a siren had called to him, and he had gone to her mesmerized, but somehow managed not to wreck himself on the rocks at her feet.

He awoke from a dead sleep at the heavy knocking at his door. He roused. It was broad daylight and he heard the muffled thumping of helicopter blades turning against the wind.

"Yes?" he called.

Artun said through the door, "Iryna goes to saddle the horses."

"I'm up," Monarch said, dressed quickly, and then hustled down the stairs to find Artun waiting for him with a cup of coffee.

"Thanks," Monarch said.

"Stable is beside helipad," Artun said, watching him evenly.

Monarch went outside. The air was warm. Insects buzzed. He heard the jingle of tack, and smelled the horses before he rounded a corner and found Iryna fitting a bit into the mouth of a big roan gelding.

"Sorry I slept so long," Monarch said.

"I understand," she said, not looking at him. "You had a long flight. Jet lag."

"Exactly," Monarch replied. "Where'd you learn about horses?"

"Constantine pays for teacher," Iryna said. "You?"

"Here and there," he said. "You sleep?"

She smiled. "I have many dreams. You?"

"Dreamless," Monarch said.

She handed him reins, saying, "I am awake, but still feel like I am in dream."

An hour later, Monarch curled over Iryna

in the aftermath of their second lovemaking, his face buried in her hair, his lips finding the nape of her neck, crazed for the taste of her. They were high above the estate, in a cedar grove that grew to the edge of a cliff. The sea far below seemed to stretch toward infinity. Iryna reached around to cradle his head, and his hunger for her blocked out the voice of warning in his head.

"I could get you out of here," he said.

Iryna sighed, as if some spell had broken. She kissed him on the cheeks with a sad expression. "You have no idea what Constantine is capable of."

"He has no idea what I'm capable of," Monarch said.

Iryna's attention passed over his face, her emotions flickering hope and fear and ultimately bitterness. "I am tied to Constantine," she said, putting on her riding pants.

"Not married to him," Monarch said.

"Not in church. But he has me."

Monarch dressed, watching her turn her back to him as she put her blouse back on. She did not look at him as she went back into the cedars, heading toward the horses.

"Does it feel like that when you make love to him?"

Iryna untied her horse's lead rope from the tree.

He stopped her before she could climb into the saddle. "Does it?"

"No," she said. "It feels safe and warm with the food I want to eat and the wine I want to drink and the clothes I want to wear."

"Is that all you want? That and the occasional thrill with one of Constantine's risk-loving guests?"

Anger blazed through her. She reached back to slap him.

Monarch caught the blow and said, "Is it?"

"I don't apologize for my life to someone I fuck twice," she said fiercely.

Monarch hesitated, knowing she was right, and then let her arm go, saying, "Fair enough. Fair enough, and I'm sorry."

But the ride down the mountain passed in an uncomfortable silence broken only by the chug of the helicopter returning mid afternoon. Belos banked the airship past them. Monarch could see Lacey in the copilot's seat. She waved at them before they landed.

When they reached the stable, Artun was waiting. He watched Monarch with his flat, unreadable eyes while taking the reins of their horses and informing them that Constantine had gone to his office to return an urgent call, and Lacey had been shown to her room.

Iryna nodded, then looked at Monarch and said, "Thank you, Robin, for coming on ride with me. It makes me feel safer."

"Anytime."

"Maybe tomorrow morning before you leave," she said. "Maybe not."

"Whatever you decide," Monarch said, and left her, heading to the house.

He found Lacey unpacking an overnight case in his room. "Robin!" she cried, and threw herself into his arms.

He hesitated, but then hugged her and went to kiss her, when she pushed back from him and looked at him strangely.

"You stink."

Monarch did not miss a beat. He laughed and said, "I didn't have time for a shower after going out on the ride." He sniffed his shirt and made a show of cringing his nose. "Horse sweat and me sweat. I'll take a shower."

Lacey shut her left eye as if aiming at something, but then turned back to her overnight case, saying, "Please. I did not sneak out of London and fly three hours in a plane and a half hour in that helicopter alone with Constantine Belos to be hugged

238

by a man who smells of horse sweat."

Monarch went to the bathroom, asking over his shoulder, "Why did you have to sneak out of London?"

Lacey did not reply, and for a moment as Monarch began stripping off his clothes, he thought she had not heard him. Then the door to the bedroom shut, and she appeared behind him as he was turning on the shower. She said, "Aunt Pat was already on the warpath over us having dinner with a Russian mobster. I did not need to make matters worse by telling her I was coming to his estate for the weekend."

"Smart woman," Monarch said. "Where does Lady Pat think you are?"

"Where everyone thinks I am," she replied. "At home, editing manuscripts, not to be disturbed until Monday evening at the earliest."

Monarch got in the shower, shut the glass door. "You think like a criminal."

Lacey laughed and said, "I read a lot of crime fiction."

"How was Constantine on the ride here?" he asked before he dunked his head under the hot water, his hand groping for the soap bar.

"Gentlemanly enough," she said. "But he makes me nervous, like he's calculating something about me."

"Calculating?"

"It was just a feeling," she said. "But it could be my overactive editor's mind. Then again, he is a Russian mobster."

Monarch heard the shower door open behind him. He turned to find Lacey naked, her ginger hair spilling around her shoulders. She was smiling at him. "I missed you."

Monarch felt shitty at a very deep level, but then moved toward her, trying to summon his leftover hunger.

He awoke in bed an hour later. Lacey was up, moving around the room, getting dressed. He was about to say something when a soft knock came at their door.

"Yes?" Lacey called.

"It is Iryna, Lacey," she called through the door. "I like to know if you want to join me for mojito?"

Monarch remarked, "I had one last night. They're excellent."

Lacey said to the door. "Of course, Iryna. We'll be down in fifteen minutes?"

"I wait for you," Iryna said. "And Robin? Constantine says he likes to talk to you in office about security plans before dinner."

25

Belos's office took up a large room with oriental rugs, modern furniture, and fine silk drapes pulled back to reveal a plate glass window that faced the cliffs and the sea. Belos was sitting in a leather executive's chair when Monarch entered. His back was to the drapes. He faced computer screens arrayed on a desk. The mobster rose, gesturing at one of the leather club chairs in front of his desk. "Please, Robin," he said.

Monarch settled into his chair and noticed Artun standing off to one side with arms crossed, and he felt suddenly ill at ease.

Belos came around the desk, smelling of cigarette smoke and vodka. He sat on the edge of his desk and looked at Monarch like he was seeing him for the first time.

"You think more of security?" he asked.

Monarch drew out a piece of paper he'd folded and put in his shirt pocket. "This sums up what I have in mind," he said, handing the paper to Belos. "I'm thinking a wall with sensors joining the sensors on the cliff," he said. "And of course, the panic room. But I don't think it can go off your bedroom area. The floor joists won't support it."

"Where is best place for it?" Belos said, putting the paper behind him on the desk.

"Where your wine cellar is now."

Belos smiled, and then he casually asked in Russian, "How much did you get for the emerald necklace?"

Monarch felt punched, but managed to pretend puzzlement at the language Belos was using. "What's that?" he said in English.

"You understand me," Belos said in Russian. "I know you speak Russian fluently and Chinese and six other languages."

Monarch blinked slowly before shaking his head and replying in English, "English would be best for me."

Belos laughed and continued. "I think either Spanish or English would be best for you, but let us speak my language. I know much about you, Robin."

Monarch licked his lips, glanced at Artun, and replied in English, "Constantine, I don't know what's going on here."

Belos's eyes went hooded. He reached over and twisted the nearest screen to face

Monarch. The screen was split. On the left Monarch saw a younger picture of himself in a U.S. Special Forces uniform. The Cyrillic writing let Monarch know he was looking at a GRU GenStaba intelligence dossier on himself. Monarch now watched the Russian the way a mongoose might a cobra.

"Your parents were very interesting," Belos remarked, tapping his index finger on his lips. "A con artist and a cat burglar. How did they meet?"

Monarch wondered how Russian intelligence had gotten that information, then replied, "On a job. They were both targeting the same old woman."

"You were part of the con, too," Belos said.

"When I was old enough," Monarch admitted.

"You moved around a lot. So many countries as a child."

Monarch raised his eyebrow. "They believed in not staying still for too long."

"Your parents were killed in front of you in Buenos Aires, revenge for swindling someone close to the Perón family."

Monarch said nothing.

"You disappeared for five years before surfacing at a U.S. Army enlistment depot in Miami," Belos continued. "You scored exceptionally high on the exams they gave you during boot camp. They discovered your language skills, sent you to the Defense Language Institute at Monterey, and you left fluent in Russian, Arabic, Farsi, and Chinese to add to the French, German, Spanish, and Italian you already knew.

"Simultaneously, you were trained as a Special Forces reconnaissance scout," Belos went on in grudging admiration. "Your job, as I understand it, was to make high-altitude parachute jumps into locales hostile to U.S. interests, blend in, and scout the target before you called in your team. The kidnappings you ran were impressive."

Monarch was frankly shocked at how much detail the GRU had on him, but he said, "I believe the word is *rendition.*"

Belos laughed again. "It's kidnapping and it was masterfully done. So was the stealing of the Iraqi defense plan before the attack in 2003."

Monarch looked disgusted. "Wish I hadn't. Shitty war all the way around."

"And now you steal jewels for a living?"

"I steal what people pay me to steal," Monarch said. "The jewels are a sideline."

"Ahh, you've gone freelance," Belos said, taking his seat behind the desk again.

"I prefer independent contractor," Monarch said.

Belos chuckled at that. He opened a humidor, drew out a cigarette, and offered it to Monarch, who declined. Belos put the cigarette to his lips before saying, "I would like to hire you to steal something for me, Robin."

Monarch shook his head. "No offense to you, Constantine, but I don't work in that capacity for organized crime."

Belos's face clouded as he grappled with the fact that Monarch knew things about him as well.

"You are like me, Robin," he finally spit out in English. "Do not think that you are not. I am criminal, yes, but I am corporation, too. This you will do for the good of my company."

"The one that runs drugs?" Monarch asked. "Or the extortion firms?"

Belos reddened. "One that does legitimate business. Caviar."

"Just what is it you want me to steal for your legitimate business?"

Belos sobered. "The triggering component to a nuclear device."

Monarch saw he was serious. "What kind of nuclear device?"

"Medium-range missile," Belos said. "Russian."

"Got some mad plan to annihilate the world, Constantine?"

Belos's face returned to that stony expression he used when he was trying to intimidate. "No," he said. "But I would not put it past the other man interested in trigger."

"And who's that?"

The crime lord leaned forward and turned the third computer screen around to show a scruffy-looking man sitting on a chair on the porch of a rough cabin. He wore workman's clothes with a turban and was wizened by the sun.

"He goes by Omak," Belos said. "He's *Obshina*. Chechen Mafia. He's the one behind the attack on me in St. Moritz. Omak has bought pieces of the rocket for years and is building it somewhere in Caucuses. Now, GRU thinks he has the missile and warhead, and now only needs the trigger system."

"What's your interest in the trigger?" Monarch asked.

"I don't want Omak to have it."

"You telling me you're doing this for altruistic reasons?" Monarch said, laughing.

Belos scowled. "Omak is a crazy man. He thinks he does God's work. Omak not only puts the world in danger, he puts my business, my life in danger."

He went on to explain that the trigger

246

Omak sought was Soviet-era, and believed to have been stolen fourteen years ago off a missile at a dismantling factory outside Murmansk. Belos said that a lieutenant in a Hungarian crime syndicate had contacted his organization, claiming to be acting on behalf of whoever had the trigger, and trying to find bidders interested in buying the device.

"Why don't you just buy it, then?" Monarch asked.

"I will try if I have to," Belos said. "But I want to be sure I get the trigger by having you steal for me first. Cheaper, too."

Monarch thought about it and said, "Pass."

"I give you five million dollars," Belos said in English.

The number surprised Monarch and gave him pause, but then he shook his head. "Look, tell your friends at GRU about this. I'll even warn the CIA for you, but —"

A knock came at the door. "Constantine?" Iryna called out. "We have mojitos!"

"Five minutes!" Belos yelled. He waited several moments and then leaned toward Monarch to say softly in Russian, "You'll do it or I'll send this file to Inspector Robillard. He'll figure out the rest. You'll be wanted by Interpol. You'll do time."

Monarch looked him in the eye. "And if that happens, you'll be a dead man."

"You threaten me?"

"I'm just describing consequences," Monarch said. "And I guarantee you I will not make the same mistake the Chechens did."

Belos thought about that and sighed. "I can be a very convincing man, Robin."

"No doubt," Monarch said, rising from his chair. "But not on this count. I'll write you a report detailing what I think you need for security here, and we'll call it good."

Belos was clearly not pleased, but he shrugged. "Have it your way," he said. "Go have a drink. I will be along."

Monarch came down the hallway from Belos's office, wondering if the night was going to be uncomfortable between him and the Russian. He could hear laughing ahead of him. He reached the great room. Lacey sat at the bar, looking remarkable in a mauve evening dress. She'd let her ginger hair down and it cascaded around her bare shoulders. Behind the bar, chattering like a professional working a favored patron, Iryna dazzled in black slacks and a high-collared sleeveless sweater. He paused there, watching Iryna prepare the mojito, and it seemed to him that she was a born actress, or at least someone like himself, able to change persona and story to meet the demands of the moment.

"I have gotten very good," Iryna boasted to Lacey with a broad smile as he walked over to them. She nodded toward Monarch. "Ask him."

"Good as you'll get in Havana," Monarch said, smiling.

"How was your ride?" Lacey asked.

Iryna did not miss a beat as she poured the club soda. "I usually ride much faster, but your Robin is not a very good . . . how do you say . . . horse man."

"That's not true," Monarch protested.

"Hah," Iryna cried sarcastically. She put a mojito in front of Lacey. "He can't keep his butt in the saddle, his weight is all over the place." She did an imitation of a drunken cowboy. "He has sores in the morning."

"I already have those," Monarch said, shifting on the stool cushion.

"I wish I could have seen that," Lacey said.

"It was not pretty," Iryna said in a conspiratorial tone.

"C'mon," Monarch protested. "I wasn't that bad."

Iryna kept talking to Lacey and patting her on the hand. "He was that bad. I only hope for your sake he's better in bed."

"Oh, he is," Lacey said, glancing at him with a smile. "A regular stallion."

"Oooh," Iryna said, appraising him and then breaking into laughter.

Monarch felt weirdly scrutinized, but smiled at Lacey, saying. "I'm happy to be your beast of burden."

Belos lumbered in. The mobster's eyes were bloodshot. "What beast?"

"Not you, Constantine," Iryna scolded.

"Oh," he said. "I hate coming in to talking late. Vodka, Iryna."

She poured him a shot, and then raised the bottle toward Monarch and Lacey, who both declined. Belos took the vodka and downed it. Monarch caught him looking at Lacey as he lowered his glass, and he swore he saw a moment of pity in the Russian's eyes before they returned to their normal flat state.

Artun entered and said, "Dinner, Constantine."

Belos and Monarch sat at either end of a dining room table with the women facing each other. Belos spent much of his meal picking at the food and swilling red wine, watching them all while Iryna played life of the party — exuberant, funny, and smart.

Iryna paid no particular attention to Belos, focusing all her exuberance, flattery, and wit on Lacey and Monarch, acting as if she were close confidante and wayward cousin, pouring them all glass after glass of Cypriot wine.

"I'll say this," Iryna remarked as dessert was served. "Robin's plans will make me feel better, Constantine."

Belos grunted, "I'm sure it makes my wallet feel worse." He was drinking coffee and keeping most of his attention on Monarch.

"The fence?" Lacey asked. "Is it necessary?"

"The men in St. Moritz meant to kill," Monarch said. "What do you think?"

Lacey nodded as if she had only just realized she was sitting in the unsecure house of a mobster who'd recently survived an assassination attempt. "A fence sounds reasonable, and a lot more," she said at last.

"Cameras. Iron screen underwater across cove, and a safe room," Iryna said, grinning at Monarch. She pointed at him. "Is all his ideas."

Lacey looked at Monarch with new appreciation. "You really are good at this."

"What?"

"Being an international man of mystery, a security agent for hire, disappearing all the time on missions, building fortresses,"

Lacey said, and blew Monarch a kiss. She looked over at Iryna, who was grinning wildly. "Isn't he something?"

Iryna shifted her attention to Monarch, sobered, sat upright, and accorded him a fair appraisal before giving Lacey a sharp bob of her head. "Yes," Iryna said. "Robin Monarch most definitely is something."

Iryna laughed and Lacey joined her, leaving Monarch feeling under the microscope again. He managed to nod good-naturedly, and in grudging wonder over how Iryna had so thoroughly disarmed Lacey through sheer radiance and good humor.

Belos coughed suddenly. He took a deep belt of his wine and set the glass roughly on the table. He leaned over his elbows and grumbled, "You want to know what Robin Monarch is? That something?"

Monarch, Lacey, and Iryna looked down the table at Belos like he was a bear just prodded from sleep, bleary, grouchy, unpredictable.

"What is he, Constantine?" Lacey asked.

"A thief," Belos said, and pulled a pistol from beneath the table. He pointed it at Monarch. "He is nothing but a thief, just like me."

"My god, Robin," Lacey cried after a moment of being stunned. "What's happening?

What's he talking about?"

"I don't know," Monarch said. His brain was calculating angles and distance and body positions. It wasn't good.

Iryna, strangely, said nothing as she watched the scene.

Belos cocked the pistol's hammer.

"Please!" Lacey said. "What's he done? What's he stolen from you?"

Belos snorted at Lacey. "The last fucking one to know. You don't even know what he steals from you and your friends."

Monarch glanced at Lacey, who was registering the gist of that information. Her cheeks quivered as she pivoted in her seat toward Monarch. "What did you — ?"

"— Nothing," Monarch said. "He —"

"— lies to you again," Belos said. "It's what thieves do. What did he tell you about the necklace of emeralds?"

Drunk as she was, scared as she was, that slapped Lacey. She found the arm of her chair, dazed and looking like she was seeing things for the first time. Her face twisted up in disgust and disbelief, and she fixed her building anger on Monarch. "You had the time," she said. "Your client stood you up."

"No," Monarch said. "I was —"

"— climbing the tower at Badrutt's Palace," Belos said, enjoying himself, still leveling the cocked pistol at Monarch.

Monarch felt himself squirm under Lacey's look of condemnation.

Her hands curled to fists. "You did, Robin. You cold, lying son of a bitch, you did, and you let us all believe . . ." Lacey looked angrily at Belos and demanded, "If he stole the necklace from Dame Maggie, what did he steal from me?"

Belos grunted in amusement and looked at Iryna, who said in a matter-of-fact manner, "He fucks me twice. Once on beach last night. Once in hills."

Lacey looked confused, then hurt, and shouted at Monarch, "Oh, my god, you *were*, weren't you? This afternoon? And you tell me the smell on you is horse!"

She snatched up her dessert plate and flung it at Monarch. He didn't duck. Just let it hit him on the side of the head and shatter. She grabbed her wineglass and whipped it at Iryna. "And fuck you, too, bitch!" It missed and exploded against the wall behind her. She glared at Belos in drunken rage. "Go ahead. Shoot them both."

Belos smiled coldly and offered her the gun. "Come, take it. Why don't you? You will feel better afterward. Justified."

Lacey looked at the gun. Her eyes crossed

and then she doubled over and cupped her palm to her mouth. "I'm going to be sick."

She made to leave the room, but Artun appeared, carrying a sawed-off shotgun and blocking her way. "Sit down," he ordered.

Lacey started blubbering. When she tried to turn, she stumbled to her hands and knees, retching and crying, "How could you, Robin?"

"Yes, how could you, Robin?" Belos said, moving laterally toward Lacey. He gestured the gun toward Iryna. "Original plan, you know, was Iryna seduces you, and I give you money to steal trigger, two carrots instead of one. But you tell me no. And then Lacey tells Iryna that no one knows she is here, not even her aunt, and we throw old plan out in favor of better one."

Lacey was trying to get to her feet. Her hand groped the tabletop for a napkin to clean her face.

As her fingers closed on it, Belos grabbed her hair and wrenched her back against him. He shoved the pistol muzzle against Lacey's head. "So go get me trigger, Monarch, or she dies," Belos said.

"Oh God, oh God," Lacey whined in terror.

Belos snarled in her ear, "Tell Robin he does what I want or last thing you know is this and worse." With that, Belos lifted her off the ground by her hair.

"Robin!" Lacey screeched. "Please. Please do what he says!"

"Do it," Iryna told Monarch. "Constantine always gets what he wants."

"Let her down," Monarch said.

Belos relaxed his grip. Lacey fell weeping at his feet.

"You do it?" the mobster asked.

"You let us walk out of here, and I'll get you the trigger," Monarch said.

Belos chortled softly and he stroked the gun barrel on Lacey's tear-spattered cheeks. "No, Robin. You bring me trigger. Then I give you girl."

Monarch's attention swung all around, looking for some attack angle he had not considered in the minutes since the Russian pulled the gun. But Belos had him covered at close range, and Artun was doing the same from the only doorway.

Monarch brought his full attention back to Belos and said, "When I was a teenager, an orphan in Buenos Aires, I survived by joining a street gang called *la Fraternidad de Ladrones*. 'The Brotherhood of Thieves.' "

Belos bobbed the pistol at Monarch. "See, I tell you we are alike, you and me."

"The Brotherhood has rules," Monarch

said. "Eighteen rules."

"Same as Vory v Zakone," Belos noted.

Monarch continued, "The Brotherhood was run by a guy named Julio. He was smart, and read about the Russian Mafia and your thieves' code in some magazine article. He changed your rules to suit his purposes and taught them to everyone in the Brotherhood, including me. We lived and survived by the eighteen rules. I still do."

"What is point?" Belos growled.

"Julio didn't like your rules," Monarch said. "In fact, he changed every single one of them in some way or fashion except one, the last one, the eighteenth rule. He kept it. It's the only rule shared by Vory v Zakone and *la Fraternidad de Ladrones*."

" 'Make good on promises given to other thieves,' " Artun said.

Monarch nodded and said, "I don't know how it works with you Russians. But in la Fraternidad, any violation of the eighteenth rule is punishable by death."

He gestured at Lacey, who was watching him from the floor at Belos's feet, horrified by what he'd become in so short a time. "If I come back here with that trigger and find her harmed in any way, I will punish you under the eighteenth rule. And, Constantine, I will show no mercy." He looked at Iryna. "No mercy to either of you."

Constantine's lip had curled. "And I give you two weeks to get me trigger. Fourteen days. If no, I kill her. Know also, I move her as soon as you leave. Very simple. You understand, Monarch?"

26

THE WILLARD HOTEL
WASHINGTON, D.C.

Jack Slattery groaned and rolled off Audrey, who lay panting on the bed, dressed in a lavender corset, garters, and stockings.

Slattery's head found the pillow, and he gasped, "You're a genius, Audrey. You don't know how much I needed that."

Audrey laughed, propped herself up on one elbow, and ran a finger through his chest hair. "You were one tense man when you came through that door," she said. "I figured I'd better release some of that built-up pressure."

Slattery sighed happily. "You found the right valve."

Audrey giggled. "So you want me to put on the skirt? Get ready for round two?"

Slattery played with that idea and was about to answer in the affirmative when the cell phone in his trousers began to ring. He rolled away from Audrey without giving her an answer and found the phone. He'd been waiting for a call on that phone all day.

He answered it by saying, "Hold on." He went to the bathroom without giving Audrey a second glance and closed the door behind her. "Talk to me."

"It is done," Constantine Belos said. "He goes."

"He took the money?"

"No," Belos said. "But I find way to make sure he does this for me."

Slattery wanted to ask the Russian how he'd turned Monarch, but instead asked, "And you gave him the information about the Hungarian?"

"He has it," Belos said. "I give him two weeks to find this thing."

"Or?"

"Bad things happen," he said.

Slattery nodded to himself. *Give Monarch a deadline. Don't let him have time to think too much.* It was smart.

"When you have the trigger, contact me immediately," Slattery said.

"As agreed, whoever you are," Belos said.

"Whoever I am," Slattery said, and hung up the phone.

The covert ops chief grinned at the mirror. It had all come together like the workings of a fine clock. The morning after the shoot-out on the bobsled run, he tracked down phone numbers for Belos through a contact at the GRU. He told the Russian that he was an American intelligence officer, and that he had information and a proposal that Belos might find interesting. He told Belos a fabricated tale about his archnemesis, Omak, trying to build a nuclear missile so he could dominate the central Asian smuggling routes. He told Belos that Omak nearly had the missile complete and needed only a trigger. Slattery said that there was such a trigger on the market and that the United States and Russia wanted it kept out of the Chechen's hands.

For reasons Slattery said were too complicated to explain, neither country wanted to commit assets to the mission. Indeed, Slattery said that there was only one man capable of stealing the trigger before it got into the wrong hands: Robin Monarch, the same man who'd saved Belos's life the evening before. Slattery's proposition was simple: If the Russian could convince Monarch to successfully retrieve the trigger, Belos would receive ten million dollars. The Russian had countered at twenty million, and they achieved an agreement at four million up front and eleven on delivery. Once the negotiations had concluded, Belos asked where Monarch was supposed to start looking, and Slattery told him he was still working on that.

He had not had to wait long. Immediately after leaving C. Y. Tilden's limousine, he returned to his office and used the CIA's filtering software to have every report arriving at the agency searched for certain keywords. A week after Ali Nassara was murdered in Odessa, *particle,* one of the key words in Slattery's search, was found in a report about a midlevel Hungarian crime figure putting out feelers to gauge interest in technology that sounded vaguely similar to Green Fields.

There was a knock on the door. "You coming out, sugar?" Audrey asked.

According to the game he'd so painstakingly put together, Slattery knew he should be making an effort to contact Omak in order to establish further pressure on Monarch, but then decided to celebrate his good fortune. He deserved it.

Slattery opened the door and said, "Start unzipping now."

27

FOUR P.M., THIRTEEN DAYS LEFT . . .
PARIS
Monarch paced in front of the Ritz on the Place Vendôme, calling a number he'd been dialing constantly and unsuccessfully on his long way to Paris.

He was about to hang up when he heard a click and then Gloria Barnett came on, saying, "Whoever the Christ this is, quit calling. I don't want to buy whatever —"

"It's Robin, and I'm in trouble," Monarch said. "I need you to take a vacation."

There was silence on the line and for a moment Monarch thought she'd hung up. But then she said, "What kind of vacation?"

"Retrieval," he said. "I can't explain. You'll just have to trust me."

"Trust you, Robin?" she cried, and then laughed caustically. "Trust you?"

"Trust me," Monarch said. "And I want you to contact the others. I'll need their help, too. I will meet all of you tomorrow night at your flat in London."

"That's not going to happen. You don't know how they feel about you."

"I can guess," Monarch said. "But tell them that I want the chance to explain what happened in Istanbul."

"And you want them to fly to London on short notice for that? Three of them aren't even working because of you."

"I'm paying," Monarch insisted. "Tell them to put the tickets on a credit card and I'll reimburse them. I'll be paying them, too. And you, Gloria. Two weeks of work, one hundred thousand dollars each."

"Where the hell are you getting that kind of money?" she demanded.

"Leave that up to me," Monarch said. "Tomorrow night. Eight o'clock."

He snapped shut the cell phone, stuck it in his pocket, and entered the Ritz.

Twenty minutes later, in a magnificent penthouse suite, Lady Patricia Wentworth went pale, sat down shakily on the couch, crying, "Lacey's a hostage?"

Monarch nodded. He'd just given her an edited version of the events that led to Belos taking her niece, including the ransom demand of a nuclear trigger, but leaving out his affair with Iryna and Dame Maggie's necklace.

Lady Wentworth was dressed in a purple satin robe. Tears welled in her eyes as she said, "Lacey's the last of the Wentworths."

"I will bring her back to you," Monarch promised.

"You've done enough, I'd say!" the billionairess cried angrily. "Didn't I tell you about the Russians?" She didn't wait for an answer. "I'll call my friends in the Foreign Office. I'll call Downing Street. They'll have the Cypriot Army in there in the morning."

"Not a good idea, Lady Pat," Monarch cautioned. "He's moved her by now. She could be anywhere."

"Then how are you going to find her?" Lady Wentworth demanded.

"By finding this trigger," Monarch said. "I've got a lead. A good one."

She studied him. "I had a shitty feeling about you from the start, Monarch."

"You did. And you were right."

Lady Wentworth thrust out her lower jaw. "What can I do to help?"

"I'm going to need money," he replied. "Enough to hire a team to help me."

"How much?" Lady Wentworth asked, her expression narrowing.

"A million should cover it?"

Her suspicions deepened. "How do I know this is not some scam?"

Monarch could see her point. "You know who I am."

"Do I?"

"My name anyway," Monarch said.

"Is it real?"

"Yes. And so are my fingerprints, the ones the Swiss took. If I'm lying to you, turn me over to Inspector Robillard."

Lady Wentworth said nothing.

Monarch hardened. "Your niece has thirteen days."

After another long silence, Lady Wentworth said in a steely tone: "Just get Lacey back to me. Then I want you the hell out of her life."

28

TWELVE DAYS LEFT . . .

LONDON

Monarch stopped, took a deep breath, and knocked on an apartment door off Picadilly Circus. Special ops teams are delicate organisms. He wondered if what he'd broken could now be fixed. He wondered how many of them would be here at all.

The door opened and Gloria Barnett looked out at him suspiciously. He had not seen his old operations runner in nearly a year and a half, and he saw the strain of what he had done to her in her face and in her carriage.

He took a step and tried to kiss her on the cheek. She accepted it with a chilly expression.

"Thank you, Gloria," he said, and then walked down a hallway into a living area.

To his relief, they had all come. John Tatupu stood against a wall, arms crossed, fingers tapping his giant biceps. Abbott Fowler nursed a beer; he'd lost weight and would not meet Monarch's gaze. Ellen Yin stood in the doorway to the kitchen, looking at him with a bittersweet expression.

Chanel Chávez put her beer down, marched up to Monarch, and slapped him across the face. "I don't care why you did it. Get one thing straight: Only one owing here is you. Chanel Chávez don't owe Robin Monarch a thing, least of all trust!"

Monarch took the sting of her slap as his due. "You deserved the truth a year and a half ago, but I believed that sharing it would bring you harm. Turns out I was right. Three weeks after I left, someone ordered my assassination. They attacked me in Algiers."

"Who and for what?" the big Samoan demanded.

"I don't know. But I don't think I was sent into Nassara Engineering after archives."

"Then what," Tatupu demanded.

"A Green Fields weapon."

Over the course of the next hour, Monarch told them everything that had happened to him that night in Istanbul, including his discovery of the designs for a Green Fields device. Until that point, none of his team had said a word. But then he described what the weapon did, and laid out the horrors that could be associated with it.

"Is it for real?" Yin asked. "Green Fields?"

Monarch shrugged. "All I know is that what I saw could be worth billions of dollars in the wrong hands and could result in the death of millions. I was happy Nassara's lab blew up. There was no point to what we were doing. No nobleness. We were just after a bigger club to hit the other guy over the head with."

The Samoan looked at Monarch as if he were mad. "We had direct orders," he said, his voice rising. "The point was that club could be used against us someday. The point was we were trained never to leave any member of the team in the field, Robin! You trained us that way!"

"I trained you to keep each other safe, and that is what I did."

Chávez yelled, "How do you know that what you saw wasn't camouflage to hide the rest of the Al-Qaeda files?"

Monarch shrugged. "I can't answer that."

"We thought you were dead," Yin complained. "We lived with that until you mailed in your letter of resignation." She shook her head bitterly. "No calls? No e-mails? We were family, Robin. All of us. Slattery forced us out. Gloria's the only one left at the agency, and they've got her reading crop reports."

Monarch saw the pain in the faces of his old comrades. He said, "Leaving like I did gave you safety. You didn't see what I saw and they knew it."

"Who's they?"

"People wanting to make money off Green Fields," Monarch replied. "Maybe Slattery. He nearly had a shit fit that night in Istanbul when I wanted to open one of the Green Fields files."

"He was having a shit fit because you were not leaving the lab," Barnett said.

"Maybe. But maybe Hopkins gave the order. Or Slattery's Turkish source gave Slattery tainted information."

"You got anything concrete on any of them?" Tatupu asked.

"No."

"You don't even know if Green Fields worked," Fowler said.

Monarch replied, "Whoever sent me in to steal those files must have believed it would work. They tried to have me killed afterwards. But none of that really matters. That's not why I came to you. A Russian mobster is holding a friend of mine hostage. Her ransom is a nuclear trigger that I have to locate and steal in the next twelve days."

"Or?" Yin asked.

"She dies. And she's innocent. And I got her messed up in it."

Tatupu said, "Does life ever slow down around you?"

"Not often," Monarch replied, shaking his head. "Here's the deal: The pay is one hundred K and a percentage of whatever else we manage to make along the way."

"Where did you get that kind of cash?" Barnett demanded.

"The hostage's aunt," Monarch said. "But I'm going to repay her out of the money I'm going to get out of the Russian before this is over."

"How?" Fowler asked.

"Haven't figured that out yet," Monarch said. "But I will."

Tatupu glanced at Chávez, who still stood there, arms crossed, chewing on all that had been said. Chávez said, "What does this friend mean to you?"

Monarch hung his head. "I wronged her, and put her in the hands of a stone-cold killer. Lacey's an innocent, good person. I owe her freedom and everything else."

"Hundred grand?"

"Minimum," Monarch said.

"I got to break laws?" Fowler asked.

"I'd imagine," Monarch said.

Barnett said, "But you have no idea where this trigger is."

"I've got a lead," Monarch said, and then pulled out a piece of paper and handed it to her. "His name is Vadas. He lives in Budapest."

Gloria took the paper, studied it, and then said, "Okay, Robin. I'll help you."

One by one, the others did the same. And for the first time since leaving Belos's estate, Monarch felt he had an honest chance.

29

NINE DAYS LEFT . . .
BUDAPEST

A raw wind was blowing out of Austria when Monarch left the Keleti train station on the Pest side of the river around four in the afternoon. He raised the collar of his wool pea coat, tugged down his black watch cap, and then picked up his canvas duffel that together with his fake Canadian passport completed his guise as a traveling merchant seaman. He'd never been to Budapest, but he had studied a map of the city on the train ride from Frankfurt, saw it clearly in his mind, and made a northeasterly loop past the opera house before heading toward the Chain Bridge across the Danube.

As darkness fell, the streets bustled with people leaving work and heading for home. Monarch did not understand a word of the Magyar chatter, and that left him feeling anonymous, which is exactly what he wanted to be, what he wanted his entire team to be as they filtered into Budapest by other means. The more they operated deep in the shadows, the greater their chance of success.

Monarch smelled the Danube before he saw it, a fouler odor than he expected. When he reached the walkway along the river, he set his bag down by the railing and appeared to be paying attention to a barge maneuvering beneath the bridge. All the while, Monarch's eyes took in everyone passing beneath the streetlamps. When he was fairly certain he had not been followed from the train station, Monarch hailed a cab and gave the driver an address scribbled on a piece of paper.

When the taxi finally stopped, Monarch was in a stretch of bars, restaurants, and theaters. He left the main drag, heading onto a street of older apartment buildings.

Chanel Chávez opened the door before he knocked. He entered quickly and she shut the door behind them. The apartment was big and almost empty and the wall plaster crumbling. The floors were old planks. A gas fire burned at one end of the living room.

"How'd Gloria find this place?" Monarch asked.

"She's the best," said Ellen Yin, who lay on her back under a long folding table, working with the various cables and plugs attached to three laptops, a printer, and a portable hard drive. There was a storage locker on the floor beside Yin, lid up, revealing cameras and other electronics.

"Where is she?"

"Out buying more supplies."

Tatupu sat in a chair at the window, holding a pair of high-power Leica binoculars, which was stuck out between the folds of the drapes.

"How close is Vadas?" Monarch asked.

"Hundred fifty feet," Tatupu said, rising from his seat and handing Monarch the Leicas. "Straight across and down. They're in there. Both of them."

Taking the binoculars, Monarch open the drapes several inches, finding it had begun to rain outside. On the other side of the narrow street, he could see the third-floor windows. The shades were half-drawn, and the lights inside were on.

He caught a flash of movement and lifted the binoculars. The light in the bedroom went off. And then another in the adjoining room.

"I think they're leaving," Monarch said, drawing back. "Chávez, you're the only one who speaks the lingua franca. Follow them. Your Hungarian cover."

Chávez reacted swiftly. She grabbed a rain jacket, then went to an open suitcase in the corner, snatched up a satellite phone, and stuffed it in her pocket. She grabbed her Hungarian passport and a set of rental car keys off the table. She clipped a Bluetooth unit to her ear as she headed toward the door. "Yin, you got me?"

"Five minutes to chitchat," Yin promised her as she clipped a cable to a portable satellite Internet link.

Monarch looked down at the front door of the Hungarian criminal's apartment building. A minute passed before Miklos Vadas opened the door for his girlfriend.

Sophia Rozsa was taller than her boyfriend and had bleached-blond spiked hair. Vadas himself was balding and nervous, smoking a cigarette. He swiveled his head as he puffed, inspecting the street. They were both dressed for a night out. They walked up the street to a Mercedes sedan, got in, and drove away.

A black Lancia coupe pulled out from directly below Monarch's window. Chávez was on them. Monarch had almost taken his eyes off the street when a tan Toyota sedan pulled out from a space to the south. It accelerated through Monarch's field of view so fast that he saw only the wipers smacking the rain-slathered windows, and the gloved hands of the driver.

"I think Vadas has a second tail," Monarch said, getting up. "Chávez needs to know."

"Thirty seconds," Yin said, getting up from beneath the table. She put on a headset plugged into one of the laptops and started typing. She paused, listened, and then handed Monarch the headset.

Monarch put it on, heard the hiss of an open line, and said, "Nice drive?"

"Crazy traffic," Chávez said.

"There's a second tail on your rat," Monarch said. "Back off, let the late-model tan Toyota four door coming at you have him."

"Roger that," Chávez said.

Monarch handed back the headset to Yin. "GPS up?"

Yin nodded and turned around another laptop so Monarch could see Chávez's position plotted on a map of Budapest. She was heading back toward the Danube.

Something dawned on Monarch. He looked at Tatupu, who was working on the third computer. "Can you get me a layout of Vadas's apartment building?"

"Already have it," Tatupu said.

"I'm going in, then."

"Now?" Yin asked.

"Whoever else is tailing Vadas is gone with him."

"You won't have full support."

"Do an infrared. Long as it's empty, it's a piece of cake. Twenty minutes tops for a basic prowl-and-bug fest."

Tatupu looked ready to argue, but nodded and looked at Yin. "How fast?"

The team's technology officer said, "Basic support, five minutes."

Monarch said, "I'm inside in twelve. Where's the stuff Gloria had delivered?"

Tatupu pointed to boxes piled in a corner. While Yin worked, Monarch found a plumber's bag. Then he stuffed the bag with the tools and equipment he would need.

Tatupu, meanwhile, had taken up the largest of the cameras, set it on a tripod, and ran a link from it to one of Yin's computers. Tatupu flipped on the camera's power as Monarch came up beside him dressed in a tradesman's jumpsuit, a black leather jacket, and a snap-bill wool cap.

Monarch pivoted to watch the computer screens, one of which showed the digital blueprints of the fifth floor of Vadas's apartment. The screen linked to Tatupu's camera was spattered with brilliant colors, blues mostly, but golds and light oranges, too. Tatupu trained the camera across the face of the building across the street, and Monarch saw the blurred mutating renditions of human forms and animals and ovens and furnaces revealed on the screen by their heat print.

Then the screen stilled. Vadas's apartment came into focus, a warm gold tone surrounded by cold blue. Aside from the hot red lines that represented the baseboard hot water registers, there was no other radiating form on the screen.

"That's it?" Monarch said.

Tatupu looked through the viewfinder on the camera. "Wall to wall."

"Then we're clean and I'm gone," Monarch said, spun around, grabbed the plumber's bag, and headed toward the door.

Monarch left his building by a rear service door that exited into an alley. The rain drummed around him. He circled the block, grateful for the lousy weather, which seemed to have emptied the streets and dulled all sound.

With a quick left and right look up and down the block, Monarch climbed the stairs to Vadas's building. He spotted the key cylinder in the iron gate and smiled. He knew the mechanism. He grabbed the picks snuggled in his wristbands and slid the larger of the two into the upper part of the lock. He gave it a jig, felt it catch slightly, and lifted. Something gave. The smaller pick found the lower grooves, probing and finally ticking. He made a prying motion with the upper pick and a downward grind with the lower. He heard a metallic click. The iron door swung loose on its hinges. Monarch picked up the plumber's bag, entered, and closed the gate behind him. He went straight to the elevator.

He got off at the sixth floor, found the stairs, and dropped down a level. He opened the stairwell door a crack and surveyed the hallway. He heard a television playing. A woman finished singing. People were clapping. The air in the hallway smelled of meat simmering in paprika, garlic, and mint.

He slipped down the hallway and found Vadas's door. Two locks, one doorknob, one dead bolt. He had them open in thirteen seconds.

Monarch pushed the door inward a crack, his eyes scrutinizing the doorjamb, looking for evidence of a security alarm. He reached for the talcum powder he always carried in his front right pocket, but then heard another door opening down the hallway.

He pushed the door to Vadas's apartment open and slipped inside. As he did so, his eyes cast downward and he saw his right leg break a tiny beam of blue light. He pivoted and shut the door. Right in front of him, mounted on the wall at eye level, an electronic access pad was blinking red. A synthesized woman's voice said something forceful in Hungarian. Monarch didn't understand the words, but he got the meaning. He had less than fifteen seconds to disarm the system before sirens would start.

Monarch snatched his iPhone from his breast pocket. He thumbed on the power, selected an application, and watched a bell curve swell on the screen. He tracked time, wanting to let the device gather as much power as it could before unleashing it. Just before the alarm was to wail, he pointed the iPhone at the security box.

He pressed SEND, felt the device lightly thud in his hand, and heard a low bass sound as an intense magnetic pulse let loose. The pulse obliterated the memory and much of the circuitry in the alarm system. It left the screen on the access pad blinking and spewing garbled gibberish.

Monarch took a deep breath and sighed. "That was close."

"What's that?" Tatupu asked.

"I had to pulse the alarms," Monarch murmured as he tugged out an LED head-lamp from his right jacket pocket.

Yin said, "The police will be on the way."

"Maybe," Monarch said. "If Vadas sprang for a phone alert."

Without waiting for a reply, he flipped on the red headlamp bulb, slipped off his shoes, and moved in stocking feet into the flat. According to the blueprint Barnett had sent, there should have been a kitchen on his right. But he found only a blank wall, and he soon emerged into a main room that was a backward L-shape. The place stank of cigarettes, perfume, and stale coffee.

"Looks like they've renovated this place recently," Monarch said into the Bluetooth. "Blueprints are useless."

He adapted, moving quickly, scanning. He spotted the computer first, a Macintosh laptop on a desk. He went to the laptop, noticing no other cable than the power, which meant the place had wireless. With a gloved finger, he tapped the laptop's touch pad. The screen sprang to life, and for a moment he thought it was going to be all too easy.

Then a prompt appeared on the screen, asking him for a password.

Monarch opened the plumber's bag and

dug out a wireless modem attached to an Ethernet cable. He snapped the cable's free end into Vadas's computer.

Monarch said, "Yin, got your modem in a Mac. I'll find the router and tap it."

"Roger that," Yin said.

"Chávez?" Monarch asked, leaving the computers.

"I'm camped on a restaurant near the river," Chávez replied in Monarch's Bluetooth. "Vadas went in with his girlfriend ten minutes ago."

"What about the other tail?"

"Up the road from me eighty yards."

Monarch went through the main room a second time heading for the hallway. He searched the closets and found the router. He unclipped the incoming cable and snapped on a bug between it and the router.

"You've been in ten minutes," Tatupu said.

"How's it coming, Yin?" Monarch asked, leaving the router.

"I'm hacked into his hard drive," Yin replied. "Doing the vampire now."

The hallway ended in a pair of double doors. Monarch opened them and found himself in a large bedroom suite that smelled of fresh paint and new carpet. He set a bug under the nightstand and another in the landline handset. He set a third in the bathroom. When he opened the walk-in closet, wires and cables hung from an open crawlspace above the shelves. Monarch left the suite, intending to place an optical bug somewhere in the main room, when it hit him: Where was the kitchen?

He went and looked around the living area, his attention coming to rest finally on the three-quarter wall that supported the home theater. He padded toward the opposite end of the wall, which he saw did not run the entire length of the room. There was something behind it.

Monarch stuck his head around the corner and felt his heart build pace. "This place has two floors," he whispered into his Bluetooth.

"What?" Tatupu asked.

"I'm looking down a staircase into darkness. Scan it."

He'd no sooner said that than he heard the distinct sound of a dead bolt being thrown and a door creaking opening somewhere below him.

"You've got competition," Tatupu said. "Two of them."

"Thought you said they were in that restaurant," Monarch hissed as he twisted around, his mind taking inventory of everything he'd done since entering the apartment.

"They are," Chávez said. "I can see them, sitting by the window."

"Get the fuck out of there," Tatupu said. "No arguments."

Monarch danced across the main room to the computer and yanked the modem.

"I'm not done," Yin complained.

Monarch grabbed the plumber's satchel and stuffed the modem in it. He went for the hallway and the door. But when he reached the foyer, he heard women arguing outside. He stuck his eye to the peephole and saw them, directly across the hallway — one of them in her doorway, hair covered in a scarf, the other with her back to him. They were both wagging their fingers at each other and arguing in Hungarian. Monarch grabbed his shoes and fl ed toward the master bedroom.

Thirty seconds later, his shoes and satchel sat side by side on the highest shelf in the closet and he was sliding feet first into the crawlspace with a silenced H&K .45 held in his teeth. He was barely able to roll over in the tight quarters, all the while fighting off the urge to sneeze. He looked across the hole and saw a square piece of plywood lying on the opposite side.

"One's coming up the stairs," Tatupu said in his ear. "You want backup?"

"Negative," Monarch murmured. "Let's ride it out."

Monarch grabbed the plywood and did his best to set it on top of the hole. Gun in his right hand, he peered down through the crack, noticing that his red headlamp was shining. He snapped it off and was enveloped in blackness.

Monarch did what he always did when he was stuck in a tight spot: He started breathing deep and slow. Then he started flexing his muscles one at a time, starting with his toes and working through his feet and up his legs, forcing his body, muscle by muscle, to relax and so to conserve energy in case he had to fight. He'd reached the muscles along the spine when he heard the door to the suite open. A few moments later, the bathroom door creaked.

The door to the closet opened. The light came on. He made his eyes slits and saw a tall blond man in a trench coat, head down, looking around the floor of the closet, a black Glock in his latex-gloved left hand, a cell phone clipped to his lapel.

Quartering away from Monarch, the man reached inside his coat and came up with a prescription bottle. He pried the cap off with his teeth before spilling two small pills into his mouth. The man swallowed, pushed the cap back on the bottle with his teeth, returned it to his coat, and turned, head still down, inspecting the boxes. Monarch saw that he did it all with his left hand. There was something wrong with his right.

Monarch no sooner had that thought than the man raised his head to look at the higher shelves, his attention focusing on the plumbing satchel. Monarch recognized him. It was the same man he'd bumped into on the way to steal Dame Maggie's emeralds, the assassin who'd tried to kill Belos, the one he'd chased down the bobsled run in St. Moritz, the man whose arm he'd wounded. The man transferred his gun to his right hand, holding it gingerly by his side as he reached up toward the satchel with his left. Monarch trained his pistol on the assassin's forehead.

A voice hissed from the cell phone on the blond man's chest, *"Vytor! Politsya!"*

Vytor moved his gun to his left hand, flipped off the closet light, and was gone. Monarch waited ten seconds, and then moved. He was out of the hatch, on the floor, into his shoes, and running with his bag inside of fifteen seconds. He heard a door slam below just as blue light began playing in the windows.

"You got police at your door," Yin said in Monarch's ear. "Single cruiser."

"Way ahead of you," Monarch said, leaving by the upper door, and relieved to find the hallway empty.

He glanced at the elevator and then at an exit sign at the end of the hall. He ran toward the sign and darted through a door into a utility stairwell he remembered from the blueprints. He heard shoes on the staircase below him. He looked over the railing and saw, one story below, the Chechen assassin looking up at him. Two stories below Vytor, one of Budapest's finest, a woman, was looking up at both of them.

30

"Halt!" The police officer shouted.

The Chechen seemed to recognize Monarch, because his face twisted into rage and he raised his pistol.

Monarch spun, heard the spit of a silenced weapon and the twang of ricochet, and he started climbing three stairs at a time.

"Get me out of here," he gasped into the Bluetooth.

"Seventh floor," Yin said. "You've got a ladder and then a bulkhead to the roof."

Monarch bounded across the landing on the sixth floor and onto the next flight of stairs, hearing shouts below him. He rounded the next landing and spotted the metal ladder bolted to the wall and a locked bulkhead at the top.

He shot off the lock and the hasp. The cold driving wind ripped the bulkhead open. He threw up the satchel and sprang onto the ladder. He made the top just as the Chechen appeared, livid, gun up and firing.

The rounds whined off the coping, just missing Monarch, who returned fire, forcing Vytor back. Monarch scrambled through the bulkhead onto the roof. He spun and grabbed the satchel.

"Gimme a direction. I got two sets of dogs on my trail."

"North," Yin said.

Monarch ran. Halfway across the roof, he glanced over his shoulder. The Chechen was up on his knees, pistol up, trying to shoot. Another man, shorter, bulkier, was coming up through the bulkhead behind him.

The Chechen fired. Monarch dodged behind an air-conditioning compressor at the last second and kept running. Behind him he heard the cracks of unsilenced shots.

"Cops are shooting at the guy who tried to kill Belos in St. Moritz," Monarch grunted. "He's shooting at me. This place is going to be crawling in five minutes."

"Jump," Yin ordered. "Ten foot drop and rollout."

Monarch spotted the low raised wall that marked the edge of the roof. He jumped up onto the ledge with his right leg and drove off it hard. The move threw him out into space in a forward dive, the satchel flung out in front of him.

He saw the second roof coming at him, ducked his head, and locked his free left arm and hand in a rigid arc up and before him. The blade of his left gloved hand struck first, then his forearm. With his chin tucked tightly into his chest, it caused him to roll in a somersaulting motion that ended in a skidding, aikido-style landing.

Monarch got the gun around, and fired back at the roofline he'd dropped from just as the Chechen appeared. The round drove the assassin back again. Monarch grabbed up the satchel and took off.

"North still?"

"Go, go, go," Yin said.

Sirens started to wail in the distance as he sprinted across the roof in a low zigzag pattern. He heard something heavy land on the roof behind him, looked back, and saw Vytor struggling to his feet.

"Bastard doesn't give up," Monarch said. He swung the pistol under his right armpit and shot backwards blindly three times, hearing the silenced rounds whacking the roof and the wall.

He saw a red laser light scribbled on the roof near him, understood it was a weapon sight, and made two radical cuts in direction. Gravel threw at his heels, and he heard the rush of the assassin's round pass him. He could see the top of the next building ahead, elevation only slightly lower.

"Ten foot gap," Yin said. "Four-story drop. But you've got a fire escape on the near side. One floor down, directly in front and below you."

Monarch heaved the satchel ahead of him over the edge, then angled slightly to the right and skidded to a stop, peering over, then looking back. The Chechen was coming, gun up, laser sight slashing. Monarch put his pistol in his teeth and dived.

He fell ten feet, caught the upper brace of the fire escape like a gymnast's high bar, and swung through hard. He slammed into a brick wall, coughed out his weapon, and went to his knees, stunned.

His instincts took over. He snatched up the gun off the grate, aimed it left-handed, and fired upward. Vytor cursed and Monarch scrambled down three more flights of the fire escape before jumping to the alley floor.

The rain had picked up again. The police sirens were getting closer.

"East," Yin said.

Monarch peered around a moment in the dim light before finding the satchel. He grabbed it up, saying, "I'll need a pick —"

The red laser dot appeared on the satchel. The shot broke the handle and sent Monarch into high gear again. As he ran, he kept speeding and slowing, angling side to side in erratic moves, trying for the shadows, seeing the laser dance around him, hearing the chug of the Chechen's pistol and the whipping of his bullets.

Vytor had the high ground. Monarch knew he couldn't stop and return fire. Stopping meant death. So he used every move he knew, every deke, juke, and stutter-step to throw off the assassin's aim. The alley's mouth gaped before him. The police sirens wailed nearby. Monarch felt like a target about to be punched.

A black sedan skidded across the mouth of the alley. The door flung open. Abbott Fowler sat at the wheel.

Monarch dived into the front seat. Fowler peeled off. Monarch gasped for air, then stuck his head out the window, seeing the shadowy form of the Chechen high up on the corner of the roof behind him.

They hit an intersection and Fowler took a hard left, heading away from the apartment where Yin and Tatupu waited. Blue lights flashed ahead in the rain, racing toward them. Fowler pulled dutifully to the side, let them pass, and then continued on.

"Where the hell'd you come from, Abbott?" Monarch gasped.

Fowler smiled. "Yin called for a pickup, and I was just driving in from Vienna."

Several hours later, Gloria Barnett kept her hands clasped firmly around a steaming mug of coffee and moved closer to the gas fireplace, looking skeptical. "You're positive on the ID?" she asked Monarch, who was sprawled on a couch. "He definitely made you?"

"Absolutely," Monarch said, sitting up. "I knew I hit him in St. Moritz."

"No wonder he had a jones to wax your ass," Tatupu said.

"So he works for Omak?" Barnett asked.

"Seems the most likely candidate. Omak and Belos are longtime rivals, and they both want the trigger, so Omak goes preemptive and tries to have Belos killed. When that doesn't work, he gets the idea to steal the trigger for himself, and sends Vytor to do it."

Barnett appeared unconvinced. She looked to Yin. "Where are we electronically?"

Yin ran her fingers through her hair. "Police haven't found any of the bugs, so we've got a pretty decent net up and active:

landlines, wireless Internet, some direct audio. No optical, though."

"What are you hearing?" Barnett asked.

Chávez had been listening. Vadas and his girlfriend played dumb with the cops, saying they had no idea why men carrying silenced weapons would break into their house, steal nothing, and then engage in a firefight with police.

"How's that going over?" Fowler asked.

"Not too well," Chávez admitted. "One of the officers was wounded before he killed the guy with the Chechen."

"No ID on the dead guy?" Monarch asked.

"If they had one, they weren't telling Vadas."

"No questioning regarding Vadas's organized crime connections?"

"Lots," Chávez said. "Vadas said he didn't know what they were talking about."

"And after the police left?"

"Tense, angry, scared. The girlfriend even more so. Before they went to bed, she kept saying that she didn't know if she could keep on living like this."

"And Vadas?"

"He told her to fuck off and have a drink."

"Nice guy."

"A real gem," Chávez agreed.

"What was Vadas doing before he found out?" Barnett asked.

"Having dinner with the girlfriend and another guy at a restaurant by the river."

"Who's the guy?"

Chávez shrugged. "No idea. But I got a picture of him. Yin's got it."

Yin made several clicks on her keyboard. On the near screen, a grainy picture appeared of a man in his mid-forties carrying an umbrella. He was bald, blockishly built, and dressed in a business suit.

Barnett and the others studied the man. Monarch asked, "Who paid for dinner? If the suit did, maybe we've got a name."

Chávez nodded. "I'll call the restaurant when it opens, claim I'm Visa or American Express, checking for fraud."

Monarch looked at Barnett. "Find anything on the trigger?"

"I did," Barnett said. "Belos's information was mostly solid. According to International Atomic Energy Commission logs, there are many Soviet-made triggers missing, all of them polonium-210 fission producers, which were manufactured in Murmansk in the sixties and seventies. Those kinds of triggers are among the oldest models the Soviets produced. It was put on hundreds of their smaller missiles. But I don't think a trigger itself is what we're looking for."

"No, it is what we're looking for," Monarch said. "Belos said so."

She shook her head. "Turns out there are enough fission producers around that I don't think someone would try to sell the mechanical parts of one at auction."

Monarch insisted, "Belos —"

Barnett held up her hand. "Hear me out, Robin. These triggers are useless without polonium-210, a radioactive isotope similar to radon, that stuff you find in old basements. It turns out that one of the most primitive methods of triggering a nuclear explosion is to take two foil packs the size of a restaurant sugar package and fill one with polonium-210 and the other with beryllium-9. When the foil packages are crushed together by the fission producer, the elements are combined, causing the nucleus of the beryllium to decay and spit out a neutron, kind of like a primer going off behind a bullet."

"The warhead goes off once the neutron is spit?" Abbott Fowler asked.

"Boom, boom, boom," Barnett replied. "Here's the rub: Polonium-210 is extremely rare. There are only four or five ounces of it made every year. All at factories in Russia, all, up until this point, bought by the U.S.

for millions every year since the fall of the Soviets to keep the stuff off the black market. Here's another thing to consider: Polonium-210 has a half-life of one hundred and thirty-eight days, which means most of the older fission producer triggers are inoperable."

"But if you had fresh polonium-210?" Chávez asked.

"You'd be able to set off all sorts of nuke devices still lying around from the Soviet era — suitcases, missiles, the shebang."

"The polonium. Is it radioactive?" Monarch asked.

She nodded. "But it's relatively harmless to humans unless you ingest it. A few years ago, a grain of polonium-210 was used to kill that Russian spy, Litvinenko, after Moscow learned he was trying to sell a dirty bomb to Chechen radicals."

"Chechens again? Are we talking Omak?" Tatupu asked.

"He had to have been part of that, too," Yin agreed.

"Unclear," Barnett said. "But if so, it would make sense they'd keep trying."

"How's it handled?" Monarch asked.

Barnett explained that polonium-210 produces alpha radioactivity, very weak. Her guess was that they were out to steal one to two ounces of polonium-210 stored in a small airtight stainless steel container about the size of a coffee can, maybe smaller.

"Coffee can in a haystack," Fowler said when she finished.

"No," Monarch said. "If Belos is right, Vadas has a line on the coffee can. We just need to wait him out. In the meantime, Gloria, can you get me a picture of exactly what these containers might look like?"

"Why?"

"I don't know. Just a thought."

31

SEVEN DAYS LEFT . . .

For nearly forty-eight hours, Monarch and his team listened, monitored, and followed Vadas and his girlfriend on the rare trips they made outside the apartment. Chávez bore the brunt of the work, taking the headphones for nearly every conversation and telephone call, translating every e-mail and text message.

They learned that Vadas had a dying mother, that Rozsa liked Hungarian soap operas, and that they both liked to drink, smoke, and bicker. Most of the latter had been directed from Rozsa at Vadas over his alleged affairs. But simmering beneath it, Chávez had caught several references to "a deal" in the works that had them both on edge. Beyond that, all communications in and out of the apartment appeared benign.

Monarch was growing frustrated. He kept thinking about Lacey Wentworth held hostage as day after day slipped by and only a week left. Would Belos really kill her? If he wanted the trigger more than anything, that wouldn't make sense, would it? This time constraint felt odd, considering the stakes.

"Think they're on to us?" Fowler asked, breaking Monarch's thoughts.

Chávez said, "Why not just tear out the bugs? Why the charade?"

"Maybe they don't have the polonium-210," Barnett said.

"They don't," Monarch said. "Vadas is not exactly kingpin material, and Belos told me that Vadas had portrayed himself as a go-between."

"But between who and who?" Yin asked.

Monarch said, "Let's ask the girlfriend that same question."

Later that day, Chávez overheard Vadas's girlfriend telling him that she couldn't stay in the apartment any longer. Rozsa was going to visit her sister in Pest. She left the apartment late in the afternoon. Chávez followed on foot. Fowler fired up a panel van they'd rented and brought it around into the alley, where Monarch and Tatupu jumped in.

"We reading?" Monarch said into his Bluetooth.

"You're clear," Barnett said in his ear. "She's taking the tram."

"Chávez?" Monarch said, glancing at a GPS device that showed a map of the city and a blinking pinpoint of light that represented her location beacon.

"In the same tram car," Chávez replied. "Get to the sister's place."

Thirty-five minutes later, they were parked down the street from the tram station closest to the sister's address. When Vadas's girlfriend emerged, she walked right at them down the sidewalk with Chávez in near pursuit. Darkness had fallen. Few people walked the commercial strip. Most stores had already closed for the evening.

Chávez timed her bump perfectly. Just as Rozsa came abreast of the van, Tatupu jerked open the side door and Chávez hit her from the side like a hockey check. Vadas's girlfriend cried out and fell in. Monarch clamped a hand over her mouth and dragged her inside. Chávez jumped in after her. Tatupu shut the door and Fowler pulled into traffic.

Rozsa started screaming and squirming until Tatupu slapped tape over her mouth. He then taped her wrists and ankles before Monarch set her up against the van wall.

Shadows crisscrossed Rozsa's terrified face. She whined, her eyes arcing back and forth. Monarch and Tatupu said nothing as they blindfolded her.

Fowler took them in a loop toward the Danube before doubling back again and picking up Chávez, who climbed into the back and put on her own hood. Fowler drove them outside the city to a forested area. Monarch nodded. Tatupu pulled off the blindfold.

Chávez said in Hungarian, "We are the closest thing to good guys you're ever going to see, Sophia."

Her eyes widened at the fact they knew her name.

Chávez said, "Don't scream. It won't do you any good."

Monarch peeled the tape off her mouth.

Tears formed in her eyes as she blubbered, "What do you want? Who are you?"

"The good guys," Chávez said. "Where is the trigger?"

Rozsa's face twisted in confusion. "What trigger?"

"The one your boyfriend's trying to sell," Chávez said.

"Miklos?" she said, bewildered. "I have not heard of a trigger. What trigger?"

"The one to a nuclear weapon," Chávez said.

"Nuclear? Miklos?" She shook her head. "He's in cigarettes. Booze. Fencing. A little pot. But a nuclear weapon? Miklos? No. He is not so brave."

Monarch spoke to Chávez in Spanish, "Tell her Vadas has been trying to attract buyers to an auction for the trigger."

Chávez did and Rozsa shook her head again. "No, that's some machine someone stole. Some kind of accelerator."

"An accelerator to mass destruction," Chávez said. "You want to be part of that?"

"No," she said. "Did you break into our apartment?"

"No," Chávez lied. "There must be others who know about the trigger."

"Who are you?"

"The people who can save you," Monarch said in Spanish. "Does Miklos have this accelerator?"

After Chávez translated, the mobster's girlfriend turned fearful. "No, a man from Moldova or Ukraine, I think. Miklos knows him. We had dinner with him the night of the break-in. Miklos is seeing him again later to night."

"What's his name?" Monarch demanded.

Rozsa seemed to understand without

304

translation. "Antonin. Antonin Duboff."

"You know where they're meeting?" Chávez asked.

Rozsa nodded and gave them the name of a restaurant.

As Fowler drove back into Budapest, Monarch said in Spanish, "Your boyfriend's playing a game far more dangerous than booze, tobacco, and a little pot. I suggest you disappear for a while. Have you got money?"

"Not so much," Rozsa said after Chávez translated.

Monarch nodded to Tatupu, who zipped open a bag and took out a wad of hundred-euro notes and handed it to her.

"Go to some island where it's warm and stay there for a month," Monarch said. "But if you warn Miklos, we will come find you, Sophia, and I guarantee we are better at tracking someone down than he is. If you don't warn him, you'll never see or hear from us again, and you've had a pretty sweet vacation."

Chávez translated into Hungarian, and Rozsa nodded in a mixture of fear and wonder at the strange and terrible good fortune that had been bestowed upon her, then climbed out and hurried down the street.

"Get us to that restaurant," Monarch said.

As Fowler pulled away, Monarch heard Yin say, "You've got a picture of Antonin Duboff coming at your cell."

Monarch dug in his pocket for the cell, saying, "Where'd you get it?"

Barnett replied, "I used my password and tapped into the agency files. Duboff's ex–Red Army, mercenary, assassin for hire. He currently works for Boris Koporski, President of Transdniestria, a breakaway republic of Moldova. Koporski is as corrupt as they come, and heavily into weapons dealing. He's suspected of having secret factories where he builds rifles, grenade-launchers, and SAMS that he sells on the black market."

"But what about something as big as a nuke trigger?"

"In Koporski's wheel house. Two years ago, one of Koporski's top men tried to sell an Azlan missle to an undercover reporter for *The London Times.*"

32

Monarch was the first to spot Antonin Duboff walking toward Miklos Vadas outside a French restaurant near the opera house. Duboff wore an overcoat, but there was no hiding the powerful body that lay beneath or mistaking his shaven block head and the coarse features from the picture Yin had sent over.

Duboff and Vadas shook hands. Chávez listened on a headset to a feed coming from the powerful unidirectional microphone Fowler had aimed out the window.

She tore off the headset and handed it to Monarch. "They're speaking Russian."

Monarch yanked on the earphones in time to hear Duboff say, "Don't worry. You're safe. No one knows where we have this thing. No one ever will except the buyer."

Vadas hesitated, and then nodded. They went into the restaurant.

Chávez and Monarch got out and followed them inside. They entered a lobby with a maîtred's station at the left and a cloakroom on the right, where a clerk was hanging up Duboff's overcoat. Monarch dug in his pocket for a tracking bug. He took off the leather jacket he wore and took Chávez's as well. "Cover me," he said.

Monarch smiled and handed Chávez's jacket to the clerk, and then slipped into the cloakroom and grabbed a hanger right next to Duboff's. The clerk started scolding him in Hungarian. Chávez called to her, turning her attention and apologizing for Monarch, whom she called a stupid American. It was enough time, however, for Monarch to slip the tracking bug up under the collar of Duboff's coat. He exited the cloakroom, saying, "Sorry. Just trying to help."

He and Chávez went into the bar and ordered drinks and appetizers. Duboff and Vadas had taken a booth in the far corner of the dining room, making it impossible to use the unidirectional on them. They left after one drink.

Monarch climbed back in the van, saying, "Time to pack up."

"Where are we going?" Barnett asked.

"I'm going wherever Duboff takes me," Monarch replied. "You and Yin get the gear together. Fowler, Chávez, and Tatupu will come back to get you. I'll call you when I've learned enough to have a plan."

Antonin Duboff left the restaurant without Miklos Vadas an hour later. Monarch followed him dressed in a gray suit and black overcoat. He'd brushed gray into his hair and wore clear glasses. He wore bud-style earphones connected to his iPhone, which was running an application that tracked the beacon on Duboff's coat. Monarch also clutched a worn leather valise filled with documents that identified him as a Ukrainian businessman, a representative of a plumbing goods company.

Duboff hustled past the opera house. Monarch shadowed him from one hundred yards back, noting that the man made no effort to disguise his intentions. He was headed to Keleti, the train station through which Monarch arrived in Budapest.

Monarch shuffled into line several patrons behind Duboff, close enough to hear him ask for ticket to Tiraspol, capital of Transdniestria.

Glancing up at the train schedule high on the wall of the train station, Monarch saw that the Tiraspol train carried on to the Ukraine. "Kiev," he said when he arrived at the counter and showed his passport.

An hour later, Duboff boarded the third car behind the engine. Monarch chose an empty sleeping compartment four cars back. The iPhone chirped softly and then stopped. The screen showed Duboff was stationary, settling in for the ride.

By the time the train lurched and rolled from the station, it was nearly midnight. Monarch rested his head against the window of the compartment, and soon drifted on the edge of unconsciousness. He awoke sometime later when Romanian border guards entered the train to inspect passports. Their coats and hats were wet. He looked out and saw a mix of sleet and snow falling. He answered their questions in sleepy Russian. They left him when they understood he was merely traveling through to Ukraine.

Again, Monarch fell into light sleep, only this time he dreamed bits of his recent life: warning Constantine and Iryna about violating the eighteenth rule; Vytor chasing him across the rooftops of Budapest; Sister Rachel crying at the money from Dame Maggie's emeralds; the sound of Iryna's breath in his ear; the look of abject terror on Lacey Davenport's face as he left.

The chirping started again. Monarch startled awake. Duboff was moving. Monarch checked his watch. Three A.M. He tugged out the iPhone, expecting to find Duboff heading toward the toilet. But instead he saw the icon linked to the bug in the collar of Duboff's coat was coming right at him.

Ninety yards. Sixty yards. Thirty. He was in Monarch's car now.

The train slowed. Monarch felt the car tilt to the rear. The wheels were grinding and squealing to climb a steep hill. Monarch heard Duboff's footsteps pass and caught his shadow behind the smoked-glass door. He watched the tracking device, seeing Duboff heading toward the rear of the car at a steady pace.

Suddenly the icon accelerated. Duboff had to be sprinting to the next car.

Monarch's brain raced. Something or someone had the Russian spooked. Something in this car. He bolted for the door and yanked it open.

The corridor was empty. Monarch loped in the direction Duboff had taken. He left his car and passed through another car, and then a third, noting on the tracking device that Duboff had not slowed.

Entering the fourth and last sleeping car, Monarch glanced at the device and felt his stomach lurch. Duboff was suddenly 150 yards away and now 200, 250, 300. He had just jumped off the back of the train!

Monarch sprinted toward the rear of the last car. He grabbed the door, opened it, and stepped out onto the train's rear platform, peering into the darkness, trying to figure out whether to jump as well.

The arm came across his throat like a vise. Monarch felt steel in his back before hearing Russian in his ear, "Who are you? Why do you put bug in my coat?"

The train reached the top of the grade, squealed, and started down another steep pitch. The action threw Monarch and Duboff off balance.

Monarch snapped his chin into his assailant's forearm, striking the ulnar nerve and causing Duboff's grip to loosen. At the same time, he dropped his center twelve inches and spun left with his elbow leading. He felt ribs crack and heard Duboff gasp. Monarch's left hand made a tight circular movement that hooked and barred Duboff's arm holding the knife.

Monarch pivoted again, slammed Duboff's head against the train car, and stripped him of the knife. That only served to enrage the Russian, who grabbed Monarch above the knee with his free hand. Duboff's probing felt hydraulic in its power and threw Monarch's quadriceps into spasm.

Monarch's leg buckled. He released his hold on Duboff's arm and tried to hit the Russian at the nape of his neck. But Duboff was too quick and bullish in his counterattack. The blow slid off the assassin's shoulder blade just before the Russian's bald head buried itself in Monarch's solar plexus.

All the air exploded from Monarch's lungs. He felt himself lifted and pile-driven onto the grate at the back of the train. Duboff outweighed him by at least fifty pounds and used that weight as an anchor while he threw blind punches at Monarch's face.

Monarch kept rolling his head and throwing up his arms to block the blows. But he could smell murder in the man, liquefied in his sweat and atomized in his breath; he'd gone primal and would kill Monarch, more out of frenzy than from anything else.

The train was going full tilt now into a series of tight curves that threw them around again. Monarch realized he'd had the knife in his left hand before Duboff hit him. It wasn't there now. He grabbed Duboff by the coat fabric at the elbow while his left hand groped for the knife.

Duboff grabbed Monarch by the throat

with both hands. "I kill you," he said. "But not before you tell me what you want from me."

"The trigger," Monarch managed.

Duboff looked confused. "What trigger?"

"The accelerator, the device you're trying to sell," Monarch said, choking. He was coming to now. His fingers groped around the grate. "I want to buy it."

Duboff shook his head. "You want to buy it, you don't put a bug on me. You come to Duboff like businessman. Not like spy. Who do you work for?"

Monarch said nothing. Duboff started to throttle him. "Who?"

Monarch's fingernail bumped into something on the grate. It slid. He snatched up Duboff's knife by the handle. He slashed upward. Duboff was amazingly quick. He released his hold on Monarch and jerked back enough that the blade barely touched his neck in passing. Still, it was enough to sliver a cut across his Adam's apple.

Duboff's eyes went wide. He blocked the second cut Monarch made, and swung his fist, trying to hit him with his right.

Monarch dodged the punch, flipped the knife to his opposite hand, and stuck the tip up under Duboff's jaw. "Where's the fucking accelerator?" Monarch demanded.

Duboff's face filled with worry and then scornful mirth. "I don't fucking know."

"Not a good answer," Monarch said, pushing the tip of the knife into his flesh.

"I don't," Duboff said, his torso lifting. "Only General Koporski knows this."

But there was something in the way Duboff replied, a flicker of deceit, that led Monarch to believe the man was lying, that he did know the location of the device Belos was calling a trigger and he was calling an accelerator.

Duboff surprised him again. In a single move, he lurched himself up and backwards, up off the tip of the blade, up off his knees to his feet. He set himself and kicked at Monarch's leg. Monarch rolled away from the blow, but the man's shoe still made hard contact with his lower hamstring. Monarch dropped the knife and used the hand to push off the grate. The second kick just missed Monarch's lower back and kidneys, setting his glute aflame. One more kick like that, and Monarch's back could be broken. Duboff cocked his foot as Monarch felt around again for the knife.

He found it and snatched it up by the point of the blade. As Duboff kicked, Monarch twisted back toward him and flung the knife. It flipped once in the air and stuck deep and dead center of the hollow above Duboff's rib cage.

The Russian assassin coughed hard and fell back against the train car, his hands rising, finding the handle of the knife and the hasp at his skin. He coughed again and this time blood sprayed out fine and pluming. He staggered to his left and hit the railing, going limbo across it.

Monarch jumped up to grab him before he fell. "Where is it?" Monarch demanded. "Where's the accelerator?"

Duboff looked confused again before retreating into scornful amusement. "Go ask the general," he said, and died.

33

NOON
LANGLEY, VIRGINIA

Jack Slattery worked feverishly in his office, poring over satellite images laid out on his desk, preparing for a fifteen-minute meeting he'd requested with the CIA director, crafting his argument so Dr. Hopkins would approve his strategy.

Late the afternoon before, Slattery had asked to see Hopkins after looking at records of recent searches Gloria Barnett had made inside agency records. She'd reviewed files on polonium-210 and Antonin Duboff. That revelation had led Slattery to seek the most recent intelligence on Transdniestria, including up-to-date satellite images. What he found in those images was enough for him to seek an audience with Hopkins.

Slattery took two of the images off his desk and put them inside a clasp envelope.

He got up, donned his suit jacket, took the envelope, and left for Hopkins's office, feeling like he was operating just ahead of the curve of events, like a surfer shooting a curl.

"What's so important, it couldn't wait until our regular meeting on Friday?" Dr. Hopkins demanded as he set his glasses on his desk and rubbed his eyes.

"Monarch," Slattery said.

"Monarch?" Dr. Hopkins said. "I thought we'd heard the last of him."

"We received intelligence yesterday through the Russian GRU that a St. Petersburg mobster named Constantine Belos has hired Monarch to steal a live triggering system for a Soviet-era nuclear missile."

"Why?"

"Unclear," Slattery hastened to say. "But the Russians believe it is part of an ongoing war the mobster has been having with the leader of the Chechen Mafia."

Hopkins pinched the top of his nose and said, "Is there credible intelligence that a triggering system is missing?"

"Yes, sir, several from Murmansk," Slattery said. "But this one is said to have the radioactive fuel that makes it work."

"Who's got the trigger now?"

"We're not positive," Slattery replied. "But

given the possible implications of this situation, I asked the NSA to monitor cell phone transmissions made last night by Monarch in Budapest. Monarch was last heard from trailing an assassin named Antonin Duboff on a train bound for Tiraspol, Transdniestria."

"Transdniestria," the CIA director said, a foul look appearing on his face. "Most lawless hellhole on earth. Is that ape Koporski involved?"

"Duboff works for the general, sir."

Hopkins sat back in his chair, twirling his eyeglasses in one hand while talking more to the ceiling than to Slattery. "What's Koporski doing with a nuclear trigger?"

"I'm betting he's a middle man," Slattery said.

"Except GRU thinks Monarch has been hired to steal it from Koporski before he can sell it?"

"That's my understanding," Slattery said.

The CIA director thought about that and then said, "Any idea where Koporski's hiding this trigger?"

"As a matter of fact, I have a strong suspicion," Slattery said. He opened the envelope and drew out the two satellite images. "These were shot about three years apart, the most recent about a week ago."

Hopkins studied the pictures. "They've done quite a bit of digging in there."

"And fortified the walls with machine guns," Slattery said.

"And you think Monarch knows this is where the trigger is?"

"Monarch is resourceful," Slattery said. "He'll figure it out."

"So what's our response?"

Deep inside, Slattery smiled. He'd been waiting for this question. He said, "We make him steal the trigger for us."

34

SIX DAYS LEFT . . .

MOLDOVAN–TRANSDNIESTRIA BOR-
DER

The train slowed as dawn gave way to steel
light and snow driven against the windows
of the compartment where Monarch sat.
He'd turned up the collar of his black
overcoat and buttoned it high on the neck
as if he were chilled. He didn't want the
border guards to spot any blood spatter he
may have failed to wash off after dumping
the corpse of Antonin Duboff over the side
high in the Carpathian Alps.

The train squealed to a halt and wheezed
a sigh in a stubble field strewn in snow and
backed by a bleak, leafless forest. Soldiers
in brown Soviet-style uniforms crimped
their eyes to the falling snow as they walked
along the train, looking under it and up at
the windows. Pale men, gaunt men, they
either cradled their AK-47s like they were

babies or brandished them as if they were tipped with bayonets. A sharp rap came at the door. It slid open. A sergeant in his early twenties with a lazy left eye entered and demanded his papers. Monarch handed them to him.

"What business do you have in Transdniestria?" the sergeant demanded.

"I have no business here," Monarch said. "I'm passing through."

"What is your business?"

"I sell toilets. We have a factory in Kiev. You've probably used one of them."

"We're lucky to crap in outhouses," the sergeant said.

Another soldier appeared over his shoulder. "He's not in the train, Sergeant."

The sergeant squinted his lazy eye and handed Monarch back his papers, asking, "Have you seen a bald man? Big. Built like a wrestler?"

Monarch appeared confused, then laughed. "I've been asleep most of the night."

The sergeant appeared ready to ask him something else when he heard shouting from the rear of the train. He turned and ran.

Monarch looked out the window across the stubble field toward the forest. Five hundred meters, he figured. But dressed in black, wearing business shoes, he wouldn't get two hundred yards before they caught him or shot him. There had to be at least a hundred people on the train, so it would take some time before they got to him. He decided to settle in to wait.

Then he realized he'd better make contact with his team. He got up, shut the door, and got out his iPhone. He typed in a text message:

AT BENDER BORDER CROSSING. FRIEND FOUND BUG. HE HAD AN ACCIDENT, GOT OFF EARLY. SOLDIERS SEARCHING. YOUR LOCATION?

He hit SEND and waited.

A moment later, the phone beeped. The message was from Gloria Barnett:

ROMANIA. OTHERS FOLLOWING. DO YOU NEED IMMEDIATE HELP?

NEGATIVE, Monarch typed in reply. GO THROUGH TO MOLDOVA. WAIT ME THERE.

ON OUR WAY, Gloria replied.

Monarch erased the messages from his mailbox.

A knock came at the cabin door, and the sergeant opened it again. "There is a problem," he said, studying Monarch with that lazy eye.

"With the train?" Monarch asked.

"Someone is missing," he said. "There is blood."

"Blood?" Monarch said, concerned. "Missing? Where? Here? In this car?"

"At the end of the last car. On the platform."

"I did not know there was one," Monarch said. "Who is missing?"

"Someone who has friends. The train will be met in Tiraspol. They will want to talk with everyone."

"But I have a meeting in Kiev in four hours," Monarch protested.

"Not today," the sergeant replied, and slid shut the door.

Monarch watched out the window. Very few soldiers were getting off. Which meant they were staying on the train. Probably going to watch the exits.

The train groaned and rumbled beneath Monarch's feet. They gained speed past the stubble field and into the forest, gray and wind twisted.

Monarch considered it likely that he had some of Duboff's blood on his clothes and there was no way to get rid of it before he was questioned. Monarch chewed on his predicament for several minutes, and then found his strategy in Duboff's last words.

The train crossed the Dniester River

toward the city of Tiraspol, which struck Monarch as a place that time seemed to have forgotten, the ghost capital of a ghost country.

The river was lined with cement buildings, most of them Soviet era, numbing in their plainness and rigidity. The people he spotted walking by the river had the carriage of animals that have known only a cage and a harsh master, bent over, hoisting with every step the heavy burden of their lot in life.

Dozens of soldiers waited on the platform when the train entered the central station in Tiraspol. Monarch scanned them, looking for the leader. He spotted him standing at the rear of the platform, a tall, broad-shouldered man with a ruthless bearing, chin up, hands clasped behind him, studying the train from beneath an olive-colored military officer's hat with a red band above the brim.

Monarch stood and left the compartment, knowing this was a dangerous play, and yet the only one he had. He spotted the sergeant near the exit, his rifle at port arms.

"I wish to talk with whoever is in charge," Monarch said. "I may be able to help."

"They'll get to you, toilet salesman," the sergeant said. "Go sit and wait."

"If I do and I tell them I had to wait to give them what I know, you could spend your life at that fuck-hole outpost on the border, freezing your ass off in the outhouse, counting the days until you die," Monarch said evenly.

The sergeant's lazy eye roamed over him before he gestured with the gun toward the exit. Monarch moved past him and climbed down the stairs onto the platform. It was bitter cold. The air smelled of strong cigarettes and unbathed men.

An officer stormed toward them, snarling, "You were told to keep them aboard."

"He says he knows something," the sergeant said.

"What do you know?" the officer said to Monarch. He wore a lieutenant's bars, had a bent-over left ear, yellow teeth, and horrible breath.

"You are not in charge, Lieutenant," Monarch said calmly. "Take me to who is."

The lieutenant scowled, but then spun in his tracks and led Monarch, followed by the sergeant, up to the tall officer standing at the rear of the platform. "Colonel Gorka," the lieutenant said. "This man says he knows something."

Up close, Colonel Gorka had dark eyes and scarred skin on the left side of his face, as if he'd been burned. He was taller than Monarch by several inches, and heavier by at least fifty pounds, a man used to using his size to intimidate.

He looked down on Monarch in mild contempt. "What do you know?" he asked.

"I'd rather we speak in private, Colonel," Monarch said, bowing his head.

The colonel glared at him for his impudence, but then jerked his head at the lieutenant and the sergeant, who hesitated before walking away.

"Talk," Colonel Gorka said.

"Take me to see General Koporski," Monarch said.

Gorka snorted. "Who do you think you are?"

"I'm the man who killed Antonin Duboff and threw him off the train near Vlad the Impaler's place," Monarch said. "And I'd like to tell General Koporski why."

35

TIRASPOL

High above the statue of Vladimir Lenin, hundreds of crows swarmed, circled, and cursed in the falling snow. The thirty-foot statue of the great comrade founder of the Soviet Republic still dominated the square in front of a forbidding cement building in downtown Tiraspol. Lenin was posed in a moment of trial and triumph, bearded chin up, bald head exposed to the elements, his body braced forward, his cape and scarf swept behind him as if he were leaning into the gales of history.

It was midmorning when Colonel Gorka hustled Monarch in handcuffs past the statue. The sky had changed color since the dawn, casting a gunmetal light on the statues and on the crows now perched and shitting on the comrade leader's shoulders.

Armed guards opened the front doors to the old Supreme Soviet building. Colonel

Gorka pushed Monarch through a metal detector into a lobby filled with more nostalgia of the communist era. There were busts of Lenin, Brezhnev, and Stalin on pedestals. The walls boasted murals that depicted the Soviet triumph: workers happily toiling in the fields, proud soldiers marching, and bold leaders on a hillside, saluting the pinko dawn.

"Ahh, the good old days," Monarch said. "You must all miss them. Where's Trotsky? No Putin?"

Colonel Gorka ignored him and pulled him along. They walked to the only elevator that was guarded. The soldiers snapped to attention and stood aside. The elevator interior was dull steel and plastic and smelled of coffee. The colonel pushed the button for the fourteenth floor.

They rose in silence, and Monarch wondered whether he'd gone too far, if he'd actually be able to pull this off, or if he'd be simply taken somewhere and shot.

The elevator opened. Four armed soldiers faced them. Colonel Gorka motioned Monarch out, and he found himself in a hallway with a fine parquet floor. They walked the hallway, surrounded by the soldiers, to a set of double doors.

The soldiers knocked on the doors and

then opened them. Gorka and Monarch entered a large, lavishly appointed foyer with gilt on the crown moldings and gold silk drapes. Three women worked on computers at lacquer-black desks arranged in a semicircle facing the elevator. The pair to either side barely gave the colonel and Monarch a glance. But the third one, who sat before a second set of doors at the foyer's center, looked up.

"This is not a good time, Colonel," she said, glancing grimly at Monarch.

"Is it ever?" Gorka replied. "I must see him. Now."

She hesitated, stood, and went to the doors. She raised her hand to knock when shouting erupted from inside, a man's voice, muffled but launching into a tirade. The secretary looked at the colonel pleadingly.

Colonel Gorka said, "I'll announce myself."

The colonel turned the knob, opened the door, and pushed Monarch through.

The office was a large rectangle. Chandeliers overhead. Rich hardwood paneling. Deep oriental rug. Landscape paintings on the walls. Two sofas and a coffee table set before a burning fireplace separated Gorka and Monarch from a desk behind which General Boris Koporski stood in shirtsleeves, his back to them, facing a pair of floor-to-ceiling windows that overlooked the statue of Lenin.

"I don't care," the dictator was shouting into a telephone. He hammered his fist on the window at the crows. "We have a deadline. It will not be missed." He listened. "Then suffer the consequences!"

Koporski spun and threw down the phone on the desk. It bounced, fell, and tumbled on the rug. The general's expression went from outrage to lividness and back to outrage when he spotted Monarch and the colonel.

"What you are doing here, Gorka?" he demanded. "Who is this?"

Koporski was a thinner man than Monarch had thought from the pictures. His face was like a feral dog's, scarred in several places. He sported a Cossack's mustache and a tight crop of silver hair. His jaw was jutted forward, showing his lower teeth, which were remarkably large and canine.

Colonel Gorka said, "His name is Vastily Petroyin. A toilet salesman from Kiev. He claims he killed Duboff and wishes to tell you why."

General Koporski stared at Gorka dumbly for a moment, then looked at Monarch, the rage draining from him, as if it had been sluiced by this news. Koporski threw his head back and laughed, low and gravelly. "A toilet man kill Antonin Duboff?" he cried, shaking his head. "I don't think so."

"It was more self-defense than anything else, Mr. President," Monarch said, walking toward the general. "It certainly wasn't my intention."

That seemed to amuse Koporski even more. "Exactly what was your intention before you killed one of the most feared assassins in the world, toilet man?"

"I followed him out onto the rear platform of the train early this morning. He put a knife at my throat and asked him why I was following him. So I took the knife away and tried to have a reasonable discussion with him. But he seemed annoyed that I took the knife away from him. He tried to kill me. I had to put his knife in his throat."

Koporski hesitated, roared with laughter, and then looked at Colonel Gorka. "Is this some kind of joke? Who put you up to this?"

Colonel Gorka shook his head. "There was blood found on the platform on the rear car, General. And Duboff was supposed to be on that train. He bought a ticket. He was seen getting on. He wasn't on when the train reached our border."

The general didn't reply as he sat in his

tufted leather desk chair. "*Were* you following him?" Koporski asked Monarch.
"Duboff?"

"As a matter of fact, I was."

"Sell toilets?"

"Not often," Monarch admitted.

"Lot of men in my country like you these
days," Koporski observed.

"Must be the climate and the swell tourist
attractions."

"What did you want to talk to Duboff
about?"

"A special, uh, trigger or accelerator said
to be in your possession," Monarch said.

"Accelerator?" Koporski said, affecting
confusion. "Who says I have an accelerator?"

"Duboff, as a matter of fact," Monarch
said. "Shortly before he died."

"You got Antonin Duboff to tell you I was
in possession of some accelerator?"

"He volunteered the information. After a
little coaxing on my part."

"I could have you taken out and shot."

"You could," Monarch allowed. "But
you'd be out a deep-pockets player in the
auction you're planning to hold for that
device."

The general's eyes turned glassy and
small, like black marbles. "Who are you?"

"Does it matter?"

Koporski studied Monarch as if he were a ticking bomb, and then shrugged. "I suppose it depends on how deep the pockets are that you claim to represent."

"Substantial enough that they hired me to follow Duboff," Monarch said.

"How deep?"

"Deep enough to inquire whether you'd be interested in saving yourself the hassle of having to hold an auction."

Koporski looked at Monarch in a new light. "You're asking whether a preemptive bid would be considered?"

"I am," Monarch said.

The general's face went slack in thought. "There'll be a floor at the auction. We won't take less than one hundred million, so your preemptive bid better be twice that."

A hundred million? Was that what polonium-210 was worth? Monarch couldn't see it at first. Then again, he supposed it was largely a function of supply and demand. Either the supply of clandestine nuke trigger materials was extremely limited, or the demand was high. Or a combo of the two.

"I'll relay your reply to my clients and get back to you," Monarch said.

Koporski gestured at a phone on the table

beside Monarch. "Go ahead. Call."

"With all due respect, General, the sum you are naming as a floor requires me to meet with my clients in person."

"Where?" Colonel Gorka demanded.

"Outside your charming country," Monarch said. "I should think I could be back here within a very few days."

Koporski seemed to find that amusing. "You think you're going to murder one of my top men and then go free?"

"It was self-defense, and, as a matter of fact, yes."

The general chuckled. "You have guts, Mr. Petroyin, or whoever you really are."

"Thank you, General," Monarch said, bowing his head slightly.

"Take his handcuffs off," Koporski told Colonel Gorka.

"You can't be serious," the colonel protested. "We have no idea who this man is, whom he represents."

"And we have no idea whether or not he actually killed Duboff," Koporski shot back. Then he smiled. "Besides, I've always enjoyed a game of chance. Take them off."

Gorka was not happy, but he came over to Monarch and roughly unlocked the handcuffs. "Thank you," Monarch said. "My phone?"

"We'll keep that," Gorka said.

"I can assure you it's encrypted," Monarch said. "And all my phone calls are automatically erased as soon as I hang up. The wonders of technology amid the ever-present war on personal privacy."

The colonel's face soured, and his tongue flickered with hostility when Koporski said, "Give it to him."

Monarch took the device and put it in his breast pocket. He rose from the chair and bowed in the general's direction. "I appreciate your hospitality and your practicality."

"Don't mention it," Koporski said.

"I'd like to return to the train station," Monarch said. "Push on to Kiev."

Koporski flicked his hand at Colonel Gorka. "See him there."

Monarch made as if to turn to leave, but then halted. "One last question, because I'm sure it will be asked, General."

The general hardened. "What is it?"

"My clients will want to know about the security surrounding the device."

Koporski nodded coldly. "It's in the most secure place in all of Transdniestria."

"And where's that?"

"Try my patience much more, toilet man, and I'll throw you in a hole so deep, not even your deep-pocket friends could ever find you."

36

FIVE HOURS LATER
KIEV, UKRAINE

As monarch walked across the plaza toward
Kiev's Kreschatik metro station, he decided
to shake the tail that had been on him since
he'd boarded the early-afternoon train from
Tiraspol to the Ukraine. They were a team:
a blond guy who looked about seventeen,
and a punkish-looking woman in her twenties.

They were quite good, actually. He'd seen
them on the train shortly after Colonel
Gorka left. The guy had earbuds in and was
listening to music. She was working on a
Sudoku puzzle. Monarch had discounted
the idea that they were Koporski's agents at
first. Instead he suspected a short, squat
man in a herringbone wool coat who'd
boarded his car shortly after he did and took
a seat behind Monarch.

But the man in the herringbone coat left

the car after they crossed the border, and Monarch had not seen him again. He spotted the Sudoku woman outside the train station, however, trailing him at a distance on the other side of the road. The guy listening to music appeared to be trying to loop in front of Monarch. He'd seen him down a side street, running and dodging through sidewalk and road traffic.

Kreschatik is the common station of Kiev's purple and red metro lines and was just starting to swell with commuters when Monarch made his move. He walked by the stairwell to the subway as if he were going elsewhere. Then he vaulted the railing and landed between a family and a couple who were shocked and almost fell.

Monarch dodged by them, ignoring their curses. He ran to the longest line of commuters trying to put their tickets in the turnstiles, jumped up on the machine, and landed on the other side. Someone shouted, but he didn't stop, just barreled down the stairs and onto the southbound platform. An electric bell was ringing. He jogged away from the staircase toward the oncoming train.

The train slowed and stopped. Monarch got on the last car and waited. His first impulse was to get off at the last second.

But then he'd still have the guy to contend with.

He stayed on for one stop and exited the train at the Palats Sportu station. But instead of following the herd toward the staircase to the sports complex, Monarch's instincts led around the back of the train and down onto the tracks. He danced across them, dodging the third rail, and sprang up onto the far platform just before the north-bound train groaned into the station. He ignored the people shouting at him that he was a fool, that he'd die if he ever did anything as crazy as that again.

Monarch climbed in the car and glanced out the window. The punk girl was glaring at him from the opposite platform, and calling on a cell phone. Monarch waved.

He got out two stops later, climbed out of the subway, and stood with his back to a wall on a crowded sidewalk, calling Gloria Barnett on his phone.

"Where the hell are you?" she asked.

"Kiev," he said. "You?"

"Chişinău, Moldova," she said. "The hotel's a hell hole."

"Find us someplace private, and closer to the Transdniestrian border."

"You found the coffee can?"

"Let's say I've shrunk the size of the

haystack it's hiding in," Monarch said.

"What's your ETA?"

"Depends on the train schedule," he said. "I'll go through Odessa."

"We'll be waiting."

Monarch flipped shut his phone, thinking he'd be smart to take a cab to the first stop toward Odessa south of Kiev to avoid the central train station again. He caught a flash of something in the corner of his eye. Before he could turn, he felt a gun in his ribs.

The short, squat man in the herringbone coat whom he'd seen on the train now slipped from the crowd on the sidewalk and was standing at an angle to Monarch, gun barrel jutting out his sleeve. "Walk or die," he said in thickly accented Russian.

Monarch considered fighting but knew he had no chance, so he did as he was told. They walked through the streets and alleys for several blocks into a deserted factory grounds with high brick buildings with blown-out windows.

There was a Mercedes-Benz parked between two of the buildings. Several men with automatic weapons stood outside and behind by a dusky rawboned man with a salt-and-pepper beard and wizened skin the color of oxblood. The man was in his late fifties, early sixties, and wore a rough woven sweater, canvas pants, and combat boots. A wool scarf was wrapped around his throat. His workman's hands rested on the head of a cane.

"Omak, I presume," Monarch said in Russian when they reached him.

Omak flicked a finger before Monarch felt something touched to his back. Electricity jolted through him. His tongue arched, his eyes bugged, and his jaw slammed shut hard before the electricity stopped, leaving him slumped over, weak and panting.

Omak said, "Vytor enjoyed that very much." The Chechen's voice was gritty, like coarse sandpaper tearing wood.

Monarch saw Vytor moving into his vision, a stun gun in his left hand.

"Are you stealing the trigger for the Russian?" Omak asked. "Belos?"

"What trigger?" Monarch asked. "And who's Belos?"

Vytor sank the stun gun into his side and fired it. Monarch twisted and shook so hard, he thought he'd torn something internally. Sweat boiled on his head and ran down his forehead in streams.

"You saved his life in St. Moritz," Omak said. "Vytor saw you in Vadas's apartment building. Some of my other men saw you at Belos's house in Cyprus. And now we see you leaving Koporski's headquarters. So I ask you again: Are you helping the Russian get the trigger from Koporski?"

Vytor flipped the Taser lazily in one hand.

Monarch said, "I'm negotiating for it on his behalf."

"How much is Koporski asking?"

"Two hundred million," Monarch said.

Omak laughed. "Constantine Belos will pay this?"

Monarch shrugged. "It's a negotiation."

Omak shook his head. "Belos will never pay this kind of money, because I would never pay this kind of money." He paused, and then fixed his gaze on Monarch. "You are stealing it for him, then?"

"Not my style," Monarch said. "I'm just a go-between."

Omak pursed his lips and then nodded to Vytor, who hit Monarch a third time with the Taser. He was feeling like he might vomit when Omak asked, "Why does he want it so much, he would hire you to steal the trigger?"

Monarch was still panting. "So you don't have it."

Omak thought about that and smiled. "How much is he paying you to steal it?"

"Five million," Monarch said. "And the life of a friend of mine."

"Where does Koporski have it?"

"Still trying to figure that out."

Omak studied him, nodded, and got down off the stool. He leaned heavily on his cane and moved awkwardly, as if he'd broken a large bone in his lower body that never healed correctly. He leaned back against the table to Monarch's immediate left. "I will pay you four million and let you live," Omak said.

"No," Monarch replied. "Belos says you've been building a nuke and all you need is the trigger to make it go. So between that and the premium he's willing to pay, I think the trigger will be going Belos's way."

Monarch braced himself for the shock. But Omak waved Vytor off. He rested the tip of his cane on Monarch's shoulders. "I have no missile. Who told you that? Belos?"

"He did."

"He's wrong."

"So why do you want the trigger?"

"So Belos does not have it," Omak said, and laughed.

"All the more reason to negotiate."

"I am not in the habit of negotiating."

"Join the real world," Monarch said. "This is an auction whether Koporski runs it or I do. Right now, the bid on my services is five million and the life of a woman I care for.

So either up the bid or let Vytor do his thing."

Omak gave him a look of dark reappraisal. "Six million and you'll have to see about this woman yourself."

Monarch thought about that and said, "Deal."

37

FIVE DAYS LEFT . . .
EAST OF CHIŞINĂU, MOLDOVA

On the overnight train ride from Kiev to Odessa to Chişinău, Monarch slept and considered, trying to see the events of the last few weeks not in the way he'd experienced them but from afar. Belos squeezing him to find the trigger. Vytor showing up inside the Hungarian's apartment. Duboff telling him it's an accelerator not a trigger. Koporski confirming possession of the accelerator. And now Omak was in the picture.

These events were troubling to Monarch because he seemed to be facing close opposition wherever he went. After much thought, some of the events struck him as more than coincidences, like someone was playing him. Indeed, the more he dwelled on it, the more he saw himself as a puppet with various strings influencing his actions. He tried to come up with other arguments to dispute this theory, but in the end he accepted it and made it the basis of his future actions because of Rule Number Twelve: Listen to your feelings. When you got nothing else, go with your gut.

He arrived in Chișinău around 8 A.M. and took a cab to an address Gloria Barnett had texted him: a decrepit villa in the countryside fifteen kilometers east of the city. The walls were stone and choked with bare vine. The roof sagged with the weight of wet snow. A raw wind blew when Monarch paid the cabdriver and went to the door. He was weak and tired, which he attributed to the three jolts Vytor had given him. He looked forward to a bed.

The door flung open before he could knock. Gloria Barnett looked wrung out and ashamed, "I'm sorry, Robin," she murmured.

"For what?" Monarch asked, concerned and stepping inside.

Barnett didn't reply. She turned and, in a wounded gait, led him down a musty passage and into a large room with peeling wallpaper and a dripping ceiling. Cobwebs hung everywhere, except near the tables that had been drawn together between two large portable gas heaters blowing blue flames of heat in the dark, dank room.

Chanel Chávez was sitting up on the back of her chair, chewing the inside of her lip. John Tatupu was in a folding chair, head bowed. Abbott Fowler jiggled a beer can, and Ellen Yin seemed desperate to avoid looking at Monarch, darting glances instead at her computer screen and at Jack Slattery, who stood by the cold fireplace dressed in a down parka, jeans, and a pair of heavy boots.

Slattery had his arms crossed. He was watching Monarch with no expression.

"How'd you find us, Jack?" Monarch asked.

Slattery gave a nod at Barnett. "Her BlackBerry. When I saw that she'd looked up information on Constantine Belos and heard that she'd asked for a vacation, I had a bug installed in it. Gloria is a great operations runner, but she was never very good at the whole day-to-day spy-craft thing and, as expected, never looked."

Barnett's fair cheeks burned as she stared at the floor.

"What do you want?" Monarch asked.

"What everybody wants: that trigger," Slattery said. "The United States is not about to let it fall into the hands of zealots."

Monarch watched Slattery, thinking that he now knew exactly who had been manipulating him. That recognition caused Monarch to have instant doubts about what he was supposed to steal. Those doubts turned into a strong suspicion about what the trigger really was. *It's Green Fields. But is that possible? Wasn't everything destroyed in the fire?*

Monarch decided he had to assume that not everything about Green Fields was gone, that some piece of it remained. That meant he had to be as smart and as canny as he had been taught to be by his parents, La Fraternidad de Ladrones, the U.S. Special Forces, and the CIA. He had to think ahead now, way ahead, anticipating every one of Slattery's moves and flushing him into the open, along with whoever was behind him.

Monarch said, "Sorry, Jack, we're already under contract."

"I could have you all declared traitors, and have you hunted down," Slattery said.

Monarch said, "Or you can pay us ten million for the trigger."

Slattery laughed scornfully. "Is that what you believe your services are worth?"

"What the market seems to bear these days," Monarch replied evenly. "It's amazing what happens when there are multiple bidders for a single coveted item."

"You'll do it for us for no pay in return

for your freedom," Slattery stated flatly.

"You're in no position to make that threat," Monarch said.

"And why's that?"

"Because I'll kill you first."

Slattery snorted, trying to laugh, but it came out forced.

"Or I will," Chanel Chávez said.

"Or me," Tatupu said.

"Watch your back, Jack," Fowler said.

"Most assuredly," Barnett said.

Slattery glanced around, trying his best not to look intimidated and not succeeding. "I'll see what I can do about a reward. But I know it's not going to be ten million. Try more like five."

"Too low," Monarch said before turning to his teammates. "We're changing strategy. We'll get the trigger freelance, and then we'll have an auction just as Mr. Koporski has planned. Find out the real value of a nuke trigger."

The CIA's chief of covert operations reached in his breast pocket and fished out a silver cigarette case. He retrieved a cigarette, snapped shut the case, put it away, and came up with a lighter. The flame flashed. He lit the cigarette, took a drag, and said, "Nope. Five million. Because I bring something of great value to the table."

Monarch's eyes narrowed. Dealing with Slattery was like dealing with a flyweight boxer, not a hooking bomb and uppercut kind of guy. He was a jabber, a feint artist. You never knew if his next move was real or designed to set a trap where you could get your head rocked.

"What do you have?" Monarch asked.

"The trigger's location," Slattery said smugly. "I mean, if you don't know where it is, Monarch, I don't care how much money someone's willing to pay you to steal it."

Monarch glanced around at his teammates.

"He's got a point," Fowler said.

"How do we know he's not lying to us?" Barnett demanded.

"Now, what would be the purpose of that?" Slattery asked.

"How do you know where it is?" Tatupu asked.

"Transdniestria is a thriving market for black market weapons," Slattery said. "You don't think we have contacts inside? You don't think we use satellites?"

Monarch considered his options before saying, "Five million and you provide support when I go to Cyprus to free a woman who's being held hostage by a Russian who also wants this trigger."

"A hostage?" Slattery said, surprised. "Unexpected, but we have a deal."

"So where's the trigger?" Chávez asked.

Slattery walked by Monarch to Yin. "May I?" he asked.

Yin got up out of her seat. A moment later, Slattery turned her computer screen toward them all to reveal a photograph of the ruins of a medieval stone castle built high on a riverbank, with battlements and four towers.

Slattery said, "The ancient fortress of Prazil. About eighty-five kilometers from here. Sits high on the western bank of the Dniester River. Built by Suleiman the Magnificent in the 1500s. Until Koporski came to power, the fortress was something of a tourist attraction. Then, three years ago, he closed it off for archeological restoration."

Monarch watched Slattery closely as he typed again. Yin's screen revealed a satellite look at the fortress. Slattery pointed to the four towers, which were girdled with scaffolding and black tarps.

"According to our sources, these towers are now equipped with 12.7-millimeter heavy machine guns, one to each tower," Slattery said, then gestured at the fences surrounding the ruined fortress. "Electrified razor wire." He pointed to the tops of the battlements where soldiers could be seen fuzzily. "And armed sentries with dogs."

"Kind of extreme for an archeological job," Barnett said.

Slattery said he believed Koporski had dug out the ancient catacombs beneath the fortress and built an underground arms factory supplying insurgencies all over the world with knock-off AK-47s, SAMS, mines, and mortars.

"And this is where you think he's got the trigger?" Chávez asked.

"I do."

Monarch studied the layout. "So you want me to get by the fences, the machine guns, armed sentries, and attack dogs to break into that fortress, go somewhere below ground into a secret arms factory, find the trigger, and then bring it out?"

Slattery looked at him evenly. "Yes, that about sums it up."

Monarch's every cell pulsed with the idea that he should leave with his team to track down the location of Belos and Lacey Wentworth and free her by force. But then he saw things more simply, in terms of fate. He was supposed to go in and steal whatever was left of Green Fields. He also felt he was supposed to figure a way to keep it out of Slattery's hands for good. His first counter-move came to him that very instant.

Rule Number Nine: Turnabout is fair play.

"What's it look like, Jack? The trigger?" Monarch asked. "Gloria says it will be in a coffee-sized container. You know, because of the polonium-210?"

Slattery hesitated, and then said, "I'm not sure what the trigger will look like."

That helps, Monarch thought.

38

Monarch crashed in a back room in a sleeping bag Barnett had brought along. He slept fitfully for three hours. His darkest dreams were of Lacey and the thought of her suffering. He awoke midafternoon and looked out a window at the cloudy sky.

Slattery had said it would take at least thirty hours to have the equipment required for the mission to be brought in from an air base in Germany. That gave Monarch time. He got up and changed into running shoes, pants, and a windbreaker.

He returned to the outer room, where Slattery was hunched over a computer and talking on a cell phone. Barnett and Yin were working at their own computers. Fowler, Tatupu, and Chávez were dozing on the couch.

"Everyone up," he said. "We're going to be cramped in here for the next two days. I want everyone loose. We're going for a run."

Slattery looked up from his computer and shook his head. So did Yin. But Barnett and the others got to their feet, stretching and yawning.

Ten minutes later, they left the villa and jogged out onto the road. When they were several hundred yards from the villa, Monarch mimicked holding a phone and shook his head. The others understood. Tatupu and Fowler tugged out their cell phones from their pockets and set them softly in leaves by the side of the road.

They jogged on another several hundred yards before Monarch said, "I think it's a scam. I don't think we're after a nuke trigger."

"What?" Chávez said.

"Past few days, I've been feeling like a web has been spun around me, forcing me from all sides to steal this trigger," Monarch said. "And Slattery coming here like this to micromanage the mission says to me that he's the spider."

"What's he really after, then?" Barnett asked, huffing to keep up with them.

"I suspect it's the same thing we were after in Istanbul."

"Green Fields?" Tatupu asked. "You said it all burned."

"That's what Slattery and Hopkins told

me," Monarch said. "But I want to prepare in case that is what General Koporski is holding in his fortress."

"Makes sense," Fowler said. "Weapons factory. Heavy security."

"Exactly what I was thinking."

"How do we prepare?" Chávez asked.

Monarch slowed his pace and told them what he had in mind.

39

THREE DAYS LEFT . . .

Monarch dressed in black special ops gear. Two H&K .45 USPs in holsters were strapped to his utility vest. Tatupu, Chávez, and Fowler were similarly dressed. They and Slattery stood behind Yin and her laptop, studying a 3-D version of the Prazil fortress, going one last time over the final steps of the plan they'd cobbled together.

"Chopper rendezvous is oh eighteen hundred," Slattery said, checking his watch.

"Fifteen minutes to pickup," Yin said.

Monarch's ground team fanned out and started grabbing the gear that Slattery had flown in from Germany. Monarch took an H&K submachine gun and went outside. A chill gusting wind was blowing. The night was near pitch black. He looked around and saw Barnett climbing out a bulkhead from the villa's basement. She was dressed in civilian clothes, wore a headlamp, and carried two shopping bags. She handed the smaller bag to Monarch. It was heavy. He did not look inside, but instead wrapped stuffed the bag and its contents into his pack.

"Everything?" he murmured.

Barnett glanced over his shoulder. "Or a reasonable facsimile."

"Where'd you get them?"

"A metal shop in Chişsinău and a college geology student."

"You're the best, Gloria," Monarch said.

"No," she said. "I'm not, Robin. I got us busted."

"Don't worry about it," he said. "Happens to the best of us."

"You sure you want to go through with this?"

"I hate being controlled, and I want to know who's trying."

Tatupu came out the front door, night-vision goggles around his neck. Chávez followed, the sniper rifle in a drag bag slung over her shoulder. Fowler came next, laboring under a load stuffed into a black rubber dry bag.

Monarch gave Barnett a kiss on the cheek. He went around the back of the house, heading toward a meadow beyond a rock wall. Even over the gusting wind, he heard the helicopter long before he saw it swing in over the meadow. The chopper landed. The helicopter's side door slid back. His teammates got on board. He took one last look back at the villa and saw Slattery standing there, watching.

Monarch dropped into a crouch and ran forward under the spinning rotor blades and flung his pack inside. The Samoan's big hand reached out and hauled him inside. In moments, he was strapped into harness and jump chair and they were lifting off.

As they raced east through the night, Monarch sorted and discarded all thoughts of being manipulated and of trying to manipulate until there was only to night, this plan and his determination to execute it. It was at these kinds of moments that Monarch usually felt most alive, singular in purpose, completely in himself, a thinking machine with a goal. Slattery could not exist. The money at stake could not exist. Even Lacey and her predicament had to be erased from his thoughts.

Twenty minutes later, they crossed into Transdniestrian airspace, flying right off the tops of the trees. The pilot swung south of the fortress ten miles and landed in an agricultural field by the Dniester River.

They were off the bird and had the gear on the ground in less than two minutes.

Tatupu wiggled into the harness of a pack frame to which a thirty-horse outboard motor had been strapped. Monarch and Fowler had to help hoist the pack until the Samoan could get to his feet. Tatupu staggered under the load toward the river.

A six-man rubber raft was strapped to a second pack frame. Fowler got into the pack's harness. Monarch helped him to his feet and then worked with Chávez to get the rest of the equipment gathered and ferried to the riverbank. They found a game trail that took them down the steep bank to the water's edge. They inflated the raft, attached the engine, and were soon moving upriver, hugging the western shore.

Two miles south of the fortress, they beached. Monarch and Chávez got out. Monarch checked his watch. Eight P.M. Ten hours to daylight. Three hours to showtime.

Monarch shouldered his pack and then looked at Tatupu and Fowler, who were getting ready to shove off. He reached out and bumped knuckles with both of them. He watched the raft until it was swallowed in the night. Monarch and Chávez climbed the steep bank using tree roots as handholds and reached the top sweating.

"That's the worst of it," he said, gasping under the weight of the pack.

"Take your time," Chávez said. "We've got plenty."

Monarch knew she was right. But Rule Number Eleven stuck in his mind: Be early on a job. Early means you can adapt.

He kept up a brisk pace through the woods.

They broke free of the forest and reached a knob above the village of Prazil at nine that evening. The smell of woodsmoke hung in the air. There was little traffic in the narrow streets. Many of the squalid row houses and decrepit cottages were already dark. Several hundred yards away, though, on the far side of the village, the ancient fortress glowed under the glare of banks of sodium lights.

Monarch got out his binoculars and sat in the grass, studying the façade beyond the razor wire fence. To form the refuge's outer walls, Suleiman the Magnificent's stone masons had cut and stacked blocks of rough rust-colored granite thirty feet high. There were medieval battlements atop the palisade, gaps in the stonework that would have allowed archers and musket men to fire on the enemies of the Ottoman Empire.

At either end of the south-facing wall, he

spotted the scaffolding and the black tarps that wrapped the upper towers. He adjusted the binocular's setting and saw movement in a slit in the tarps. A soldier was altering the angle of a heavy gun.

"Look like 12.7 millimeters, just like Slattery said," Monarch said, lowering his glasses.

"Nothing my girl here can't take care of," Chávez said. She'd retrieved a silencer from her pack and was screwing it into the muzzle of her rifle.

Monarch raised his glasses again and spotted the bell tower of an Orthodox church about two hundred yards south of the fortress. "You okay with that high ground?"

Chávez set the rifle down and looked at the church through her own binoculars. "Nah," she said. "First place they'll look. I like that big tree in the graveyard."

"You lose twenty feet of elevation."

"Thirty feet up, I'm level with the wall," she said. "I can't help you once you get over it, even from the bell tower."

Monarch saw her point and nodded.

For the next hour, they sat on the knob, watching the fortress, seeing the rhythm of guards walking the parapets with dogs. Because of the tarps, they couldn't tell how many guards were in each tower, so they went conservative and figured three.

At ten fifteen, Fowler's voice came over the headset. "Fireworks at eleven."

"Roger that," Barnett said from the villa outside Chişsinău. "You copy, Robin?"

"Loud and clear," Monarch said. "We're moving into position."

"Cameras on," Jack Slattery's voice ordered in his ear.

Monarch hated wearing the camera. It caused those watching to question his perspective and instincts. And in situations like this, you lived or died by your perspective and instincts. Still, he groped the side of his headset and rotated the slender digital video camera forward so the lens was by his right eye. He thumbed a switch on the camera and caught a flash of red in his peripheral vision.

Sixty-five miles away, in the farm house outside Chişsinău, the CIA's director of covert operations stood with his arms crossed, headset on, watching the larger of Yin's computer screens. He saw static and shadows.

"You got me?" Monarch asked.

"Too dark," Slattery said. "Shift to night vision."

The screen jumped to the milky green

suggestion of the streets of the old village.

"You're go," Slattery said to Monarch. He cupped his mic with one hand and told Barnett, "Bring up the others."

Barnett typed on her keyboard and quickly her screen divided into quadrants. Upper left showed Monarch's perspective. Upper right showed Chávez's camera and the distant fortress bathed in sodium light. Lower right displayed Fowler's view as he attached explosives to the electrical station that fed the fortress a quarter of a mile away. In the lower left screen, Tatupu was moving through dense cover, the brilliant lights of the fortress showing through limbs and branches ahead.

But then Slattery's attention focused on Monarch and Chávez as they slipped down into the village. The streets were empty and dark as they padded along hedgerows, heading toward the Orthodox church. They parted outside the fence that surrounded the churchyard. Chávez climbed the fence and slipped through the graveyard to a towering fir tree.

Monarch found his point of attack in the stairwell of an abandoned row house a block south of the road that fronted the fortress.

"Two sentries in a guard shack at the razor wire fence," Monarch said. "Two others and a dog at the big oak gates. Everyone looks relaxed."

"Good," Slattery replied, satisfied. "In a few minutes, there should be just enough confusion to make this happen."

Chávez spoke. "I'm up at the height of the wall."

Slattery's attention jumped to Chávez's feed, just as she said, "We got trouble: Tanks, two of them, camouflaged at the southeast and southwest corners of the fortress. Guard on each."

Over the years, Monarch had learned that penetrating a high-security facility was as much an art as a science. If you were lucky, everything went according to plan and it was all science, tactics, and disciplined execution. But as often as not, the science was flawed, or the plan incomplete, or the tactics inappropriate, and the disciplined operator had to improvise. And therein lay the art and the artist.

"John, you with me?" Monarch asked. It was three minutes to eleven.

"Just getting there," Tatupu replied, breathing hard. "And we've got tanks on the northwest and northeast corners as well."

"Take the northwest tank out at oh

twenty-three hundred," Monarch said.

"It's a T-37. I'm gonna have to be right on top of them," Tatupu said.

"Attack and retreat," Monarch said. "Lots of noise. And Chávez, pin down the sentries at the fortress gate."

"Roger that," Chávez said. "Tower guards?"

"Only if they light up," Monarch said. "Abbott? You drive a Soviet T-37?"

"I think I could figure it out," Fowler said.

"Have fun with that."

Monarch shifted under the weight of the pack and then took it off before he heard the revving of motorcycles and the chug of a diesel engine. Headlights swung into the road behind him. He ducked down against the side of the stairwell.

He peered through a gap in the wall and saw two soldiers on motorcycles leading a black armored SUV-styled limousine that had small flags mounted on the hood.

"Big swinging dick at the gate," Chávez said.

"Came right by me," Monarch said. He was up on his knees on the top stair, training his binoculars on the limo. The front passenger window rolled down. Monarch caught a glimpse of Colonel Gorka and heard him shouting something at the sentry.

367

The sentry snapped to attention. The other began to fumble with the outer gate. The sentries beyond were calling for the oak doors to open. Monarch saw his chance, snatched up his pack and exploded from the stairwell just as a dull thud became an explosive roar to the northwest of the fortress. Every light in the place went out.

He drew one of the .45s from its holster, held it at his side while running in a loping arc toward the limousine's taillights, seeing the sentry at the first gate groping for a flashlight amid the first cries of alert and the baying of dogs up on the battlement.

Ka-ruumph! Monarch heard the missile leave Tatupu's SAM a split second before an explosion rocked the north side of the fortress. A ruby fireball flared against the night sky. A heavy machine gun opened up from the north. A third explosion from the northwest muffled the sound of the limo revving its engines and popping into gear. The vehicle barreled forward, pinning one sentry against the gate before exploding through.

Monarch sprinted after the retreating vehicle. The limousine skidded and slammed into the old fortress's huge oak doors just as Chávez touched off from her position in the tree by the church. Monarch didn't hear the suppressed crack of her rifle, but he saw the sentry on his right arch and fall away from the limousine, dropping his hold on the leash to his dog and grabbing at his leg. The driver threw the limo in reverse. Monarch dived toward the limo and rolled over. The vehicle slid over him.

"Open the gate!" he heard Colonel Gorka shouting. "The president is inside!"

The dog came snarling and biting under the car at Monarch. The limo driver slammed the vehicle back in gear. Monarch stuck the handle of his pistol in his mouth and snagged hold of the limo's frame a split second before the vehicle burned rubber through the open gate and into the fortress yard.

It was wet and muddy in the darkness beyond the gate. The limo slid in a violent fishtail that threw Monarch free of the undercarriage. He tumbled, rolled, and came up on all fours, peering around, seeing an excavating machine. As he was scrambling in behind it, his attention darted from the sentries closing the gate and soldiers running with flashlights on the ramparts to the brake lights of the limousine skidding to a stop before the only structure inside the fortress walls: a low, bunkerlike building.

"I'm inside," Monarch said into his microphone.

40

Back in the safe house outside Chişsinău, Jack Slattery nodded at the screen showing Monarch's feed.

"We can see that," Slattery said. "Well done. Fowler, you are go."

Fowler's screen showed his view in infrared. He was racing from the north, firing at the Russian soldier guarding the tank. On Tatupu's screen, the machine guns on the fortress's north side opened up in chops and rattles, trying unsuccessfully to kill Fowler before he managed to get inside the hatch of the tank. Then the safe house echoed with the groans of a diesel engine starting.

Lying in the mud inside the fortress grounds, Monarch heard it, too.

"That my tank, Abbott?" Monarch asked.

"Roger that," Fowler said.

"Take it west, then come around south

and take out those other tanks."

"Let you know when I'm close," Fowler said.

"We got soldiers trying to get to the tanks on my side," Chávez said.

"Don't let them," Monarch ordered. "And Tats, I could use a little distraction right about now."

"Christ, you're needy," Tatupu said.

The machine gunners in the north towers slowed their fire and stopped. There was a pause, and then shouting rose throughout the inner fortress. Monarch glanced at the limousine, seeing General Koporski and Colonel Gorka getting out of the vehicle and moving quickly toward the front of the bunker.

Monarch looked back toward the gate and spotted two sentries hugging the wall to either side of the oak doors. Monarch let go his pack. He got to his feet and was running toward the closest sentry when — *harrumph!* — Tatupu fired his second and last SAM missile.

Monarch caught the flare of it streaking at the northwest tower before the blast sent shock waves across the inner fortress. The sentry threw himself flat at Monarch's feet. Monarch grabbed him by the neck and hit him near the temple with the butt of his pistol. The sentry crumpled. Monarch dragged him back toward the excavating machine.

The northeast tower was burning now, throwing flames and black smoke. The machine gunner in the northwest tower had opened up again and was hailing bullets on the tree line, where Tatupu was mounting his assault.

Then the southeast tower machine guns opened fire.

"They made me," Chávez said. "Changing position."

Monarch spotted General Koporski hustling through the bunker's steel door. Colonel Gorka was shouting at soldiers gathered around him, demanding that generators be turned on. Two soldiers followed Koporski, while Gorka ordered the tanks and several of the machine guns on the fortress's south side brought north. Soldiers were shouting at him that the attackers had snipers killing anyone who tried to get at the tanks.

Monarch wrestled the unconscious sentry out of his long wool coat. He put it on and the sentry's hat as well. He fished in his pack and came up with a small bomb made of plastic explosive and a timer detonator. He stuffed it under the excavator's seat.

■ ■ ■ ■

Back on the Moldovan side of the border, Slattery grimaced with impatience and demanded, "How are you going to get below ground?"

"Working on it," Monarch said before he grabbed more bombs, set their timers for twenty-five minutes, and tossed them beneath various pieces of construction equipment.

"Gloria, keep count. I am minus twenty-four forty-five."

"Got it," Barnett said.

Slattery glanced at Fowler's screen, seeing the tank advancing toward the south wall of the fortress. "Take them out, Fowler," he said. "Now."

Monarch heard those orders as generators fired to life and the sodium bulbs began to glow over the inner yard. Monarch threw his pack on and trotted at Colonel Gorka, who was alone, moving toward the bunker, listening to a handheld radio.

Behind Monarch and beyond the gate, Fowler touched off the first round from the tank's cannon. The ground shook at the explosion. A fireball rose behind Monarch, silhouetting him in electric light as the lamps gathered power and cast the inner fortress in a strange aluminum glow.

Gorka had ducked to one knee at the cannon blast. He looked wild-eyed up at Monarch before recognizing him. "You!" he grunted in Russian.

Monarch showed him the pistol. "Take me inside."

Slattery watched Yin's computer screen as Monarch picked Colonel Gorka up by the collar, stripped him of his weapon, and pushed him toward the bunker. The colonel opened the bunker door, revealing the sort of bulletproof pods seen in super-max prisons. Inside the pod, two soldiers leaped to attention.

"Open the gate!" Colonel Gorka roared in Russian.

"It's tee time," Abbott Fowler said.

Slattery glanced at Fowler's feed to see his weapon sight centered on a second tank. A boom. A rush of fire. The tank heaved and gushed smoke and flames.

He looked back at Monarch's screen and saw the soldiers in the pod cringing.

Colonel Gorka was shouting, "I've got to get the president away from here! Now open the goddamn gate and get out there and fight!"

One guard slapped a button inside the pod. The steel gate in front of the colonel swung open. Monarch followed Gorka through the gate to an elevator. The elevator door opened. They got in. The door closed. The colonel looked at Monarch in amazement. "Why do you attack us with an entire army?"

"Rich people don't like to pay full price if they can help it," Monarch said.

"You'll never find it," the colonel said.

"I've got a Geiger counter," Monarch said. "I'll find it."

Slattery frowned and looked at Barnett "Geiger counter? I never saw that on the manifest."

"A last-minute request from Robin," Barnett said in an offhand fashion.

"For what?" Gorka asked, puzzled on the screen.

"Tracking the radioactivity," Monarch said.

"It's radioactive?" Gorka said, suddenly looking at his hands.

"Koporski didn't tell you?" Monarch said.

Slattery triggered his microphone. "You don't have time to search with a Geiger counter. Lean on him, Monarch."

The screen showed Gorka looking at Monarch with a sickening expression.

Monarch said, "I was hoping you'd show me the accelerator's location in return for your life. Be a shame to die in an elevator like this, Colonel. Active, smart man such as yourself. A few good years left to live, I'd imagine, even with the radioactive exposure. And certainly, now, you have no allegiance to the general."

"Beautiful blend of bullshit and threat," Slattery commented.

"Nobody does it better," Yin agreed.

On screen, the elevator dinged. The camera angle switched to the doors opening, revealing a pair of sentries turning to look at them, weapons up.

"I'm quicker," Monarch muttered.

"Who's he talking to?" Slattery asked.

"The colonel," Barnett said.

"Where's the president?" Colonel Gorka demanded as he brushed by the sentries.

"I don't know," one sentry said.

"But you do," Monarch murmured, tight to the colonel's back.

In the bunker beneath the ancient fortress, Colonel Gorka led Monarch through a set of swinging doors onto a staircase that overlooked a room filled with machine tools.

Rows of AK-47 knockoffs stood in racks beside wooden crates.

"Koporski's arms factory," Slattery said in Monarch's ear. "Intel is dead on."

Monarch ignored this irritation and followed the colonel as they descended the staircase and walked among the lathes and workbenches littered with guns in various stages of manufacture. He took inventory, seeing what he might use should he get caught below ground.

Off the factory floor and down another staircase, Gorka led them through a warren of passages to a steel door. He knocked and called out, "It's me, General."

Monarch heard muffled voices inside before the door opened two inches. He pushed Gorka and shoved his pistol in the face of the soldier at the door handle.

The soldier went cross-eyed and moved backwards. They entered a room without windows. A shelf and the wall behind it had been pulled aside. General Koporski was emerging from behind the false wall. The dictator held a metal case in his hand.

Koporski spotted Gorka first. "How many are there?" he demanded. "Should we get out the — ?" The dictator saw Monarch and froze in recognition.

"I told you we should never have let him

go," Colonel Gorka said.

"Put the case on the table, General," Monarch ordered, yanking shut the steel door behind him. "Then sit against that wall, your back to me, hands behind your head. You, too, Colonel. And you, soldier."

Koporski flexed his shoulders like a pit bull setting to fight, but put the case on the table and started to move toward the wall. "You plan to execute us as you did Duboff?"

"Consider this an armed assault," Monarch said, picking up the case. "No homicide intended. I get what I want, you live. So I'd like the combination, General."

Monarch thumbed back the hammer on his pistol with a stiff click and aimed the gun at the side of Koporski's head. "I either get into it here or I get into it later."

The general was straining to look over his shoulder at Monarch. Evidently he saw the dead seriousness in Monarch's eyes because he said, "Zero, six, six, seven, nine."

"Good," Monarch said. "Now sit down, hands behind your back."

Monarch came up behind them and cinched their wrists with plastic zip ties before returning to the case.

Inside the safe house in Moldova, Slattery studied the case on screen, feeling a swell of excitement. "That it?"

Monarch did not reply. He fumbled in his pack, opened the shopping bag Barnett had given him, and came up holding a device that looked like a cigar-shaped microphone attached to a heavy coiled electrical cable.

"What is that?" Slattery demanded.

"Geiger counter," Monarch muttered.

"Forget the Geiger counter!" Slattery roared. "Open the damn thing."

The spymaster watched, fascinated, as Monarch's fingers rolled the tumblers of the lock. Thumbs levered open latches. Hasps snapped. The lid split, lifted, and for an instant, gave a peek at something shiny and steel before the screen went black.

"What the hell's going on?" Slattery roared.

"I don't know," Yin said, typing furiously on the keyboard.

"What's wrong?" Monarch's voice came over the headset.

"Your camera," Slattery said. "It's out."

"I don't know," Monarch said. "Let me try reconnecting. . . ."

Deep in the bowels of Koporski's arms factory, Monarch was staring at the contents of the foam-padded interior. *My god,* he thought. Green Fields was real. Nassara actually built the son of a bitch. *No wonder Slattery wanted me to steal it. Too bad he's not getting it.*

That thought buoyed Monarch and he snatched up the contents of the case and stuffed them into the side pockets of his pack. He reached in the shopping bag and came up with a rough replica of the kind of canister used to transport polonium-210. He laid the canister on the foam before flipping on his camera again.

Monarch's feed on Yin's computer blinked back to life, revealing the open case, the foam, and the stainless steel canister.

"You reading me now?" Monarch asked.

"Yes," Slattery said, catching his breath at the sight of the canister.

"That look like what we're looking for?" Monarch asked.

"Open it," Slattery said.

"No chance," Monarch said. "I'm picking up radioactivity. Probably the polonium-210."

Slattery frowned, but then ordered, "Take it and get out of there."

"Roger that, coming out," Monarch said. "Gloria, what's my count?"

"Twelve minutes thirty seconds, Robin," Barnett replied.

381

Monarch picked up the canister. Koporski said, "Who do you work for?"

"A consortium," Monarch said.

"How much are they paying you?" the dictator demanded.

Monarch said, "High bid's currently six million on delivery. Latest bid was a lot less, but there were kickers thrown in that make it a compelling offer."

"I'll pay you seven million, right now, to leave without it," Koporski said.

Inside the safe house, Slattery straightened. There was a moment's hesitation before the screen showing Monarch's camera feed went black again.

Slattery stared in disbelief and then shouted, "Monarch? You bastard! Monarch!"

41

Sixty-five miles away, deep inside Koporski's bunker, Monarch smiled to himself, thinking of the rage that must now be boiling in Slattery's veins, the threats of damnation and of incarceration. He asked the general, "Can you pay now?"

Koporski nodded at Gorka. "He can do it. Give him an account number. Use my computer in the bag there."

"You're serious?"

"Dead serious," the dictator said, attempting to rise.

"Not so fast, General," Monarch said, pressing him down. "Just the colonel."

Gorka grimaced, but with Monarch's help, struggled to his feet. Monarch fished out the laptop computer from the general's bag. He set it on a table in the corner. He tapped the muzzle of his pistol against Gorka's cheek. "Nothing funny."

The colonel stiffened, but nodded. Monarch snipped the plastic restraints. Gorka looked at Koporski. "From what account?"

"The factory's," the general said.

"In euros, then," Gorka said. "The account number?"

Monarch rattled off the number of an account at a bank in Dublin. Gorka went to work, and in a few minutes time had authorized a payment to Monarch's account for the euro equivalent of seven million U.S. dollars.

"Pleasure doing business with you," Monarch said, strapping the restraints back on Gorka and shoving him on the ground.

"Wait! You're taking it with you?" Koporski demanded. "Have you no honor?"

"Haven't you heard? There's no honor among thieves," Monarch said, just before he hit the dictator behind the ear with the butt of his pistol. The general crumpled.

Monarch struck Gorka with a similar blow, stuffed the canister and the Geiger counter back in the main pouch of his pack, and headed to the door. As he did, he turned on his radio headset and camera.

"Is anybody reading me?" he called. "This is Monarch, do you read me?"

Inside the villa in Moldova, Slattery was venting his wrath on Barnett and Yin. "He won't get away with it!" he vowed. "Monarch's selling out the country! I'll have him arrested for treason! I'll have you all arrested for treason!"

"He's not an agent of the U.S. government anymore," Barnett reminded him.

"I'll tell you what he is. As of right now, Robin Monarch is a wanted —"

"— This is Monarch, do you read me?"

Slattery spun toward the laptop, seeing the screen filled with Monarch's herky-jerky video feed. Monarch was running through the arms factory. He was carrying the case. Slattery could see it flash and disappear in time with Monarch's arms pumping.

Yin snatched up her headset. "Loud and clear, Robin."

"I'm coming out," Monarch gasped. "Abbott, you think you can knock the front gate down for me?"

"Affirmative," Fowler said. "You give me the go."

"Gloria, what's my count?" Monarch demanded as he bounded up the stairs off the factory floor.

"Three minutes ten seconds," Barnett said.

Monarch burst through the swinging doors. The sentries at the elevator stood. Monarch barked at them in Russian, "The

385

colonel wants you in the factory. You're to help guard the president."

The sentries hesitated, but then ran toward the factory. Monarch got in the elevator and it closed.

"You didn't sell out to Koporski?" Slattery demanded after several moments.

"What, and be an asshole?" Monarch huffed before aiming his pistol at the doors.

The doors opened. Monarch exited saying, "Count, Gloria?"

"One minute," Barnett said.

Monarch went through the open steel gate and peered through the window. The lights were still running dim on the generator. Though the active shooting had stopped, Slattery could still make out soldiers crouched up on the battlement.

"Thirty seconds," Barnett said.

Slattery watched Monarch drop the clips in both pistols and reload them with spares. Just as he finished, Barnett said. "Twenty, nineteen . . ."

Inside the bunker, Monarch listened to Barnett voice. "Fifteen, fourteen . . ."

At ten seconds, Monarch went through the bunker door, moving laterally toward the fortress's east wall. In his peripheral vision, he could make out at least one soldier in the southeast tower moving his machine gun in his direction.

"Five, four, three . . ."

Monarch threw himself on the ground.

Tatupu's first time bomb exploded north of the fortress. Monarch's first bomb blew out the cab of the excavator. Soldiers on the wall shouted. Dogs snarled and barked. Burnt cordite fouled the air. Another bomb exploded outside the north walls, and a third before Monarch's last four went off in quick succession, blowing lumber and debris high into the air above the bunker. In the stunning silence that followed the blasts, Monarch was sprinting toward the wall to the left of the wooden gate.

"Gimme a way out of here, Abbott," he ordered.

"Exit stage center coming right up," Fowler replied.

Monarch threw himself down again and covered his head. The tank cannon thundered. The shell hit the gate on the seam of its two halves. The oak disintegrated inward. Monarch lurched to his feet and charged the smoking, gaping hole. He heard machine gun fire and felt rounds clipping at his heels. Despite the uniform and hat, one of the men in the towers now suspected him. Or Gorka or Koporski had aroused and sounded the alarm. In any case, Monarch went into a tight zigzag before he leaped through the hole, shouting, "Chávez, shut that gun down."

He landed and rolled toward the trashed razor wire gate. He caught a glimpse of a machine gun from the southeast tower swinging toward him before he thought he heard a slapping sound. The gunner in the tower hunched up and pitched forward into a dive. Monarch got to his feet and sprinted toward the Soviet tank rolling out to meet him.

42

TWO DAYS LEFT . . .

Shortly before dawn, the helicopter landed behind the villa outside Chişsinău.

"Refuel and you're back in an hour," Monarch told the pilot.

Chávez, Tatupu, and Fowler were already climbing out the side of the bird, all of them looking bone tired. Monarch felt about the same, but forced himself alert when he spotted Slattery, Yin, and Barnett standing in the mist, waiting for them. He went straight at Slattery, feeling the anger pulsing in him. But instead of letting it rule him, he used it to fuel his own ruthlessness.

"Where is it?" Slattery demanded.

Monarch said, "First there's a bill payable."

"I'll see that it happens."

"Now," Monarch said. "The pilot's coming back for us in an hour."

"The hostage?" Slattery asked.

"I'll call and tell you when it's over," Monarch said.

"Us?"

"I'll need the entire team with me. Part of the deal."

Slattery hesitated again, but then nodded. "Done," he said.

They went inside. Monarch reached in his pack and pulled out the steel canister. Slattery looked at Monarch. "Did you examine it?"

Monarch shook his head. "I'm not about to mess around with a radioactive substance. But if you want to, Jack, be my guest. Just wait until we're long gone."

Slattery looked at the canister differently, but then said, not quite sure, "Okay."

"The money," Monarch said while his team started gathering gear.

The CIA covert chief went to Yin's computer and spent several minutes typing and responding to prompts before saying, "Where do I transfer the money?"

Monarch gave him the same account number and routing information to the bank in Ireland. Several minutes later, Slattery bobbed his head. "Done."

Monarch considered his old boss a moment before replying: "Wish I could say I enjoyed working with you, Jack."

"Feeling's mutual," Slattery said coolly. "But no hard feelings."

Monarch nodded at that lie, and then turned to help the others. He moved close to Barnett, who huddled in her down jacket, and murmured. "Still have those extra two canisters? And more of that stuff in the basement?"

"I do," Barnett said.

"Good," Monarch said. "We're going to need them."

An hour later, Monarch and his team lifted off. Slattery watched them go. The pilot would return for him later in the day, which was fine by him. Indeed, as he walked back toward the villa, Slattery felt swelled with the infinite possibilities that Monarch had just presented to him, sure that he was bound for great and glorious times.

Buzzing on that idea, Slattery shivered on his way inside. He pulled a chair close to the gas heater before pulling out his satellite phone, feeling as satisfied as he'd ever been as he punched in a rarely used number.

It rang three times and a woman answered, "Yes?" Campaign music played in the background over the roar of clapping and whistling.

"Virginia?" Slattery said. "It's Jack Slattery."

There was a pause before the congressman's wife asked, "Can you hold, Jack? Frank's working the room."

"Of course," Slattery said.

Listening to the crowd and the music, looking at the canister on the table, Slattery suddenly felt jittery inside at what he'd accomplished.

"Jack?" Frank Baron said a moment later.

"Tell our mutual friend that the object of his desire is in hand," Slattery replied.

"Is that right? You're actually holding the thing?"

"Right here. It's giving off low levels of radiation."

"Really? Is that how it works?"

"I'm no expert," Slattery replied. "But I'd like someone who is to handle it."

"I'll have it arranged," Baron said. "I'm going to C.Y.'s beach place for the weekend. How soon can you get to Grand Bahama?"

Slattery checked his watch. "Late tomorrow afternoon, your time."

"We'll have experts present and waiting to take it off your hands."

43

SEVERAL HOURS LATER . . .
KÖROĞLU MOUNTAINS, NORTHERN TURKEY

"Slattery's going to be very unhappy in a day or so," Monarch said.

He was sitting in the front passenger seat of a Land Rover. Fowler was driving. It was raining outside and they were heading west from a drop point on a winding two-lane highway deep in the mountains east of Istanbul.

"Screw that lying piece of shit," Tatupu said. "Let's see it."

The rest of Monarch's team looked at him expectantly from the rear seats. He dug in the side pockets of his pack and tugged out the items he'd taken from the case inside Koporski's fortress. The first item out appeared to be a semiautomatic pistol with an open metal frame instead of a grip. The second item was a laser sight. The third was a cartridge that featured a thumb switch and a raised tubular rib that looked like an upside down Q with the tail pointing straight up.

Monarch snapped the cartridge into the frame of the pistol grip. "This must have been in that case I saw Nassara carrying. His nephew killed his uncle for it, and then it got into Koporski's hands."

Fowler glanced over at Monarch. "Why call it Green Fields?"

"A cover? I don't know," Monarch said. "But this is definitely a miniaturized version of those bigger gizmos I saw bolted into the floor inside Nassara's lab."

"All small particle accelerators?" Chávez asked.

"I think so," Monarch said. "Nassara was turning the pure science he did as a younger man at CERN into revolutionary weapons."

"For who?" Yin asked.

"Whoever would pay the most for it, I'm sure," Monarch said. "If it works, it's groundbreaking stuff. An army equipped with Green Fields weapons would be virtually unstoppable against conventional armaments."

"If it works," Barnett said. "I mean, it's all been for nothing if it doesn't work."

Monarch looked at Fowler. "Find a side

road where we won't be bothered."

Ten minutes later, Fowler stopped the Land Rover on a dirt road deep in the forest. Monarch exited, holding the Green Fields weapon in his left hand. The others got out, watching him. Chávez flipped open her phone and prepared to video.

"You think it's safe?" Yin asked nervously.

"If not, I'm going to be vaporized pretty quick," Monarch said.

He thumbed the switch on the cartridge, felt the pistol vibrate to life, aimed through the laser sight at a stump about fifty yards away, and squeezed the trigger. The gun bucked, let loose a sharp buzzing report, and Monarch saw a hurtling flash before the stump exploded, leaving smoking cinders. Monarch's jaw dropped.

"Motherfucker," Chávez whispered, lowering the phone. "Is that for real?"

"Motherfucking yes," Tatupu said. "Impulse gun. No bullet. No gunpowder."

"Just bolts of energy," Monarch said.

"Total shock and awe," Fowler said.

Yin was still staring at the smoldering stump. "And you think this could be built to all sorts of scales?"

Monarch nodded. "Think of a cannon or a machine gun like that."

"Long as they were on our side," Barnett said.

"You know it doesn't work like that," Monarch said.

Tatupu bobbed his head in understanding. "The Koporskis of the world will get it sooner or later, and start mass-producing it."

They looked at Monarch.

"What are you going to do with it?" Barnett asked.

Monarch dismantled the gun. "Let you know when I do. You get that, Chanel?"

She looked at her phone and then nodded. "Whole thing. Jesus, Robin, if you're right about Slattery, he and whoever else is working with him will come for that gun."

"I expect so," Monarch agreed, heading back to the Land Rover.

They climbed into the car. Fowler got in the driver's seat and said, "Where now?"

"Where it all started," Monarch said. "Istanbul."

"Wait a second," Yin said from the backseat. "Slattery paid you five million. How much do we get of that, Robin?"

"Ten percent. And ten percent of the seven million I took off Koporski."

"That's one-point-something million each," Fowler said.

"Give or take," Monarch said, "though I expect there will be much more after we meet with Belos and Omak."

"And you get the rest?" Tatupu asked. "Fifty percent?"

"No, I'm taking ten percent, and the other forty's going to a friend of mine, Sister Rachel. She helps street kids in Buenos Aires. The poorest of the poor."

They all studied him. Barnett got it first. "Like Robin Hood or something?"

Monarch cocked his head. "Yeah, something like that."

Chávez grinned. "Anyone ever tell you you're a natural-born criminal?"

"Nearly everyone, Chanel," Monarch said, "starting with my mother and father every night before they laid me down to sleep."

44

THE FOLLOWING NIGHT . . .
CONFLUENCE OF THE BOSPORUS
STRAIT AND THE SEA OF MAMARA
Monarch saw a light flash twice ahead in
the darkness. He nodded to Fowler, who
stood in the wheelhouse at the helm of a
small fishing boat they'd stolen from a marina down the coast. The sea was rough,
misting and foggy. Yin was in the wheelhouse as well and looked ready to be sick.
Fowler gunned the engine. The boat shuddered against waves breaking against one
another from opposite directions, wind-
driven south off the strait itself and piling
north with the currents off the Sea of Marmara.

"Use the light," Monarch said.

Fowler threw a switch. A powerful spot
threw a corridor of light across the pitching, foggy sea. For a second, Monarch
thought about abandoning his plan and opt-

ing for a more conventional setting for the complicated little exchange he had in mind.

But then the spotlight revealed the side of a huge dredging barge, rolling slowly in the chaos at the mouth of the strait, straining against its chains and anchors. Tatupu appeared in the soft light cast by the red warning beacons at the corners of the barge. Chávez appeared beside him. They wore neoprene wetsuits and carried guns.

Monarch went forward onto the front deck and grabbed hold of the rope Tatupu tossed to them. Fowler threw the engines in reverse and cut the wheel, causing the vessel to come about on the swell. The boat bounced against the tire bumpers on the barge's wall before Chávez and Tatupu hauled on the ropes and snugged her in place.

Fowler cut the engine. Monarch climbed the ladder onto the swaying barge, taking in the pilot's house, the crane at midship, and other dredging tools and equipment neatly stacked and lashed across the remaining deck.

"Any problems?" Monarch asked Tatupu.

Tatupu shook his head. "Security detail of four. We've got them restrained belowdecks. No shots fired."

Monarch got out his cell phone and

activated the GPS software. "I'm sending them our position." He waited until he had a lock, copied the coordinates, and texted them to two phone numbers. A moment later, he heard two beeps to let him know that both messages had been received and opened.

"How long we got?" asked Yin.

"Ten minutes. Maybe fifteen in this weather," Monarch said.

"That's enough," Yin said before following Chávez toward the wheelhouse. She climbed a ladder to the roof of the wheelhouse. Yin went inside and turned on a light.

Tatupu said, "I'll be over your right shoulder, northwest."

"You hear that Gloria?" Monarch asked into his Bluetooth.

"Roger that," Barnett said in his earpiece. "How's the weather out there?"

"Rub it in," Monarch replied. Barnett was, at the moment, encamped in a luxury suite at the Four Seasons six miles up the shore of the Bosporus.

Monarch looked up on the wheelhouse roof, seeing Chávez settle into position in the shadows beneath a lifeboat. When he glanced back at Tatupu, however, the big Samoan had already disappeared into the clutter on deck.

The chugging sound of a boat came from the west: Omak. Then Monarch heard a second boat, a higher tone in its engine, cutting from the east: Belos.

Monarch said into his mic, "Lights, Yin."

The lights went out in the wheelhouse before the two boats emerged from the fog. Vytor, the Chechen, stood in the bow of one boat, and Artun occupied the prow of another. Both men had machine pistols and aimed them one at the other as the boats drifted and sputtered toward the barge. Monarch could make out a pilot steering Omak's boat, but not the Chechen warlord himself. He strained to spot Lacey in the other vessel, but saw only Belos emerging from the wheelhouse onto the aft deck.

Monarch caught the bow and stern lines from both boats and lashed them to cleats. Then he backed up across the rolling deck and stood there waiting as first Artun and then Vytor came aboard. Belos got up on the deck next, wearing a heavy black wool sweater and watch cap.

"Where is it?" Belos growled in Russian at Monarch. "I'm not bidding on anything unless I can inspect the goods."

"I wouldn't have it any other way," Monarch said.

Omak climbed up onto the deck now,

drawing Belos's full attention and part of Monarch's. The Chechen wore a gray wool tunic and fez, and carried a briefcase. Upon seeing Belos, his face rippled with barely contained hatred. Belos looked just as agitated, his hands flexing, his shoulders bunching. The men genuinely despised each other.

Monarch said in Russian, "Just so everyone understands the rules, you should know that there are sniper rifles aimed at your heads."

The Chechens and the Russians flinched and looked around uneasily.

Monarch said, "Now it's show-me-what-you've-got time."

"The trigger first," Belos demanded.

"Not until I see you have the goods to negotiate."

Omak held up the briefcase. "I have the passwords and codes to an account that is ready to transfer."

"Excellent," Monarch said. "Constantine?"

Belos scowled before turning and looking over the side of the barge at the fishing boat he'd arrived in. "Bring her out," he commanded.

A man appeared, holding Lacey Wentworth, who wore the same clothes he'd left her in nearly two weeks before. She was filthy, and there was a hood over her head. Her arms were bound in front of her.

"Bring her up," Monarch said.

"The trigger," Belos said.

Monarch walked over, retrieved the knapsack, and drew out one of the metal canisters. He showed it to both men.

Belos looked at it suspiciously. "How do we know it's real?"

"It's what I stole from Koporski's arms factory," Monarch said.

"Does not answer the question," Omak said.

Monarch got out the Geiger counter. He flipped it on and passed the wand over the canister. It began to click and whine in a rhythmic pattern.

"That's the radioactive signature of polonium-210," Monarch said. "The accelerator necessary to trigger a nuke using a Russian-made fission producer."

Belos licked his lips. "It doesn't come with one of those fission producers?"

"Those are a dime a dozen on the black market. Isn't that so, Omak?"

Omak was gazing at the canister with open desire now. "Five million," he said. "That's my bid."

Monarch looked to Belos. "And your offer?"

"The girl."

Monarch shook his head. "Girl plus five million."

Belos looked over at Artun. "Kill her."

"The girl and five million," Monarch said calmly.

"Six million," Omak said.

Belos looked like he wanted to punch someone. "Girl and five million."

"Deal," Monarch said.

"Deal?" Omak cried. "There is no deal!"

"There is," Monarch said.

"Kill him!" Omak roared at Vytor. "I want that trigger!"

The Chechen made to swing his gun at Monarch. But before he could get it around, a silenced rifle shot flashed from atop the pilothouse, and the machine pistol flew from Vytor's hands and landed at Artun's feet.

"The next one will be between your eyes, Omak," Monarch said. "Both of you on your knees, hands up behind your heads. Now!"

Vytor looked like he was about to sip battery acid, but lowered himself onto the rolling deck of the barge. Omak sat on the deck. "I cannot kneel," he said. "My hip."

"You now, Artun," Monarch said. "Throw the gun over to me."

Artun did not move until Belos nodded. His bodyguard kicked the machine pistol across the deck to Monarch.

Belos said, "Give me the trigger now."

"Let's get Lacey up on deck and that money transferred. Then it's all yours."

Belos hesitated, and then called over the side of the barge. "Bring her up."

A few moments later, Belos knelt, reached down, and hauled Lacey up onto the deck of the barge by her wrist. "You're hurting me!" she whimpered, still hooded.

Belos threw her down at his feet. "Where do I pay?"

Monarch said, "In the pilothouse. One of my men will assist you."

"Robin?" Lacey cried from under the hood. "Robin, is that you?"

"Right here, Lacey," Monarch said. "You're going to be fine. Just stay where you are a couple more minutes. Are you all right?"

But Lacey had begun to cry and could not answer.

Belos stepped over her and by Vytor. But as he passed Omak, his boot shot out and clipped the Chechen Mafia boss in the ribs. Omak made an *oomph* noise and rolled over on his side, groaning.

"That's for trying to have me killed in St. Moritz, you lousy Muslim fuck," Belos said, and then marched to the wheelhouse, where Yin had turned on the light.

Ten minutes later, Belos emerged from the pilothouse and walked to Monarch. Over Belos's shoulder, Yin was giving the thumbs-up.

"The trigger," Belos said.

Monarch tossed him the canister underhand. Belos caught it uncertainly.

"It's radioactive?" he demanded.

"Mildly," Monarch said. "You wouldn't want to get your hands on what's inside, but it's safe enough to travel with."

Belos handed it to Artun, who was getting to his feet, before looking back at Monarch. "I haven't forgotten the eighteenth rule," he said.

"Neither have I," Monarch replied.

Artun scowled, but then cast off the lines and jumped onto the deck as the fishing boat's engine throttled up. Tatupu appeared as Belos's boat disappeared into the fog.

"Get Lacey into our boat," Monarch said.

"You made a big mistake giving him the trigger," Omak grunted, sitting up again when Monarch approached. "He is insane."

"He says the same about you," Monarch

replied. "But who cares? Belos doesn't know it, but Koporski had two canisters of polonium-210."

It took a moment for the Chechen to understand. "You have another?"

Monarch went to the backpack and retrieved the last canister. He turned with the Geiger counter and ran the sensor over it. As before, the detector clicked. "Polonium-210," Monarch said in Russian. "Did you know it is the second radioactive isotope Madame Curie discovered after radon?"

Omak stared at him like he was speaking another language, and then his attention drifted to the canister. Desire was building in his face again.

"This is a bargain at five million, a million below your last offer because — and I want to be straight with you, here, Omak, because I respect you — the polonium in this canister is two weeks older than the one Belos took. Polonium-210, as you know, has a relatively short half-life, so you better be planning on using this stuff fairly soon."

Omak cocked an eyebrow. "How soon?"

"Six months at the outside."

The Chechen thought about that and then said, "Four million."

Monarch thought about that and said, "Euros?"

Omak hesitated and then nodded. "Euros."

"Deal," Monarch said before gesturing at the pilothouse, where Yin was watching. "She will help you make the transfer."

45

THAT SAME DAY . . .

GRAND BAHAMA ISLAND THE BAHA-
MAS

Cocktail hour at the exclusive offshore fund-
raiser for Frank Baron kicked off around
four that afternoon on the expansive lanai
of C. Y. Tilden's waterfront estate.

Waiters moved through the crowd, offering drinks and tuna sashimi. Large-screen
televisions on either wall showed the first
cut of the ad campaign Baron intended to
use in the months leading up to the Georgia
primary elections.

As a rule, Jack Slattery did not favor this
kind of affair; he was more comfortable
celebrating alone or with hired talent. Today
was different. Today, he'd decided, was his
day of days, and he plucked a rum concoc-
tion off a passing tray. Slattery sipped from
it, thinking that he had taken risks for today,
great risks. But on this, his day of days, he'd

come through in a monster way on the biggest risk of his life.

Tilden's engineers already had the Green Fields device. Within minutes, the bank account he had opened upon his arrival on Grand Bahama would be flush with enough money to let him do whatever he wanted for the rest of his life, maybe even buy a place like this one.

"How does it feel?" a soft male voice asked behind Slattery, who turned to find C. Y. Tilden looming over him.

The chairman of Allied Energy wore dark sunglasses, a white long-sleeve shirt, matching pants, and a wide-brimmed straw hat. He had smeared his exposed skin with thick sunscreen that made him even paler than Slattery remembered. Tilden smiled and removed his sunglasses and let his pitted silver eyes roam all over the CIA officer, while his lips curled in pleasure, as if Slattery was the billionaire's newest favorite thing. Slattery almost extended his hand, but remembered Tilden was a germophobe.

Instead he said, "It hasn't quite sunk in."

"It will," Tilden said. "Freedom is a remarkable state of being. And will be for you, especially."

Slattery found Tilden's eyes unnerving, but he said, "How so?"

"It will give you freedom from the memories of your father, for one."

Slattery cocked his head back. "You knew my father?" he asked after a moment.

"I know enough about him," Tilden said. "Damian Desmond Slattery, career U.S. Army master sergeant who lost his wife in your birth. He never forgave you, did he, for that and for attending West Point?"

Despite years of having built defensive walls around himself, Slattery was caught flatfooted. For several moments, he did not know whether to punch the man or to walk away. Slattery said, "My father was an angry drunk. That's about the best you could say about him."

"And poor," Tilden said. "He made a good salary, but you and your stepmother lived poor because he drank, gambled, and whored his way through money every chance he got. That's what got to you, and drove you to West Point, didn't it? The shabbiness of your existence?"

Tilden seemed to take some delight in this, which hardened Slattery. "Who likes being poor?" he said. "But what's your point, C.Y.?"

"The point is, I'm genuinely interested in people and their motives," Tilden replied. "I've found that it is crucial when doing business. And I wanted to know why you would allow yourself to be corrupted and then go to such lengths to get Green Fields. So I hired some people to figure out your motivations."

"And?"

Tilden sniffed. "Money and mommy-love. Hardly unique. I'd hoped for something more, actually, but that was it," the billionaire said. "You have an important job, Jack, and have a decent standard of living. But in your childhood dreams, there was more than that — a rich life, one where you could fully indulge these games you evidently play in your head all the time, especially this game with the woman in the A-line skirt. I figure it's some image you've invented to represent your real mother."

Slattery was dumbfounded. He'd never spoken about these things to anyone except —

"Audrey, that beautiful redheaded prostitute you brought to the Smithsonian?" Tilden offered with great satisfaction. "She was more than happy to tell my people all about you in exchange for quadruple her hourly fee. Who is she playing for you? Is it dear dead Mommy? Or someone else?"

Slattery felt cornered. "Fuck you, C.Y.," he snarled. "You want *me* rooting around in *your* past?"

Tilden smiled. "Why be angry, Jack? Be happy. You have seen your dreams realized. Ten minutes ago, I transferred your fee to your bank account. You are officially a wealthy man. You can hire as many women as you want to wear A-line skirts for you."

Slattery sank on his heels, feeling the rage that had been building in him ease; and in its place, he felt a sense that a fortress had been raised up around him. "Fifty million?"

"To the dime," the billionaire replied, only to be interrupted by clapping and then cheers behind them.

Congressman Baron was coming out the French doors onto the lanai, and people crowded around him to shake his hand. Baron worked the room like a pro. Virginia, the former Miss Georgia, moved behind her husband radiating gentility.

Slattery felt a familiar pang of envy at the sight of the perfect couple, but then realized with satisfaction that for the first time, he had something Baron did not. His friend the congressman had a beautiful, smart wife who came from some money. They were comfortable, but hardly someone of his current high net worth.

"Did you feel it when you first met him? Frank?" Tilden asked.

"The way people just seem to like him?" Slattery replied. "Sure. He's never stepped in shit once in his entire life because of it."

Tilden laughed softly. "There's something I missed in your profile. Resentment."

"Not anymore," Slattery said, and then changed the subject. "I hear people think Frank will win the Senate seat in a landslide."

Tilden shook his head. "Maybe the primary. But in the general election, he'll be running against Helen Porterfield. She's smart, she looks good on television, she sits on the Intelligence Committee as well, and she's a black leader in Georgia. Frank will have to be on his toes for that fight. Now, if you'll excuse me, your work for the day is done. Mine, however, is just beginning."

The billionaire angled across the lanai toward Baron. Slattery snagged another drink from a passing tray and walked into a garden that ran out toward a sea wall.

He looked across the wall to the water. It was late afternoon, almost dusk, and the sun had become a fireball in the sky. A yacht sailed beneath, blaring calypso music and filling him with a general sense of victory. He wanted to pump his fist at the sky. Then he imagined himself dancing . . . no, pissing on his father's grave while holding wads of money. *Who's the big gambler now? Who took the big score?*

Slattery took a deeper drink of the rum and thought to himself that he should celebrate. At the very least, he deserved a woman tonight, one of great and exotic beauty, or maybe two; and more rum; and maybe a card game first. He'd heard the local casinos were quite good and imagined he might find female companionship there as well.

"Slattery!" C. Y. Tilden shouted, jolting him from his happy games. The billionaire was hurrying through the garden to him, his face a livid red.

"What's wrong?" Slattery asked.

"My office," Tilden said, barely in control. "Frank will join us shortly."

Selena Carter was middle-aged with a twist of brunette hair, no makeup, and black-framed glasses. She came into C. Y. Tilden's personal office at his beachfront estate shortly before Congressman Baron did. Slattery watched as Baron's eyes swept the room, taking in him and Tilden, who glowered behind his desk, before alighting on Selena Carter. She was the only person he didn't know, so Baron walked over to her and shook her hand. "Frank Baron."

Carter looked flustered and did not seem to know what to say.

"Selena Carter, Frank," Tilden said. "Head of my reverse engineering team."

"On Green Fields?" Baron asked. "Wonderful to meet you, Ms. Carter."

Carter nodded. "Yes, of course, Congressman."

"Tell them," Tilden rumbled.

The tycoon's lead research engineer pushed her glasses back up the bridge of her nose, and said, "The contents of what you brought us, Mr. Slattery, in no way constitute the alleged capabilities of Green Fields technology. What you have is several cups of radon-contaminated soil, just radioactive enough to set off a Geiger counter. There's no particle accelerator."

"It's a sham!" Tilden roared, and pounded his fist on his desk. "I've been conned! You fucking conned me out of fifty million, Slattery!" The tycoon's face swelled, reddened more, and he coughed and hacked.

Baron moved toward Tilden. "Calm down, C.Y., your heart."

"Screw my heart, Frank," Tilden snarled. "I've been conned, and I want my goddamned money back."

Slattery imagined this was what being gutted felt like. "I did not con you, C.Y."

"Then who the hell did?" Baron demanded.

"I don't know," Slattery said, thinking out loud. "Monarch said Koporski was under attack and he went for that case. It was the most important thing to him. It had to be Green Fields."

Tilden demanded, "How do you know for sure that Koporski went for that canister specifically when he came under attack?"

"I saw it myself on a satellite feed," Slattery replied. "All agents on operations like that carry a fiber optic video and infrared camera clipped to the brim of their . . ."

Slattery stopped, flashing on how Ellen Yin's computer screen had gone black just as Monarch was opening the case Koporski had given him. He felt like he was looking toward a horizon that was growing sharper even as his distance from it increased.

"Monarch," he said, feeling sick. "Koporski had the Green Fields device in that case, but Monarch substituted it with a phony canister. That thieving son of a —"

"Find him," Tilden said, cutting Slattery off. "I don't care what it takes. Find Monarch and get it. And until then, I want my money back."

"So do I," Slattery said.

46

THE SEA OF MAMARA

The stolen fishing boat curled away from the barge around three that morning. A wind had picked up, blowing the fog away, revealing a moonlit, starry night.

Monarch climbed belowdecks, finding himself in a small galley. Lacey Wentworth sat in the booth, a mug of hot tea in her hands, a blanket on her shoulders.

Chávez boxed up their medical kit, saying, "She's got bumps and bruises, but I think she'll be all right."

Lacey acted as if she didn't hear. Chávez moved by Monarch and out of the galley.

Monarch slid into the booth across from Lacey. "That right, Lacey?" he asked. "You okay?"

Lacey's hands gripped the mug so tight, he thought it might break. Then she lifted her head. Her eyes were teary and blazing. "Before you, I always thought I knew what okay was. You have destroyed that, Robin Monarch."

"I came back for you," he replied. "You're free."

"After being your afterthought," she snapped. "I was a pawn in the twisted games you people play. Belos was right. You're no different than he is. A thief."

"We're thieves, but we're different," Monarch said.

"Where do you draw lines?" she shouted. "You just make it up. No truth."

"There is no one truth, Lacey. There are just rules, and we make them up for ourselves as we go along."

She looked at him anew, as if he were a feral dog. "Is that how you look at life?"

"At times," Monarch said. "I also believe in loyalty and living up to my word."

"That's a laugh," she said bitterly.

"You're alive, Lacey," Monarch said, growing colder. "I could have just left you with Belos and told your Aunt Pat I had no idea where you were. I didn't. Be grateful."

"You stole Dame Maggie's emerald necklace," she said.

Monarch considered how to play that before answering, "I did."

"Why?"

"For money, Lacey," Monarch replied.

"What else would I do it for?"

The boat shuddered as Fowler down-throttled the engine, and then it rocked slightly as if they were drifting.

"We'll need to get you ashore," Monarch said.

A few moments later, Fowler had the fishing boat tied into a slip in a deserted marina. Chávez helped Lacey onto the dock. Monarch climbed after her, saying, "Chanel will get you into the city, get you clothes and a ticket back to London. Tell your aunt I'll be wiring her the money I borrowed from her to mount your rescue effort, plus interest."

"And you, Robin?" Lacey asked archly.

"That kind of depends on you, Lacey."

"I could alert the authorities in Switzerland and Interpol that you stole that emerald necklace from Dame Maggie," she said.

"You could," Monarch said. "And I wouldn't blame you. But believe me, everything I've done is for a greater good."

Lacey gazed at him in disbelief, and then in defiance. "I like you not knowing what I'm going to do," she said at last. "I want that not-knowing to haunt you, Robin, the same way this nightmare you dragged me into is going to haunt me." She turned and followed Chávez off the dock and into the darkness.

Tatupu, Fowler, and Yin came over to Monarch. The Samoan asked, "What emerald necklace?"

"Long story," Monarch said. "Hell, I'll probably send it back."

"So what are we going to do?" Yin asked. "They'll be on our trail soon enough."

Monarch nodded. "I was thinking that we'd better figure out a way to ambush whoever was behind all this before they can do us any harm."

"You got an idea where?"

"More like how," Monarch said, and explained.

When he finished several minutes later, Yin touched her lips in disapproval. "We can't let you do that, Robin. You don't know how they might respond."

"I know," Monarch said. "But it's the only way I can think of. They won't be expecting it at all."

47

THE NEXT AFTERNOON . . .
OFFICE OF THE CIA DIRECTOR
LANGLEY, VIRGINIA
Dr. Willis Hopkins looked over the top of his glasses at Jack Slattery with an irritated expression. "You're sure?"

"It's in that report from the lab," the covert operations chief replied in ready fury. "Radon-contaminated soil. No polonium-210. No trigger. We were taken. Make that *I* was taken. I let it happen, sir. I accept full responsibility. You can either accept my resignation or allow me to try to get the five million back."

The CIA director rubbed the back of his neck and continued to regard Slattery as if he were some theoretical math problem he had yet to crack. "Get the money back, Jack," Dr. Hopkins said. "And bring Monarch to me."

48

TWO DAYS LATER . . .

LONDON

Jack Slattery left his hotel in Kensington after three hours' sleep and took a cab to the U.S. embassy. Dawn was coming on, and he passed through parks and by palaces. It had been a week since Robin Monarch conned him, seven days since Monarch snatched away his victory and threatened everything. Monarch and his entire team, save one, had vanished. Slattery had watches out for the rest of them in every major airport and train station in the world, giving all their known aliases and passports. He had agents working Monarch's bank account in Ireland. So far, they'd come up with nothing substantive beyond the fact that the money had been split ten ways and transferred to a host of other financial institutions in known money-laundering centers around the world.

To make matters even more enraging, Russian GRU had just sent over a communiqué, indicating that Constantine Belos was claiming to be in possession of polonium-210 for a nuclear trigger. He was looking to auction it to the highest bidder.

Worse still, the night before, during his flight over from Washington, Slattery had gotten word from his men in Damascus that Omak was also claiming to have a cache of polonium-210 for sale. He was supposedly talking to Tehran about it.

The taxi pulled up in front of the embassy shortly after sunrise. Slattery ground his molars thinking of Monarch swindling them all. Monarch would get his due. Slattery promised himself that would happen. He paid, got out of the cab, and marched up to the U.S. Marine standing at the gate. He showed him his identification and was passed inside to the officer on duty.

Ten minutes later, Slattery was sitting inside the utilitarian office of Gloria Barnett, the only member of Monarch's team to have surfaced. She'd reported for duty three days before, on the exact date she was due to return from a twenty-one-day leave.

Slattery glanced out the window down through the chestnut trees just starting to bud with leaves and saw Barnett walking up to the gate. He wanted to shoot the bitch on sight, but held off, telling himself that would get him nowhere closer to Monarch or the accelerator. So he sat down in the chair in the corner, looking right at the door, wanting his presence to upset her, throw her off balance.

Her key scratched at the lock before the door swung open. "Hi, Jack," she said before flipping on the lights.

He scowled.

"I do work here," Barnett said, putting her purse and briefcase on the desk. "Why do I have the honor of your company so soon?"

He studied her for any pretense. "Where's Monarch?"

She shrugged before pulling her arm from her coat. "I haven't seen or heard from him since we left you that day in Moldova."

"Where is he?"

"I don't know. The evening after we left you, we went our own ways. I stayed on at the Four Seasons in Istanbul for two days of luxury before I returned here."

Slattery remained motionless, taking in every tic in her face, every shifting of her carriage, before saying, "Where's the Green Fields weapon?"

Appearing genuinely puzzled, she said,

"The what?"

"The trigger," Slattery said, barely containing his rage.

"Uh," she said, taking off her raincoat, "the last time I knew you had it.

"I had a fucking thermos filled with radon-contaminated dirt!"

"What?" Barnett replied, wholly incredulous.

"You were all in on it. You're all going to suffer for it."

"Whoa, whoa, whoa," Barnett protested. "I was in on nothing but a straight snatch. Jesus Christ, Jack, you were right next to me during the entire attack on the fortress."

"You're saying you didn't know Monarch was pulling a scam?" Slattery said.

"That's exactly what I'm saying," she replied, now getting visibly angry.

"Where's the money I paid him?" Slattery asked.

"How should I know?" she said. "I was paid a flat fee up front."

"How much?"

"Fifty thousand."

"I want it. Where are the rest of them?"

"Like I told you, we split up the night we left you. I don't know."

"I don't believe you."

Barnett raised her palms. "If I were in on

some big scam, don't you think I'd have gone to ground somewhere a bit less conspicuous?"

"Unless Monarch sent you here to try to find out what I'm doing," Slattery said.

"Exactly how was I supposed to find out what *you* were doing from London?"

"Because Monarch knew that I would come to talk to you if you surfaced first," Slattery said.

"What goes on in that brain of yours, Jack?" she retorted. "Aren't you acting a little narcissistic, casting everything in terms of you, you, you?"

Slattery turned icy. "Don't cross me, Barnett."

"I wouldn't dream of doing that, Jack," she replied. "I know my place."

Slattery watched her, not believing her, but unable to dispute her. "Your computer hard drive will be coming with me."

Barnett gestured at the desktop. "Have at it. Thing's infested with viruses."

He grimaced as he stood up. "Your cell phone, too. And you're being reassigned."

"Where?" she asked.

"Langley," he replied. "Where I can keep my eye on you."

"When?" she asked.

"Now," he said.

"I'll have to go to my flat, get packed," she said.

"We'll have movers do it all for you," he said.

49

BUENOS AIRES

On a chilly morning, Robin Monarch landed at Buenos Aires International Airport on a flight from Peru. Someone would be watching the airport by now. It was just logical, and it made Monarch feel as if he were a rabbit and there were hawks circling when he debarked the jet and moved toward immigrations and customs, carrying papers that identified him as Edgar Vincente, a Paraguayan textile representative with a trim beard, eyeglasses, and silver-tinted hair.

Monarch wove through the crowded airport on alert, scanning for evidence of the watchers he'd spotted and shaken on his last trip. A woman at the newsstand was paying for a magazine. Two taxi men to his right held up placards for incoming tourists. And there was a crowd waiting for friends. No one seemed to take much notice of him at all.

Still, Monarch stayed on alert as he left the mezzanine and took the escalator down to the baggage carousels. He passed rental car desks and ducked out a side door used by porters. He hurried up the sidewalk, hearing cars honk, buses sigh open their doors, and motorcycles whine like chain saws.

He got in line for a cab, watching his back trail. When he climbed into the taxi, he was fairly certain he'd come through clean, and he let his shoulders drop.

"Where to, *señor*?" the cabbie asked.

"The Melia," Monarch said.

"A fine hotel," the cabbie said, looking at Monarch as if he knew him.

Monarch smiled. "Especially for a boy from Villa Miseria."

50

"Keep the drones high," Jack Slattery told Agatha Hayes.

"Four hundred feet," Hayes said. "We're just birds in the sky."

Slattery was in the special ops center, watching the image of a taxi rolling toward the center of Buenos Aires from high overhead. He was feeling good. At last, something had gone his way.

The unmanned drone aircraft followed Monarch to the Melia Hotel, where agents in cars and on motorcycle took up a vigil. They did not have to wait long. Two hours after he checked in, midafternoon, Monarch left the hotel, hailed a cab, and crossed town to the neighborhood of Boca, where he hired a rowboat and headed across the river.

Monarch almost shook Slattery's men with that move. But by then, Slattery had ordered in another five men to the detail trailing Monarch, using hand-offs and circling vehicles and motorcycles, changing clothes constantly in order to keep him moving unaware of the operation that swirled around him.

Two agents on motorcycles sped across the nearest bridge and picked Monarch up leaving the river and heading on foot to a luxury apartment building high on a hillside overlooking Buenos Aires. They spotted him ringing the buzzer of Claudio Fortunato.

"Who is this guy?" Slattery demanded.

Hayes tapped on her screen. "Says here he's a painter. Got a lot of rich people all over the world buying his stuff."

"Priors?" Slattery asked.

Hayes went back to her keyboard and a few minutes later said, "Yup. When he was a young, starving artist, he was a gang member arrested for receiving stolen goods."

Slattery rubbed his hands together. "Once a fence, always a fence."

51

BUENOS AIRES

Claudio Fortunato sat on a bar stool in his studio, wearing shorts, flip-flops, and a paint-spattered sweatshirt. He turned the Green Fields device over in his hands, his fingernail running along the raised tubular upside-down Q, saying, "And this slides into the magazine of the pistol?"

Monarch nodded. "I left the gun itself in a safety deposit box in Istanbul. But that is the heart of it."

"Gotta be worth a lot," Claudio said.

"Twenty-one million dollars already," Monarch said, holding a beer.

Claudio was dumbstruck as Monarch explained, and agitated as the tale closed.

"So you've conned the U.S. government, a Russian mobster, and a Chechen warlord out of twenty-one million dollars?" Claudio demanded.

"Don't forget the dictator–slash–arms

dealer," Monarch reminded him.

Claudio groaned. "You're screwed, Robin. I don't know how. I don't know when, but you are screwed. Didn't you learn anything I taught you?"

"I hear you," Monarch said. "I'm going to get that money into Sister Rachel's hands, and then go to Patagonia."

Claudio looked at the Green Fields device, frowned, and scratched at his head. "I'm kind of nervous having this thing in here," he said. "My paintings are selling, you know, Robin? I can't hold this for you."

"I'm not asking you to, Claudio. I've got a much better place in mind."

52

CIA HEADQUARTERS

A hemisphere away, slattery ate a sandwich at his command station in the special ops center while trying to game out all the ways that this could go.

But before he could develop anything in a meaningful way, Thompson, his chief asset in Argentina, called over Slattery's headset: "Monarch and Fortunato just left the apartment building. Monarch got a taxi and is heading back to town. We're on him. Fortunato left in a late-model BMW and headed in the other direction."

"Put a tail on the painter."

"Done. He's heading west toward the mountains. He's got golf bags with him."

Slattery slid into his chair. "Give me whoever's on Monarch."

"Thompson, coming up," Hayes said.

Slattery's screen jumped to reveal a motorcyclist's-eye view of a crowded street in Buenos Aires. Ahead several cars, Slattery could make out a taxi and the silhouette of Robin Monarch in the backseat.

"Where's Fortunato now?" Slattery demanded.

"Still heading west," Hayes said.

Slattery barked, "Thompson, how many men you have at Fortunato's?"

"Dobbs and Fernández are still outside the apartment building."

Slattery said, "Tell them to crawl that apartment. Now."

Fifteen minutes later, Agatha Hayes looked over at Slattery, who was monitoring the motorcycle feed on Monarch and the feed from the agents who'd broken into Fortunato's apartment building through a utility door and were now working to pick the lock on the artist's apartment.

"Shit," Hayes said. "We lost Fortunato."

"Goddamn it, how?" he roared.

His operations runner cringed. "Tractor trailer jackknifed on the highway right in front of our guy, lucky he wasn't killed."

Before Slattery could give that more thought, Thompson's voice came over his headset: "Looks like Monarch's going on foot. He's heading into a cemetery."

"Stay with him," Slattery ordered, watching Monarch enter the cemetery.

"Close as we dare," Thompson said.

Ten minutes later, Slattery watched a long-range image of Monarch kneeling before a black gravestone. He removed the old flowers in the vase and replaced them with new ones he'd bought at a kiosk near the main gate. He fussed with the arrangement.

Slattery's attention jumped to the feed coming from Dobbs and Fernández, the two operatives who had managed to pick the locks on Claudio Fortunato's door, disarm the alarm, and were now creeping through the artist's studio.

"Pretty amazing stuff," Fernández was saying, his camera drifting over the canvases of Buenos Aires at nightfall.

"I don't give a damn about the art," Slattery said.

"We don't even know what we're looking for," Dobbs complained. His feed showed him snooping in the large supply closet off the studio.

"I'll know it when I see it," Slattery snapped.

Dobbs was moving back rolls of canvas stacked against the wall of the closet. He knelt as if inspecting the floor. His hand reached out and pried at the boards. Suddenly, Dobbs's camera whipped around, revealing Claudio Fortunato with a golf club and a maniac expression on his face.

He roared something in Spanish and swung.

The camera feed lurched and went dead, but Slattery heard the slick crack all too clearly. The painter could swing a driver and Dobbs's head was a big ball.

"Fortunato is inside with you, Fernández," Slattery said calmly. "Dobbs is down."

Fernández did not reply, but his video feed showed him moving at an angle across the studio, away from the windows and the paintings, toward the hallway that led to the closet and the front door.

The golf club was a flash on Slattery's screen, but he heard it connect somewhere on Fernández's body, and heard the agent grunt with pain. The camera lurched wildly as he fell to the floor. The lens found Fortunato raising the club up chopping style again.

"Don't —," Slattery started to say.

But the chug and spit of Fernández's silenced 9mm cut him off. Fortunato's hands let go of the golf club. His body stuttered a moment in disbelief before crashing backwards onto the paint-spattered floor.

"Leave him," Slattery ordered. "Dobbs was on to something in that closet. A loose floorboard or something."

Fernández's feed showed the agent coming to his feet slowly, and Fortunato unconscious but still breathing.

"Go to the closet," Slattery said again.

Fernández and his camera moved down the hall to the closet and focused on the crumpled figure of Dobbs lying on his side, his head bashed in, before turning to the floor. A moment later, the floorboard was removed, showing the safe.

"That's where they've got it!" Slattery crowed.

"I can't crack this," Fernández said. "I don't have the right equipment."

Slattery gave it only a moment's thought before he saw an angle that might lead him to the contents of the safe.

"Take all ID off Dobbs, grab two of those paintings, and get out of there," he said.

"Monarch's on the move again," said Thompson in Slattery's headset. "Heading north back toward Fortunato's."

Slattery's eyes darted to the other screen, seeing the rear of a taxi again through the windshield of the motorcycle. He could make out the smudge of Monarch's head.

"So much the better," he said.

53

BUENOS AIRES

Monarch unlocked the front door of the loft. *Claudio golfing,* he thought as he pushed the door open. *Where did that come from?*

He immediately spotted legs jutting out of the storage room. He dropped into a crouch and shut the door with his heel, tugging out the pistol Claudio had given him. He slunk forward, angular to the outer room, now able to see the dead stranger.

He heard the gurgling noise of a sucking wound before he spotted Claudio on his back in the main studio, holding his hands tight to his chest, blood pooling on the paint.

"Claudio!" Monarch cried, and ran to his side.

Claudio was looking at his paintings. His eyes rolled lazy and tearful toward Monarch. "Will I be remembered, Robin?" he asked.

Monarch tore at his friend's bloody shirt.

"Don't you give up on me."

He saw the two bullet holes — one through the meat of Claudio's right shoulder, and the other in his lower right chest. Monarch heaved Claudio over on his side and found the exit on the lung wound, a hole that spat out Claudio's blood with every breath. Monarch ripped Claudio's shirt and rammed the patch into the exit wound. He laid him flat on the floor, hoping the pressure would hold it. He tore another strip and stuffed the entry wound.

"Am I dying?" Claudio asked.

"You're a brilliant painter with a lot of years ahead."

Claudio smiled, crying. "I came back for my golf shoes. They were here."

"Who are they?" Monarch demanded.

"Don't know. The other one took paintings."

"I'm calling an ambulance," Monarch said.

"Go," he said. "Take the money in the safe. Give it to Sister."

Monarch was up and heading toward the phone. "Give it to her yourself."

Less than five minutes later, after calling emergency services and reporting a gunshot wound, Monarch exited the front door of

Claudio's apartment building. He carried a knapsack over one shoulder. He panned down the street and up the other side, seeing nothing but taxis, cars, and motorcycles.

He set off on foot, feeling a rush of guilt at having to leave his oldest and dearest friend, his brother, wounded and maybe dying. But then he heard ambulance sirens coming and believed he would see Claudio again. Claudio was strong, a former captain of La Fraternidad, a painter now but still as tough as they come.

Monarch hailed a cab and climbed in. "Villa Miseria."

As the cabbie wound his way toward that dreadful neighborhood of Buenos Aires, Monarch's thoughts were all answers to a single question: Who had attacked Claudio?

Monarch quickly came up with two scenarios. The first had Claudio, famous and wealthy now by Argentine standards, the target of a straight-up burglary. The crook shot him after he'd managed to tee off on the first guy. They were after money, and some of Claudio's canvases.

The other scenario was more troubling and more expected. It had Slattery or Belos or Omak or Koporski aware of his presence in Argentina. Monarch focused on the likelihood that he was under surveillance and prepared himself for what might come.

As they approached the edge of Villa Miseria, Monarch shouted, "Stop here!" threw money at the cabbie, and jumped free of the vehicle.

He looked behind him down the scruffy boulevard, searching the late-afternoon light for evidence of anything he'd seen so far that day, a face, a vehicle, a —

The motorcycle rider in the boulevard's far lane glanced at him from behind a tinted helmet shield. It was enough to trigger Monarch's quick entry into the slum, hooking through the warren of shacks, beneath the amplifiers blaring Bolivian rock and Peruvian hip-hop, heading in the direction of *el ano* along the same route he'd taken his very first night in the Village of Misery.

At dark, Monarch came to the intersection where he'd found the paco smokers during his last trip to see Sister Rachel. Ten minutes later, he walked to the edge of the garbage pit. He glanced behind him, seeing nothing out of the ordinary. He looked up the hill toward the clinic and decided he would go nowhere near the place, for fear of putting Sister Rachel in jeopardy. He would wait for whoever was trailing him. He stood on the edge of *el ano* and watched the wretched, the dispossessed, and the lost claw through the dump, searching for anything to fill their stomachs.

Monarch saw himself again as Robin, that newly orphaned boy, beaten, bleeding, and starving, and Claudio, saying, "Rule Number One: You have the right to survive."

The vividness of the memory in light of what had just happened so transfixed Monarch that he let down his guard and had very little understanding of who or what was around him. He was drifting in the world of twenty years ago, leaving the pit with Claudio several weeks after his parents were murdered.

Back inside the CIA, Slattery watched a grainy thermal image of Monarch standing on the edge of a dump in the worst slum in Buenos Aires.

"Shoot him," he ordered.

A gun barrel appeared and fired with the sharp burp of a high-powered air gun. Monarch stiffened, dropped the bag he was carrying, staggered, and reached up toward his neck to grab at the dart that had hit him there.

"You got him," Slattery said. "Nice shot, Thompson."

"We aim to please," Thompson said as Monarch went to his knees and then pitched off the side of the slick ditch, down into *el ano.*

"Search him," Slattery said.

Agatha Hayes was on her feet, beaming. "Congratulations, Jack."

Slattery was suddenly breathless and imagined that this was what hunters felt after facing down a Cape buffalo charge and killing the beast, or at least hitting him with tranquilizers strong enough to take him off his feet and out cold for a very long time.

Thompson said, "He's got a lot of cash in a knapsack, three fake passports, and not much else."

"We're looking for a metal thing."

"There's nothing like that," Thompson said. "What do you want us to do with him?"

Slattery felt like kicking in the screen. Monarch had stashed the Green Fields device somewhere. Or he had left it in that safe at Fortunato's. He had no choice now.

"Take him to the airport," Slattery said.

"Roger that," Thompson said.

"Where are we having him transported, Jack?" Hayes asked.

Slattery hadn't even given it consideration. Then he saw a certain irony at play in the game that had led to Monarch's darting, an elegant way to possibly achieve his ends without getting his hands any more wet than they already were.

PART IV

54

THREE DAYS LATER . . .

Monarch came to consciousness at a primal level, where he did not know his own name. His head rushed in pain, swelling like a wave. His tongue felt thick and dry. He smelled wet wool, opened his eyes, and felt his lids slide against fabric before seeing only darkness. He came more alert, understanding his head was in some kind of hood, it was very hot, and he was on his back on something flat and hard.

He tried to move his arms and felt them restrained. His feet and chest felt the same way. He listened and heard only silence at first. Then he caught the rumble of thunder followed by the patter of rain, which built into drumming.

"Water," he said in English. It came out like a frog's croak. "Water." He repeated the request in Spanish, then in Russian and Arabic, and on through every language he knew.

No one replied.

At first, Monarch had no idea how he'd gotten into this predicament. Then he remembered staring at the dump in the Villa Miseria, and then feeling something hot and sharp sting him in the neck. He remembered slapping at it and then falling.

Dart, he thought.

Monarch's brain conjured up drugged memories, snapshots taken in those moments between being darted in Buenos Aires and this moment: the low roar of an air transport, needles jabbed into his arms, the crunch of gravel under a tire. He'd been moved far, far away from the Village of Misery. He could be anywhere.

"Water," he said again, louder this time.

For several moments, Monarch heard nothing. Then he caught the clank of a bolt being thrown and the scuff of feet approaching. The hood came off. Monarch squinted at harsh light that made his head feel like it had been cleaved in two. A short, stocky figure in dark clothes and a black ski mask stood over him, holding a paper cup.

"You want water?" the hooded man asked in English tainted with an accent that could have been Russian or Chechen or just as well some CIA spook disguising his voice.

450

The hooded man moved the paper cup over Monarch's face and dribbled some water on his lips. Monarch opened his mouth, but the water stopped falling.

"Tell me, where is Green Fields?" the man asked.

"What's Green Fields?" Monarch asked.

The rest of the water was thrown in his face, and his hood was wrenched down. He heard the door slam shut and the bolt thrown. Monarch dissected the entire encounter and came away with one clear meaning: They meant to make him suffer. The only question remaining in Monarch's mind was whether he could last long enough to make the suffering worthwhile.

55

ELEVEN DAYS LATER . . .
PRIMARY ELECTION NIGHT SAVAN-
NAH, GEORGIA

The packed ballroom of the Doubletree Hotel erupted into cheers and applause when CNN declared Congressman Frank Baron had won his party's nomination to the U.S. Senate.

"Baron! Baron!" the crowd chanted.

After a few moments, the congressman appeared, running up onto the stage, hands overhead, clasped in victory, while his wife and two children trailed in behind him.

Jack Slattery watched the victory speech from the rear of the ballroom, admiring the practiced charisma his buddy had developed. He wondered at the fairness of life, sometimes, what one man could do with ease and while another man had to fight for it.

"News, Slattery?" C. Y. Tilden asked

coldly. The pale billionaire loomed beside him. His lips were purplish from wine.

"I was going to tell you both after the speech," Slattery said.

"I think it prudent if we left Frank ignorant of certain details from now on."

"He's a member of the Intelligence Committee," Slattery said. "Legally, he's the only one with a legitimate right to know. Not you."

"I still hold the purse strings. Has he cracked yet?"

Slattery felt slightly nauseated. "No."

"What do you mean *no*?" Tilden said. "What have they done to him?"

"Starvation rations. Confined to total darkness."

"Maybe he doesn't know."

Slattery shook his head. "We've since had direct discussions with Koporski. The Green Fields accelerator was in the case when he handed it to Monarch."

Tilden said, "I think you need to go straight to the rough stuff with Monarch. Sounds like it's the only language he speaks."

Slattery shook his head. "Monarch has a tremendous will. If they get too rough with him too fast, he would withstand it, and then they could go overboard, and hit him so hard, he could just die on us. In which case, we'll be nowhere. It may take a while to soften him up. But I assure you, he will break eventually."

Tilden studied him with his pitted eyes. "You better damn well hope so."

56

THE FOLLOWING MORNING . . .
CIA HEADQUARTERS LANGLEY, VIR-
GINIA

Gloria Barnett slouched in a windowless office before a computer she was sure was
compromised, reviewing the history of
security protocol in encryption, a make-
work job that seemed designed to drive her
either insane or to sleep.

She yawned and ran her fingers through
her shock of red hair, feeling her muscles
ache because she had been unable to walk
her routine five miles that morning due to
the insolent, not-so-little handler with
whom Slattery had stuck her.

The door to Barnett's office opened. Agatha Hayes stood there, adjusting her glasses.
"We should have lunch, Gloria, get to know
each other."

"I don't eat much during the day, Agatha."

"We should have lunch," Hayes repeated.

Barnett sighed and got up, following the little woman with the big shoulders to the CIA cafeteria. She got a salad. Hayes bought a roast beef sandwich with horseradish and fries. They sat at a table by a window that overlooked the courtyard that held *Kryptos*, a black granite-and-copper sculpture in a shape that suggested an open book. There were two thousand characters embossed on the sculpture, a code that had not been broken in more than twenty years. For a long time, Barnett had been obsessed with the sculpture and spent many hours studying it, trying to decipher the message. But today, she scanned the lunch crowd instead. She'd been away in London for only fifteen months, but she was still surprised at how few people she recognized.

"What's he like?" Hayes asked after taking a bite of her sandwich.

"Who?"

"Robin Monarch," Hayes said. "He's kind of a legend around here."

"Is he?" Barnett replied. "I didn't know people talked about him."

"In certain circles," Hayes allowed.

"Jack Slattery's circle?"

"I wouldn't know about him," Hayes said, and then looked away, dabbing horseradish from the corner of her mouth.

Barnett may have washed out of the field officers' program, but she did understand when she was being lied to. Rather than challenge Hayes directly, she asked, "Where do you normally work, when you're not watching me, Agatha?"

"Here, uh, in the building."

"Right," Barnett said. "Slattery's office? Or the special ops center?"

Hayes's eyes flickered before settling. "You know I can't tell you what I do."

"That's where I used to work," Barnett offered. "Special ops center. Before Slattery buried me in London."

Hayes did not offer comment, but then asked, "What's the one thing people don't know about Robin Monarch?"

Barnett studied Hayes for several silent moments, evaluating, trying to read behind her questions. Finally, Barnett replied, "They don't understand how incredibly tough he is. The more difficult the situation, the better he gets. Uncatchable. Unbreakable."

She said these last words with premeditation, wanting to see what Hayes's reaction might be. She saw a flicker of smugness when Hayes replied, "I don't think such a man exists."

That response sickened Barnett, and she pushed aside her salad. "I'm not feeling well all of a sudden. I've got to use the ladies' room."

She got up and hurried through the crowd out of the cafeteria, down the hall toward the museum and the restrooms. Hayes's response had told Barnett that if Monarch was not captured, he was about to be. He'd been right all along. He told them all the last time he saw them, on the docks off the Bosporos Strait, that he would be hunted, that they all would be hunted, and they had to take measures to protect themselves.

She entered a stall, closed the door, and hung her head between her knees, knowing that she had to alert the others. That was going to be easier said than done. Before they disbanded, they'd made a pact to keep in touch at appointed hours through an encrypted Web site that Ellen Yin had put together. Barnett had missed the first appointed hour because she'd been flying from London to Washington, D.C., under Slattery's watch, and the second appointed hour passed because she could not get access to a computer she could trust.

The third and next appointed hour was that very evening at seven. But again, she didn't have a clean computer. She sat on the toilet, trying to formulate and analyze the possibilities. The first involved her staying late and pirating onto another computer inside the agency.

She could do it. In her early years with the CIA, after she flunked out of the field officers' program, Barnett had toiled in the thankless world of information technology at the agency. She had worked on a team devoted to developing a new and more powerful method of encrypting passwords and user names in the agency's computer system.

Among the various benefits of that job — and also completely illegal — was that she had managed to compile a list of user names and passwords of almost a hundred midlevel CIA officers. She kept the list in a safety deposit box at a bank in Reston, Virginia. Over the fifteen years since, Barnett had rarely used the user names and passwords, and only when she wanted to snoop around in files she wasn't authorized to inspect.

She knew that if she could get to a free computer inside the agency, she could use one of the names and passwords to gain access to the Internet without raising suspicions. But that plan had its challenges. It demanded she get out from under Agent Hayes's nose, which had proved highly difficult so far. It also demanded she have a way to get into offices without triggering Slattery's attention. He'd undoubtedly flagged her badge, so anytime she entered a restricted area, it would notify him. She shook her head and decided she could not take the chance of using an in-house computer with the scrutiny she was under.

So what other way? For several minutes, Barnett could not come up with an answer that filled her with the likelihood of success. If she got free of Hayes, she could go to a public library and use a computer, but that would be awkward in the long run should she have to use the Web site again. If she got free of Hayes, she could go to a Staples or a Costco and buy a computer. But she'd leave a record using her credit card or her debit card, and she was sure Slattery had all her bank accounts flagged, which meant any cash withdrawal large enough to buy even a netbook would look suspicious. In the end, she decided to try to think like Monarch, and when she did, a plan laid itself plain.

Barnett would have to steal a computer.

At five o'clock, Barnett shut off her agency-issued desktop computer after four hours of reviewing the protocol surrounding data lost or corrupted, and stood up from her desk, waiting. A knock came at the door before it opened, revealing Agatha Hayes.

"I can give you a ride back to the apartment, Gloria," Hayes said.

"I'll take a cab or ride the bus," Barnett said.

"I can give you a ride," Hayes insisted.

"You can't keep me like this," Barnett said.

"Like what?" Hayes asked.

"Under house arrest," Barnett said.

Hayes said, "I'm just trying to be helpful."

"Then I need to go to a pharmacy or a Walmart or something on the way to the apartment," Barnett said.

"Done," Hayes said, and stood aside to let Barnett out.

Barnett glanced at Hayes, saw she was amused, and felt something change inside her. It was true Barnett had never been a field operator, but she suddenly knew without a doubt that she could and would kill this woman to help Monarch. It shocked her at some level because she had never felt herself capable of violence before.

But that feeling was still present when she and Hayes took a bus from CIA headquarters through the security gate to a satellite parking lot where they retrieved Hayes's Toyota. Hayes fumbled with her keys opening her door and dropped them. It occurred to Barnett that Hayes was probably as physically awkward as she was. The only difference was that Barnett had had quite a bit of training before she washed out. She bet that Hayes had none.

"There's that drugstore next to the Starbucks in Arlington," Barnett said. They'd stopped at the coffee shop every morning Hayes had driven her to work.

Hayes nodded. "I'll take you there."

When they reached the shopping center that housed the pharmacy and Starbucks, Barnett got out, moaning, "I could use a latte with a shot of hazelnut."

Hayes half laughed. Latte with a shot of hazelnut was her coffee recipe of choice. "I could use one myself," she said.

"Get me one?" Barnett said. "I'll be right out."

Hayes hesitated, and then said, "Sure."

Barnett headed inside the pharmacy, picked up a shopping basket, and angled past the cashier's area, snagging a lighter and a small can of butane fuel as she passed. She made as if to put them in the basket, but instead slipped them inside the cuff of her blouse before heading to the medical supply aisle and finding a box of latex gloves. She tore the box open and drew out a pair, put them up her sleeve, and then headed toward the back, past the men's shaving gear aisle and the antacid aisle, where she found a door that led her into a stockroom. She went out a fire door into an alley.

She slipped up to the back entrance of the Starbucks and peeked through, seeing a hallway, and a trash can near the door, and newspapers strewn over several tables in the room beyond. She could also make out a college kid sitting on a stool and working at a laptop computer. Beyond the kid, Hayes was already at the register, paying for her drink.

Barnett tugged on the rubber gloves. She wiped the butane canister against her blouse to remove her prints and did the same with the lighter. Adrenaline flooded through Barnett. She peeked in the door again and saw Hayes with her latte, back to her, heading toward the front door. It was now or never.

She counted to five and then moved up and through the door into the hallway. The restrooms were to her right, both closed. She stuck the butane canister into the newspapers bulging from the trash can, sprayed for a count of three, and flicked the lighter.

The papers caught fire with a whoosh.

Barnett dropped the butane canister into the fire, turned, and hurried toward the front of the coffee shop with the air of a harried mother in need of a caffeine fix. She could see out the window that Hayes was entering the pharmacy carrying the two lattes. Two other women were in the Starbucks, both of them carrying briefcases and occupying the attention of the barista working the counter.

Barnett circled behind them and to the side of the kid working the laptop.

The smoke alarm went off at the same time the butane canister detonated with a low, thudding boom. One of the women screamed.

Barnett screamed.

The kid kicked away from his chair, scrambling low and toward the front door.

Sprinklers went on, spraying. The customers and the baristas were screaming and trying to get out as well.

Barnett grabbed the kid's computer, yanked out the plug, and with them both cradled in her arms, walked dead ahead, straight into the smoke.

57

THAT SAME DAY . . .

Monarch forced himself to eat slowly, even though he was nearly starving and the impulse was to gorge. But he knew enough about deprivation through personal experience and training to understand that after so many days with no food and very little water, his stomach would reject nourishment if he gave it too much too soon.

His head spun slightly as he broke bread and added cold meat and cheese, and took a small bite, chewing and drinking cold water from a jug. Barely aware of his stark surroundings, he ate and drank with the sole purpose of swallowing everything they gave him and keeping it all down. He'd lost strength since he'd awoken with the hood on his head, however long ago that was. Ten, maybe twelve days, he guessed.

He thought about what he'd just endured, the long, long time in darkness. It had been maddening at first to be kept in the dark with little food and water, with no sense of time or place, a fan running so he could not hear much, and left to soil himself.

But Monarch had surrendered to the ordeal eventually and went through a series of mind–body exercises he'd been taught in SERE school that would allow him to slow his pulse and so his metabolism and so his hunger, and achieve a state of mental hibernation where his inner core could not be touched.

He'd survived the experience, but not by much. If they had not started increasing Monarch's water ration about midway through his time in the hood, he would have succumbed eventually. But then they started giving him water and the questioning intensified: *Where is Green Fields?*

The darkness in the hood and the questioning had gone on, day after day, until just about an hour ago, when the short, squat jailer entered his cell, unstrapped him, pulled him to his feet, and with Monarch's hands manacled behind him, dragged him somewhere between three and four hundred feet from where he'd been held. There he'd been ordered to strip, which he did as best he could after they removed his restraints. He was standing on cement of some kind, and over the foul smell of his soiled clothes, he smelled mud and heard chickens clucking.

The spray had hit Monarch with the strength of a fire hose, blowing him back off his feet and slamming him against a wall. He fell over writhing as the blasting water stripped whatever waste remained on him. He was pulled roughly to his feet and sprayed again, this time with less force. Then they took off the hood.

He was in some kind of farm bay, cement beneath his feet, a high cement wall at his back, flaring cement arms tapering down from the back wall out toward a gravel drive, a green field, and a hardwood forest in full leaf beyond.

Two guards covered him with rotary-magazine shotguns. One was the short, squat one he was used to seeing. The other was taller, thinner, and staying well out of reach when he tossed Monarch a pair of threadbare denim shorts and a stained blue T-shirt. Once he'd dressed, Monarch was ordered by the tall guard to sit cross-legged, his hands interlaced behind his head. They handcuffed him.

Then they marched Monarch back to his cell without his hood. He passed through a barn and saw stalls with horses and cows.

They took him to an extension of the barn, with a cement-walled hallway and steel doors off the hall. They opened one and pushed him through.

The tall guard covered Monarch with the shotgun. The stockier one had Monarch sit on a straw mattress on a rough wooden cot by the wall, and then locked his left ankle into a steel cuff attached to a heavy chain that ran out to a stout anchor set in the floor. The tall one left and returned with a plate piled with dried meats, cheese, an orange, several dates, a loaf of brown bread, and a jug of cold water, all of which he set on a card table that had been placed in the room beside a metal folding chair.

"Eat," the stocky one had said. "Drink. Get back your strength."

"Fattening me up to meet Mom and Dad?" Monarch asked.

The tall one said, "You tell us location of Green Fields, we bring more, food, wine, women, anything you want."

"Like I told you, it was gone when I got there," Monarch said.

"Then have long rot in hell," the stocky one said, and left the room.

The tall one had followed, slamming the door behind him. Monarch heard the famil-iar sound of a bar being thrown, and got up off the bed, moving slowly so the manacle would not rub and blister his ankle, making his way to the table, where he'd begun to eat his first real food since his capture.

His stomach soon felt filled. Monarch slowed his eating to take in the rest of his circumstances. Besides the cot, the straw mattress, the table and chair, the only other objects in the ten-by-fifteen foot room were a steel bucket that they'd stuck by the door and a roll of brown toilet paper.

Overhead, nine 100-watt bare lightbulbs blazed. On the far wall, opposite the cot, was a pair of padlocked green shutters. It was hot and humid in his cell, but nowhere near the stifling heat he'd suffered under the hood. His legs ached. So did almost every muscle in his body, protesting at the fact that he had not moved or stretched in such a long time.

Monarch left the remaining food and goaded himself to his feet. He would exercise as best he could, and then eat again. He stripped off the T-shirt and used it to pad the ankle iron so it would not tear him up.

Monarch began slow ballistic movements to stir his muscles into firing, then slowly worked into sit-ups, squats, and push-ups, less than half what he would ordinarily do in a workout, but he was still gasping and bathed in sweat when he finished.

Monarch dropped back into the chair, chest heaving, feeling the endorphins starting to kick in, and drank straight from the jug before starting to eat again. He glanced up at the glaring lights and suddenly understood.

Feeding him meant they were taking a different tack. They meant to torture him in some way other than starvation, which oddly enough gave him a sense of satisfaction. Changing the method meant he'd won this round, at least. But this fight was not over by any means, he decided. Not even close.

58

TWO HOURS LATER . . .

FALLS CHURCH, VIRGINIA

Gloria Barnett lay on the couch in her running gear in the living room of the apartment she was being forced to share with Agatha Hayes, watching the *Charlie Rose* show on PBS. The lock threw and the door flung open.

Hayes entered, looking at Barnett in angry disbelief. "Where the hell did you go?"

Barnett answered earnestly, "Out the back of the pharmacy. The sirens starting sounding and one of the clerks said there was a fire next door in Starbucks. I looked around for you, couldn't find you and took a cab back here."

Hayes sniffed suspiciously. "I smell smoke."

"It was all over that alley," Barnett said, nodding. "I even took a shower before I went out for a run."

Hayes shook her head. "I think you set that fire."

Barnett looked at her like she was an idiot. "Why would I ever do that?"

"To escape."

"Escape? Escape what? Is this a prison, Agatha? Is this what I willingly escaped to? This might be a prison, but I did not escape."

Hayes scowled. "I don't know what you're up to, but I'm going to find out."

"Don't be so paranoid," Barnett said, returning her attention to the television. "You'd think you were in the CIA or something."

Hayes made a huffing sound and stormed toward her bedroom. Barnett acted as if she were engrossed in the show, but inside she was gloating. Using a shopping bag, she'd gotten the kid's computer into the bathroom, which she'd previously checked for all evidence of fiber-optic cameras, finding none. She had discovered several audio bugs, but foiled them by using the shower as cover noise while she'd hacked into the kid's computer and got herself onto an open wireless Internet system that someone on the apartment floor was using.

She gained access to the secure Web site Yin had put together, entered her passwords at precisely seven o'clock, and was linked to an instant messaging system. John Tatupu had been online from Samoa. Chanel Chávez was typing from Mexico. Abbott Fowler was in Jamaica. Yin came on from the mountains of North Carolina. They'd all been worried about Barnett and Monarch.

HE'S BEEN TAKEN, Barnett typed. LAST KNOWN LOCATION: BUENOS AIRES.

Tatupu replied, WE ARE IN MOTION. WE'LL START THERE.

They agreed to a time to be online the next day before Barnett shut down the computer and hid it at the back of the top shelf of the linen closet, under a towel behind soaps and shampoos.

She looked up from the television toward Hayes, who had emerged from her room and was now loudly rummaging in the kitchen, making herself some eggs. Barnett felt breathless at the risk they were all taking, especially Monarch. She couldn't imagine what he was going through, and she vowed it would last not one minute longer than it had to.

59

THREE DAYS LATER . . .
BUENOS AIRES

It was late afternoon when John Tatupu, Chanel Chávez, and Abbott Fowler stepped from a cab at the outskirts of the Villa Miseria. The air was cold enough to drive the people of the slum to leave the streets and shut their doors. Weak, slanted sunlight shone on the tin roofs and threw the dirt lane in shadow as the taxi drove away.

"You know you're in trouble when the cabdrivers won't enter," Fowler said.

"Where else do you help the poor?" Chávez asked scornfully. "Beverly Hills?"

"I think he's saying this could get rough," Tatupu said, noticing a busted broom in the gutter. He picked it up by the handle and broke off the head completely.

Chávez shrugged and glanced at an iPhone locked into a GPS application, showing the way through the maze of streets to the Clínica de Esperanza, the "Clinic of Hope."

It had taken them only a day after their arrival in Buenos Aires to track down Sister Rachel Diego del Mar through a state social service office. Sister Rachel, it turned out, was as Monarch had described her: She belonged to a religious order called the Sisters of Hope, which worked in the worst slums in South America, offering medical assistance to the poor and shelter for orphans. Chávez had called the Hogar de Esperanza, but was told that the sister was taking an extra shift at the clinic in the Villa Miseria.

They walked along the narrow streets of the slum, which were still muddy from rain earlier in the day. The air smelled of frying food and woodsmoke. Behind closed doors, they could hear tinny music playing. Then the wind changed, and despite the cold, they smelled *el ano.* Chávez choked. Fowler threw up his hand to cover his mouth.

"What the hell is that?" Tatupu demanded. "Smells like a slaughterhouse."

"Worse," Chávez said.

"And you'd know that how?" Fowler asked.

"There was an abattoir in my town," Chávez said, coughing.

They rounded a corner in the slum and saw the pit and the hills of garbage at its center. Toddlers, children, teens, and adults scavenged through the refuse, trying to find something, anything, to survive.

"Jesus," Chávez said.

"How can people live like this?" asked Fowler.

"They don't for very long," an unfamiliar voice said to them in Spanish.

All three of Monarch's comrades spoke the language, and they turned to find a woman in her fifties, wearing jeans and an embroidered blue blouse. She had braided silver hair, a handsome face that seemed both weary and wise, and a doctor's bag in one hand.

"Why?" Chávez asked, sensing something solid about the woman.

"Because they die," the woman said. "*El ano* is a petri dish of disease."

"Do you live here?" Tatupu asked.

"I work here," she said. "I have a clinic up on the hill."

"Sister Rachel?" all three exclaimed.

The woman startled and stepped back. "Yes?" she said uncertainly.

"No, don't worry, Sister," Chávez said. "It's just that we've come such a long way to find you."

Sister Rachel looked more suspicious. "Why have you come to find *me*?"

"Robin Monarch told us about you," Fowler said. "We're friends."

Sister Rachel seemed even more taken aback. "Robin?"

Chávez said, "Is there somewhere we can go to talk?"

After a long moment's indecision, she gestured with her head toward the hillside beyond the dump pit. "My clinic is up there."

Sister Rachel led the way back around the rim of the pit. "Is Robin all right?"

"We don't know," Tatupu said. "We were supposed to hear from him, and we haven't — for almost three weeks now."

"That's the way he is," Sister Rachel said. "I don't hear from him for months, and then here he is. I would not worry. He's had many challenges in life and survived them all." They'd reached a hairpin among the shacks that looked down over the pit. Sister Rachel stopped, pointed, and said softly, "That's where I found him, you know? Robin? He even lived down there for a while."

"He lived in that pit?" Fowler asked, stunned by the idea.

"For a time," Sister Rachel said. "Then he

was taken into a street gang that was once powerful here. *La Fraternidad de Ladrones,* 'the Brotherhood of Thieves.' He became one of the leaders. But there was a power struggle, and a knife fight right down there in *el ano.* Robin killed a boy in self-defense but was stabbed in the side. Someone came to the clinic and got me. I found him lying in the garbage, bleeding, barely holding on to life. I stitched him up and convinced him to come to live with me at Hogar de Esperanza. He ended up bringing many of the gang boys to me, so many that the Brotherhood of Thieves just fell apart."

A line of people waited on a bench outside the closed door to Sister Rachel's clinic. As soon as they saw her, they began to clamor and call her name. She went to them one by one, asking the nature of their ailment. When she was satisfied that none was life threatening, she told them she would open the clinic in fifteen minutes, and then led Tatupu, Chávez, and Fowler inside. Sister Rachel shut the door behind them before gesturing them to the plastic seats in the waiting area.

"How did you come to be friends of Robin?" she asked.

They told her part of the truth: that they had been part of a special team inside the

U.S. military. Monarch had been their leader. They had continued to work together as a team for the CIA until they were disbanded.

"We're all still close," Chávez explained. "That's why the silence worries us."

"Maybe he has gone on vacation somewhere," she said. "Maybe he is in love?"

"Robin's not the loving type," Tatupu said.

Sister Rachel frowned. "That's not true."

"He doesn't like to complicate his life, anyway," Chávez said.

"I find it strange that he has not spoken of any of you to me," Sister Rachel said.

"Never?" Fowler said, surprised.

"I knew he was a soldier for many years. But he never gave me any particulars." She paused. "I suppose he would not want me to worry." She looked all around at them. "Why did you think I would know where Robin is?"

"Because the last time we all saw him, he told us he was coming to see you, to give you a sizable donation to your orphanage," Fowler said.

Sister Rachel reddened. "That was seven or eight weeks ago."

"No, he was coming here when we saw him last, three weeks ago."

Sister Rachel was adamant. "I haven't

seen Robin since mid-March."

Chávez asked, "He hasn't written? Called? E-mailed?"

She reddened again. "Isn't it awful? I don't e-mail, and he hasn't written or called. Then again, he rarely did. He'd just show up one day, out of the blue."

Monarch's teammates stole glances at one another. A dead end?

"Well, then, Sister," Chávez said. "We won't take up more of your time."

"I can see the worry in your eyes," Sister Rachel said. "Is he in trouble?"

"We don't know," Fowler said. "Do any of the other boys you took in with Robin still live here? Someone he might have contacted more often than you?"

Sister Rachel's face darkened. "Claudio. Robin's oldest friend, the one who brought him into la Fraternidad. But he has only just been released from hospital."

Claudio Fortunato lay in a hospital bed that had been set up in the middle of his art studio. Two nurses were hovering around him when Chávez, Tatupu, and Fowler entered later that evening. The lamps were dimmed inside so Claudio could watch the shimmering lights of Buenos Aires. But his attention was fully on his visitors, as if he were intent on remembering their faces.

"You said you are friends of Sister Rachel," Claudio rasped.

"And close friends of Robin Monarch," Tatupu said. "We heard you are, too."

Claudio considered that. "If you are so close, why has he never talked of you?" he asked, and then looked at Chávez in particular. "I mean, if Robin had friends who looked like you, I think I would have known."

Chávez smiled and blushed. Even recovering from chest surgery, Claudio was terribly handsome and he knew it. She dug in her purse and came up with a snapshot of Monarch and the team on a beach, drinking beers and laughing. She gave it to him, saying, "Robin, it seems, has many secret lives."

"Don't we all?" Claudio asked, looking at the picture. "I almost lost all of them."

"During the burglary?" Fowler asked.

"During whatever it was," Claudio said. "The one who shot me stole several of my newer paintings."

"You think they were after something else?" Chávez asked.

Claudio raised his eyebrows. "Could be."

"When was the last time you saw Robin?"

Claudio glanced at his nurses. "Could you

481

leave us a few minutes?"

When they'd gone, Claudio said, "Robin was staying here when I was attacked."

Over the course of the next half an hour, the painter laid out the events as he knew them, all leading up to the fact that Monarch had been on his way to see Sister Rachel to give her money when Claudio last saw him.

"He never made it there," Chávez told him.

"I know," Claudio replied. "Sister Rachel came to see me in the hospital."

"So somewhere between here and the clinic, he disappeared," Tatupu said.

"Big, big city," Fowler remarked, looking out the window.

"A light for everyone," Claudio said appreciatively.

Chávez asked, "What are the police telling you?"

Claudio coughed and then rasped, "To them, it is a burglary of someone who makes enough money to afford a better security system."

"So you don't know the identity of the man who clubbed you?" Chávez pressed.

"No," Claudio said. "But I did remember something yesterday: The man who shot me spoke in English. He was speaking into a radio."

"You tell this to the police?" Tatupu asked.

Claudio shook his head. "It was just yesterday that I remembered."

"Don't tell them for a while," Chávez said.

"Why should I?" Claudio said. "No one has told me anything."

There was silence except for the painter's breathing for several moments before Fowler asked, "Did Robin have the Green Fields accelerator with him when he left?"

"I don't know. The only thing he left behind was an emerald necklace."

60

FOUR DAYS LATER . . .

Monarch rolled onto his side away from the brilliant lights. He kept his hands cupped over his ears, trying to block out the grinding strains of a Russian techno rock group that screamed incessantly about anarchy and revolution.

They were feeding him twice a day now, giving him enough to drink, and even emptying the bucket in which he relieved himself. But they were keeping the lights blazing and the music pounding twenty hours a day from speakers they'd bolted into the corners of his cell.

During his Special Forces training, Monarch had been subjected to sleep deprivation and taught techniques to deal with it. He was able to stay strong the first three days simply by learning the lyrics to the music and singing along with them; and at least once an hour he'd stick his head into his folded-up straw mattress, trying to give himself ten to twenty minutes of muffled screaming and semidarkness in which to rest. The four hours of quiet and darkness were the cruelest part of the torture. He would no sooner sink into deep, deep sleep than the lights would blaze and the techno would start again, pulsing through his head.

Only now, after more than a week of this, each bass note was like a saw pulled through his head, each synthesized screech like the saw bucked back through again, so his brain felt roughly parted. There were moments when he questioned who he was and why he was holding on so tightly to the location of the Green Fields accelerator.

Part of it was that by nature, Monarch was disinclined to yield to any man in battle. And that was what this was. The stocky one and the tall one and whoever was giving them orders were locked in a battle for Monarch's mind.

But the other part of his stubbornness came from his conviction that by enduring this torture, he might unmask the people who'd been trying to control him, and then destroy them. Along the way, he just might make more money to give to Sister Rachel. He hung on tight to that argument as the torture went on, the blaring and the lights and the screaming until he felt wasted to the point of breaking.

All of a sudden, the music stopped.

The lights in the cell dimmed. Monarch drank more water and lurched for the straw mattress, knowing how much he needed rest or risk going mad. After he'd collapsed, already plunging toward sleep, the door to his cell opened.

It was the tall one. "Where is Green Fields?" he demanded.

Monarch gazed at him, hallucinating that his torturer had wings.

"Where is Green Fields?" the tall one shouted.

"At death's door," Monarch said, and blacked out.

61

EARLIER THAT MORNING . . .
FALLS CHURCH, VIRGINIA

Gloria Barnett sat on the toilet in Agatha Hayes's apartment, looking at the e-mail message Chávez had left her on the secure Web site. Chávez had gone to the police in Buenos Aires on Claudio Fortunato's behalf and was told that the man he had killed had been positively identified as Frank James Dodd, an American import–export executive.

"Can you search agency files for him?" Chávez wrote. "Also, Tats and Fowler want to see if you can determine identity of Slattery's Turkish source for Green Fields."

A knock came at the door. "I need to get to work," Agatha Hayes called from outside.

"Be right out," Barnett replied, flushed the toilet, and ran the water in the sink while she hid the computer.

When she exited the bathroom, she looked

at Hayes and said, "I need to stop at my bank. It's on the way."

"What for?" Hayes demanded. "You've got direct deposit."

"I need to get into my safety deposit box," Barnett said. "My mother's living will is in it. She's sick, Agatha, and has been for months. She lives in a home in Queens. You can check if you'd like."

Hayes hesitated, but then nodded. "You better make it quick."

Twenty minutes later, Barnett opened her safety deposit box, took out her mother's living will, and asked the clerk standing outside the door if it could be copied for her. As soon as the clerk left, Barnett dug deeper and came up with a list of names, user names, and passwords.

She ran her finger down the list, looking for one in particular. When she found it, her heart began to beat faster. She wrote down Jack Slattery's user name and password and tucked them in her purse. The clerk returned and handed her the original of her mother's living will and the copy. She put the original in the box, locked it, and returned it to the clerk.

Barnett left feeling the way she used to as a child before taking a roller coaster ride.

There was no clean way to do this. Slattery had to have some way to monitor who had access to his files. He'd know if she got inside and started snooping around. If there was incriminating evidence, he might have reason to do her harm, maybe even kill her.

But as Barnett left the bank and walked toward Agatha Hayes's car, she found that she did not care. Robin Monarch was risking everything. She would risk everything. She felt dangerous and giddy as she climbed into the car, holding the copy of the will.

"Got it," she said. "Thank you, Agatha."

62

NOON . . .

On many hallways in CIA headquarters, there's a single nondescript door that opens with an electronic pass and lets the user enter a no-frills conference room with a table and chairs, an audio-video unit, and a desktop computer in the corner. Barnett entered the conference room down the hall from her basement office at five past twelve, when Agatha Hayes took lunch. She told Hayes she was going outside for a walk, and then slipped down the hallway to the conference room.

Her heart pounded again as she sat at the keyboard. She prayed that Slattery was not on his computer and had gone to lunch, too. Her hands shook. But then she fixed on a memory of Monarch laughing, her friend of nearly ten years. She got resolve again and entered Slattery's user name and password.

The screen hesitated and then jumped to a guest desktop. Barnett bit her lip, forcing herself to think like Monarch. She realized she should check his records first. But when she searched his name in the CIA personnel database, she got a message that read HELD FOR DIRECTOR/ACCESS DENIED.

She frowned and then typed in her own name. Her file popped up. She opened it and found a memo from Slattery that described her as COMPROMISED AND SOMEONE WHO RIGHTFULLY, THEREFORE, OUGHT TO BE TERMINATED IN THE NEAR FUTURE.

Barnett's frown deepened. So she was getting canned. Fifteen years. She had felt it coming, but still it was a shock. Then she shrugged. It really didn't matter. She had money offshore now, enough to last her a good long time if she was careful.

Barnett scanned a few more pages of her file, then went back to the agency's search engine and typed in CHANEL CHÁVEZ. Her file came up. She opened it and discovered that the first notation said WANTED FOR QUESTIONING. CONTACT CIA COVERT OPERATIONS DIRECTOR IF DETAINED.

She typed in John Tatupu's name and then Abbott Fowler's and Ellen Yin's, and found the same notation in their files. Then she typed GREEN FIELDS.

A single file came up. She opened it and found a running chronology of events surrounding Green Fields, including commentary by Slattery, all of it predicated on the notion that the files at Nassara Engineering were, indeed, the archives of Al-Qaeda. She also found a summarized account of a phone discussion between Monarch, CIA Director Hopkins, and Slattery that included Monarch's contention that he was sent in after something besides the archives. In brackets, Slattery had called the idea PREPOSTEROUS. There were also notes from Slattery that indicated that he had met with U.S. Representative Frank Baron about the case, and with C. Y. Tilden, a Georgia industrialist who had extensive ties in the world of Turkish engineering.

Then, deeper in the file, Barnett discovered a translated copy of a Turkish National Police Report by Muktar Otto, head of its criminal intelligence group. Otto's report quoted an anonymous employee of Nassara Engineering who described how he had stumbled onto the files in Abdullah Nassara's personal computer when the inventor had forgotten to sign out. To look at this file, Slattery was telling the truth. Monarch had been sent after the archives. Everything he'd done since was based on wrong assumptions.

But Monarch had come out of Koporski's fortress with a Green Fields weapon, not polonium-210. These files were all part of a whitewash. Slattery's role was being documented to create an illusion of reality that did not jibe with the one Barnett knew to exist. Slattery had taken his operations black. He was part of the plot to steal the weapon. She was sure of it now.

She searched Slattery's computer directory, hoping to find a list of recently opened documents. But none seemed linked to Monarch, or to Green Fields. She searched the word TRIGGER, however, and found three files. She opened them and scanned them, finding translated GRU documents that described a missing "hot" nuclear trigger, and Russian intelligence's belief that Omak was trying to obtain it in order to complete a missile he'd been assembling.

The file also described a discussion with Dr. Hopkins about Monarch working for Belos in an effort to retrieve the trigger and the CIA director's approval of an effort to turn Monarch. The last notation was a report from the CIA lab on the canister Monarch had exchanged with Slattery.

Below the report was the word SWINDLED! in red ink.

The last thing she found in the file was a signed directive from Hopkins authorizing the arrest and interrogation of Monarch with the goal of retrieving the five million dollars — and then nothing more. No description of Slattery's efforts to find Monarch. No reports of sightings. No musing on his whereabouts. Nothing.

Barnett almost signed off, but then she remembered the name of the American Claudio Fortunato had hit with the golf club in Buenos Aires. Frank James Dobbs. She typed it in and got an immediate hit. Dobbs was indeed a cover for a CIA field officer who worked covert operations in Central and South America, mostly involving narco-terror. There was no mention that he'd been dead for almost four months.

Why not? Because it had not been reported. Which meant that Slattery ordered the forced entry of Claudio's studio, probably figuring to steal the accelerator. When it went wrong, Dobbs got killed, and then another operator snatched Monarch.

She glanced at the clock and saw in a rising panic that she'd been rummaging in Slattery's files for almost forty minutes. She almost signed out, but then in a last-ditch effort called up the general directory of Slattery's work area. It spit out more than five thousand files. Inspecting each one would take all night, but Barnett did not have to because the directory was in alphabetical order, and the fourth file read, AGATHA.

She opened it and found a copy of Agatha Hayes's personnel file. She was, as Barnett had suspected, a field support specialist who worked directly for Slattery in the command center. Ten years with the agency. Work reviews as stellar as Barnett's own. Hayes looked honest and straightforward by this paper. But then she saw a comment Slattery had made in the file: a four-word query that read, WEAK LINK IN GAME?

Barnett stared at those words for several moments before their possible meaning became clearer. "She knows," she muttered. "Agatha knows."

63

FIVE HOURS LATER . . .

Monarch rolled over on his straw mattress. He heard a rooster greet the dawn. He opened his eyes, wondering if the sound was real or a dream. It was dim in the cell, but not black and not so brilliantly lit that it threatened his sanity. And it was quiet enough to hear a cock's crow.

A lazy smile crept to Monarch's lips. They'd stopped the sleep deprivation. He'd beaten them again. He had not talked. They had no idea where the Green Fields accelerator was. As he came fully to consciousness, he realized that he'd been asleep a very long time and that he was ravenous. A plate of food sat on the table, dried meat, hard-boiled eggs, figs, and carrots.

He sat up, scratched at the beard that now snarled his face, and pushed back the hair from his eyes, before getting up and moving to the table. He dipped his hands in the water jug and splashed his face.

Monarch sat before the meal, closed his eyes, and intertwined his fingers, thanking the power that is for helping him through the ordeal. He shook with gratitude and felt tears come to his eyes. That emotion was enough to lift whatever traces of sleepiness still wafted in his brain. He was alive and that said a lot. After what he'd just gone through, there had to be a reason, some meaning to his existence.

In the last few days of sleep deprivation, Monarch had wondered bitterly about his life, born to a con artist and a cat burglar, witness to their murders, a castaway in the streets, a gangbanger, a soldier, a spy, an impostor, a burglar, a thief, a grifter, a killer. His mind got so close to imploding that for a while he believed he was meant for nothing but chaos and mayhem.

But then Monarch grabbed at the memories that seemed most valid, especially those of Sister Rachel and the paco boys he'd rescued. They deserved more of everything. And so his mind had held to that one thought, and through that one thought he survived. He bowed his head, gave thanks again, and ate.

When he finished, he felt energized. He wondered how long he'd been in the cell. A month? More? Time had evaporated at some point, and he thought that this was what life must be like for people who try to set records for staying in caves, cut off from the rise and fall of the sun, adrift of their circadian rhythms and looking for anchor.

He thought about his team. Did they know he'd been taken? Were they searching for him? Had they found anything to make his suffering worthwhile?

He heard the slap of shoes in the outer hall. Monarch steeled himself, understanding that the men who held him, whoever they were, would not quit, not if they'd taken his torture this far already.

No, Monarch decided as the dead bolt was thrown, now it was going to get brutal.

64

FOUR HOURS LATER . . .
FALLS CHURCH, VIRGINIA
Barnett signed off the computer after posting a report on the encrypted Web site detailing what she'd found in Slattery's files. She put the computer in an overnight bag she'd brought into the bathroom. Then she picked up the knife she'd snagged in the kitchen.

She slipped to the door and yanked it open. Agatha Hayes startled and almost fell over. She'd been listening.

Barnett pounced over her, pressing the butcher knife to Hayes's neck. "I hate you, Agatha. I honestly feel like killing you."

Hayes trembled. Her eyes were crossing. "Please, Gloria, don't —"

"Where is Robin Monarch?"

"I don't know," she sobbed.

"You do. You know."

"I don't."

Barnett pressed the knife tighter to Hayes's throat. "I'm giving you one more chance to tell me where he is, Agatha, and then I'm slitting your throat."

Hayes began to hyperventilate. Barnett heard her piss herself. "I swear, I don't know where he is," Hayes sobbed. "Some operatives darted him in Buenos Aires, and they took him to the airport. I don't know where they took him after that. I don't."

Barnett glared at Hayes. "One word of this to Jack, Agatha, or to the police, and someone, maybe not me, but someone will be back and you *will* die." She picked up the overnight bag, snatched the keys to Hayes's car, and headed toward the door.

Hayes got up and sneered after her. "Jack knows you were in his files today. He's got men coming for you, Gloria. You're a hunted woman. You won't get far."

"Watch me," Barnett said, and left.

Barnett began to run, thinking that she had to get away from there as fast as possible and that she was going to need money to rescue Monarch, wherever he was. She had cash offshore. So did the others. But it was not easily accessible.

Then she thought of someone who might give them a quick loan, and she sprinted toward Hayes's car.

65

AN HOUR LATER . . .
THE WILLARD HOTEL

Jack Slattery took a long draw on a rum and Coke, and listened to the new girl getting ready in the bathroom. He wished she'd hurry. He needed something to tame the stress he felt cinching in around him the last few weeks.

Gloria Barnett had gotten away in Agatha Hayes's car before his men arrived. Hayes had told her that Slattery was behind Monarch's disappearance. What would he do if he were Barnett in this situation? She was one woman working alone. Or was she?

He doubted it. He considered the idea that she was in contact with the rest of her team, and tried to cross-reference that with the files she had opened in his work area while he'd been at lunch. But he made little progress.

Lying there in the hotel bed, Slattery kept

flashing on images of Monarch, thinking that the man might never succumb and reveal the accelerator's location. Five weeks. The man was not human. And the longer he held on, the more Slattery felt as if all his scheming might eventually come crashing down around him.

But then the bathroom door opened. The statuesque redhead appeared wearing lavender lingerie, and Slattery's worries drifted off into the periphery of his consciousness, and he allowed himself to smile in anticipation of welcome pleasure.

His cell phone rang. He gritted his teeth, but then picked it up and answered.

"He *does* not break," a Russian male voice said in reply.

The new girl eased onto the bed beside him. Slattery wanted to shatter the phone against the wall.

"Do you hear?" the Russian demanded.

"I hear you are a fucking incompetent."

"Hey, we do you favor, asshole. We get nothing in return."

"Neither have any of us."

"Then we go to extreme," the Russian said.

The new girl was unbuckling Slattery's belt. He looked down into her green eyes, and then glanced over at the chair in the corner, seeing the A-line skirt there, waiting. He gave no more than a fleeting thought to C. Y. Tilden, Frank Baron, or Gloria Barnett. Fuck them. Just for a little while, fuck them all.

"Whatever it takes," he told the Russian in a mild groan and hung up.

66

TWO DAYS LATER . . .

ISTANBUL

It was dark and close to 10 P.M. when Muktar Otto, head of criminal intelligence for the Turkish National Police, pulled his BMW up to the gate of his villa in the hills above the west shore of the Bosporus. He keyed in the security code. The gate opened.

Muktar Otto drove in, glancing at his wife's lush gardens lit by soft landscape lights. One of his sons' bikes lay in the driveway, blocking the garage. He thought about moving it, but he was too tired and he parked in front of it.

The squat, balding police intelligence chief got out, smelling his wife's orchids, scanning the yard, and seeing nothing out of the ordinary. He went to the front door and used his key to unlock the security gate. He swung it back and opened the inner door. The foyer was dark. He expected to hear the dog, a Rhodesian ridgeback.

But Muktar Otto heard nothing except a radio playing. He squinted and reached for his gun in its shoulder holster. He got out the weapon and moved deeper into the house, toward the kitchen and the radio.

"Fatima?" he called. "Are you there?"

He stepped into the kitchen and turned toward the table where his family ate their meals. His wife stared at him wide eyed and petrified. Her mouth was taped shut. One of the biggest men Muktar Otto had ever seen held a gun to Fatima's head. Otto's children, two boys about six and ten, were seated at their mother's feet, hands tied behind them, tape across their mouth, equally terrorized. Otto felt a gun at the back of his head.

"Drop it," Chávez ordered in English.

Muktar Otto's wife began to squeal and cry behind the tape. The Turkish cop let the gun fall. Chávez kicked it across to Abbott Fowler, who'd emerged from a back room.

"You're making a mistake," the police intelligence chief said. "Do you have any idea who I am?"

"We know exactly who you are," Tatupu said.

"What do you want, then?" Otto demanded. "We are people of modest means."

"Quite the house for someone of modest means," Chávez commented. "We figure you're on the take big-time. But that's the least of your worries."

The Samoan nodded. "If you don't give us what we want, and immediately, we are going to shoot your sons, one by one, and then your wife."

Chávez said, "We want to know about the report you wrote and fed to the CIA about Nassara Engineering being a front for the archives of Al-Qaeda."

Muktar Otto looked at her like she was a poisonous snake. "What about it?"

"Nassara Engineering had nothing to do with Al-Qaeda, did it?" Tatupu asked, thumbing back the hammer on his pistol.

The criminal intelligence officer grimaced until his wife started to sob again. "No," he said at last. "It didn't."

"Give it to us," Chávez said, clicking on a tape recorder and setting it on the counter in front of Muktar Otto. "All of it, or you watch your family die, one by one."

67

THIRTY HOURS LATER . . .

Monarch choked and hacked up water and mucus, coming alert in stages. His consciousness fed on the violent spasms in his lungs and airways. His eyes ran with tears. His throat felt burned. His head pounded. His wrists ached. So did his ankles. He was flat on his back, bound to a sheet of plywood raised and locked into a level horizontal position. He was weaker than he'd ever been, true exhaustion, virtually reptilian in his brain function and response.

Then Monarch felt again that burning in his throat, and he gagged at a tugging in his lungs. A tube was yanked from his throat. He coughed and choked and rattled his way into a full understanding of his plight: He was in the chamber where his torturers had water-boarded him for the fifth time. He had not drowned. He'd been spared yet again. His eyes opened and slowly focused.

Never give up. Go down fighting. Rule Number . . .

The smaller hooded man held a suction device. He saw Monarch come around and said, "You do not think we let you die like that? So easy? No, Monarch, you die much harder than that."

Monarch's chest heaved. He coughed again hard and spewed out the last of it, pale crimson with a taste like copper.

"Looks like you blow up something in there," the tall guard commented. "You tell us where is Green Fields accelerator and no more water."

Monarch heard the clatter of the metal bucket on the cement floor. He stared dumbly at his torturers like a patient might a dentist in a nitrous nightmare. His vocal cords would not respond. He managed a weak whine.

"Yes?" the hooded man asked. "You tell us?"

Monarch's voice box rattled, and he coughed again.

"Yes," the hooded man said, crooning in Monarch's ear, "you tell me now."

Monarch's chest heaved for air. "Gone," he managed. "Gone."

His torturer's gleaming eyes dulled, "Not gone. You take it. Koporski says this."

Koporski? Monarch's brain still felt at sea, and he closed his eyes at this information, hoping to still the seething waves in his head. *Koporski. Are they his men?*

"Don't have it," he whispered. "Gone when I got there. Gorka maybe. Switch."

The other torturer appeared. "Not true. You take gun."

Monarch opened his eyes, seeing the room swirl. "Kill me. Won't change story."

"Then more water," the shorter guard said. "How many times you come back?"

He went for the bucket and the towel. But the taller one stopped him. "No. I believes him now. Accelerator was gone."

Monarch nodded blearily. "Was gone."

The taller torturer nodded. "So we no need you now, Monarch. Tomorrow morning, you die. No water to die. Worse. We show what really happens when thief breaks the eighteenth rule."

Later, Monarch lay on his bug-infested cot, thinking about that last threat and the invocation of the eighteenth rule. It meant Belos was involved. If Monarch's guards were using the rule as a way to mentally torture him, it would not work. But if they were telling the truth, masked men might come for him at dawn. They might drag him to a place where his screaming would not be heard and then execute him. With a gun if he were lucky. But maybe with a rope. Or a chain saw.

Monarch fought these visions by forcing himself to look at the table where a steak, uneaten, greasy and cold now, sat on the tin plate beside a bottle of vodka, a stack of paper, and a pen. A last meal. A last opportunity for confession.

The shorter of his two torturers had brought these things to him an hour before. "You write," he had said. "We send to relatives."

Outside, on the other side of the metal shutters, Monarch could hear the wind picking up. Branches slapped the side of the building. He smelled rain. Monarch looked again to the paper and pen on the table. He would not make a confession, but he did want someone, somewhere to know his fate should death indeed come for him in the morning.

Monarch was still shaky and weak from the water-boarding, but he managed to get to the chair and sit in it. He looked at the steak that he'd ignored since they brought it to him. Now, he tore into it, filling himself with the cold steak and taking several deep belts of vodka before picking up the pen.

My Dear Sister Rachel, he began.

My hope is that somehow this letter will find its way out to you so that you might understand what became of me. Five or six weeks ago, I was shot with some kind of tranquilizer on my way through Villa Miseria to find you. I have been held captive and tortured ever since. Where, I do not know. By whom, I do not know. Why, I do not know, either, though I have strong suspicions.

This was my doing. I have secret enemies and I was trying to flush them out into the open where friends of mine could deal with them. But my strategy has backfired. They tell me that tomorrow morning I will be executed. I never thought I would die like this. But there it is.

Monarch stopped a moment, and then wrote,

My situation is enough to drive a man mad, Sister. It's enough to drive a man to question every moment of his life, or at least the pivotal ones, the ones that changed him forever, turned him into who he was, maybe even doomed him. I know my moment of doom. It was when I spotted the Russian's woman that cold, sunny afternoon before the attack.

He wrote into the night and early morning, trying his best to summarize the events leading up to his capture and confinement, without revealing details or names in the extreme likelihood his captors would read the document before ever mailing it.

Finally, with eyes bloodshot and head drooping, Monarch took another shot of vodka and scribbled,

As my end draws near, Sister, I hold tight to the fact that I did this all for you and for the forgotten and abandoned children of Villa Miseria. Bless you for rescuing me, and the others. You were our mother when we needed one and wise counsel ever since. I only wish I could have given you all that you deserve.

Love,
Robin

68

FOUR HOURS EARLIER . . .
NORTH OF PAPHOS, CYPRUS

Iryna Svetlana feared nights like this one, moonless, summer nights that drew her toward drowsiness and nightmarish sleep, where the sins of her past lived and haunted her. For weeks now, Iryna had suffered a recurring horrid dream in which she imagined Robin Monarch being tortured. In every one, he promised to punish her under the eighteenth rule of the Brotherhood of Thieves.

After one of these nightmares, Iryna would awake sweating and feeling like she'd run for miles. She had begun to drink more heavily than normal. By 9 P.M. that particular evening, she'd already polished off a bottle of wine and poured herself a brandy. She kicked off her sandals and took the brandy through the darkened halls toward Constantine's office. She knew what might take her mind off her nightmares.

She reached his door and pushed it open. Constantine Belos had his back to her. He was holding a phone, standing behind his desk, and looking out across the lit terrace toward the darkness and the sea.

He was saying, "And then you add an extra bullet so there's two, and fire. No man could take more than two rounds of such insanity."

The Russian hung the phone up and tossed it on the desk. He reached for an open bottle of vodka and took a swig. Then his eyes caught Iryna's, and they glistened. He knew that saucy look she got when she hungered.

"My love?" he said.

"Does he talk?" she asked.

"He will," Belos replied.

"You said that a month ago."

"Because I thought I could rely on others to do the job correctly," Belos said, shrugging. "With a man like Monarch, you have to go at him creatively, and show him conclusively that the only thing to do is to talk."

"And you do that how?" Iryna asked.

"A tale for later, I think. Come here. I want you on my desk right here."

Iryna stiffened. "I was thinking upstairs,

Constantine."

Belos hardened. "We are safe, Iryna. There is security everywhere."

Iryna drained her brandy and crossed the room, unbuttoning her blouse.

Offshore three hundred yards, Tatupu let the current work for him as he swam in a neoprene suit and scuba gear toward the reef. Chávez trailed him. As the Samoan navigated, his mind clicked through the reconnaissance Fowler and Yin had performed around the perimeter of Belos's estate.

The security wall was almost up, and there were cameras all around the house. Four armed guards. Two dogs. It was all according to the security plan Monarch had described to Tatupu and the others before they'd disbanded in Istanbul. So the Samoan assumed the pressure sensors had been installed on the cliffs, and perhaps the iron fence had even been hung across the reef, though he prayed that not be the case.

Tatupu checked the waterproof GPS unit on his wrist. He made a stabbing motion upward to Chávez. Together they breached the surface into light swells. Ahead of them, waves crashed across the reef toward the cove below Belos's estate.

Few lights shone in the house. But strings of lights glowed on the perimeter fence and within the grounds. Tatupu swam toward the lights until a swell picked him up and hurled him toward the reef. He body-surfed down the wave. In the moonlight, he caught a glimpse of the steel fencing before slamming into it. He grabbed hard to the rungs with neoprene gloves. The wave exploded over his head.

The sea ebbed. Beside him, Chávez clung to the fence, which rose six feet to a coil of razor wire — a nice touch, and one that forced them to submerge and crawl down the side of the fence to where it met the reef.

Tatupu switched on a waterproof red headlamp that turned the bubbles thrown by the waves iridescent and swarming like hornets. The Samoan cast the beam on the fence six inches away, and together he and Chávez inched along the bottom of the barrier. Several moments later, they found the gate. An iron bar, hasp, and lock on the other side of the fence held it tight.

They had anticipated this possibility. Tatupu retrieved a small package of plastic explosive from his utility belt, slapped it against the gate between the hinges, and used zip ties to cinch it in place. Chávez pierced the package with the wires of a waterproof timing device. She activated the timer and they swam wildly away. It went off with a powerful thud that vibrated through their chests. They swam back to the gate, which flapped open.

Tatupu hoped that they'd used just the right charge to take out the gate, powerful enough to cut through steel, quiet enough that the explosion would have been ruled nothing more than a particularly large wave bursting on the reef. They turned off the lights and swam through. The reef fell away into the deep pool of the cove.

They flutter kicked upward. Tatupu surfaced first, letting his head glide free of the water, hearing the surf behind him, but seeing nothing on the beach or on the cliffs above them. He breathed a sigh of relief. He had not wanted to fight his way out of the cove. It would have been like shooting fish in a barrel, and he'd have been one of the fish.

Tatupu spit out the scuba mouthpiece, then rid himself of the entire system — vest, tanks, and hoses — and let them fall toward the cove bottom. Chávez did the same.

He whispered, "Watch for pressure sensors under the cliff."

Chávez nodded, and swam toward the

north side of the cove. Tatupu went south and soon climbed from the water and up onto the rocks. He rested for several moments before opening his dry bag and fishing out a .45 with shoulder holster, ten loaded clips on a bandolier, a silencer, and a radio headset. He screwed the silencer on, stuffed the gun into the holster, and put on the headset. He said, "Reading?"

"Got you," Gloria Barnett said. "Everyone's on."

Barnett was five miles offshore in a fishing trawler with Ellen Yin.

"I've got two guards," Fowler said. "Outside the wall, northeast."

"Take them first," Tatupu said. "You are go."

"Roger that," Fowler said.

The Samoan started to climb up the jumbled pile of rocks that formed the south cliff, going slower as he approached the rim, peering everywhere for evidence of trip wires and pressure sensors. He spotted one about ten feet below the rim, got around it and up to a flagstone terrace. He slipped forward in a crouch, careful not to crush the brittle leaves strewn there.

Tatupu took several steps and then locked up at the sight of an attack dog, a Doberman, loping toward him. A growl boiled in the dog's throat before it dipped its head and launched, his mouth open and snapping.

The Samoan stooped, turned sideways, and shot his right arm forward and beneath the animal, almost to its back legs, so the dog overshot him and ended up with its belly over his shoulders. The instant Tatupu felt the dog's weight on him, he heaved upward and twisted to his rear with all his might, flinging the attack dog back and over the side of the cliff. He heard its snarling bark turn to a yelp of fear, and then nothing.

Tatupu trotted toward the north wing of the mansion, sticking to the shadows, ready at any second to hear —

Two rifle shots cut the night.

Inside Belos's office, he and Iryna were scrambling to dress. They'd heard the thud and passed it off as thunder or a large wave. But then they'd heard the dog yelp followed by the two shots.

"My god, Constantine," Iryna whined as she struggled back into her pants, hating the booze fogginess that plagued her.

Belos had gone to a cabinet, opened it, and pulled out a pump shotgun. "Go," he said. "The panic room."

"It's not done!" Iryna complained, near tears now.

"It locks," Belos said, moving by her even as shooting started up again outside.

Iryna ran after him, haunted by her nightmares. "Who is it?"

"Does it matter?" the Russian grunted as he ran hard down the hall toward the foyer, the bar, the solarium, and the door that led to stairs and the panic room.

Belos shifted the shotgun to his left hand and reached for the door handle as Iryna pressed in behind him.

Tatupu stepped from the shadows, thumbing on the high-intensity flashlight taped to the bottom of his pistol. "Drop the gun," he ordered in English.

The Russian stiffened, glanced to his right, and saw the silhouette of the huge Samoan training the .45 on him. He dropped the shotgun. Iryna held up her hands and began to cry. "Please," she said. "I am innocent. He makes me do these things."

"You lying bitch," Belos said.

"You're not innocent, lady," Tatupu said. "You both set Robin Monarch up. One thing about Robin: If he tells you he's going to invoke the eighteenth rule, he's going to follow through. Even if he has to have someone else see the penalty carried out."

Iryna sobbed. "I was not a part of his torture. I am many things, but not that."

Tatupu swallowed. Monarch tortured. The worst scenario had come true.

"Where is he?" the Samoan demanded.

"I don't know," Belos said.

"Then she dies," Tatupu said, swinging his gun toward Iryna.

She pointed at Belos and screamed, "He knows! He knows!"

Chávez appeared just as the Samoan aimed his pistol at the side of Belos's thigh and fired. The Russian buckled, screaming. "Your balls with be next," Tatupu said, leaning over him. "Where is he?"

Writhing on the ground, Belos grunted, "A farm Koporski owns south of Tiraspol along the river. That's all I know."

"Who ordered him kidnapped?" Chávez asked, picking up the shotgun.

Belos said nothing.

But Iryna cried, "An American! He is intelligence officer. He calls Constantine the night after Monarch saves us in St. Moritz. He says we can make much money if we get him to steal trigger that Omak supposedly wants. But then Monarch tricks us. The American calls Constantine again, tells him he is fool."

"Shut up!" Belos snarled.

She ignored him. "The American says to him, 'You want money back? I have Monarch. Take him. Make him tell where is trigger.' "

"The American's name?" Chávez demanded.

"I don't know," Belos said, capitulating at last. "But he had Omak and Koporski involved, too. Monarch swindled us all. We joined forces."

Tatupu looked at Chávez, who nodded. They made to move.

Belos started laughing, "Why hurry? He'll be dead before you get there."

"Not if your friends never hear from you," Chávez said, and casually shot the Russian in the groin, leaving a hysterical Iryna to tend him.

69

NINE HOURS LATER . . .

THIRTY KILOMETERS SOUTHEAST OF TIRASPOL, TRANSDNIESTRIA

Four hooded men came for Monarch in the dark, opening the heavy cell door and shaking him from where he'd collapsed on top of the letter. They put him in plastic wrist restraints and released the iron at his ankle. Then they blindfolded him, and marched him barefoot out of the cell.

"My sister," Monarch said in Russian. "She's a woman of God. Send my letter to her. The address is there."

"Of course," said one of his captors. "A last wish granted."

Something about the way the man had said that gnawed at Monarch, made him think he'd heard this man speak before. "Who are you?" he demanded.

"To you, I am death," the captor replied.

They halted. A door was opened. Monarch

felt chill dawn air. He could smell mowed hay now, and heard chickens clucking and stirring on their roosts. He shivered, but forced himself to keep smelling the hay and listening to the birds. These were not bad things on which to focus in the last moments of your life, he decided.

Monarch stubbed his toes on rocks, got hung up in weeds, and stumbled several times. Each time, he was hauled to his feet. They led him onto a dirt road. He heard more men fall in around him.

They crossed some kind of ditch and climbed a steep bank before descending again onto a flat of matted grass. Monarch smelled cows, and heard the neighing and puttering of horses.

They pivoted Monarch and pushed him up against a wall. He had the bitter thought that he did not want to die this way, hands locked behind his back. He wanted to die fighting. He wanted salsa music playing, and a fine woman beforehand, and then a fight among equals before he died.

"Take off the blindfold!" Monarch shouted. "I want to see who will shoot me."

There was a long hesitation before that captor with the familiar voice said, "Yes. He should see this coming."

Someone removed his blindfold. Monarch

squinted in the first light of a pale dawn. Stars still flickered. The crescent moon was setting. A tree line marked the darkness about two hundred yards away. He was at the edge of an overgrown field, up against a wall that smelled of moss. Rusting old farm implements hulked in the periphery of his vision.

Five men in uniform stood before him about thirty yards away. Kalashnikov rifles lay in a pile before them. To their right, another four men stood, hoods off. Even in the low light, he recognized them: Colonel Gorka; General Koporski; Vytor, Omak's soldier; and Artun, Belos's right-hand man.

"Interesting coalition," Monarch said before nodding to Artun. "Death."

Artun's shoulders hunched before he said in English, "You have last chance, Monarch. Tell us where is Green Fields?"

"Constantine got better things to do than to watch me die?"

Artun glowered, then held up a camera. "He sees you die. Again and again."

Vytor held his camera up as well. "A many-million-dollar death."

Koporski scowled and demanded, "Where is my money?"

"Where it's doing some good," Monarch said.

"I shoot you myself, then," Koporski said, growling and setting off toward the five hooded men and the guns.

"No," Artun said, grabbing him by the elbow. "You've had your chance. We do this Constantine's way now."

The dictator looked ready to fight, but then shook off Artun's hold. "I could have you shot for touching me like that."

Artun stiffened. "Of course, Excellency. My apologies."

Koporski stalked away. Artun moved toward Monarch, gesturing at the guns and saying, "Constantine thought you like a game of chance. Only one gun has bullet. Men shoot straight ahead. If bullet is in gun of man in front of you, you die."

"And if it's not?"

"You live until next round. Shooters rotate. Second gun is loaded into mix."

"Clever," Monarch said.

Artun put his finger to his head. "Constantine. Very smart."

Vytor seemed to have had enough playing second fiddle to Artun. "Where is Green Fields?" he demanded.

"Where you can't get at it," Monarch said.

"Aha!" Colonel Gorka cried. "You admit you have it!"

"I admit nothing," Monarch said.

"Then take a chance," Artun said before motioning to the hooded men.

They came forward and picked up the guns, one by one. They lined themselves up so the third man in line, the middle man, was standing directly opposite Monarch, thirty yards away, his AK-47 held at port arms.

"Ready?" Colonel Gorka said in Russian.

The five hooded men brought their weapons to their shoulders.

"Aim!"

Monarch looked beyond the guns to the tree line and then to the fading stars. If this was to be his last impression of life, he wanted it focused on the unknowable, to be humble and accepting of his fate. He'd taken a risk. It had not panned out.

"Fire!"

The shot rang out. Before Monarch could flinch, he heard the bullet wallop a plank to his right. Splinters sprayed the side of his face. Then he flinched. Hard.

Despite his every effort to stay calm in the face of death, Monarch hadn't prepared for living. Adrenaline deluged his system. Black dots swam before his eyes. Every muscle went rubbery. He went to one knee, sure that he'd puke.

"Where is Green Fields?" Artun asked in

Russian.

"Gone," Monarch said. "I threw it away."

"Liar!" General Koporski roared.

Monarch's vision came back, but he retched and hated himself for it. He did not want to give these men the satisfaction of knowing they'd reached something in him, something beyond his training, his only fear, the random orphaning moments of life.

Vytor grabbed Monarch by the collar and shoved him up against the wood-and-earth backstop. "Tell us!" he bellowed. "Or you no have burial. We feed you to dogs."

"Anyone ever tell you you're kind of twisted?" Monarch asked.

The Chechen released him and reached back as if he meant to punch him. Colonel Gorka pulled him away, saying, "The guns are ready."

The hooded men were picking up the rifles again.

Artun said, "Two bullets this time. Twice the chance to die. Ready, Monarch?"

As the executioners raised their guns a second time, Monarch forced himself to look once more to the tree line, now turning a charcoal gray, and then up to the building light of sunrise. The moon and stars were already gone.

"Fire!"

The shots were simultaneous, thundering and both to his left. The crack of the bullets exploding into the wooden planks and damp earth threw Monarch down once again, onto both knees this time. He was hyperventilating, wondering how long he could hold on before the last defenses of his mind were breached and overrun. His entire body trembled as Colonel Gorka and Vytor hauled him to his feet.

"The gun," the colonel said.

"I threw it into the Bosporus," Monarch gasped. "That kind of weapon should not be put in the hands of ignorant men. Any men."

That seemed to take them aback. But then Koporski said, "I don't believe you."

"Three bullets," Artun said, holding up the rounds.

Everything felt dizzying to Monarch now. He'd survived the roulette twice. The odds of three bullets going to his left or right, however, were long. His resolve began to disintegrate like a stone wall crumbling in an earthquake.

"Ready?" General Koporski shouted.

Shaking now, Monarch raised his eyes a third time toward the forest, wanting nothing more than to reveal the locations of the two pieces of the Green Fields gun and thus live. But as he opened his mouth to yell the truth, he swore he caught a glint high in the tree line.

"Aim!"

In a split second, Monarch reacted, gathering all his remaining strength and — just as Koporski was yelling "Fire!" — hurling himself forward toward the executioners.

Time slowed for Monarch as he traveled through space and began falling.

He saw surprise in the eyes of the shooter directly opposite him. The other rifles fired. The shooter opposite him swung his gun barrel toward Monarch just before the man's head snapped backwards, as if the base of his skull had been whipped with chain, and blood erupted from his throat and nose.

PART V

70

Monarch crashed to the wet ground, watching his would-be executioner drop as if into a hangman's trap. His rifle went off. The bullet bit the soil right next to Monarch's head. The weapon discharging so close disoriented Monarch at first.

But then his fathomless will to survive took over. He rolled to his left and up to his feet, expecting to be met with force. But his captors and the four remaining members of the firing squad had all spun toward the tree line, crouching or trying to get to cover. There was a flash and a flat bark from high in the trees. Monarch heard a soft noise, like a pillow plumping before General Koporski hunched up and fell.

"Robin!" Tatupu sprinted in from his left, dressed for war, a submachine gun held at his shoulder.

Monarch, still in plastic wrist restraints, ran in an awkward lumbering gait at the

Samoan.

"Get to the trees," Tatupu ordered.

Monarch ran as best he could, looking over his shoulder in time to see his captors grasp that the attack was a rescue attempt. Colonel Gorka shouted, "He's escaping! They've killed the general. Kill them! Kill them all!"

Two of the executioners tried to reload their weapons. Tatupu shot them and then retreated. Monarch got around the corner of what turned out to be an old barn and slowed. His legs, inactive for so many weeks, felt weak, wobbly.

Tatupu sprinted around the corner, grabbed Monarch by the shoulder, and dragged him toward the trees. "I told you to run!"

Monarch stumbled along with the Samoan, hearing shouting behind them. Automatic gunfire started up to their south.

"Atta boy, Abbott," Tatupu gasped into his headset. "Keep 'em pinned down."

A rifle shot from behind them smacked a sapling next to Monarch before Tatupu plunged them into the brush. He slowed in the dim light, snatched a knife from his scabbard, and sliced the plastic restraints binding Monarch's wrists. He sheathed the knife and handed Monarch an H&K .45 USP.

"Headset?" Monarch asked.

Tatupu shook his head, saying, "Best I can do."

Behind them, they heard vehicles start and come screeching in their direction.

"They're after us," the Samoan grunted. "Move."

"I can't go far," Monarch said. "My legs are shot."

"Eight hundred yards," Tatupu said. "That's all I'm asking."

"They've got jeeps," Monarch grunted as they ran through the woods to a hill.

"We've got better than jeeps," the Samoan said, and urged him to climb.

"Where are we?" Monarch demanded as he fought to scramble up through the vines and bracken that choked the hillside. "Where am I?"

"Koporski's summer place, north of that fortress we attacked."

Monarch kept slipping and falling in the wet leaves and grass. Tatupu grabbed him beneath the armpit and hauled him to his feet just as four men entered the trees below them, carrying AK-47s.

Tatupu spun around and fired at them. Monarch slammed up against a tree, aimed at one of his pursuers, and shot. The man bucked and fell. The others had taken cover and were shooting at the hillside.

Of all people, Yin and Barnett appeared on the hillcrest, carrying H&Ks. They opened fire on the flat below. Barnett yelled, "Get him out of here!"

As Tatupu dragged him farther into the woods, Monarch started to cramp and felt close to retching again. But when he almost couldn't go on, he thought of the cell where he'd spent the last few weeks of his life, he thought of the brutality they'd put him through, and vengefulness welled up in him and gave him new strength.

They crossed a grassy lane in the woods, the Samoan leading, Barnett and Yin covering their rear. "Heads up," Tatupu said. "This place is laced with these little roads."

They ducked into a pine grove on the other side of the lane, waded a creek, then scrambled the opposite embankment. They came to where five or six of the wood lanes merged into a round clearing, like the spokes of a wheel joining a spindle.

Monarch heard engines somewhere nearby in the forest, several large throaty ones and another far softer. Monarch spotted Chávez sprinting up one of the lanes toward him, her sniper rifle held at port arms. Fowler was ripping along behind her, riding a green Rokon motorcycle.

Super quiet, lightweight, and equipped with balloon tires that allowed it to float, an all-wheel-drive Rokon could go virtually anywhere, across stumps, over rocks, through passages jeeps and ATVs could never fit through. Monarch loved them.

Tatupu and Yin pulled two more Rokons from the brush. Tatupu jumped aboard one and hit the ignition. Yin started the other. Monarch climbed aboard with his back to Tatupu, his feet up on separate pegs, while Barnett did the same behind Yin.

The Samoan threw the machine in gear just before the gunfire started. Jeeps swept into three of the lanes about two hundred yards away. Two of them had machine guns mounted on frames behind and above the drivers. The third one did not. But it was closing fast on Chávez, who was now sitting with her back to Fowler on his Rokon. She threw up her rifle and shot at the closest jeep.

The vehicle's windshield exploded. Artun stood above the frame of the windshield and tried to aim a pistol at Chávez. She ran the bolt and shot again. Monarch caught a glimpse of Belos's right-hand man jerk and fall from the jeep. Tatupu gunned their

Rokon up to speed out of the clearing.

Yin swung her motorcycle after Tatupu with Fowler coming hard on her tail. Monarch expected to see the other jeeps chasing. But they did not follow.

"We lose them?" Tatupu shouted as they bounced through ruts and then accelerated down a long straightaway.

"They're probably flanking us," Monarch said.

"Can't flank if they don't know where we're going," the Samoan replied. He slowed and drove them off the lane and into dense woods.

The motorcycle groaned and then caught traction and soon they were bushwhacking through the forest. A mile passed and then a second. During that time, they crossed twelve of those forest lanes and did not see either of the jeeps.

Monarch heard Tatupu say, "Bird, we are ten minutes out. Repeat, ten minutes out." He was calling a helicopter pilot, telling him to prepare for extraction, and Monarch was suddenly so exhausted, he did not know if he could hold on another ten minutes.

"We're coming to the burn," the Samoan announced.

Monarch looked over Tatupu's shoulder, seeing that the thick hardwood forest was giving way to the charred trunks of trees standing amid a tangle of high grass.

"I'm tired, Tats," Monarch said. "Really tired."

"Hang on five minutes more, Robin," Tatupu said as he maneuvered the motorcycle down a bank and onto a path through the burn. They disappeared into the high grass and slash, crossed a lane, and disappeared again. Despite his fatigue, Monarch's instincts triggered and he got his gun up just as the Samoan juiced the engine and sped across the second logging road. Left, right, nothing. They were back into the grass.

"Tell me when we're coming to another one of those roads," Monarch said.

"Now," Tatupu said, and accelerated. Left, right, nothing. They were back in the grass and now almost across the burn, heading toward a wall of thick spruce.

"Road," the Samoan said, and punched the accelerator.

They flew across the opening. Left, nothing. Right . . .

Jeep a hundred yards away. Colonel Gorka behind a machine gun. They disappeared into the grass again. Machine gun fire sliced after them. Tatupu sped and then slowed in a stand of burnt trees. Monarch jumped off the Rokon and took cover behind a charred tree trunk at the edge of the lane.

Yin and Barnett were coming. Monarch could hear their motorcycle's engine and see the high grass waving before they appeared on the other side of the lane. He signaled at Yin to accelerate and pointed to his right. Yin caught his meaning and sped up, with Barnett shifting her weapon so she could shoot southpaw.

Monarch leaned around tight to the tree, trying to time his shot, trying to see through the grass to Colonel Gorka's position. A split second before Yin and Barnett sped across the opening, Monarch fired four shots. Barnett fired her own burst, and they roared past Monarch into the stand of burnt trees. The machine gun chiseled the soil all around Monarch, then stopped.

Tatupu crawled up beside Monarch. Monarch thought he heard Gorka telling his driver to move forward. He looked over and spotted Fowler and Chávez sitting on their Rokon about a hundred feet back from the crossing, watching him, awaiting his call.

Tatupu said into his mic, "Abbott, you are go in ten seconds. We'll give you cover where you're twenty feet out."

Monarch heard Gorka's jeep start to move at the same time Fowler ducked low over the handlebars of the Rokon and hammered the accelerator. They shot forward.

Monarch gauged their speed, then said, "Now!"

Tatupu sprang up, firing over the top of the grass, while Monarch crouched. Monarch heard screams, and his rescuers were by him and up the trail in a flash. Monarch waited a count of two, then rolled out into the lane, pistol up. The windshield of the jeep was blown out. Steam and smoke spit from the engine. Colonel Gorka, covered in shards of glass, was trying to get back up behind the machine gun.

He spotted Monarch lying prone in the lane, aiming, and had a moment of terrible disbelief before Monarch shot, catching the colonel in the throat, causing Gorka to grab at the machine gun as he fell, his finger finding the trigger and touching off a burst of gunfire that sprayed the morning sky.

Monarch got up, his brain feeling seared. He walked toward Tatupu, knowing how dead his eyes must look, and not caring. He'd survived. Gorka had not. That was all that mattered for today.

"Let's get out of here," Tatupu said. "There's still another jeep around."

Yin and Barnett led now, with Fowler and Chávez second, and Tatupu and Monarch bringing up the rear. They crossed the last two lanes that cut through the burn and powered up the spine of a ridge. Monarch scanned the ground below, seeing only Gorka's jeep and the colonel's corpse hanging out the back.

They reached the ridgetop and turned onto another logging road.

"Three minutes," Tatupu said into his headset.

"Gimme a fresh clip," Monarch said.

The Samoan handed him one over his shoulder. Monarch dropped the empty and slammed the new one home.

Monarch spotted the third jeep swinging into the lane behind him about eighty yards away. Vytor was up on the front seat beside the driver, trying to aim his machine gun.

"Gets steep here," Tatupu warned.

They rolled over the brink of a hill and headed down so fast that Monarch was thrown back against the Samoan. Vytor and his jeep disappeared from view.

"Shit," Monarch said. "It's the Chechen from the bobsled run."

"We're here."

Monarch looked over Tatupu's shoulder and saw the extraction zone. The others were already on the flat, heading toward a yellow construction helicopter sitting in the middle of a large marshy area by the river, its rotors twirling. The side doors to the big bird were open with ramps extended.

Monarch realized that Vytor would have the high ground. They'd all be massacred before they reached the chopper.

The moment Monarch felt the lane level off, he said, "Get inside the bird, Tats. I'm right behind you."

Monarch stepped off the Rokon and raised his pistol just as the jeep crested the hill and rocked forward, throwing Vytor off balance. Monarch shot three times, seeing the driver hit and the Chechen thrown back.

The jeep went out of control and came pell-mell down the hillside, bouncing straight at Monarch. He threw himself into a depression at the edge of the marsh. The careening jeep smashed front first into the compression where the hill turned flat.

Vytor was ejected and flung through the air into cattails.

Monarch staggered to his feet. Fowler and Yin already had their Rokons in the helicopter's hold. Tatupu was driving toward the ramp. Monarch went on autopilot, wading through the marsh grass and cattails, head down, left arm thrown up to block his eyes from the chaff and stalks the rotor wash threw. He was forty yards away when Tatupu drove the last Rokon inside the hold of the helicopter. Chávez ran out to help him.

The blade wash whipped around him and he slowed, feeling slightly disoriented, as if he might faint before he could make his escape. Chávez got him under his left elbow and helped him toward the bird. They bent over to get beneath the whirling blades. Monarch caught movement in the cattails to his right. He tried to turn and swing the .45, but knew it was already too late. Vytor, covered in mud and blood, was aiming a pistol at him and smiling.

But before the Chechen could pull the trigger, a burst from Barnett's gun rattled Vytor's chest and knocked him down dead.

71

Monarch watched out the side of the helicopter until he could no longer see the farm where he'd been held. The late June air that rushed in had never smelled sweeter. He bowed his head several moments in gratitude, and then turned to face his team. They were harnessing themselves into jump seats. Seeing the gear, the motorcycles, and the weaponry inside the helicopter, Monarch became aware of the daunting logistics that had to have been associated with his rescue.

"Who put this together?" he demanded. "Who found me? Who paid?"

The copilot got up, ducked through the door, and tugged off her helmet and visor.

"They found you," said Lady Patricia Wentworth, shaking out her hair. "I paid."

Monarch was flabbergasted. She was the last person he'd ever expected to see.

"How?" he said. "Why?"

"Why?" Lady Wentworth said, as if it

should be obvious. "Because as much of a scoundrel and a cad as you are, Monarch, you saved my niece's life twice. And after I heard the whole story from your friends, including how you'd let yourself be kidnapped and tortured, I figured I could repay the favor at least once."

As they flew southeast toward Greece, Monarch heard about the events that had unfolded during his long captivity, up to and including Agatha Hayes's confession that Slattery had ordered Monarch taken. Barnett escaped to Canada, crossing over from Vermont before boarding a flight to London, where she tracked down Lacey Wentworth. Barnett told Lacey that the emerald necklace was being returned to Dame Maggie. She also described the predicament Monarch was believed to be in. Lacey balked, but then went to her aunt and asked her to fund the mission to find and save Monarch.

Lady Wentworth shot Monarch an imperious glance and harrumphed, "Robin Hood, my ass. I should have known you were a socialist, Monarch."

"I'm no socialist," Monarch said. "Just trying to even things out a bit."

Lady Wentworth looked like she wanted to argue, but let it go with, "At least we got

Dame Maggie's necklace back, dreadful thing that it is, completely over the top. Who does she think she is, Nefertiti?"

Monarch shot an annoyed look at Barnett. Climbing Badrutt's Tower had been treacherous. But he said, "Glad it got back to her."

Lady Wentworth pursed her lips, seeing that was all Monarch was going to give her in the form of an apology, then bobbed her head curtly.

Over the next hour, they told Monarch about their investigation, how it had led them back to Belos, and on an overnight journey from Cyprus to Transdniestria on Lady Wentworth's private jet and the helicopter she rented.

"We weren't even in position when they played the first round of Russian roulette," Tatupu said.

Chávez nodded. "I was climbing that damn tree as fast as I could once I realized what was going on with the firing squad. When that second shot went off, I couldn't see you, and I almost got sick."

"I was cracking," Monarch admitted.

"I made sure there was no third round," Chávez said.

Monarch patted her on the leg. "Amazing shot." He looked around at them all. "I can't tell you how much I appreciate what you did for me, all of you, but especially you, Gloria, the best spy of all of us."

Barnett beamed. "I couldn't just have you die, now, could I, Robin?"

Monarch sobered. "Where's Slattery now? We have unfinished business."

"Probably still at Langley," she replied. "But he's not the only one in on this."

She explained about seeing the reference in Slattery's Green Fields files to his college friend, Georgia Congressman and U.S. Senate candidate Frank Baron, and to Baron's biggest political backer, C. Y. Tilden, a billionaire industrialist who owned a large stake in two big U.S. ammunition companies.

Monarch nodded. "They have to have been a part of it."

Lady Wentworth peered at him. "So, this accelerator. Do you still have it?"

"The accelerator and the gun are both in safe places."

"Is it as bloody revolutionary as your friends make it sound? Worth a fortune to whoever holds it?"

"Only if whoever holds it is willing to sell it."

"And you're not?"

Monarch shook his head. "I've got other plans for the Green Fields gun."

"Such as?"

"I'm working on them," Monarch said, drifting toward sleep. "Gloria, I'm going to need everything you can find on Congressman Baron and C. Y. Tilden."

72

THE FOLLOWING DAY . . .

GRAVELLY POINT PARK, VIRGINIA

Jack Slattery looked like hell when he drove his car across the bike trail, blocking it and stopping Congressman Frank Baron in his tracks. Slattery had the passenger window down.

"Get in," he said. "We've got big problems."

Baron scowled and climbed in the front seat. "What the Christ now, Jack?"

"Monarch," Slattery said, driving on. "He's escaped."

"Escaped?" Baron said. "From where?"

"C.Y. didn't tell you?"

"C.Y. told me to mind my own business, that I was better off not knowing."

"He was being held in the Balkans," Slattery said. "His men came for him. They broke him out."

Baron looked shaken. "What does that mean?"

"It means we've got one angry and dangerous man and a highly trained team out there. Monarch was tortured, and now I'm betting he's out for revenge."

"Tortured?" Baron cried. "Who authorized torture?"

"No one authorized it. The guys who held him acted on their own."

"So what are you so worried about? Maybe he'll go away."

"A few of his men paid a visit to a Turkish police source of mine a few days ago at his home in Istanbul. They terrorized him, his wife and children. They got him to admit that the intelligence report about the Al-Qaeda archives was made up. They got him to say that I asked him to write the report."

The congressman thought about that. "But I'm okay, right? I mean, Monarch might be after you, but he can't trace anything to me, can he?"

"Nice of you to think about yourself, Frank," Slattery said bitterly.

"Can he?" Baron said.

"I don't know, Frank."

"What do you mean, you don't know?" Baron cried. "I can't have this. I just got word yesterday that Carney is out. His wife has cancer, and he's retiring tomorrow during the threat-assessment hearing. Do you know what that means?"

"I'm not an idiot," Slattery said. "Your hearing gets big-time media coverage because Hopkins comes to testify, and you become chairman of the House Intelligence Committee in front of those cameras before the election, which helps your stature so much, you win the senate seat against Porterfield."

"That's goddamn right!" Baron shouted. "So you have got to stop this guy, Jack. I don't care what you have to do. You stop him, and anybody with him!"

73

TWO HOURS LATER . . .

OFFICE OF THE CIA DIRECTOR

Slattery looked at Dr. Hopkins and said, "Monarch's surfaced."

Hopkins tapped a pen against his lips and said nothing.

Slattery felt his stomach churn. One false step, one wrong word, and it was over.

"He was evidently involved in a shoot-out in Transdniestria yesterday," Slattery began. "He killed six people, including General Koporski."

"The dictator?" Hopkins said, surprised. "Why wasn't I apprised of this?"

"Because we only just learned that he was one of the victims," Slattery said. "The Transdniestrians are keeping Koporski's death under wraps because there's a power struggle under way internally, and the Russians are involved, of course."

"Why Koporski?" Hopkins demanded.

"Why would Monarch kill him?"

"Because Koporski got to Monarch before we did," Slattery said. "We believe he was holding Monarch and trying to convince him to return the millions Monarch evidently swindled from him. But then it appears that Monarch's old team rescued him, and during that rescue, they killed Koporski and five of his men."

"So what does that have to do with us?" Hopkins demanded.

Slattery shifted in his seat. "Sir, I have reason to believe Monarch is bent on revenge. He believes that we, the agency, had a part in his imprisonment and torture."

"Torture?" Hopkins cried, then leaned across his desk at Slattery. "Did we?"

"Absolutely not, sir," Slattery said. "But he thinks we did."

Hopkins studied Slattery. "And you think, what, that he'll try to kill you?"

"Yes, sir, and perhaps you, too."

The CIA director's eyebrows lifted. "Me?"

"One of Koporski's guards, a man who was wounded during Monarch's escape, said he heard Monarch tell Koporski before he shot him that he was going to kill everyone who had a part in his being held and tortured, beginning with the Director of the CIA."

Hopkins's lips formed into an O before he said, "What do you recommend?"

"Monarch and his men are extremely dangerous, sir. I don't think we should underestimate what they are capable of, especially if we are in a defensive posture. I suggest we go on the offensive. Against all of them."

The CIA director tapped his pen against his lips several more times before he said, "I want them captured if possible, but if not . . ."

In the silence, Slattery nodded. "Understood, sir."

74

LATE THAT SAME AFTERNOON . . .
BUENOS AIRES

Monarch wore no disguise when he left the
cab in front of the cemetery late that chilly
Monday afternoon and bought flowers at
the kiosk. He wanted to be seen.

That thought filled Monarch with vengeful wrath as he took a looping path to his
parents' grave, scanning the cemetery to see
if anyone was watching him. To his mild
dismay, he saw no one. But as he approached his parents' graves, Monarch
noticed something different about the big
pine tree on the other side of the knoll. A
bird house had been fixed to the trunk of
the tree facing his parents' graves. That sight
was enough to set Monarch grimly at ease.

He knelt with his head bowed for several
moments in front of the headstone before
leaning over to the brass vase embedded in
the earth. He dug out the dried grass and

leaves that clogged it until he felt the Green Fields accelerator. He tugged the device out, put his hand in his pocket, and then brought it back out. Then he set about arranging the fresh flowers in the vase.

75

FORTY MINUTES LATER . . .
CIA HEADQUARTERS
LANGLEY, VIRGINIA

"That's it!" Slattery cried, pointing at a computer screen inside the covert operations center and pictures of Monarch on his knees at his parents' grave, fishing a black object from the vase and putting it in his pocket before arranging the flowers.

"Right under our nose," Hayes said admiringly.

Slattery's enthusiasm dampened for a moment as he studied the pictures again. Had Monarch taken the Green Fields accelerator, or had he just appeared to? He looked again. No, he defi nitely took it.

"Where is Monarch now?" Slattery asked.

"He left the cemetery and went to a private hangar at the international airport. He boarded a jet that belongs to Lady Patricia Wentworth. Brit nobility. Billionaire."

Slattery immediately feared that Monarch was selling the accelerator to Lady Wentworth. "I want a flight plan."

"Already got it," Hayes replied. "They're coming here. Dulles Airport."

76

THE FOLLOWING MORNING . . .
DULLES INTERNATIONAL AIRPORT
CHANTILLY, VIRGINIA

Slattery parked the black Suburban and motioned to his passengers, who slipped out wearing airplane mechanics' jumpsuits and identification that would give them access to the runways and hangars for private jets.

Slattery adjusted his earpiece and said, "Are you reading me, Hayes?"

From the backseat of the SUV, where she was working on a laptop, Agatha Hayes said, "Loud and clear."

Slattery got slowly out of the van, meaning to follow his men, knowing that they were all operating inside the United States, a federal crime for CIA officers. But what was he going to do? Bring in the FBI? No, this had to be handled the right way, the final way. When Monarch left the jet, he would be shot and the Green Fields accelerator retrieved and life would go on, and his dreams would be realized.

Slattery was rounding the back of the Suburban when the rear passenger door flung open.

Hayes looked like she'd touched a live wire. "They diverted course," she said. "They landed at National."

"What?" Slattery cried in fury. "When?"

"Ten minutes ago," Hayes said.

"Monarch must have suspected we were on to him and . . ." Slattery's voice died as his mind linked National Airport, Gravelly Point Park, and . . . "They're five minutes from Capitol Hill!"

Hayes said, "We've got to warn Dr. Hopkins. He's testifying up there today!"

Slattery jumped into the front seat of the Suburban and fired it up. Hayes leaped in beside him. He yelled at his men, "Get a taxi back to Langley!"

Then he squealed out of the parking lot, shouting at Hayes, "Call the director's secretary! Have her patch me through to his cell, or the cell of whoever is with him."

77

AN HOUR LATER . . .
CAPITOL HILL

Monarch left Union Station and started toward the U.S. Senate office buildings north of the U.S. Capitol. He'd dyed his hair gray and put in tinted contact lenses that made his brown eyes look as blue as the ones in his fake Spanish passport. He wore a business suit and carried a briefcase, both purchased minutes before, inside the train station.

At the front entrance to the Hart Senate Office Building, Monarch showed his identification to the U.S. Capitol Police, telling the guards in halting English that he was a businessman in to see a staffer on the Commerce Committee. The officers put his briefcase through the scanner. They patted him down, and then inspected him with a wand, but found nothing. They waved him through.

■ ■ ■ ■

A wall of screens showing various entrances to the Capitol and House and Senate office buildings flickered inside the Capitol Hill Police Watch Commander's office as Captain Barbara Meeks handed Jack Slattery back his identification.

Meeks, a tall African-American woman, said, "How can I help the CIA today, Mr. Slattery?"

Slattery was sweating from the running he'd done since Hayes dropped him off beyond the barricades on the House side of Capitol Hill. He'd run all the way to Meeks's office, upset because despite Slattery's warning about Monarch, Willis Hopkins had refused to cancel his appearance before the Intelligence Committee.

"I believe there may be an attempt on Dr. Hopkins's life before, during, or after his testimony before the House Intelligence Committee this morning," Slattery said.

"Kind of a vague timeline, isn't it?" Meeks said.

"I believe the attack is imminent," Slattery insisted. "One of our former agents went rogue two years ago. He cracked and blames his breakdown on the director and myself. I've been tracking him. He got off a private jet at National about an hour and a half ago with a team of his followers. Hopkins is testifying this morning."

"Name?" Meeks demanded.

"Robin Monarch."

"What kind of work did Monarch do for you, Mr. Slattery?"

"He was a thief and an assassin, a legend at the agency before he —" Slattery stopped in midsentence, his eyes transfixed by one of the screens, seeing Barnett standing in line, waiting for security. "There's one of them!" he cried, pointing at the screen.

"West entrance, Dirksen," Meeks said, and picked up a radio.

Slattery's eyes were darting at other screens. He spotted Yin. "There's another!" he said. "She just went through security!"

78

Monarch, meanwhile, had taken an elevator to the basement of the Hart Office Building and worked his way through several hallways to an underground passage and the subway to the U.S. Capitol Building. He sat in the rear car next to two Hill staffers who were talking about a finance bill set to reach the Senate floor. Monarch read a folded copy of *The Washington Post* that he'd purchased at the train station.

When the train halted, Monarch got out and positioned himself behind the two staffers. As they passed the officers guarding the subway, Monarch wove to the outside of the staffers, acting as if he were late for a meeting, and blocking a clear view of his face.

Monarch put his Bluetooth earpiece in, got out his cell phone, and made a call. The connection was marred by static, but serviceable.

Tatupu answered on the first ring. "You through?" he asked.

"In the basement hallways of the Capitol Building," he said. "Heading toward the House side. Tell Fowler I'm running three minutes late."

"Got it," Tatupu said.

Captain Meeks gave crisp orders over the radio, telling her men to detain Barnett and Yin. Then she looked at Slattery, who was studying all the other screens, and demanded, "You have a picture of Monarch?"

Slattery nodded, pulled out his Black-Berry, and said, "Give me two seconds to send it to you. But Yin and Barnett are decoys. We want to be wherever that hearing is being held, or wherever Hopkins is right now."

"Rayburn House Office Building," she said, moving out the door, barking into it as she went. "Rayburn, we are on alert. I want four more officers to move to the Select Intelligence hearing room. You'll be getting a picture of a person of interest sent to your station in the next minute. If you spot this man, I want him detained."

Monarch kept his cell connection open, but put the phone in his pocket. He looked at

566

the escalator that dropped down another level to the pedestrian tunnel and subway to the Rayburn Building. But he had no intention of going anywhere near the Intelligence Committee hearing, much less that Rayburn Building. Instead, he took a step toward the tunnel that led to the Cannon Building just as two men passed him, heading to the escalator. Monarch recognized them: C. Y. Tilden and Frank Baron, thick as thieves.

For an instant, Monarch turned homicidal, but held the urge to attack them in check. Revenge was best served ice cold. He hurried on, checking his watch, not bothering to look back at the men he was about to destroy.

79

Slattery and Captain Meeks reached the subway tunnel that led to the Rayburn House Office Building. "How far?" Slattery demanded.

"Five minutes," Meeks said. "I've already got men —"

The watch commander stopped in her tracks, listening to a transmission coming in over her earbud. "Where?" she demanded, hesitated, and then said, "I'm on my way." Meeks made to turn around.

"Where are you going?" Slattery demanded. "Rayburn's this way."

"Someone set off a bomb in the trees behind the Hart Senate offi ce building," Meeks said. "I have to shut this place down."

"It's Monarch or one of his team," Slattery insisted. "He's trying to draw your forces to the Senate side of the Hill. We need to get to that hearing room. Now."

■ ■ ■ ■

Monarch reached the third floor of the Cannon Office Building.

"You're sure she's there, right?" he said
into his Bluetooth.

Tatupu said, "She's receiving constituents
until the committee hearing."

"Here we go, then," Monarch said, and
walked down the hallway toward an open
doorway marked with a simple, small metal
sign that said 8TH DISTRICT, GEORGIA. REP.
HELEN PORTERFIELD.

Below and to the side of the sign stood a
beefy Capitol Hill Police officer who was
looking intently at his BlackBerry. Monarch
went straight to him. The cop looked up.
Monarch caught confusion, and then recognition in the officer's eyes. The cop went for
his pistol, but Monarch's reflexes were too
fast. His hand shot out and pinned the officer's wrist to his waist, his fingers finding a
pressure point. The officer grunted in pain
and released the pistol grip. Monarch's
other hand dropped the briefcase, snatched
out the cop's gun, and pressed it to the officer's stomach.

"Be reasonable now, Officer Kesaris,"
Monarch said, reading the name on the

badge. "I'm not here to hurt anyone."

"What do you want, then?" the cop asked, flushing red at the fact that he'd been stripped so quickly of his weapon.

"Just a few moments with Congresswoman Porterfield," Monarch said. "Now."

"Or?"

"Shoot you in the foot? Cause a ruckus when there really doesn't have to be one?"

A moment later, Monarch walked behind the Capitol Hill cop into the office's reception area. The gun and his right hand were in his suit coat pocket, the muzzle pointing at the back of Officer Kesaris's leg. A blond woman in her early twenties was taking a phone message. She looked up, saw the cop, smiled, and went back to work.

They took a left into a narrow hallway past several cubicles where staffers were working before the doorway at the far end opened, revealing a plump man in his forties followed by his wife and two children. A severe-looking woman in her late thirties trailed them and stood in the doorway.

"We're so glad you came," she said. "Eva at the front desk will get you your White House tickets."

Beyond the woman in the doorway, Monarch spotted Congresswoman Helen Porterfield, a petite woman of color, standing with her reading glasses on, perusing a stack of documents.

The aide finally noticed Kesaris coming at her. "Phil?" she asked. "Something wrong?"

"Let's go inside, Lydia," Kesaris said. "Mr. Monarch here wants to talk with the congresswoman."

Lydia tried to look around the cop at Monarch, saying, "He's not on the list for this morning, Phil. Tell him to —"

Monarch put the barrel of the pistol on top of Kesaris's shoulder and pointed it at her face. "Do as the man says, Lydia. Now."

Lydia panicked and backed up, her hands in the air, starting to cry. Monarch pushed the cop through the door and shut it with the heel of his shoe.

"What's going on, Lydia?" Helen Porterfield asked, looking up in alarm.

The congresswoman's administrative assistant threw her arms wide and backed up in front of the congresswoman, saying, "You'll have to kill me first!"

"I'm not an assassin, Lydia," Monarch growled. "I'm a thief."

That took everyone aback. Porterfield asked, "What are you stealing?"

"Nothing from you, Congresswoman," Monarch replied. "I'm here to tell you what I stole on behalf of Jack Slattery, the CIA's chief of covert operations, on behalf of Congressman Frank Baron, and ultimately on behalf of C. Y. Tilden."

"Baron and Tilden?" Porterfield said. "What did you steal for them?"

Monarch set the briefcase on her desk, and, with the gun still on Officer Kesaris, used his free hand to snap it open and retrieve a disk. "Put this in your computer and play it," he said. "This device led Baron, Tilden, and my old boss at the CIA to engage in bribery, collusion, kidnapping, and torture."

"Torture?" she said. "Of whom?"

"Me."

Porterfield took the disk gingerly and then slipped it into her computer. A video appeared, showing Monarch holding the Green Fields gun. There was a thump, and then a bolt of light hurtled from the gun across an opening and blew up the stump, leaving only dust in the air.

"Motherfucker," the congresswoman gasped.

80

The hearing room was already jammed when Slattery and Captain Meeks passed through the phalanx of Capitol Hill Police guarding the door. There were at least fifteen television cameras and twice that many still photographers in the room. Slattery heard reporters discussing the rumor that Jim Carney of Oklahoma, the venerable chairman of the House Intelligence Committee, was stepping down because his wife had been diagnosed with terminal cancer. At the witness table, Slattery saw Dr. Willis Hopkins flipping through his prepared testimony. He wanted to go talk to the CIA director, but various congressmen were already settling into their committee seats.

Frank Baron entered and shook the hand of an ashen Jim Carney with practiced concern before taking the seat next to the chairman. Baron looked into the audience and nodded. Slattery spotted C. Y. Tilden sitting two rows behind Hopkins next to Baron's wife, Virginia, who looked polished to a shine.

Slattery let his attention roam all around the room, trying to see if Monarch had somehow managed to get inside in disguise before Meeks shored up security.

"I don't see him," Slattery said at last and with great satisfaction.

Chairman Carney picked up his gavel and gave it a sharp rap to settle the room just as Congresswoman Helen Porterfield entered through a back door, carrying her purse. She took her seat on the side opposite Baron.

Carney smiled wanly as he said, "I'm afraid these cameras are not all here for you, Dr. Hopkins, as popular as you are."

The CIA director said, "I didn't think so, Mr. Chairman."

Carney looked out at the reporters crowding the small hearing room. "As some of you have probably heard, my dear wife, Charlotte, has been diagnosed with cancer," he began in a halting voice. "As much as I love this job and my life in Washington, I feel that I must be at Charlotte's side — and so with a heavy heart and effective immediately, I am announcing my retirement as chairman of the Intelligence Committee, and as representative of the Fifth District of the great state of Oklahoma."

There was a minor uproar in the room, with several reporters darting out the door to file their stories and other bystanders beginning to dissect the political meaning of this news, all of which caused Carney to wield his gavel to restore order.

When the room quieted, Carney looked to his left. "In the interim, before the majority leaders can meet to formally nominate a new chairman in the next congress, and unless there is any objection, I will turn over temporary leadership of this committee to my friend and colleague, a great patriot and American, the honorable Representative Frank Baron of Georgia."

That set off another gentle hubbub in the room as Baron stood to shake Carney's hand and to pat him on the back. The chairman offered Baron his gavel.

But before Baron could take the gavel, Helen Porterfield leaned into her microphone and said, "Mr. Chairman, I object."

There was a moment of stunned silence before many of the cameras swung from Carney and Baron to the congresswoman from Georgia, the minority legislator with the least seniority on the committee.

Baron's concern became a livid scowl. Carney held on to the gavel and said, "You object, Congresswoman Porterfield?"

"I do, Mr. Chairman," Porterfield said. "Most strenuously."

"On what grounds?" Baron demanded.

Slattery's attention shot from the dais toward C. Y. Tilden, who was straining forward, his pale skin flushed, his hands gripping the seat in front of him.

Porterfield said, "I object on the grounds that you, Congressman Baron, knowingly colluded with Mr. C. Y. Tilden and a top CIA official — whom under federal law I unfortunately cannot name in an open forum such as this one — in a scheme that involved bribery, robbery, kidnapping, and the solicitation of torture and murder."

Baron was stunned. The room erupted into pandemonium: "A top CIA official?" "Is it Hopkins?" "Torture?" "Murder?" Reporters headed for the exit, pulling out their BlackBerries, calling their news desks, while others in the audience watched the scene in open shock. Slattery was one of them. He glanced at Captain Meeks, who was studying him.

"I don't know what she's talking about," Slattery told her, but he was almost overcome with claustrophobia.

Baron regained composure, shaking his head as if he could not believe how low his esteemed colleague had sunk. "That is a pack of lies, Helen. It is all lies, and this is a despicable political stunt that denigrates not only me, but also our great state of Georgia and especially Chairman Carney in his hour of grief and need."

"I've got proof," Porterfield said, holding up the disk Monarch had given her. "I have a film here that shows a so-called Green Fields gun, a revolutionary weapon that uses a miniature particle accelerator to throw bolts of energy instead of bullets. A Turkish national, a man named Abdullah Nassara, invented the weapon.

"Congressman Baron's biggest benefactor is Mr. C. Y. Tilden, a billionaire from my home state who made his money manufacturing conventional weapons and bullets. Someone inside Nassara Engineering talked about the Green Fields gun, and Tilden found out about it. Tilden stood to lose a fortune if Green Fields weaponry replaced conventional guns and bullets. He also stood to make untold fortunes if he were the first to bring such a weapon to the market. But how to get that gun? And for cheap?

"Well, it turns out Congressman Baron has an old college buddy who holds a high rank in the Central Intelligence Agency," Porterfield went on. "Maybe a bribe was offered, I don't know — but in any case, this man was coopted, and a scheme to steal the gun was hatched, using unwitting U.S. operatives to carry out the deed. Along the way, these three men condoned murder, robbery, kidnapping, and torture. That, Mr. Chairman, is why I object to Congressman Baron taking the chair of this committee."

Porterfield took her eyes off Baron, who looked rocked by the depth and accuracy of her barrage. She peered into the audience and said, "Isn't that right, Mr. Tilden?"

The media suddenly realized that the billionaire in question was right there with them and swung their cameras at Tilden, whose pallor had turned scarlet. Dumbstruck by Porterfield's assault, Slattery looked over drunkenly at his boss. The Director of the CIA was staring directly at him.

Tilden, meanwhile, choked and began to claw at his neck. Then the industrialist gagged out something unintelligible before collapsing into the lap of the former Miss Georgia, who screamed and stood up. Tilden fell off her to the floor.

In the melee that followed, as reporters and cameramen jostled for position and Captain Meeks and other Capitol Police moved forward, Slattery woke from his shock and decided it was high time to leave. He needed to go fast and far away from this room, from this city, from this country, maybe even this hemisphere.

81

TWENTY MINUTES LATER . . .

Monarch watched a live C-SPAN feed of the hearing in Helen Porterfield's office along with Lydia, the congresswoman's administrative aide, and Kesaris, the Capitol Hill Police officer. The screen showed medics who had rushed into the room and were working on Tilden. Frank Baron, meanwhile, stood there watching an EMT put an oxygen mask on his wife's face. The congressman's mouth hung open, and he looked punch-drunk as Porterfield resumed her narrative of the nefarious deeds that had been done in the name of Green Fields weaponry.

Officer Kesaris and Lydia were glued to the screen. Monarch set the cop's pistol on a table and left. He walked down the narrow hallway past the oblivious members of Porterfield's staff who were all glued to several screens showing the cable news network coverage of the fiasco.

"You know what this means, don't you?" one said. "Helen's gonna be a senator."

"Could not have happened to a better person," another replied.

Monarch smiled, feeling almost as good as when he handed money to Sister Rachel. *Maybe that old saying is right,* he thought as he moved into the crowded hallway and headed toward the staircase, *maybe it is better to give than to take.*

"Robin Monarch," a woman's deep and unfamiliar voice said behind him. "I thought I might find you here."

Monarch stiffened, stopped, and looked over his shoulder at a tall African-American woman in a police uniform. She was standing a few feet away. She held a pistol loosely in her left hand and a radio in her right.

"My name is Meeks, Captain Barbara Meeks of the Capitol Hill Police."

"A pleasure, Captain," Monarch replied. "Can I help you?"

"You sure know how to cause a shitstorm on short notice."

"It is one of my specialties," Monarch allowed.

"I can see that," she said. "Tell me, Mr. Monarch, was Jack Slattery the CIA official that Congresswoman Porter could not name?"

Monarch winked and said, "Rule Number Thirteen: Keep your secrets secret."

"How's that?" she asked, confused.

"Captain, it's a federal offense to reveal the identity of a CIA field operative."

Captain Meeks smiled. "I've heard that. He's gone by the way, Slattery. He scurried out of the hearing room when my back was turned after Tilden dropped dead."

"Scurrying away sounds like Jack," Monarch said.

"And this Green Fields weapon?"

"Somewhere safe from little boys," Monarch said.

She thought about that. "Probably smart."

"I think so," Monarch said. "A Green Fields weapon is not one of those things civilized folks would want lying around. By the way, do you have a couple of friends of mine in custody?"

Captain Meeks nodded.

"Feel like letting them go?" he asked. "We're done here, and it would be embarrassing to Dr. Hopkins if you were to find out that one of them is still active CIA."

She thought about that a moment, and then lifted her radio and called in the order to release Barnett and Yin.

"Thank you, Captain," Monarch said.

She nodded. "What about Slattery?"

"Oh, if I know Jack, he'll turn up somewhere."

He turned to leave, but she stopped him, saying, "Monarch?"

He looked back at her. "Yes, Captain?"

"It's nice to know some legends are real."

Monarch smiled, laughed, and walked away, saying, "Listen to me talk like a politician: I categorically deny that the stories circulating about me are true."

82

SEVENTEEN DAYS LATER . . .
BUENOS AIRES

In the hour before darkness fell, a man with dyed-black hair and two weeks of beard exited a bus wearing brown contact lenses, jeans, and work boots with a blue Windbreaker, sunglasses, and a slouch hat. He hunched over as he entered the cemetery, as if he were carrying a great weight. When he passed a kiosk that sold flowers, he happened to catch his reflection in the glass. No one would ever recognize him like this.

He walked deeper into the cemetery and saw a young Argentine woman emerge from the gravestones. She was beautiful and she'd been crying, but it was her black A-line skirt that caught Slattery's eye. For the briefest of instants, the life of the CIA's former chief of covert operations was different. He was not a fugitive. His life was not destroyed. His future was not bleak and dark. He was just Jack, a sixteen-year-old kid watching the redheaded hooker with the lavender lingerie his marine father had hired for his birthday as she squeezed herself back into her A-line skirt.

But then the Argentine woman was by him and gone, and so was the vividness of the memory, replaced by the crushing reality of his situation. There was an international manhunt out for him. It had taken every bit of his skills to avoid being caught as he had made his way by car, train, and bus, seventeen days, from Virginia to Argentina and this cemetery in Buenos Aires. The graveyard was his last-chance game, his only remaining hope for redemption.

Slattery approached a hearse and limousine on the path and a group of mourners, men in dark suits and women in black veils, gathered around a casket and grave. But then he spotted the knoll where Monarch's parents were buried. The hearse driver stood by, watching from behind dark sunglasses as Slattery walked up the hill toward their graves, feeling shaky with anticipation.

He saw the birdhouse on the pine tree. He moved to the side of the tree, where the motion detector would not notice him, found the switch on the camera, and shut it off. He walked to the grave. His eyes scanned the black monument and the fl at stones in the grass before coming to rest on the wilted and dried flowers jutting out of the vase at what seemed to him an un-natural angle.

Slattery's breath caught in his throat. He fell to his knees, yanked out the flowers, and threw them aside. With trembling fingers, he reached down into the vase and felt something metal and rectangular. He pulled out the device and saw a raised tubular upside down Q on the surface.

Slattery wanted to cry. He wanted to scream for joy. What ever he'd done would be forgiven now. All people would care about was the accelerator. He'd bargain his way to freedom and to riches. He'd live the life he'd dreamt of. He'd beaten Monarch, and now, at long last, he would benefit. *End-game,* he thought. *Fucking endgame!*

Slattery wanted to stand up and dance like a vengeful lunatic on the graves of Mon-arch's parents, but he knew it would draw too much attention. He should just leave. But spite rose in him as he pocketed the ac-celerator, stood up, and looked around. Two groundskeepers were raking leaves with their backs to him seventy-five yards away. And the burial party was moving toward the hearse and limousine a solid 150 yards away.

Slattery unzipped his pants and fumbled. He laughed caustically and began urinating all over the headstones and the monument. "Fuck you, Monarch," Slattery chuckled. "And fuck your stinking, thieving parents, too. I piss on their graves! I piss on you!"

He heard a cough from somewhere above him.

"You know, Argentines frown on desecration of the dead, Jack," Monarch said, "and most thieves draw the line at grave-robbing."

Slattery startled and ducked at the sound of Monarch's voice, horrified and dribbling on himself as he looked high into the pine tree. Monarch was perched on a limb about twenty feet up, aiming. The Taser hit Slattery in the chest, blasting him backwards off his feet. His world lurched to woozy impressions where time had no meaning.

Slattery saw Monarch standing above him. The groundskeepers joined him. They were both Latin men, darker than Monarch. They reached down to pick him up. When they did, he saw that they had the same tattoos on their forearms: a hand poised to snatch something above the letters FDL.

He heard gravel crunch. The hearse. The door opened. He was thrust in the back with four men from the burial party. One zipped him up. One stuffed a handkerchief in his mouth. They wrapped his wrists together with duct tape, and his ankles, too. He heard a car door slam.

Monarch said, "Drive, Claudio. Manuel, strip him clean."

The hearse started to move. Slattery felt their clever hands in his pockets. They found money, a fake passport, a money belt, eight gold coins sewed into his waistband, bus stubs, and the Green Fields accelerator, showing them all to Slattery one by one.

The Taser's effect on Slattery was weakening with every moment. His body no longer felt sapped, and his mind was clearing. By the time they'd driven several miles, he felt strong enough to offer some token resistance when the hearse stopped. He heard doors opening and slamming shut. The rear of the hearse opened. The four men lifted Slattery and passed him out into the waiting arms of John Tatupu and Abbott Fowler. They picked him up, walked him several feet, and slammed him down in a wooden chair facing a sledgehammer that stood upright a few feet away on the concrete floor. Tatupu kept one beefy hand on his shoulder.

Slattery looked around. They were in an abandoned warehouse that smelled like petroleum. The men from the hearse moved to one side as the other members of the burial party filtered toward him from the limousine. The women raised their veils. Chanel Chávez. Ellen Yin. Gloria Barnett.

Monarch came around in front of Slattery holding the Green Fields accelerator. He leaned one hand on the sledgehammer before nodding to Fowler, who tore the gag from Slattery's mouth.

Monarch flipped the converter with his free hand. "Friends of mine spotted you coming across the border from Chile earlier today," he said. "I had a feeling you'd come see if I really took the converter from the vase."

"Fuck you."

Monarch smiled. "We trusted you at one time, Jack. We didn't like you, but we trusted you, and by that I mean everyone, from Dr. Hopkins on down. You betrayed that trust. You sold it. And then you lied to us and put us in your schemes. You put all our lives in danger. You caused the deaths of innocent people. You had me kidnapped and tortured. And now you're going to suffer for it."

Slattery blinked and then got angry. "You can't do this," he said. "You have no jurisdiction, Monarch. I'm an American. I've got rights! You can't just mete out justice."

"You're among thieves," Monarch said, still flipping the accelerator. "You have no rights. We'll take from you anything that we want. Perhaps even your life."

Slattery's eyes darted around at the faces watching him in silence. He felt sweat roll down his face. He was trying to come up with a game, some way out of his situation, and then saw a way.

"You understand why I did it, don't you," Slattery said to them all as if they were comrades at a bar. "You thieves, I mean. You want money, don't you? All thieves want money. Well, I'm like you. I wanted money, a, uh, a certain way of life." He gestured at the accelerator in Monarch's hand with his chin. "That device he's holding is worth more than any of us could ever dream of. Billions, potentially. I know people who know people. We can put the past behind us, Monarch. We'll sell it, and take the profits and —"

Monarch dropped the accelerator on the concrete. He picked up the sledgehammer and smashed it again and again until it was flattened and bits of electronics had scattered out its ends. Slattery's jaw hung open as he looked at what was lost.

"We'll do nothing of the sort, Jack,"

Monarch said, and set the sledgehammer upright beside him again. "Things like Green Fields weapons should not exist, because they corrupt men like you."

Slattery sneered at him. "You're a thief, Monarch, a goddamned thief. Who are you to fucking lecture me about corruption, about wanting more for yourself!"

"Even thieves have rules, Jack," Monarch said. "Principles to live by. You have none." He looked around at the others. "How say you?"

"Guilty," they all murmured.

"What?" Slattery cried. "No! You can't just —"

Tatupu stuffed another gag in his mouth, and Slattery felt himself lifted again. The four men from the burial party carried him to a pickup truck that he had not seen before. Then they set him in the front seat. Claudio got into the driver's seat. Monarch climbed in beside him. Tatupu, Fowler, Yin, Chávez, and Barnett stood outside watching.

"I'll see you up there in the morning," Monarch said to them.

They nodded as Claudio put the truck in gear and drove out of the ware house into an industrial area that gave way to commercial strips and then neighborhoods of wealth and ornate architecture. Slattery kept looking outside, and then in around the cab of the truck, trying to figure a way out.

But there was none, and in a matter of minutes and miles, the cityscape had turned to wretched poverty, tin-roofed shacks lit by lanterns, filthy people in tattered filthy clothes, open sewers and a stench that poured in the open windows of the truck when they turned directly into the slum.

Claudio wove them slowly through the muddy lanes as the shuddering reality of the place pressed in on Slattery from every side. Drugged prostitutes called to them. Dealers slapped the hood of the car and asked, *"Paco? Paco?"* Slattery wanted to shout to them for help. But the gag kept him quiet and breathing through his nose, inhaling that awful smell that seemed to just get stronger the deeper they traveled into the slum.

At last, they rounded a corner and Slattery could see lights ahead, lights that appeared to be moving around on what looked to be steep hillsides. The odors in the air were so rank, he thought he'd retch.

Monarch pulled a knife, reached down, and cut Slattery's ankles free. Then he yanked out the gag. "This is where you get out, Jack," Monarch said.

Claudio stopped the truck, letting the headlights play out across what had been hillsides, now revealed as towering piles of garbage. People with flashlights and lanterns were climbing in the refuse, children and women and men foraging for an existence.

Slattery was suddenly filled with a fear greater than he'd ever known, face-to-face with an existence the exact opposite of the one he'd dreamed of as a boy. "No!" he shouted when Monarch opened the door. "You can't leave me here!"

Monarch said, "You have no money. No identification. You're a hunted man, likely to be shot on sight by the agency's assassins. You've got nowhere else to go, Jack. This is your life now."

Slattery tried to kick at Monarch. But Monarch pushed the blow aside, reached in, and dragged Slattery out and onto the muddy road. He took his knife, cut Slattery's hands free, and then kicked him in the testicles.

Slattery fell over on his side, his eyes bugging out, groans that didn't even sound like his own echoing around him as Monarch climbed back into the truck and drove away, leaving him sprawled in the mud at the edge of hell on earth.

83

ELEVEN WEEKS LATER . . .

PATAGONIA

Monarch went out on the terrace of the hacienda he rented on a vast and remote estancia. He liked to sit outside and have a drink at the end of his day, a chance to gaze up at the impossible beauty of the Andes, a chance to smell the sage and pine trees, a chance to give thanks for another day in the solitary paradise he'd created for himself since he'd left Buenos Aires.

He sat in a wicker chair, watching the snow-capped peaks, as the spring sun set and the moon rose and another day passed into memory. It was the longest period of Monarch's life spent in solitude, and he'd found it suited him. Being alone for this long had allowed him to look into his past, relive it, and discard it in a way that had not been possible before. There was one memory, however, he liked to revisit at least once a day.

It was morning the day after he dumped Slattery in *el ano.* Monarch led his team through the gates of the Hogar de Esperanza. Claudio was with them, too, walking with a cane and one arm around the shoulder of Chávez toward a group of kids playing pickup soccer barefoot on a dirt field.

One boy stopped playing, pointed, and shouted at Monarch, "I know you!"

Monarch recognized him as one of the paco smokers. "Do you like it here, Juan?"

Juan nodded. "I have a bed and food. And I've read a book all by myself!"

Monarch tousled the boy's hair and said, "Good for you. Where is Sister Rachel?"

The boy pointed at the main building. "Out back there, working in her garden."

Monarch and the others found Sister Rachel on her knees planting seeds. "Hello, Sister," Monarch said.

Sister Rachel looked up, saw him, and her face exploded into happiness. "Robin!" She scrambled to her feet, rushed him, and hugged him. "You're alive!"

"I am, Sister," Monarch said, hugging her back.

She spotted the others. Her face fell, and she pointed to them. "Your friends came here a few weeks ago," she said. "They were worried about you. I was worried about you. I've prayed for you every night since."

Monarch felt shaken inside. "Your prayers worked, Sister," he managed to say. "They got me through some tough times."

She beamed and kissed him happily on both cheeks before looking around at the others, who were greatly enjoying the sight of Monarch being mothered.

"Claudio, you're on your feet!" she cried, before gesturing at Barnett, Fowler, and Yin. "And who are these other fine people, Robin? And why are you all here?"

"They're friends, Sister, good friends," Monarch said. "We're here to make a gift to the orphanage."

He handed her a cashier's check. Sister Rachel took one look and fainted.

The memory of her joy afterward, however, was enough to complete Monarch in a way he had never known. Yes, he had done some horrible things in his thieving life, stolen from men, conned them, and killed some of them when it was necessary.

And yes, terrible things had been visited upon him as well and at an early and innocent age. But now he'd done this thing, taken millions of dollars from crooks and despots and given most of it to Sister Rachel to fund her good work.

As darkness fell across the Andes, and the moon rose, and the air cooled, Monarch felt at last that his life had come into balance, that he'd done enough good to weigh against the bad.

He got to his feet on the terrace, meaning to go to the kitchen to cook his dinner, and perhaps pour another drink, but no more than that. He planned to get up before dawn and climb up into the mountains.

Later in the year, perhaps, he'd make a short trip back to visit a pack of boys in Algiers and a certain beggar girl, if he could find her. But other than that he had no ambitions for the foreseeable future.

But after Monarch went into the hacienda and lit the gas fireplace to take the chill off, he heard his satellite phone ringing. He frowned. The only people who knew the number were the members of his old team, and for the most part, they had honored his request not to be bothered unless it was some kind of emergency.

He got the phone and answered. "Yes?"

"Monarch? It's Willis Hopkins. I got your number from Tatupu."

"Dr. Hopkins," Monarch said, surprised. "Uh, I thought we were good?"

"We are good," the CIA director replied. "But I wanted you to know that Jack Slattery has been taken into custody and is being extradited to the United States. He was found delirious and near death in a garbage pit in a slum in Buenos Aires last week."

"Seems like a fitting end for him," Monarch said.

"Yes," Hopkins said. "He'll join Baron in prison soon enough."

"Is that all, sir?"

The CIA director coughed and cleared his throat. "No, Robin, as a matter of fact, it's not. I spoke with the president about an hour ago. He would very much like for you to steal something for him."

ABOUT THE AUTHOR

Mark Sullivan is the author of several internationally bestselling thrillers on his own as well as the coauthor with James Patterson of the #1 bestseller *Private Games* and *Private Berlin*. He lives in Bozeman, Montana.

The employees of Thorndike Press hope you have enjoyed this Large Print book. All our Thorndike, Wheeler, and Kennebec Large Print titles are designed for easy reading, and all our books are made to last. Other Thorndike Press Large Print books are available at your library, through selected bookstores, or directly from us.

For information about titles, please call:
  (800) 223-1244

or visit our Web site at:
  http://gale.cengage.com/thorndike

To share your comments, please write:
Publisher
Thorndike Press
10 Water St., Suite 310
Waterville, ME 04901

L